Ashe

C000049418

Ashes
by
Stephanie Harbon

ISBN: 978-0-9574346-4-6

To Anna,
I hope you enjoy my book!
Best wishes,
Stephanie Harbon

Ashes
by
Stephanie Harbon

ISBN: 978-0-9574346-4-6

Published by

i2i Publishing. Manchester.
www.i2ipublishing.co.uk

Second Edition July 2013

Acknowledgements:

This book has been a long hard journey which I could never have travelled alone. I would just like to show my thanks and appreciation to those who helped me along the way:

For Lionel and the team at i2i Publishing; for having faith in my writing when no other publisher did.

For my Sister; for reading me bedtime stories when I was young and terrifying me with her home-grown horror stories. Without her I would never have developed such a vivid overactive imagination.

For my dad; for always being a constant reliable figure in my life and supporting me both financially and emotionally throughout the years.

For my Gran and John-Dad; for their boundless enthusiasm and love for me and my work.

For all my friends; for putting up with me and my day-dreams during school, college and Taekwon Do and for giving me inspiration for my scenes and characters.

For Calum; for forever being there, eager to help with ideas and suggestions, and for not getting too jealous of Kieran and Jayson.

And finally for my mum; without her I would have never got this far. She has read every single piece of work I have ever written-rubbish or not-and has been there to encourage me every step of the way. Without her I would have given up on getting published a long time ago. She gave me the confidence to persevere and believed in me no matter what.

Thank you all.

Steph

Dedication:

This book is dedicated to my Grandpa, who inspired me to write in the first place and gave me my mantra 'You only get out of life what you put in to it.'
To be able to dedicate this book to you is payment enough for everything I've put into it.

Steph

Preface

Fire hums. I never knew that until now, but it's true; it does.

I guess if you listen hard enough and open your mind to the possibilities, you'll discover what you never even attempted to acknowledge as possible. Perhaps you'll learn things you once considered unimaginable or personally unachievable. Perhaps you'll learn that things aren't always what they seem.

That pretty much reflects my life recently.

It turns out that my beliefs of what is possible and impossible are actually wrong. For example: I'm dead; so technically I shouldn't even be thinking this, should I? Wrong again. I know for a fact I'm dead because I was the one who felt the fire. The fire that had been burning me since the moment I was born, I just never noticed. Small, insignificant changes are easily missed. Death, however, is the kind of thing you never forget.

I remember the blaze burning my skin, charring my flesh with vicious licks of flame like a dragon's acidic tongue. I felt the excruciation of my skin as it burned, then my limbs, then my organs, and then whatever was left. I remember distinctly the way it gnawed at my consciousness, stripping away my body until only ashes remained. I remembered the pain. For a long time there was nothing but a perpetual stretch of darkness, like an eternal night.

So how is it I am thinking again?

I can't see, I can't feel, I can't smell and I can't taste, but I can think and I am starting to hear again. How the hell does that work?

My confusion was pointless; I would never have an answer.

Fire hums. How strange it was, knowing I never even realised.

The sound was beautiful, like the gentle swaying of ocean waves or the flutter of delicate butterfly wings against a breeze. It was intricate too, thousands of different melodies intertwined into one magnificent chorus. Patterns so detailed that they would perplex any curious mind who attempted to decipher them. The noise was irresistibly compelling and seductive. It made me want to join in. It made me want to listen more.

It was like the cry of a Phoenix.

It made me want to live again.

Chapter One

It was an exceptionally cold Wednesday for early November. Inside the Black Swan, the busy pub I've worked in for nearly a year now, the heat in the kitchen was ridiculous. The unreliable ovens roared in protest as I shovelled hundreds of sausage rolls and samosas into their fiery stomachs, in preparation for the public outside. It was karaoke night, my least favourite night -*ever*- to be at work and the drunken song interpretations were about as pleasant to listen to as a howling chorus of banshees. I think it's worse hearing appallingly bad music when you're a musician yourself. Well, that's not entirely true, I can't play any instruments. I did, however, inherit my mother's natural gift for singing; along with her crimson hair. My mother had been good at everything as well as being mesmerizingly beautiful, almost impossibly so, with lashes so long they brushed her high cheekbones and a voluptuous figure worth dying for. Of course this was a long time ago, before the brain tumour had drained all the luminosity out of her skin, the vibrant colour of her hair and, inevitably, her life.

Her death had hit me and my dad very differently. My dad became a workaholic, spending all his time at the office and on extended conferences, leaving me to continue on alone. I soon became independent; with my dad constantly away I was the one who had to look after our small house, nestled on the edge of the forest that lingered around our town in the Lake District.

Not for much longer though. Soon I'll have saved enough money to leave. It doesn't matter where, just anywhere but here. Anywhere but that dark depressing house which sparked nostalgic memories of a time when I was happy, when Mum was still around; when I still thought of Dad as a father.

"Ruby?" Tanya called, snapping me out of my own thoughts. She stood by the door, her hands pressed against her hips, frowning, "Take a break darling; you look like hell."

I yanked open the oven again, hearing the deafening screech of its hinges as I cautiously placed the last tray inside. Once I'd finished I turned to Tanya and smiled exhaustedly, "Thanks. I'm just a little tired that's all."

Her expression grew sympathetic, "Still having trouble with your Dad?"

I nodded, despite his apparent lack of interest in me, every time I mentioned leaving home, he flipped. It's like he's trying to keep me near, but not to actually be with me; more out of duty or something. Sometimes I wonder if he even is my father. We look absolutely nothing alike and his cold indifference is enough to arouse suspicion. There's no point confronting him about it though. I think I'd regret asking.

I realised I'd drifted off again and answered Tanya, my boss, "It's just never the 'right time' to talk to him about it. You know what he's like."

Tanya sighed, coming over; placing a comforting hand on my shoulder, her eyes were large and wrinkled with laughter lines. "You listen to me Ruby. You need to make him listen. You can't stay cooped up at home all your life."

"I know," I said, "I will, I promise."

"Go on," she waved, "I'll take over."

I rushed out of the kitchen, sweeping past the wooden tables piled high with empty pint glasses and the makeshift stage where a man was currently massacring Robbie's much favoured *Angels*. Behind the bar Lauren looked at me with a *run while you can* expression. Twisting the brass knob I opened the heavy stained-glass door that lead to the car park. I breathed in the rich country air.

Looking up into the night sky, I noticed dark clouds grumbling over my head. Raindrops fell like crystal tears from the sky, drenching my upraised face and washing the perspiration from my forehead. I was shivering slightly from the cold and moved under shelter.

Suddenly I heard the deep thundering roar of motorbikes turning into the car park. There were two, a Suzuki and a Ducati, and that's about all I knew; I guessed that they were very fast and very expensive. They were big, menacing-looking things with polished metal and gleaming paintwork, coming to an abrupt stop not far from me. The first man who stepped down off his bike was extremely tall, clad in black leather. When he removed his helmet his face was surprisingly young, with black haunted eyes.

The second man wore only leather boots and trousers and a black t-shirt. As he took his helmet off, his back to me, I could see the rippling bands of muscle that wrapped around his darkly tanned arms. As I watched another man and two girls walked out of some nearby trees and made their way over to the bikers. I frowned slightly, wondering why they'd been walking through those trees; there was nothing behind them but forest and hills, it wasn't a shortcut into town or anything. I shrugged mentally. They all looked very similar, with tanned skin, dark hair and earthy coloured eyes, perhaps all in one family.

Then the second biker turned around and I saw his face.

Suddenly a weird sensation filled my stomach, tension raised the hair on the back of my arms and I stared harder, fascinated by this unusual creature.

He had this *presence* about him, like he was...not important exactly...more powerful. It was the way he stood, the cocky lean in his stance and the look of lazy contempt on his astonishingly gorgeous face. He was tall, tanned and muscular like the other two men. His hair was blacker than a raven's wing and kind of in an indie style with choppy edges. It suited him like that, though perhaps it didn't quite fit the biker stereotype. He had a face that any male human would cherish with pride of possession; high cheekbones, square jaw, perfectly symmetrical...

That wasn't why he kept my attention though. I mean, I'm not that shallow.

Under incredibly long black lashes, his eyes were a shocking emerald.

He turned away, unaware of me lurking in the shadows of the shelter. When he spoke his voice was deep, husky and brimming with an amused arrogance, "Well, can you imagine our luck, its karaoke night," he said, falsely enthusiastic, flashing a set of sparklingly white teeth. "Shall we go in and send off for hearing aids tomorrow, or save time and just cut off our ears now. I have a knife on me if anyone wants to go first."

"Is it really?" the first biker groaned, "Can't we go somewhere else?"

"I'm not changing again," complained a girl of around twenty, with hazel eyes and a tumbling mass of brown hair.

"I'm sure it won't affect the taste of the beer," said the last man, wearing jeans and a t-shirt which didn't quite hide the chiselled muscle underneath. "What does everyone want? We could sit out here."

They all shared a strange accent I couldn't quite place. They were definitely new to the area.

"But it's starting to rain," moaned the youngest girl with hair like dark chocolate and an athletically built body.

"Somebody fetch an umbrella, quick," said the green-eyed biker fanatically, his eyes exaggeratedly wide, "We have about four seconds before she melts."

The girl shot him a look and it was at this point I decided I shouldn't be eavesdropping and silently crept back inside. There was nobody on stage at the moment, thank God, but then Tanya rushed over to me and I wished there was someone up there. I could see the intention in her eyes.

Before she could open her mouth to speak I interrupted "No. I know what you're going to ask and no. I did it last week." Whenever there was a long gap in-between songs she asked me to sing, just to keep things moving.

"Please," she pleaded, the fine wrinkles around her eyes fanning out. "People like it when you sing, it makes listening to everyone else bearable."

I shook my head decidedly, "Ask Lauren."

"She sounds like a dying cat when she sings," Tanya complained. "Plus she's busy; come on Ruby." I was about to shake my head again but then she made things interesting, "I'll let you leave early."

I paused, a slow smile starting across my face, "How early?"

Her eyes narrowed; we'd done this before, "Ten minutes."

I deliberated momentarily, "Twenty."

She frowned and then reluctantly sighed, "Fifteen, that's my final offer."

I grinned, "Deal. Where's Charlie?"

Charlie, Tanya's husband, organised the karaoke. When he saw me coming he breathed a sigh of relief, "Thank God,

I don't think I can stand anymore bad singing. I think I might just stop karaoke night."

I grinned, "You say that every week."

"I know," he sighed, then smiled, "What do you want playing?" he gestured towards the song book.

"Have you got your guitar with you?" I asked, ignoring the book as well as the sound systems, microphones and screens I didn't know how to work.

"It's in my car," he grinned, knowing me well, "I'll go fetch it."

Minutes later I was standing in front of the chatting audience, Charlie beside me with his acoustic guitar already playing familiar melodies; his fingertips fluttering rhythmically across the strings. The room hushed instantly; the crowd was waiting, a strange hunger enchanting their eyes, growing ravenous as they recognised who it was illuminated under the stage lights. Someone even shouted my name. I think they were drunk though.

So I took a deep breath and began to sing.

At first I felt a little nervous but eventually I used my voice to its full potential, thanks to the encouraging familiar faces. I soon hit each note perfectly, the pitches ranging from almost impossible highs to intense lows. Constantly I changed the volume and texture of my voice to entertain the crowd, like Mum had taught me. They clapped and cheered obligingly. My voice rang as a piercing beauty, almost mournful in essence; like the cry of a songbird. Charlie had chosen what my friends would call a 'neggie' – or negative, to anyone else - song. I quite liked it.

Then something changed as the tone of the song dropped and slowed.

Apprehensive silence fell on everyone inside the pub.

People now watched me with an absorbed and slightly dazed expression as my voice dipped into a low almost sedative murmur. I could feel my body begin to tremble. My skin felt hot and sweaty and a series of burning sensations trickled down my spine. Something felt wrong. From the corner of my eye I noticed the strangers from outside join the crowd. The young biker seemed to whisper something to the others.

They shook their heads immediately. 'Impossible' mouthed the youngest girl. The biker glanced at the fascinated, blank faces surrounding him, eventually returning his gaze to me. He started to move closer but the oldest man held him back with a restraining hand on his shoulder. His knuckles whitened dramatically, as if he were clenching tightly.

Panic crawled up my legs in vigorous convulses now, but my voice remained hypnotic and untarnished, as smooth as a placid lake. It didn't feel like I had any control over my own voice, it was leaking from me without permission. I could see people's eyes closing in synchronisation with each other, becoming deeply unresponsive, almost as if they were falling asleep. Was this a big joke? If it was it wasn't funny. What was *wrong* with them?

I continued the song; but Charlie wasn't even playing his guitar. He gazed at me dumbly like everyone else; all except the fierce new arrivals. They had to be all in on some horrible practical joke or something. They couldn't seriously all be falling asleep? They were tricking me. That's not nice at all.

At least that's what I thought initially.

However as the crowd seemingly slipped unconscious their necks flopped down like a broken rag dolls, their arms went slack and the pint and wine glasses they held slipped from their grasp, smashing loudly into a thousand diaphanous splinters on the hard wooden floor. I cringed at the noise but then the situation intensified as the people who had been previously standing literally collapsed, crashing into tables and injuring themselves in the process. Was there some sort of gas leak or something in the room? I decided now would be a good time to stop singing. But I didn't stop.

No, I *couldn't* stop.

I felt powerful, I felt strong. I felt *alive*. I had never felt this... *wrong* and yet completely right. This had never happened before. I *couldn't* stop.

What was happening? Was I speaking English? I was frightening myself; what the hell was happening? *Why* couldn't I stop? Why were they asleep?

My heartbeat echoed inside me, imitating the way my voice bounced off the walls of the pub. Feverish sweat clung to my skin like a persistent itch. The music flooded everywhere; filling the darkest corners and cracks in the floorboards. I could almost see it dancing and twirling through the air, intoxicating everything into a fatal numbness. I'm sure if I tried I could reach out and grasp it... but then what?

I gasped the final note abruptly. It was over.

Immediately staggering forwards as exhaustion smacked into me, my vision blurred. Strong arms caught me. I weakly craned my neck up, looking into smouldering green eyes. The whole world spun but those eyes remained as still as the constant stars. They were the most beautiful shade I'd ever seen, brighter than emeralds which turned coal black at the perimeter of the iris, like a ring of onyx. It was surreal. It was wrong.

They reminded me of weapons; brilliantly terrible.

I remembered that specific colour. I'd seen it before, in a dream. Something intuitive clicked in my mind, screaming that this stranger was dangerous. Really dangerous. Not fast-food dangerous but serial killer dangerous. A familiar danger. A danger I recognised. Those eyes guessed at the truth. The truth *I* didn't even know yet. Then a blinding surge of agony exploded through me, tracing from my head down to the bottom of my spine in a blaze of excruciation. I winced, a gasp escaping my lips. I fell again, just managing to catch a glimpse of everyone waking up before my vision blackened as I fainted.

I groaned as my eyelids grudgingly opened, my back throbbed and my head ached. I was sitting outside up against a cold brick wall.

What the hell just happened? I wondered in frightened astonishment.

Did I really just…sedate people? Was I imagining it?

Tremors rocketed though my exhausted system. I couldn't understand it. What logical explanation would make people act like that? Were they all in on some cruel practical joke or something?

And then it hit me, how the heck did I get outside?

I suddenly realised that I wasn't alone. Off to my right were the two bikers and their friends from earlier. It was the green-eyed biker who captured my attention immediately. He stared at me for a long moment, scrutinising my face as if he were searching for something. Then his eyes met mine and an overwhelming shudder of *–something-* passed over me; almost recognition but more complex. One word flooded into my mind; *enemy.*

He opened his mouth but the older biker with black eyes cut him off.

"Don't even think about it," he warned severely.

The green-eyed biker shot him a significant, dirty look. "Go home, brother." he ordered fiercely "Now. Don't make me count to ten."

They stared savagely at each other, ostensibly having a silent conversation. They were brothers? Well, that wasn't entirely shocking, but it was the way the younger brother seemed to have...*authority* over the older brother which surprised me. Every ounce of him streamed with unspoken power and danger; definitely danger; that warning light hadn't yet faded.

Eventually the older boy spat, "Fine."

He stormed off, his shoulders stiff with hostility as he climbed onto his motorbike and sped off without another word. The younger brother stared flatly after him until he disappeared around the corner.

"I hope you know what you're doing," said the shortest girl. With that, she nudged the other two and all three of them dashed off the way they'd come.

While this was happening, I shakily tried to stand up.

The biker turned to me, his face abruptly plastering on an easy-going smile. "I'm Kieran," he introduced himself, utterly calm, "You need to tell me who the hell you are and what the hell you're doing here."

"I'm sorry," I said, my mouth dropping open in astonishment, "What?"

"You need to tell me who you are, girl," He enunciated each word with deep condescension.

My anger ignited like spraying deodorant over a naked flame. "Why should I?" I demanded, "And don't call me girl, I have a name." Sexist pig.

He rolled his eyes, "Hence the point of my questions." He abruptly changed the subject, "Was that some weird Derren Brown crap in there or what?" He smirked mischievously, "Do you always... well, sing I guess, here?" "No," I crossed my arms over my chest, "Sometimes on karaoke night. Not that it's got anything to do with you." I really didn't like this guy.

He leaned against the wall opposite me with a look of quiet indignation, "Let me guess, your mother or father taught you to do that, right?"

"My mum's dead." I snapped. "And I don't know what you mean."

He seemed to consider this, almost curiously, then changed the subject again, "You're not from round here. Where were you born?"

"How do you know I'm not from around here?" I blurted thoughtlessly.

He rolled his eyes impatiently, "I recognise you. I'm not from around here."

I recognised him too, though I didn't know where from. When I was younger I was in a car accident. Apparently I'd hit my head pretty badly and lost most of my memory; I can't remember anything before I was seven. I might have seen him before then and forgotten until now...?

Ignoring my silence he continued "How old are you? Seventeen?"

I stared at him for a moment, then decided to think better of it and began to walk off. I did not have to answer questions from a random stranger. My head spun as I moved and I staggered slightly.

"Hey!" He reached out and grabbed my wrist and where his skin touched mine sparked burning electricity. "I wouldn't do that it if were you, Princess."

"Don't touch me," I snapped, yanking my hand back. "I do Taekwon Do." It was a lie but he didn't know that; I could secretly have sweet ninja moves.

Kieran held his hands up as if in surrender, "Alright, calm down. Most girls want me to touch them..." he shrugged casually, "but okay, whatever."

I stared at him blankly for a moment, forgetting I was leaving. "What?"

"I'm incredibly attractive," he sighed, "It's my only true flaw."

"How about lack of modesty?" I offered, "Or manners?"

He looked down at me superiorly from his impressive height. "If I had perfect manners as well as my looks, intelligence and high regard for personal hygiene, I'd be too good to be true. And nobody wants that."

"Are you always this annoying?" I wondered.

"On the contrary," he answered immediately, "Most people find me perfectly charming, but more about you. Do you burn?" He asked casually.

The question caught me off guard, "What?"

"When you touch fire, does it hurt?" he elaborated.

I just looked at him. This guy was crazy. "Of course I burn, doesn't everyone?"

"You haven't tried, have you? You've never actually touched it."

I felt completely dumbfounded. "Why would I, if it will burn me?" then I shook my head; *what's this got to do with anything?* "What idiot would stick their hand into fire to see if it would hurt?"

"But you won't know until you do." He was staring at me closer, his full lips curving into a knowing smile, "There's something about fire that's always intrigued you,

but something is stopping you, isn't it?" He leaned closer, as if trying to understand my features, "It's in your eyes."
"What's in my eyes?" I demanded, bewildered.
"Curiosity," he shrugged casually. He stared down at me with sudden amusement, "You're scared of me aren't you?" "No," I lied curtly. "I think you're crazy."
"What are you scared of then? You're sweating like a pig." he said it so softly I barely heard the insult. A knowing flicker glinted in his eyes. "That wasn't supposed to happen in there; was it? When you were singing."
I tried to look away from those intense eyes, mumbling "No."
"Whatever it is that you did won't shock me," his voice was deceitfully soft: like silk. "You can't deny it; I saw everyone's reaction. Falling unconscious like that isn't natural, I know you did something to them."
"I didn't do anything," I stated firmly; having had enough. "And you know what? As much as I'm enjoying this conversation," I said, now feeling completely agitated, not to mention confused and frightened. "I need to get back to work."
"I'll be around when you want to talk about it," he said confidently, moving over to his bike, as he climbed on it he reached into his pocket.
"Talk about *what*?" I demanded but he wasn't listening.
He withdrew something from his pocket and threw it at me; I caught it instinctively. "Let me know how it feels," he smirked, and then revved his engine. The motorbike growled as it raced forwards, disappearing almost instantly.
I looked down at what he'd thrown; it was a lighter.

Chapter Two

I was groggy and dazed as I went to get breakfast the next morning, last night's bizarre events already long forgotten, grunting when I realised I was out of bread. Like most teenagers, my mannerisms in the morning are similar to a caveman's. I grumpily got dressed, muttering petulantly about food shopping; then I grudgingly ventured outside to walk my dog. Once I returned I caught the bus to college and spent the most of the day trying furiously to finish my English essay which had been due in a week ago.

It was a long gruelling day of hard work, especially with my French teacher lecturing me as well. I could read French almost fluently now but for some reason this irritated my tutor, who thought that I should remain at the same level as the rest of the students rather than want to learn complex vocabulary at degree-level. I'd always had a knack for languages. When I'd hit my head in that car crash and lost my memory I'd forgotten English entirely, though I'd strangely remembered most of my mother's native language. You see my mother had been born on a remote Island in the Pacific, where they spoke an old language similar to Latin.

She'd taught me that beautiful flowing language before she'd taught me English, so perhaps that's why it was English that I'd had to re-learn. I used to have a slight inherited accent, but Dad had hated it and eventually when she died, so did my accent. My mother's teachings helped me develop a talent for communication and I'd learnt quickly that once the building blocks of a language are established, the rest comes fairly easily.

I was sitting in the library when my friends Alex and Katie came to find me.

"Why are you still in here?" demanded Katie. She'd always been the prettier out of us two, with dyed blonde hair that rippled down past her shoulders and blue eyes like uncut sapphire; we'd been friends for years now. Alex was also blonde, but naturally with springing curls that wound around his slightly pointed ears. He was lanky, thin and apparently had fancied me for years, despite my gentle rejections. I had no interest in boys at that moment; I didn't have the time for them, though for some strange reason quite a few seemed to have time for me. I don't know why, I'm short and ginger. The only thing I have going for me is my voice.

"I'm nearly finished," I said, "Two more pages. Wait for me?"

As I finished the chapter I was on, the others chattered excitedly about Friday's party. Every year Alex hosted his notorious bonfire party. It was known for being amazing, with an epic bonfire of dangerous proportions and his rich parents spending hundreds on fireworks. Every year I was invited but never allowed to go. My dad had a serious phobia of fire ever since we'd been in that car crash. Something in the car had exploded and set it alight; we'd nearly suffocated from the fumes. Nowadays he determinedly avoided any situations in which we'd come into contact with fire. He wouldn't even let me take chemistry because of the practical lessons; not that I'd ever voluntarily take chemistry. All the cookers in our house are electric; we don't own matches or a single candle and the massive fireplace in our lounge had never been lit. He was extremely particular about me staying in on the most fire-hazardous night of the year.

Nevertheless Alex asked me again, for the millionth time this week, as we made our way out the building towards the bus stop, "You coming, Ruby?"

"I'd love to, but you know my dad won't let me," I sighed.

"You should invite the new kid," Katie suggested.

"There's a new kid?" I wondered.

"Yeah, she's quite cool, been put in my tutor group. Has a funny accent though; not really sure what it is, maybe Irish," explained Katie.

"Good idea," said Alex, "I'll go ask her now. Come with me, Katie, if you know her; I don't want her to think I'm hitting on her."

She laughed, "Yet." She added, "Though I doubt you'd have a shot."

"I could get any girl," he exclaimed, looking hurt.

Kate glanced at me ironically, and then smiled, "You coming?"

"Nah," I replied, "I better get back."

"Okay, see you later then," they both waved as I waited for the bus.

Once I arrived home my fearsome German shepherd whacked his tail excitedly on the floor, indicating that it was time for a walk. I sighed, smiling at his predictability; then grabbed his lead. I took my usual route through the forest behind my house, following the path I'd made over the years. The trees surrounded me protectively, their ancient branches dancing and swaying in the breeze, crisp leaves rustling. Sunlight filtered through the leafy canopy above, creating a lush atmosphere of green. Finally I discovered my river.

Cautiously climbing over polished boulders, I settled on a rock at the edge of the gushing water. The menacing roar of the distant waterfall sounded in my sensitive ears; sometimes I trekked up the hill to see it, but not today.

The water was crystal clear as it swept past; lively waves and ripples sparkling as if they carried a thousand floating diamonds. In the fathomable water beneath my feet, fish darted mercurially along the riverbed and frogs camouflaged themselves in slimy greenery. Dragonfly's electric-blue wings contrasted with the dull reeds underneath a draping willow tree; casting long mysterious shadows over the reflective water.

Abruptly I heard a loud *crack*. Max started barking frantically, dashing off into the trees. What just happened? I shouted, chasing after him, but before he returned, I stumbled onto a large clearing.

I stopped so sharply I nearly fell over.

There, in the centre of the field, was a man. Not just an ordinary man, this was one of the dark bikers from last night, and he was throwing knives randomly into the air. *Knives*, he was throwing *Knives*.

Max bolted towards him and before I could grab him back, the man noticed. He strode angrily towards me, still carrying one of the knives. The sharply curved blade, no larger than eight inches, gleamed in the sunlight.

Then my senses kicked in.

"What are you doing here!" thundered the man, who I now realised was the eldest biker I'd seen yesterday. I flinched back instinctively. He was close, just a foot or so away. Max snarled at him, protectively baring his sharp teeth.

Those intimidating black eyes barely glanced at Max. My heart was beating erratically as I consumed his glaring expression, the menacing bands of muscle, and the pulsating artery in his neck. He was built larger than any rugby player, towering over my fragile frame like a lighthouse over the sea. I edged backwards cowardly, my throat binding together, thinking he was going to use that blade to make me into a kebab.

"Calm down Adrian," cautioned a lazy voice from behind me. I whirled around, stunned. Kieran's flawless lips slowly stretched into an arrogant smirk, "Oh, look who it is. Had a play with my lighter yet, Princess?"

"You gave her a lighter?" Adrian whirled on Kieran with a thunderous look. As he drew in a sharp breath he said, "You really are asking for it."

"Why are you here?" I demanded, confused, "Are you following me?"

Kieran snorted with conceited laughter, "Don't flatter yourself. I'm way out of your league. If anything, you must be following me."

"So what *are* you doing here?" I asked incredulously.

He picked up a long curved blade that was in a bag of weapons beside his ankles. He ran his fingers tentatively along the blade's edge with a wicked gleam in his eyes, "Waiting for a pretty young girl to wander past," he said, dangerously, winking. "Of course."

I stared at him for a moment before deciding he was joking. I think.

"Is that dog going to try to bite me?" Adrian asked, putting a noticeable emphasis on the word 'try' as Max growled defensively.

I bent down to stroke his furry ears, glad he was there.

"Nah," I said. "He's just an overgrown teddy bear really." To prove my point Max calmed after I muttered a soothing word.

"What did you just say?" Kieran asked sharply, shocked.

I turned my gaze back to him, "I said he's an overgrown teddy bear really."

"No, no, after that," he waved impatiently.

My frown deepened, "I didn't." I insisted.

"Yes you did. What did you say to the animal?" he demanded.

Comprehension hit and I blushed scarlet. "Um, *Sungha*. I made it up years ago; it seems to calm him down." I explained, mentally kicking myself. Why did I say that? That word wasn't even in my mother's language. It was just a stupid word I remembered from nowhere.

"You made it up?" Kieran asked slowly, a peculiar note in his voice. "Aren't you a little old for a secret language?" The brothers shared a meaningful look.

"Look I have to go," I muttered, my cheeks flushing. I whistled Max over and walked off awkwardly.

"There's no path that way," Kieran called.

"I don't need one," I called back agitatedly over my shoulder, "my house is a mile past the river." Great one, Ruby, now they know where you live.

"There is no river up here," he argued defiantly.

Anger flickered like a broken light. "Yes there *is*," I contradicted. What was with him? Why did he feel the need to argue about nothing?

I heard muttering behind me but ignored it as I made my way home. What the hell were they doing there, and with live weapons? I went in my room, instantly rummaging in the pocket of the trousers I wore last night, for the lighter Kieran had given me. In all honesty I'd completely forgotten about it. I knew if Dad discovered I had a lighter in the house he'd go mad so I'd have to hide it. As I sat down on my bed I stared at it. It was a big metal thing with a flipped-back lid and a worn-away inscription on the side.

I stared at it for a long time, unsure what I was doing. What did I expect? That it'd explode? That if I light it and touch it the fire won't burn me? Why did Kieran give it me in the first place? This was ridiculous. Why would I be any different to anyone else? Of course I burn. What a stupid question. I put the lighter in my pocket, shaking my head at my own stupidity.

By the time Dad arrived home that night it was already dark. Outside I intermittently heard the ear-splitting screeches and booms of various fireworks. Bonfire night wasn't for another day but already fireworks were being lit. I watched from my bedroom window, just catching glimpses of them whizzing into the atmosphere in the distance, their bright sparks shattering into innumerable florescent splinters that decorated the night sky like glitter on black paper. It was while I stared; longing to get closer to the action, to the beautiful shimmering displays, that I concluded that maybe Dad would've changed his mind and would let me go on Friday.

I'd been allowed to go to a couple of Alex's parties before and they'd always been amazing fun, despite being *very* messy; but his bonfire party was *known* for being great. I really felt like I was missing out.

So I decided I would actually try to talk to my dad about it. I went downstairs, to where he was slouching on the sofa watching a program on the TV about architecture. I spoke as he glanced up. "Dad," I tried to sound casual, "Alex is having a party tomorrow which he invited me to; can I go?"

"I work late Fridays," he frowned, pulling together his brown eyebrows. Every part of my dad was some unspecialised shade of brown, his hair, his skin, even his clothes; he looked nothing like me. I didn't get my black eyes from him either: my mothers were gold, that inheritance was a mystery.

"That's okay," I said quickly, "Katie's already said I can stay around her house after. I know its short notice, but I've only just realised I'm not working. I thought I couldn't go when he asked me before."

He looked at me suspiciously, "Isn't it November the fifth tomorrow?" he questioned sceptically. When I nodded he shook his head instantly, his dark brown eyes flashing with anger, "No Ruby, you know how I feel about you going to bonfire events! They're so dangerous, with all the fireworks..."

"I'll be completely fine," I said stubbornly, then tried to smooth my irritated voice, "I'll stay inside if I think things look dangerous."

"No," he stated decidedly, picking up the TV remote and flicking through the channels; indicating that this subject was no longer up for discussion.

I hadn't finished yet though, "Why not? Give me one good reason. I'm nearly eighteen years old, I'm not a kid. I know not to play with fire."

"Oh do you?" demanded my dad, violently slamming the remote down onto the coffee table with a menacing glint in his eyes. "I don't think you do." Then he paused suddenly, "What's that in your pocket?" he ordered.

I looked down at myself, realising there was a lighter-shaped object in my pocket. I battered myself internally; why didn't I hide it somewhere? I stammered under pressure, "It's a-"

"Show it to me, Ruby," Dad interrupted, sitting up straighter with a deadly serious expression and holding out his hand, palm upwards, expectantly.

There was no way of getting around it, I yanked the device out of my pocket and shakily handed it to him, explaining frantically, "It's not mine. This boy gave it me. I swear I've never used it."

My dad's tanned fingers curled around the object, his knuckles clenching white, he spoke with quiet infuriation "You've lit this, haven't you?"

I shook my head, "No, I swear-"

"After everything I've told you!" his voice exploded into a thundering yell, "You know when we were in that car crash the flames nearly killed us all. You know how I feel about you messing about with fire."

"I haven't even touched it, this boy-" I began.

"I don't want to hear your excuses!" he shouted.

"But I-"

"No, Ruby. You're not going anywhere." His voice was growing louder still, "I made a promise to your mother that I'd look after you and that's what I'm going to do, God damn it! Why do you make it so difficult?"

I stared at him for a long moment, sucking in a shocked breath, "You promised Mum?" I repeated, "You mean, you didn't want to..." I trailed off, unable to finish that sentence.

"If you go tomorrow Ruby, that's it," he said finally, "You're on your own."

"What do you mean?" I asked shakily.

He just looked at me, his eyes were like deep emotionless pits, "I can't look after you anymore. It's too hard to keep you from the inevitable."

"You never looked after me anyway." I snapped.

"Don't speak to me like that. I've put this roof over your head!" He yelled right back, "Don't be so ungrateful."

"I should be grateful?" I scoffed "For what? All you do is work, I see you for about an hour a week. You don't know anything about me at all. The only time you take even a remote interest in me is when I tell you I want to leave!"

"You're right," he said maliciously, "I don't know you, and do you know what? I don't think I want to. I've had enough of this."

"Had enough of what?" I questioned sharply, standing straighter and glaring at him with all the force built up from the years of neglect, "Not being a father? You've *never* been there!"

"You are such a spoilt little brat," he snapped incredulously, "All the money I've given you over the years... and you're throwing it back in my face?"

"It's not money I want Dad." I said curtly. "But you don't get that, do you."

The look he gave me sent chills to my core. It was a look of deep hatred; a hatred that I'd never seen from him, or anyone, before. I always knew he didn't love me, but I never thought he hated me. The realisation of that cut through me like a sharp knife stabbing through my heart.

He walked out of the room then, slamming the door shut behind him and as I watched the door handle rattle from the impact, I gave up the long hard struggle to love the man who was supposed to be my father.

For the first time in my entire life I slept through my alarm. When I eventually awoke from a deep dreamless sleep it was midday; I'd slept through the only two lessons I had on a Friday.

I rubbed my pounding head, I felt slow and exhausted. Sweat soaked the sheets I was lying on and my body felt ridiculously feverish. I shakily tried to stand up and my head whirled. What was wrong with me? I'm *never* ill.

I felt a little better after a shower; well, I felt cleaner at least. There was no point in me going to college and I felt rough and still upset from last night's argument, so I decided I'd visit my favourite place in the world. It was the highest point within walking distance, the top of the waterfall that cascaded down a steep hillside to eventually formulate the river I walk Max by every day. The hike was long, made worse by the heat evaporating from my flesh and the ferocious aching of my back.

Then I arrived at the top of the hill and I was free.

The wind howled like a lonely wolf. It was freezing; sinking slowly into my pores. It felt nice in comparison to the blistering temperature of my forehead.

I'd never been remotely afraid of heights-which was perhaps for the best as I dangled my legs over the three hundred-foot drop. Beside me the river moved with a striking grace, gently running until it suddenly churned with fear as it contemplated its crashing fate below. It was a dangerous place to be, but not for one moment did I feel unsafe. For me this was home.

My mother preferred being high up too. She used to bring me up here, especially if I was upset. It was here where she told some of her most gripping stories. She was always speaking of her imaginary adventures, her particular favourites being that of a burning city built from sparkling alabaster in the middle of a desert, or of the terrible monsters with horns like goats that lurked deep in the mountains.

It seemed so long ago now; a different lifetime.

It was while I was thinking this that I saw Max's ears twitch. He sat up alertly, staring with almost a quizzical expression to the space behind me.

"What is it boy?" I asked curiously, turning to see what he'd spotted.

I'd expected to see a rabbit or something, but what I saw definitely wasn't a cute furry animal. No, it was rather large, muscled and glistening with sweat as it ran, obliviously, across the plateau behind me.

Kieran didn't seem to realise I was there as he sprinted past where I was sitting, partly concealed behind a gigantic oak tree. He didn't slow as he continued towards the ledge, where the earth was extremely precarious and the chances of slipping were too high for comfort. I stood up, wanting to warn him, but he skidded to an abrupt halt and before I said anything I froze in confusion.

He stood there for a moment, as if deliberating, and then slowly he began to tug his shirt off. I watched in fascination as the bulging muscles of his shoulders strained as he lifted his arms. He dropped the shirt to his side and with his back still towards me he slowly began to peel off the bottom half of his clothes until he was standing there entirely naked.

Blood gushed to my face, spreading across my cheeks like wildfire. I'd never seen a properly naked man, in real life anyway, and even though all I could see was the back half of him, I couldn't stop myself from staring. His body looked like it had been sculpted by Michelangelo and then touched up on Photoshop. And he had a really nice ass; just saying.

He stood there for a moment, gazing distantly at the horizon, as if he were searching for a future made impossible by divine intervention. It was like he was wishing for something he could never have, or something he had previously let slip through his fingertips. He looked heartbreakingly and anciently sad, longing for something I couldn't even imagine. Then he did something I didn't predict. He turned slightly towards his left, barely twisting his long athletic body, and kicked his clothes off the edge of the cliff. He sprung forwards, diving headfirst over the edge.

He disappeared from sight immediately; before my scream even had chance to unleash into the suddenly dark atmosphere. I leapt to my feet, hurtling over to where he jumped; Max dashing ahead of me, barking frantically. I couldn't believe what I just witnessed. It was a vertical drop for at least three hundred feet, possibly even more, there was no way he'd survive such a fall. He must have known that.

I came to a skidding stop as I looked over to where he'd jumped, astonishment breaking across my features. I saw no evidence of his fall but there were lots of bushes and brambles his body could've been concealed in. Panicking, I paced up and down trying to think it over and eventually got out my phone and dialled 999. I asked for mountain rescue and while I waited for them to arrive I crawled closer to the edge, trying desperately to see a body. Nothing was visible from this position. I wasn't foolish enough to climb down and risk the same fate. My mind was a buzz of nonsensical thoughts. My lungs gasped frantically, I was hyperventilating. I had no idea what to do. I was experiencing shock for the first time.

Someone had just committed suicide in front of my eyes.

Chapter Three

When the mountain rescue team arrived they raced about frantically; some asking me questions of what I'd seen, some judging how safe it would be to climb down the side of the hill, others racing back to their helicopter for more equipment. I soon became invisible as the bodies rushed about, until finally one of the mountain rescue team came up to me; shaking his helmeted head.

"I'm sorry, but we can't find a body, or any evidence of a fall." He told me.

I stared at him with wide eyes, "What?" I asked, absolutely dumbfounded, "But I swear I saw him jump off the cliff!"

"We believe you miss," he said with evident concern, "But as of now we still can't see anything. We'll keep looking though; do you know the person?"

I hesitated, "Not really, I've met him before but very briefly. I work at the Black Swan in town, you see."

He nodded, "Well there's no point in you staying here. We have all your details. We'll let you know as soon as we find something."

I nodded distantly, trudging my way down the longer but less steep path to the bottom of the hill, wandering through the forest with Max until we reached my empty house. I sat around, unsure of what to do, flicking through the channels on the TV; my mind completely elsewhere.

I must have fallen asleep for a while because I awoke to a loud persistent knocking on the front door. I'd been curled up on the sofa with my head buried in Max's thick ginger fur and as I stood up I realised my backache had returned with a fierce vengeance. I stumbled exhaustedly over to the door, glancing at the clock on the wall along the way. I'd been asleep for *five hours?* How the heck had that happened, normally I'm a borderline insomniac. I shook my head, continuing to the door and yanking it open without thinking.

There were three men standing there. One had a shaven head, tattoos covering his scarred arms, and the other two who flanked him were both dark-haired and thick-built. They wore torn jeans and dirty shirts and their eyes had noticeably dilated pupils. As I inspected their similarly pale, drawn features and the tiny red scars on the insides of their arms I became instantly suspicious that they were into something heavy.

I wanted to slam the door shut and lock and barricade it, but the last thing I wanted to do was to irritate them. Hopefully I was overreacting. They were probably just normal guys selling something or another similar activity. I was probably being paranoid. So instead I straightened my aching back, attempting to look strong and fearless, and said, "Can I help you?"

It was the guy in the centre who spoke first, in a low harsh voice, "Are you Ruby Swift? The girl who saw someone jump off a cliff earlier today?"

I nodded uncertainly, intimidated.

"We want to ask you some questions," he said darkly.

"Who are you?" I demanded with a brave intention that evaporated the moment I saw the flash of dangerous fury spread across his face.

"I think you should answer my questions before you start asking your own," he said with an acidic bite, purposefully opening up his jacket to display a nasty metal gun that gleamed like teeth in a murderer's smile.

I gulped; my mind buzzing with disturbed thoughts. My first impression was right, so now what? My heart raced rapidly. Three unpredictable men were standing on my doorstep threatening me with a gun, do I have options? "Don't worry," he added silkily. "If you answer our questions we won't touch you." I could hear Max barking, desperately trying to open the door which I'd stupidly shut behind me when I went to answer the door.

Stay inside, I prayed to my most faithful companion, *don't open the door.*

The man was speaking again, "Describe what he looks like."

"He's tall," I began, panicked, trying to flick though my little memories of him, "very good looking with black hair, tanned skin and green eyes."

They looked from one to another, then the tattooed guy spoke again, "How did you meet him? Who was he with?"

"Erm," I struggled under pressure, "At the Black Swan, I've only seen him twice. He was with a few others."

The man stepped forwards, I stumbled backwards away from him but he followed me inside: bad idea. His eyes were like empty pits, fathomlessly deep and dark. Sweat matted the back of my hair, dripping down my spine. I was shivering with terror. Max was still barking; the door handle rattled as he attempted to knock it down with his giant paws. Should I run? What do I do?

"What did they look like?" demanded one of the other men; his hair was inky black and greasy. When he waved his hands at me threateningly I saw that his nails were crusted with dirt, like little brown crescents.

I looked around frantically, stuttering "I, err, don't remember-I..."

"You better start remembering," the tattooed man pulled out his gun, delicately caressing its polished surface, like it was something greatly precious. It wasn't, it was a malicious-looking thing. I cowered away from it.

"There were two girls," I racked my brain frantically for information, "Two boys, all in their late teens or early twenties. Dark skinned and dark haired."

"What do you know about them?"

"Nothing, I don't know anything, I swear!" I said as he lifted the gun towards me, "I only met Kieran twice. For about two minutes. I don't know!"

"What has he told you about him?"

I shook my head, terrified. The two built guys were shuffling closer.

"What has he told you about him?" the man yelled suddenly, pointing the gun towards my head. I stumbled back frantically, but the other two men grabbed me and hauled me against the wall. I screamed as my head collided with the concrete. I could feel warm blood streaming down my neck.

As my head whirled, my stomach lurched nauseously. I could feel the cold weapon press against my temple. I could smell the cutting metallic scent of it.

The man was whispering in my ear, but I couldn't understand his words. He was muttering threats I couldn't comprehend in my shock.

Then he shouted, breaking through the protective shell of numbness surrounding me. "Can you hear me? Where does he live? You tell me or I'll pull this trigger." He grabbed a handful of my hair, wrapping the tangled curls around his dirty fingers and pulling hard.

I tried to pry his hands away but I heard the soft dooming click as he loaded the gun and stopped struggling. I closed my eyes trying to think through my panic and assess the situation. But then I realised there was nothing I could do, I didn't know the answer, I couldn't move.

"I don't know," I said honestly, my head still spinning. "That's the truth."

"What did you see this morning?!" he screamed.

"I saw him jump-" I began, but another man interrupted, his ugly snarling face so close to me I could smell the vile stench of his breath.

"What else?" He demanded, "What happened exactly?"

"I didn't see!" I cried, "I just assumed he fell down the cliff."

"What about before he jumped what did he do?"

Just then the door swung open, Max had managed to knock down the handle and push his weight forwards to open it; I'd seen him do it a hundred times before. I was horrified that he'd done it now. He charged closer, baring his sharp teeth as he growled and sprung at one of the men pinning me to the wall. My heart leapt, though in relief or terror I didn't know, as Max sunk his teeth into the man's leg. The man screamed in agony and Max held on.

This distracted the other two just enough for me to duck down, my instincts taking control as I shoved my elbow into the tattooed man's stomach with a surprising amount of force. He doubled over, dropping the gun to the floor, winded. Max then jumped at him, snarling and biting and sending him hurtling to the floor under his impressive weight. I kicked the gun out of the way just as the black-haired man dived for it, accidentally kicking him in the teeth in the process-an amazing fluke.

Unfortunately I'd sent the gun skidding in the wrong direction. The third man reached down for it in a blindingly fast motion, sweeping it up and holding it in a way that made me think he wasn't accustomed to handling it; his fingers looked as if they were attempting to contain a handful of rice.

Max let go of the tattooed guy, racing over to stand before me. His back was arched, his pointed teeth glistened and his piercing golden eyes flickered from man to man. I was in the corner, looking desperately at the man who was pointing the gun at me, his eyes were wide and I could see faint tremors in his fingers. He was afraid. A low threatening growl rumbled from Max as the other two men struggled to stand up. The tattooed man had deep bleeding gashes across his face, the other limped badly as he walked over to the man with the gun. Max barked furiously, standing his ground.

Just then the tattooed man snatched the gun off the hesitant man, aimed and fired. I closed my eyes, anticipating the pain, flinching at the sound of the bullet exploding from the barrel. I felt a sudden surge of agony, but it wasn't from a bullet, it was from the excruciated squeal that cut through the air like a polished blade. My eyes darted open. Down on the floor there now lay my most loyal, loving companion in a rapidly-growing pool of his own blood. The bullet had punctured straight through his skull; killing him instantly.

"We'll come back tomorrow," Stated the tattooed man with a deadly emotionless voice, "and you better have an answer by then."

Before he shut the door behind him, the limping black-haired man turned back to me and said, "Oh, and we'll be watching you as well, just in case you decide to run to the authorities." And with that he shut the door.

A terrible silence filled the house; it seemed to evaporate from the cracks in the floorboards, from the very foundations of the building. My back felt embedded into the wall, sinking deeper like a coffin being lowered into the earth. My chest heaved as I tried to stop myself from hyperventilating. I collapsed to my knees before Max, folding myself into his fur. I cried hysterically for what seemed like hours, eventually my broken sobs fading into silent devastated tears. Only a short time ago I'd been lying on him like this, his steady heartbeat constantly thumping in my ear. Now I heard nothing. Only a short time ago his body was warm and comforting underneath me. Now it was cold and lifeless, like his beautiful empty eyes. I couldn't believe it. Max was dead. He was the one soul in this world who was always there for me, the one stable figure in my life. I loved him more than I loved anything else, without him my world suddenly seemed empty. I had never felt so unbearably alone.

I didn't know what to do, but I began with burying my dog. I spent hours digging in the forest behind my house, until a deep enough grave formulated. I ignored the chilling feeling of eyes on me, straightening the hairs on the back of my neck. The process took longer than I thought and the sweat and tears ran like tracks through the dirt on my face. He was heavy, nearly eight stone; which as a dead weight wasn't that easy to move. I ended up wrapping his lifeless body in a bed sheet, saving his collar, and half-carried, half-hauled it over to the grave; suddenly wishing I'd dug it closer to the house. As night fell and the final shovel of dirt was added to the pile, I stood for a moment that soon became a minute, which soon turned into two, then ten, until finally I made a decision. I was leaving.

I knew someone who'd just moved to Manchester for University, so I rang her up to see if I could stay with her for a couple of days. She'd said yes immediately, that would be fine, so I booked train tickets. The only tickets I could get at such short notice were for tomorrow morning. I'd have to stay at someone's house until then; I'd stay at Alex's as he was closest. I packed everything essential and of emotional value; which turned out to not be that much really, then eventually I conjured enough courage to pick up the phone.

His office phone answered on the second ring. "Dad, I'm leaving." I told him seriously. All emotion had drained from my voice, I was beyond caring.

There was a long silence. Eventually his voice came. It was quiet and hopeless.

"I knew you would eventually...When you found out." There was a pause "Are you wearing your mother's chain?" he asked, surprising me.

I glanced down unnecessarily; I knew it was there. My mum always used to wear a golden chain which was coated in interlocking symbols that appeared to be burnt into the metal. From it hung a stone, richer in colour than any ruby, though it blatantly wasn't part of the original necklace. Before she died she gave it to me and made me swear I'd protect it; it was important.

"Of course I have it," I frowned, "I always have it."

"Good, keep it with you. It'll help you with the change." He told me.

His words didn't make sense, but as I was about to ask he interrupted me.

"I know I've not always been there for you Ruby, in the ways you most needed, and I'm sure you know the truth by now, but I did try to protect you from it all." He said deeply, "I did try."

I took a breath then whispered, "You're not my dad are you?"

There was a pause, then a nearly inaudible, "No, just a servant of a higher authority." Then he spoke again, and I knew in that moment this would be the last thing I ever heard from him. "Be strong and fly free, little fledgling." Then the phone clicked off.

I didn't understand anything that he said, so I tried to ring him back. The line was dead. So I forced it to the back of my mind for now.

My suitcase was loaded with my clothes, larger items and toiletries; I dragged it downstairs while picking up my backpack from the landing. Inside my backpack were all my savings, my legal documents, photos and all my other essentials. I carried them all with me as I took one last sweeping glance of the house, then I locked the door with a sinking feeling in my chest.

I was beyond tears as I dragged my things to Alex's, my thoughts a confusing blur, uncomprehending of today's events. This was really it, I was leaving. I was entirely alone. It hurt to think what I'd do now.

Alex's house wasn't far from mine. He also lived on the edge of the town, though in a massive luxurious home that just cut into the forest. After about ten minutes walking I arrived and went to knock on the door, noticing the sign that said, 'go around back.' I wound my way around the side of the building into his backyard, immediately being ambushed by hundreds of teenagers. Most I knew from college but some I barely recognised at all. There were girls in ridiculously skimpy outfits, dancing about 'sexily' to the drum and bass booming from the impressive sound system.

Oh right, the party. I had completely forgotten about that.

Apparently the party was outside on the roofed wooden decking that dominated a space the size of my whole garden. There were steps that led down into the actual garden where a gigantic bonfire was just being lit.

The atmosphere was electric. All around me everyone was dancing and screaming lyrics. Massive fishbowls of cocktails, which people were gulping down through giant straws at an inevitably treacherous rate, were scattered across a table. At the far edge of Alex's garden, I could just make out the fireworks speared into the soil in preparation for later.

I could see Alex now, rushing off the decking and into the house. I left my suitcase in the corner, clutching my backpack firmly, trying to make my way through the heaving crowd. No one would shift and eventually I was forced to shove and elbow my way through the sweaty bodies.

That was until I came to a human barrier that wouldn't move at all. I looked up and to my horror saw the dark perfect face of Kieran.

My scream was lost over the blasting noise of the speakers.

I couldn't believe my eyes, but he was there, standing before me like a figure conjured from a haunting dream. How was it possible? I saw him jump over a three hundred foot cliff barely hours ago, he should be dead. I scanned my eyes frantically over his perfect form, there wasn't a cut or blemish on him.

I shook my head, staggering backwards, this wasn't real. I was imagining it.

But I wasn't. "How are you *here?*" I said; overwhelmed by shocked horror.

He grinned naughtily, those full lips curling and flashing teeth I swear were pointed like fangs. "Plus one babe," he nodded over to where a girl was dancing; she was beautiful with cheekbones that would cut through ice. I recognised her immediately from the other night at the pub. Kieran continued, "Apparently the new girl got an invite."

She must be the new girl my friends were talking about. This thought flashed and disappeared across my mind so quickly it barely registered. The only thought I could concentrate on was how the hell was Kieran alive?

"You should be dead," I breathed, so quietly it was nothing but a whisper.

How Kieran heard my voice over the music I had no idea, but he grabbed my shoulder and practically hauled me through the crowd. I pried his fingers off my skin but he yanked hold of my wrist and pulled me into Alex's vacant dining room. "What makes you say that?" he demanded, his face suddenly so serious and fearsome it was like looking into the eyes of a hunting predator. His face was inches from mine, his skin stretched taunt over flesh and bone.

I shook my head, ripping my wrist free of his iron grasp and shuffled back from him. "I saw you, I saw you jump," I muttered, trying unsuccessfully to piece together the possibilities of this notion. I'd had too many shocks today, I'm pretty sure I might spontaneously combust any moment now.

His mouth shut and whatever he was going to say was lost. The marble contours of his face had relaxed of emotion completely, liquefying.

I looked up at him, so tall so strong, and for the first time saw a weakness.

"I saw you jump off a cliff, I saw you strip off your clothes then dive over the edge. It was at least a three hundred foot drop. I rang mountain rescue and there was no body. You should be dead. Why aren't you?" I asked firmly.

He looked at me as if I'd gone mad, but I saw through it instantly. I was right. He said, "I think you've had a little too much to drink, Princess."

"Ruby," I said.

"What?" he looked at me.

"My name is Ruby." I tried to sound unafraid; secretly my heart pounded.

He said nothing, instead turned and started walking away.

"They're here," I called after him; he paused slightly. "Whoever is after you; they're here. They came to my house. They shot my dog." My bottom lip trembled on the word *dog*. I held back stinging tears with a determined fury.

I walked up to him, stood before him, looked straight into those dark emerald eyes and saw a different world entirely lurking beneath the surface. "I have a right to know why my life is suddenly in danger." I said bitterly.

"You are not my responsibility," he growled, the sound as vicious as the crack of a whip. "Stay away from me if you want to live."

He just pushed past me. I stood there for about three seconds before I chased after him; still clutching my backpack. He shoved his way through the crowd outside, grabbing hold of his friend and saying something in her ear; she nodded then went off in another direction. I pushed my way through the crowd, struggling to follow him as he dashed off down the patio stairs. The bonfire was blazing furiously by now. Alex's little sister, Lucy, in her pyjamas, winter coat and woollen mittens, was standing near it, waving a sparkler. Alex was kneeling on the grass beside her. I guessed it was past her bedtime and she was staying up to see the fireworks.

Kieran rushed past them, towards the edge of the garden, where the dark forest loomed mysteriously. I was about to dash after him but I caught a glimpse of something in the corner of my eye that halted me in my tracks.

Alex's Dad was rolling a propane canister towards the barbeque as a drunken girl from the year below me staggered towards him. I saw the look of irritation on his face as she came closer, but then her heel sunk into the grass and she tripped over. Alex's Dad dropped the propane canister and caught the girl just before she smacked her head, but in doing so the canister hit the floor and rolled down the garden towards the bonfire.

Alex, seeing this, tried to stop it, but it was a steep hill and the canister picked up speed and he ended up helping it further along. It crashed deep into the bonfire, burning splinters of wood and effulgent embers scattered everywhere, like petals of exotic flowers.

I had no choice really, my instincts had already begun taking over.

I knew I had to get the canister out of the fire before it cracked and exploded. Lucy, oblivious to what was happening was still happily waving her sparkler around as Alex sprung forwards, lifted her into his arms and ran. There were others loitering around, I knew what I had to do.

I launched my body forwards, automatically reaching my arms out and into the furious flames. I wasn't thinking. My actions didn't catch up with me until I felt the searing pain shoot up my arms. A noise escaped from my mouth, high and shrill, as I continued to dig through the blackened wood, my eyes stinging as if someone had poured vinegar in them. Then I discovered the canister. The heat was incredible, stabbing into my skin, imitating the way the excruciation was tearing through my flesh. My fingertips grasped the burning metal, pulling hard. I screamed, my face scrunching up in agony as I forced it from the fire with my nails; ripping some of them clean off. My heart compressed as I heaved up the boiling canister with a sudden spurt of strength, then dropped it, kicking it away from the fire and people.

I was free of the flames, but the pain was engulfing me still. My vision was blurring around the edges, tension seemed to be building in my skull, like a migraine and I collapsed as my legs gave way underneath me. I felt my whole body convulsing with violence. I shrieked as the pain intensified, like a knife down my spine. I could feel myself being lifted; then everything went black.

Chapter Four

I felt a strange rocking motion chorusing through me. It was disorientating, like being on a little boat in a storm or on the back of a galloping horse; it was a sickening feeling. I could feel myself becoming more conscious, my body shooting into action like I'd been zapped with electricity. My eyes sprang open. It was dark, too dark for my eyes to adjust instantly. The world was bathed in shadow and mystery. My aching back was arched, unsupported, as my body was battered about in that nauseating swaying movement. As my eyes finally settled, I managed to make out the clawing fingers of branches as they swept past. Straining for vision hurt my eyes. My neck rolled painfully. Gazing upwards, I could just make out the night's sky dusted with distant galaxies, like a fine sprinkle of icing sugar on a rich chocolate sponge. I turned my head, tucking it against something warm.

The next thing I noticed was a quick repetitive thump beating into my ears. A heartbeat, I realised. I truly awoke then, my eyes reopening and actually seeing this time. I was clutched in the strong arms of a man, and he was running. His eyes were deep green, his hair darker than the night sky above.

He was speaking in a voice barely breathless, "Can you run?"

I looked around, why were we running? What were we running from? I focused on his question, could I run? My legs felt numb, would I fall?

I was so confused but I managed to mumble, "What's happening?"

"We are stopping," Kieran answered, suddenly halting. "You have your own legs, start using them. I am not a donkey."

He set me down onto the floor, my legs barely held me. "Where are we?" I didn't recognise this part of the forest, "Why have you brought me here?"

"Because you, stupid girl, have gone and made yourself my responsibility," he snapped angrily though gritted teeth. "I can't abandon my own."

"Your own...?" I asked. He ignored my question.

"You just threw yourself into a bonfire to retrieve a propane canister. Now look at your arms and tell me what you see," he demanded.

I looked down at my arms. There was nothing there to see. My skin was pale in the dim light, scattered with golden freckles and covered in stripes of black ash, but obviously unflawed. "Nothing," I said, shocked.

"I gave you a lighter to touch, a *lighter*, not a bloody bonfire!" he yelled suddenly, his face a mask of fury. "If you were immune to a tiny lighter flame it wouldn't have mattered, I was just curious to see if I was right, but *this*. There's no going back from this. You've screwed me over, Princess."

"Immune?" I repeated, unable to digest such a word.

"More than immune," he said, "You'll have affinities, if you survive that is."

My eyes widened "I might die?"

He shook his head; his voice was so casually factual that it made me think that no emotion could sink through such thick skin. "No, you'll definitely die. That's a fact. You'll have just over a day before the flames come."

I was about to respond when the faint sound of running footsteps stopped me short. "Who's that?" I whispered anxiously.

"You know those people you were telling me about, who came to your house?" Kieran asked, I nodded frantically, "Well, it's most likely to be them."

"Most likely?!" I repeated. "How many people are after you?" I demanded.

"You'd be surprised at the numbers," He grinned, "even if you exclude the long line of women who are just chasing me in a desperate hope that I'd have changed my mind and suddenly become available."

I stared at him for a moment, was he being serious? He was screaming at me a minute ago and now he's full of conceited remarks. What is wrong with him? Are there really people coming or is this just one big joke?

"Why are they after you?" I asked slowly.

"I accidentally slept with one of their wives." He explained casually.

"Accidentally." I repeated.

"Okay," he surrendered, "Maybe it was deliberate; but the guy was a dick. He thought just because he's some big Manchester drug lord he could get away with putting a bullet through my chest over a little misunderstanding. It pissed me off. So I slept with his wife. She was *way* too hot for him anyway."

"He put a bullet through your chest?" I repeated, horrified.

"Yeah. He was a bit surprised when I got back up and broke his nose."

"What? How-" I began. Then I heard the footsteps drawing closer and asked hysterically "Do we run?"

He deliberated. "Nah," he shrugged eventually "I'm bored of this game now; if they want me they can come and get me."

"What about me?" I asked, petrified.

He looked me over, "You? They wouldn't want you; I've seen the girls these guys get. Obviously I saw a little too much; but you get my point."

"I meant what am I supposed to do?" I glared maliciously then added as an afterthought "Did you just say I'm unattractive?"

"Typical female behaviour," he noted with analysing, quizzical eyes. "We're about to encounter some very stroppy men who spend far too much time examining the wrong types of joints, and all you are bothered about is whether the handsome stranger thinks you're attractive or not."

"Has anyone ever told you that you're a complete arsehole?" I asked.

"That's your comeback?" Kieran said, appalled. "Seriously?"

"Why don't you just..." I began, but my words fizzled out as the running footsteps stopped and silence fell like snowflakes on the living world.

As I waited I glimpsed the deadly details of the forest. It was a whole different place now, a darker more sinister environment. The sharp fingers of branches grew out crookedly to catch and claw at me. Leaves in the canopy above held precariously balanced raindrops that would inevitably fall, coating the surfaces with a slippery trap. A sense of impending doom clouded my mind. The shadows seemed to be multiplying and expanding, draining the last few spots of surviving colour. My flesh chilled, my heart thumped.

The sound of a twig snapping pierced my eardrums and my neck twisted towards the source. My eyes widened as I saw the three men from earlier, accompanied by several more; I counted eight altogether. I cringed.

The quiet was broken by Kieran, stepping forwards and announcing loudly, "Look Baldy," he held up his hands, palms forwards like he was stopping traffic. "I know your wife has probably bragged about how good I am in bed and you're probably here for a taste, but you're just not my type. I'm sorry."

"It's over, Angel," snarled a man with eyes so light blue they looked unnervingly white.

"Would you stop calling me Angel," Kieran sighed, "I've told you before; my preferred pet name is sweetheart." He smiled innocently, explaining to me in a conversational tone, "That's what Mummy calls me."

"There are eight of us, one of you." continued the white-blue eyed man.

"Great," Kieran replied, "Now turn around, fetch twelve more people, then maybe I'll consider this as a challenge."

Why wasn't he afraid? These men were obviously dangerous, they blatantly wanted him hurt, or worse, and he was mocking them? What did he know?

The man with tattoos and a shaven head stepped forwards, his eyes were lost in pupils and his face was dirty. Rage pulsated in my veins at the sight of him, anger thrashing inside me like an eagle trapped inside a cage; unleashing an awesome stream of power. In a scary, mad way, I liked it. I felt confident and powerful, my former terror crystallising into infuriation.

"You," I screamed suddenly, emotion overwhelming me. I wanted to rip this man to pieces. I moved forwards yelling,

"You killed my dog! Who gave you the right to..." but I was stopped mid-sentence by Kieran pinching me.

"*Ouch*," I glowered at him.

The tattooed man smiled a truly murderous smile, "I see you're not so afraid now are you, little girl, now you have the Angel backing you."

"For the millionth time I'm not a bloody Angel!" Kieran threw up his hands in exasperation, "My wings are black, I have a dick—ask your wife, she'll tell you," he added to the tattooed man, "And trust me I'm the last person here who'd be able to get into Heaven; including the knicker-sniffer over there."

I stared at him; dumbfounded. *My wings are black?* What?

"So now you admit it?" demanded the tattooed man.

Kieran smiled. "Admit what?" he enquired innocently.

The man glared, "That you have wings?"

Kieran shrugged, "I never disputed that."

"Show us them now!" He yelled, I could see the fury pumping in the artery on his forehead, exaggerated by Kieran's untouchable mocking demeanour.

"No wonder your wife was so unsatisfied, I can't imagine anyone being turned on by such displays of aggression." Kieran noted, looking at the man as if he were something he found on the bottom of his shoe.

"Enough," screamed the tattooed man, purposefully looking back to his friends and nodding, "If you don't want to co-operate, we'll make you."

"Oooh, scary!" Kieran winked, "Look at me; I'm shaking with fear."

Suddenly I felt hands grab at me. My heart lurched as I was thrown backwards against someone's strong body. I sucked in a sharp breath as something cold and metallic pressed against my forehead for the second time today.

Glancing up frantically, a man towered over me. I couldn't see his face properly but I noticed unkempt stubble and the faint stench of urine.

Damn-it, there had been nine men.

"You might not be scared," commented the tattooed man to Kieran, "But she certainly is. You either do as I say or she dies."

"What makes you think I care if she dies?" Kieran wondered curiously. "I barely know this girl. What's your name again?" he asked me.

I swallowed nervously, "Ruby."

"Ah yes," he remembered, "Ruby. The name matches the hair."

"Enough!" screamed the man, "Tell us what you are or the girl dies."

Kieran smiled a smile so small it was barely noticeable, "If you don't let her go within five seconds I will kill each and every one of you."

From then on there was this silence. It was an intense silence, filled with a contrasting mixture of uncertainty, fear and confidence. The smell of oil and metal wafted into my nostrils, intensifying my terror. A new bead of sweat formulated on my skin with every beat of my racing heart. In those five seconds nobody moved, I doubted anyone even breathed.

And then time was up and it all happened very quickly.

Kieran reached underneath his shirt in a flash, retrieving something that gleamed in the moonlight like rain on pavements. My brain barely had time to register that the object was a small, immaculately sharpened knife, before it catapulted towards me. I closed my eyes instantly, hearing the dull thud as the knife penetrated flesh. My eyes darted open as the grip on my body severed and a scream pierced the night. I turned my head just in time to see the gun go flying towards a tree. The hand it had been previously clutched in had been thrown back; a reaction to the knife embedded in its wrist.

I heard one word then, it came from Kieran. It was *run.*

Hey, I didn't need to be told twice. I ran as fast as my legs would carry me, darting between the trees and jumping over slippery surfaces. I could hear gunshots behind me, the shrill sounds of agony and clashing metal. I ignored it all, I just ran, each fearful step like a ticking bomb. Unfortunately I wasn't the quickest or most agile sprinter and those footsteps soon caught up with me. Someone hurtled into me like a brick wall, sending me flying to the ground. I landed hard, my arm awkwardly twisted underneath me, the joints popping in protest. I struggled from under the heavy mass, my face pressed into the mud, but someone caught my ankle.

Clawing fingernails raked down my skin like chalk on a blackboard, creating upraised lines of colour. I kicked out automatically, my foot slamming into a man's teeth. This victory was short-lived as another man was already grasping my shoulder, pulling hard. I cried out unwillingly, stumbling to my feet. I knew I had no weapon, but the man who'd yanked me up had a knife as cold and grey as his eyes.

He lunged at me, raising the knife high; it glittered with threat. I darted out of the way just in the nick of time, unfortunately landing myself in the path of the man I'd just kicked. His arms stretched out, clutching my legs, making my balance waver precariously. I struggled to remain upright, but the man pushed my knees and I toppled over. Pain lanced up my arms as I landed on my hands, rocks slicing deep into the soft flesh of my palms.

I just managed to roll onto my back as the man with the knife brought the shining device down towards me. I screamed, seeing the knife coming, then screamed again as another whistled through the air and landed in the man's back. The knife fell from his grasp as he screeched and collapsed backwards, but I just managed to roll out of the way before it landed on me.

"Still alive, Ruby?" Kieran called from a distance. Another gun shot.

Before I could react to this, the first man had already stood. He moved unnervingly fast, roughly planting his foot into my ribcage. The wind blew from me and I just caught a glimpse of Kieran racing towards me, followed immediately by four other men holding weapons.

Then as I observed, dazed and incomprehensive, I saw something that would remain imprinted onto my soul for the rest of my life.

"Okay," Kieran stopped suddenly, his back to me and the man who was pinning me down, "You want me to show you what I am?" he continued, spreading his arms questioningly, "Fine. It will be my pleasure."

He had this frighteningly wicked grin playing about his lips, this naughty gleam in his emerald eyes as he glanced back. He winked at me then turned, placing his arms above his head. From that moment me, the man pinning me down and all his fellow accomplices, couldn't take our eyes off Kieran. I watched, absorbed and fascinated, as Kieran's skin slowly began to fill with strange black patterns, like tattoos coiling up his arms. As I stared the pattern's striking familiarity intensified so much that my eyes stung to embrace it. I closed them, seeing the marks imprinted onto my eyelids.

I heard the sound of tearing material, then after a couple of seconds my eyes fluttered open as curiosity clouded my judgement. I gasped in astonishment at what I saw next. I fought against the painful intensity of the marks, just catching a glimpse as black wings shot out from Kieran's shoulders. They were huge, and they wrapped around his body. I blinked reluctantly and when my eyes reopened Kieran had transformed.

I screamed as I saw the terrifying creature before me. It was some sort of gigantic bird of prey, twice my height with an astonishing wingspan and deep black plumage that covered its entire body except the tips of its wings and sweeping tail feathers; which had seemingly been dipped in crushed emerald. My eyes latched onto the image of its sharp curled beak and dinosaur talons. And those eyes; those piercing, unforgettable emerald eyes.

The sound that erupted from it was terrifying, like a deep shriek.

Then it sprung, spreading those gloriously deadly wings and leaping at the men who were suddenly frozen in petrification. Suddenly the man pinning me down turned back to look at me in terror. Acting on impulse he reached out to gather up the knife the other man had dropped. As his weight lifted off me momentarily, I scrambled upright and backed away from him.

I looked around frantically for a weapon but found none. The bird – Kieran? - was busy disembowelling the other men with sweeping lashes of his wings and claws, making a horrifying screeching noise as he did so. The man charged at me; instinctively I dodged to the side but he was faster and moved again. I slapped the flat side of the blade away with my palm before it struck my skin, but the man swung again. The first swing of the blade missed me by inches, the second didn't. I felt a searing pain cut through me and I immediately clutched my stomach.

When I removed my hand there was blood there.

I turned and ran. I could tell the cut wasn't too deep, I'd survive the wound, but the pain was slowing me down and before I had a chance to move more than several feet away I'd once again been tackled to the ground. I fell on my back with the man on top of me, his eyes glinting madly in the reflection of the blade. I had nowhere to move. I struggled, but his weight was overwhelming. He backed off slightly sitting up, balling his free hand into a fist. The punch was as solid as steel, the pain exploded, blood poured from my nose. The man smiled sadistically as I withered, trying desperately to get out of the way, then he brought fist down into my stomach.

I heard snapping before I felt it, too stunned from the impact I suppose. Then I did feel it, and the agony cascaded onto me like boiling water.

Then the knife came down too, and this time it cut deep.

I screamed but that only made it worse because as my lungs expanded, my skin ripped further. I tried to scramble back in vain. Excruciating, that was the only word to describe the pain. I couldn't move; the pain surrounded me, and he stabbed again, two inches down from the first bleeding wound. I could feel my body slipping away, losing consciousness as my mind was screaming.

I soon sank underwater, plummeting deeper into unfathomable depth. I felt heated liquid trickling over my ruined body. I imagined a sandy peaceful beach stretching everlastingly to the horizon. My only company was the sea waves lapping perpetually across the undisturbed shore.

But I wasn't there yet. I was just in darkness; in a place between the worlds of life and death. It was a thin strip of land, no wider than a needle.

I wanted to find that beach.

Then I mentally shook myself, *don't give up!* I screamed inwardly. I flung open my eyes, which had closed without permission, ignored the blurring vision and tried to struggle back.

A sharp tug pulled at my stomach as I tried to move away. The blade was holding me securely like a splinter-thin tooth; I was covered in blood as it began shredding me apart, scattering bits of my flesh across the grass.

Suddenly I heard a loud whistling noise.

A faint glint of hope flickered in my dying body. I watched distantly as a spear with a strange yellow glow illuminating from it darted just inches above my head. It was so fast and beautiful it reminded me of a shooting star.

The spear continued its course and shot straight at the man who was still jabbing at me, piercing straight through his neck. He flew off me like a hurricane had struck. I heard a horrible crackling sound and agonised screams but they soon died down. I caught a glance at the sky.

I glimpsed that beautiful, terrible creature and thought; *you better save me, Kieran. Or I'm going to haunt you for the rest of your life.*

Then unconsciousness overwhelmed me.

I was back between the worlds of life and death.

Chapter Five

I don't think I'll ever remember what happened in the next few hours after that. I was too far gone; too close to death to comprehend what occurred around me. My mind was trapped in strange revolving nightmares. But I did awake; eventually.

My eyes struggled open. As they slowly adjusted an unexpected scene materialised before me. I awoke not in a hospital bed, nor on a sofa attempting to heal my broken body. No, instead my vision settled on the posh expensive interior of what must have been a very *fast-and-furious* car indeed. The scent of leather filled my nose with almost a nauseating strength and the sound of a rapidly accelerating engine drummed into my ears. I shut my eyes quickly, pretending to still be asleep as I thought over the situation. Okay, I'm in the back seat of a car. I don't know who is driving and I have no idea where I am.

In a flash, memories of the last time I was conscious crashed into my system. Images flooded into my mind like a tidal wave. My heartbeat picked up speed, imitating the car's noisy engine. What if I was in one of those drug dealers cars? Then that crucial memory came. Kieran, Kieran was a bird-monster. What if I was in his car? What did they want with me? I could feel the panic bubbling up through my chest. Then I suddenly thought; I had been stabbed several times when I was last conscious, why wasn't I in pain?

Very slowly I pulled my fingers over my stomach, squinting through my eyelashes to see. I could just make out that the shirt I was wearing had been intermittently shredded; frayed around the edges. The fabric had absorbed numerous pints of blood, which had dried and crusted, flakes coming loose in clumps like gory scales. I gently probed my fingers underneath the material, finding to my astonishment, not an open wound or even bandages, but rough raised flesh with the unmistakable texture of scarring. Okay, now I was scared. Why have I healed so quickly, this wasn't right? How long had I been unconscious? I had to get out of this car. I opened my eyes again slightly, but didn't recognise the person driving through my blurry vision; or the person in the passenger seat, or the forested environment outside the car.

I tried to relax deeper into the seat, attempting to look asleep, waiting for the right opportunity to flick down the lock on the car door and escape.

Then suddenly the silence evaporated as the people in front started talking.

"I still can't believe it," muttered a deep masculine voice, "Caylic Fire."

"I know," this voice was light and female, bell-like. "I wouldn't have believed it if Adrian hadn't told me. I mean, it's not like it's possible for Adrian or Kieran to do it." There was a brief pause, then, "I hate it when Kieran's right."

"Me too," agreed the first voice, "Well it's still all backfired on him." His tone wasn't specifically harsh, just factual. "There's only one way to deal with the girl now. And unfortunately that involves dragging us all into it."

My body froze. *There's only one way to deal with the girl now.*

I opened my eyes. Dawning realisation hit me as I glanced around, noticing what was piled up in the massive open sports bag next to me; weapons. Curved blades, daggers, spears, bows and arrows, throwing stars and Sai knives were bursting out from the canvas material. There were these complicated strap things made from thick bands of leather tied together with giant metal buckles and various other items that looked more like they belonged in a bondage shop than a sports bag. I cringed at the sight, my heartbeat thumping. What the hell were they going to do with me?

I didn't wait to find out. I took a deep calming breath then sprung. Moving my body in a blindingly fast motion I reached for the door of the car, yanking on the handle and pushing it open just as the people in front realised that I was awake. The car began skidding to an abrupt halt two seconds too late; I was panicking and thoughtless, already recklessly flinging myself out of the car.

For a brief moment I was suspended in midair, as if time had frozen, then too quickly I crashed into the cold hard tarmac. The impact was astonishing, I'd underestimated the speed in which we'd been travelling and I automatically pushed my hands out in front of me, unsuccessfully trying to protect my face. I felt my forehead blaze as it collided with the rough gravelled surface. My palms scraped across the ground, small sharp stones digging into my soft flesh like fragments of shattered glass. Then I was spinning, tumbling in a chaotic mess of my own limbs. The wind was blown from my lungs, but when I finally stopped, I was gasping frantically.

I didn't have time to recover; the car had nearly stopped, so I darted up, my body screaming agonised protests, and I started to run. I was slow, limping. Even then I knew I didn't stand a chance of outrunning anyone. Still, I persevered on sheer determination, struggling to dash through the trees. I would have to hide. I stumbled, glancing back for a moment, seeing what I'd feared; a tall muscled man I didn't recognise was gaining on me. He was right behind me.

"Stop!" he yelled, "We won't hurt you, we just want to talk."

Ignoring this, I ran faster, however fate was apparently against me as I tripped over an upraised root on the forest floor, landing face first into the mud. My aching muscles screeched as I attempted to stand, but the man had already reached me. The prominent biceps on his arms were stretched like thick cords as he grasped my shoulder with an inhuman strength and pinned me down.

I was gasping, my lungs contracting frantically for oxygen, but he looked barely out of breath. He looked earnestly into my eyes; his were a soft milky brown with long curling lashes. His voice was low and unruffled when he uttered, "Its okay Ruby." His tone had the kind of calm that would reassure a frightened child.

"My name is Nikolas. I won't hurt you. I know you've been through a lot, but you need to listen to me." It was only then when my brain clicked on; he was one of the men with Kieran at the pub.

He seemed trustworthy; was it genuine or was he just a really good liar? He had an honest open face, handsome in a way Mum would have called 'traditional' with his crinkly eyes, sun-kissed skin and gentle mouth.

"Why should I trust you?" I asked sceptically; my voice shaking.

Nikolas smiled sadly, letting go of his tight restraint on my shoulder and said, "Because you'll be in a lot more trouble if you don't."

There was one thing I remembered specifically from last night, other than the transformation of Kieran and being stabbed like a cocktail sausage, and that was Kieran's dooming words.

"Is it true?" I wondered to this strangely sensitive man "Am I going to die?"

Nikolas looked at me, then away before I could decipher his expression. "I'll answer all your questions inside the car. Please. You need to listen to what we have to say." He stood up slowly, offering a supportive hand.

I stared at it suspiciously for a moment.

"You need help," he persevered, "You're bleeding. Please Ruby, I won't let anyone hurt you, I promise."

My head was swimming, my vision blurring. In the end I had no choice but to take the risk and reluctantly take his offered hand. He cupped his hand just under my elbow, carefully avoiding the pouring scrapes on my palms. I needed his help more than I'd anticipated; when I attempted to walk I staggered, my head whirling and he caught me quickly, sweeping me up into his arms in an effortless motion. I protested, but in vain, and Nikolas carried me back through the forest. When we reached the road I realised we weren't alone.

Kieran, his brother Adrian and the two women I'd seen before were stood at the roadside. Kieran and his brother's motorbikes were positioned just in front of the flashy expensive-looking car I'd been in and the younger of the two girls clutched a helmet in her hands; she must have ridden on the back of one of the bikes. I only noticed this for a second before my eyes settled on Kieran and a sudden fear lurched in me. I struggled in Nikolas's arms, trying to wrench free.

"What is it?" he uttered, purposefully being quiet so the others couldn't hear.

"Kieran, he's…" I trailed off, grasping for an appropriate word. Surrendering, I settled with "A monster."

"We are all monsters Ruby," Kieran's eyes darted towards me, hearing what I said. "Every creature that holds a fragment of humanity in its heart is part monster; it's just that not everyone has claws like mine." He winked.

"She jumped out of the car, Kieran," Nikolas began.

"I can see that," he noted, looking out across the side of the road, "She's painted the pavement a nice shade of red."

"The gash on her head seems pretty deep," Nikolas continued. I could feel his chest rising and falling like ocean waves as he spoke. That motion was all I could concentrate on, my mind was spinning. I was losing consciousness as the blood persistently spilled from my forehead, leaving rivers through my eyebrows. "And there are cuts on her palms and elbows."

Kieran sighed bitterly, "Translation; fix her Kieran."

"You might as well," snarled Adrian with a sudden maliciousness, "You've already broken the laws of the High Covenant by healing her once."

Kieran turned to his brother with a deep frown, "We've *all* broken the laws; of this world and ours. What's the harm in breaking one more?"

"She'll die." Adrian spat, his gaze sweeping over me like a cold breeze, I shivered. "And what if she never rises? Or worse, what if she does? Then what are you going to do? We'll be trapped. We are free now where we are, I say we stay. What difference is it where she dies anyway? It's inevitable."

"I will not allow that." This time it was Nikolas who spoke, his tone held a softness that was subtly laced with poison. "Ruby is a Daughter of the Ashes."

"It's not the same. She's not even one of us. She's of *fire*." Adrian protested.

"It's worse than that," Kieran admitted, "She's a Swartette."

There was a sharp intake of breath by one of the women, the other looked shocked and while I was hanging there, still clutched in Nikolas's arms, something finally registered in my agonised brain; Swartette. I knew that word.

I tried to say something but my words tripped over my tongue. Nik noticed this and said to Kieran, "If you're going to heal her do it now."

Kieran's beautiful face transformed, becoming utterly devoid of emotion, his black pupils expanding across his iris. I followed the darkness, stretching my mind across the contours of the fathomless space; slipping into unconsciousness.

"Ruby, Ruby..." somebody said abruptly, I looked up unfocusedly. All I saw was brown skin before the picture evaporated. "Ruby!" I opened my eyes – did I shut them? - And saw milky brown eyes mere inches from my face. I heard a quiet sigh of relief, "Kieran will..." the words slurred, and my vision blurred again...

"Ruby, wake up," Kieran demanded. Something mercilessly hard struck my cheek. My eyes opened in surprise. Kieran was glaring at me fiercely, "you need to stay strong." He barked instructions, "Chara, check the skyline for people on the road. Nik, lower her down, but keep her upright. Briseis, fetch me some water and cloth. Adrian..." he paused. I opened my eyes, trying to prevent the lids from drooping disobediently. Kieran had a deadly serious expression as he glanced at his menacing brother and said, "Fetch me a Snickers bar."

I could see Adrian glower, making a deep rumbling noise in the back of his throat, almost like a growl of frustration as he and the others stomped off; obviously irritated by Kieran's orders but in no position to refuse.

I looked at Kieran then, sensing him before he lowered himself to his knees. A moment later I heard a girl's voice confirm that the road would be clear for at least ten minutes. Kieran nodded, swiftly moving forwards. I flinched back instinctively, but then I noticed something that made me freeze in awed fascination. As I watched, strange dark patterns advanced over Kieran's hands, spreading rapidly up his forearms and disappearing underneath his shirt; they looked like intricate tribal tattoos materialising from under his skin.

He lifted his hands towards me and I saw that the marks, although at first glance they appeared black, were a rich green that seemed dusted in crushed emerald. Kieran leaned closer, delicately pressed his fingertips to my temples, rubbing soothing circles down my bleeding forehead. I winced initially as he touched the cut, then I relaxed almost immediately. The pain and dizziness washed away, extinguishing the blazing fire in my mind. Eventually my sight and hearing sharpened; Kieran moved to the scrapes on my palms, fluttering his fingertips over the tattered flesh. My body was tingling with a bizarre sensation.

Kieran's eyes were nearly black, his beautiful skin pulled taut across his strong features; its cinnamon colour dulled lifelessly. Kieran's hands fell to the tarmac, supporting his heavy convulsing frame. His muscled arms were as tense as his clenched jaw. He shuddered then, his expression composed into bleak emptiness.

His pupils shrunk and I could see the bright green of his iris again.

A girl, the younger one, came forward carrying a wet cloth. I felt the arms withdraw from underneath me as I was lowered onto the ground. The girl helped me upright. I didn't fall though my balance wavered slightly, and she smiled as she wiped the drying blood off my forehead. I noticed her hands were small, her fingers slender and her fingernails coated in green polish. When she finished with my forehead she poured more water onto the bloody cloth from a plastic bottle. Red water spilled from the cloth and she squeezed most of it out, then wiped at my hands. To my astonishment, underneath the crusting blood was scarred but otherwise flawless skin.

I gaped in confusion, glancing up at Kieran, who was now wincing as he struggled to stand. "How did you do that?" I asked quietly.

He looked at me and for the first time I think he actually saw me. His eyes were calm, the green of a placid tropical ocean, as they stared into mine with a deep, almost sad, intensity. "With much controversy," Kieran answered.

"Ruby," Nikolas said suddenly, "You need to know our names. For a start you know my name's Nikolas, this is my wife Chara," he gestured towards the older girl, his eyes suddenly affectionate. Chara smiled at me, warmth building under necessary guardedness. Nikolas continued "This is Briseis..." He nodded to the younger girl, who grinned an unusually dazzlingly smile. "You've seen our always polite and lovely Adrian," he gestured at the dark figure of Adrian, who glared accordingly. "And you obviously know Kierakai." Nikolas finished.

I frowned. "What?" I blurted unthinkingly. I hadn't seen anyone else, unless he meant... I looked sharply at Kieran. "Your name's not Kieran." I stated angrily.

He smirked. "No it's not. My name's Kierakai Ashaik." He announced, as if *I* were stupid for not guessing. I scowled at him; but he was now scowling at Nikolas, "I really wish you would just call me Kieran like everybody else, Nik." His eyes darted back to me, "I changed my name, so you can still call me Kieran. Nik just seems to forget that I'm not who I once was."

I stared at him hard, anger blazing behind my tired eyes. He winked at me, infuriatingly at ease, my emotions were everywhere. I wanted to cry and laugh hysterically; I didn't know what was happening, where I was, who to trust...

"Well, now that you know everyone..." Nikolas said awkwardly after a short silence, "Can you explain how you got here, Ruby? Can you remember?"

I stared at him, "I remember being stabbed by men with knives and guns if that's what you mean."

Nikolas shook his head, "No, that's not what I meant," he explained, "I meant do you remember how you got here from Kariak?"

A vague flicker of recognition darted through the haze that clouded my mind. I managed to mumble, "I remember that word."

"Her memory's gone," Briseis said. "It must have been part of the curse."

"What are you talking about?" I said, even more confused.

She nodded, as if expecting that. "You are one of us, Ruby."

"Well, technically you aren't," snapped Adrian bitingly, "You're a Swartette."

I stared disbelievingly at Kieran, "I am not like you. What I saw last night isn't normal...What even are you?" I demanded, half terrified of his response.

"Surely you've heard of Phoenix before?" Adrian spat aggressively. Okay, I was really starting to get annoyed at his perpetual bitterness.

"Phoenix that I've heard of are, you know, *mythical*," I retorted.

Kieran raised one eyebrow. "Do you want proof?" he asked invasively, "Proof I can give you." Roughly he began to yank at his shirt, pulling it up.

"Put it away, Kieran," Nik huffed, rolling his eyes, "honestly, you take any opportunity to take your clothes off."

"I don't mind," Briseis offered.

Chara admitted, "Me neither."

"Chara," Nikolas reminded her, "You are married. *To me.*"

"See," Kieran smirked, "you all want to see me naked."

"I can say, without a shadow of a doubt, that I don't want you to take *anything* off." Adrian said absolutely.

Kieran looked at his brother "You've no idea how glad I am that you said that."

"Were getting off track here," Nik interrupted. "Look, we are Phoenix, there is no denying that. Do you really want proof?" It sounded like a challenge.

I shook my head "But I have never looked like you," I pointed out. This was too much. Why were they saying all this? *I am not a bird woman.* I'm from England, I work in a pub and shop at Tesco; I am not a Phoenix. I'm normal…

"Just for a moment," Kieran said obnoxiously, "pretend you have an imagination and go along with it, because if you don't you'll never wake up."

I stared at him suspiciously, "What do you mean, wake up?"

"Once the process of the Change has been triggered, a person–usually a young child of ten or eleven-will deteriorate physically in one or two days," Kieran explained factually. "They'll first get severe aches, fevers, and eventually will become crippled with fatigue and entirely lose co-ordination. A fire will ignite within them and boil their blood, charring their internal organs until nothing but Ashes remains. Then, if strong enough, they'll rise from the Ashes, a Phoenix."

My mouth dropped open in astonishment, "You've got to be joking."

"We've all been through it," said Chara sadly, tucking the brown strands of choppy hair behind her ear. "We've all died once. It's not that bad."

I shook my head, "Do you have any idea how crazy you sound? This is ridiculous. I am not going to die. I've just got a little fever."

"Nik, show her." Kieran stated.

Nik came closer slowly; I guessed so that he didn't frighten me. He gestured towards my arm questioningly. I nodded, unsure how he was going to proceed as he tugged up my shirt sleeve to my elbow. My skin underneath the fabric was still splattered with patches of dried blood, but as he touched the bare skin, sweeping his fingers up along my forearm, there appeared strange black patterns. They were similar to Kieran's except they glittered with gold dust rather than emerald and were more elaborately intertwining, more intricate and delicate like the curling whips of smoke from a blazing fire.

"You are the lost Swartette, Ruby," Nikolas said, as I stared up at him in shock and dawning terror. "We've all heard about you. You were taken away from our homeland when you were a child because you shared one of the most sacred and most terrible gifts given to our kind. Our gifts are passed down from a parent, and somehow you survived obtaining it from both of yours, but it was killing you, as it had killed your brothers and sister.

"Your father wanted power, and he was prepared to use you to get it. When your mother realised this she took you to a very skilled healer who performed something called the Ultimate Curse. This Curse stripped you of your natural affinities; your gifts, your ability to Change naturally, but it was precarious as you were only a fledgling; usually such a curse is performed on adult criminals. It also came at a price, ensuring your mother would slowly and sacrificially die.

"No one knows how you left Kariak. You were the first to ever do it, but your mother took you for your own safety; from your father, from Kariak and," he added finally, "most importantly; from yourself, in case the Change triggered."

"What would happen then?" I whispered, barely breathing.

"Well here's the thing," Nikolas admitted, "We haven't worked that out yet. The only way we can help you is by going back and hoping you're strong enough to survive the Change and whatever happens after that."

"Going back?" I repeated incredulously. I can't leave with these people.

"You can't stay here," Chara explained. "You're still cursed; you won't be strong enough to Rise unless we find the Healer who cursed you initially."

This is too much. I can't take it. A sticky film of perspiration had surreptitiously crept along my skin, I placed my hand to my temple; it throbbed hotly under my palm. A nauseating wave of pain was constantly bashing against my bones, my heart pumped erratically as I stared at where the weird interlacing marks had appeared earlier. I heard something then, the faint unmistakable sound of accelerating engines. I glanced up as the others exchanged a meaningful look.

"Time to go," Nik said. "They've caught up with us."

Chapter Six

There was a quick exchange of glances between this strange, rather terrifying family, and then it was time for action. Kieran, of course, being the annoying dictator he was, started barking out orders which immediately everyone followed.

"Nik, Chara, take the car following the east road then loop around the lake the way I showed you on the map." Kieran instructed seriously.

"Adrian take Briseis the back way, following the side roads and country lanes. I'll go the direct route through Lyon. At night ditch the roads completely and head to Toulon. We'll meet there for the crossing. We don't have much time."

The others instantaneously set to work and had driven off within seconds; after Chara had fetched a helmet which she thrust instantly into my hands. Kieran ushered me over to his big menacing bike and I shook my head, backing away. "You've got to be joking; I am not getting on *that*."

"Don't call her *that*," he practically growled. "Do you have any idea what a beautiful piece of engineering she is? Her life's worth more than yours, hands down. Hell, possibly even mine."

I glowered at him then remembered what he had said earlier, "Lyon? As in France?" My eyes widened dramatically, "Am I in France?!" I demanded.

Kieran rolled his eyes, "Look," he sighed, "You were unconscious. I figured you'd want to come with us so yes we're in France. We won't be staying here long either." He looked down at me with a deep condescension; like I was a child. "Now, are you going to sit and complain much more, because, if you do I'll need time to find something to gag you with before we set off."

I stared at him for a long uncertain moment, judging those beautiful green eyes.

Then he said, "By the way, that was a rhetorical question."

He lifted me effortlessly into an iron embrace. Ignoring my embarrassed kicks and protests, he plonked me onto the back of his bike, practically cramming the helmet on to my head. As he swiftly slid in front of me I heard more engines growl, joining the roar of Kieran's bike. We both glanced over our shoulders, seeing three cars merely a hundred metres away devouring the concrete road. I gasped in terror when I focussed on the man leaning out of the widow of the first car, brandishing a gleaming gun. Then I spun away, tucking my head into Kieran's broad shoulders. Great, I was his human shield.

He laughed a deep rumbling chuckle that vibrated through me. I felt his body twist and he muttered, "Watch this. That guy isn't even aiming." Then he grasped his own helmet firmly in his hands, holding it like one would a basketball about to be dunked then launched it through the air at the man.

Within a split second we bolted forwards as Kieran accelerated. Unprepared, I unbalanced slightly as we flew, unused to being on a pushbike let alone on such a motorised monster. I flung my arms around Kieran, gripping desperately onto life as I heard the helmet he'd thrown come into contact with the rough gravel. Bravely I took a fast fleeting look behind me and saw the man had disappeared from the window and there was something suspiciously metallic disappearing into the distance. We sped onwards, faster and faster.

It was hot and uncomfortable inside the helmet; outward noises were muffled by whatever material surrounded my face, though the overwhelming roar of the engine still managed to be heard. It growled deeply, like an angered lion. Powerful vibrations reverberated from my skin to my bones, making me feel lightheaded.

Another sound that cut through the protective shield of the helmet was greatly unwelcome; the sound of firing bullets. I heard them explode from their barrels, racing through the air and travelling too close to me for comfort. I held onto Kieran harder than I'd ever held onto anyone before. The strain on my fingers as they gripped his jacket was immense, it numbed and discoloured them. I was cold too; my exposed flesh trembling. This didn't feel real. Did this really happen to people?

Maybe I'll be like Alice and wake up out of Wonderland soon; hopefully.

The cars seemed to be getting closer. I could hear them closing in. I didn't dare turn around. Kieran drove faster and faster, how fast was it now? One hundred, one hundred and fifty, two hundred miles an hour? More?

I screamed as another bullet shot through the air, this time agonisingly close. My sudden breath made condensation on the plastic screen of the helmet. I felt Kieran's body tense underneath my hands, the muscles tightening; another gunshot. This time Kieran really did flinch. He veered off abruptly and I struggled to remain on the bike. My balance wavered as we left the road entirely and dropped down into a shallow ditch. Luckily Kieran was quick to react and carried on driving with what seemed like great effort. He must be injured. We drove through the trees, darting between them with mere inches to spare. I cringed as we just scraped into one, cutting through the surface of my right arm. I looked down at where I'd hit the tree, my shirt had been lightly torn and fresh blood spilled from a massive graze.

Kieran didn't slow down. Driving off road was no way near as pleasant as concrete, even without men shooting at you. We were constantly launched upwards and slammed downwards, weaving through the various obstacles. Eventually after a few minutes there was a thinning of the trees and several fields appeared before us.

The sun was just beginning to set on the horizon, painting the sky a warm red. Normally this colour would have seemed nice, but now it reminded me of blood; bitter metallic blood. The ride was smoother on the grass, but ahead of us there was danger. The road we had been on had a turning that went directly into our field, and I could see a terrifyingly familiar car pulling in and stopping.

Kieran stopped suddenly. It was a waiting game; a test to see who'd go first.

I froze where I sat, my heart pounding and my head spinning, listening for the next engine to suddenly roar. It was Kieran's.

The motorbike shot forwards, picking up incredible speed within seconds. I knew what was coming next; I could tell. That's probably why I unleashed a petrified scream. My already fierce grip on Kieran tightened; I buried my face into his strong shoulders. I knew the cars had already begun in our direction, I knew what Kieran was planning: he was going to jump over them.

A sudden sharp incline of the ground appeared under the tyres and then there was only air. I felt the bike lift up off the ground as my stomach dropped. I opened my eyes at the last second, seeing merely centimetres below a flicker of the black exterior of the car. I noticed Kieran twist his body unexpectedly, flinging his arm out into open air. In that moment no comprehensive thought flashed through my brain. Adrenaline punctured through my skin like a needle, filling my veins with its essence; pumping immediately around my body to my heart. I was all senses in that instant, the feel of the vicious wind on my bare arms; the smell of petrol and rattling of overworked engines.

But then gravity worked its magic.

The ground came, far too quickly, into reach. As the first tyre hit the earth we jolted, as the second tyre came down we were launched skywards. The landing was rough, painful, shooting splinter-like pangs up my legs and back. The bike didn't stop and as I recovered from the impact of the landing I realised we'd yet again sped up. We raced out of the field onto the same road we'd been on, seconds before I heard an almighty explosive boom. It erupted into the air like clap of thunder. I glanced behind me, seeing spiralling wafts of smoke.

"What did you do?" I wailed over the roar of the engine.

Kieran heard me. "Threw a grenade through the window," he yelled back.

My eyes widened, "Where the hell did you get a grenade?" I screamed. What kind of maniacs had I associated myself with?

"My pocket," he answered. I heard a manic grin in his voice.

We continued down that road for several miles. The adrenalin seemed to have drained away all the energy in me. Exhaustion pinned me down. I felt dizzy and dazed, my head burning up with a blazing headache. We only slowed when we went round sharp corners and until we eventually saw other people on the roads. Civilisation advanced before us. The street signs said we were heading directly into Lyon.

Though it was growing dark there was still a significant amount of traffic.

Not for us though. We weaved through the cars, buses and taxis at a dangerously fast pace, getting beeped and sworn at intermittently. After half an hour I stopped searching the street signs and searched my own mind for answers.

How could this have happened to me? Only four days ago everything was fine. Now I'd lost my father, well, I guess he wasn't even that. My dog is dead. I'd nearly died. I'd witnessed someone change into a monster and to top it all off, I was apparently going to die and become a monster myself. I wouldn't believe it if I hadn't seen it all myself, heard it, felt it. I didn't know what to think.

I didn't notice that we'd left the city. I was losing myself in my own thoughts and pains. The blistering in my head never subsided and the next few hours dragged on painfully. I wanted escape from it all. I wanted to drift off into a deep dreamless slumber and wake up to normalcy. I knew it wasn't going to happen.

I always knew I was different.

I just didn't realise how different.

We eventually stopped at the coastline, it was extremely dark now, but I could hear the sound of crashing waves. There was a cliff ledge only three or four metres away. My butt was numb as I stumbled down from the uncomfortable seat. My stomach lurched uncontrollably and I felt bile rise in my throat. I doubled over abruptly, violently spewing whatever had been settled in the bottom of my stomach. I heaved until there was nothing left to heave then I cried furiously; trying to hide the tears.

I felt awful; every bone in my body ached, my head burned. I swear each beat of my heart was becoming more and more of an effort. I wiped my mouth, feeling disgusted, and looked up at Kieran who, bizarrely, looked empathetic.

"What's wrong with me?" I whispered brokenly.

I had never felt so ill in my entire life. I could barely breath it was such agony, like there were shards of glass wedged between my ribcage.

Kieran looked down, so that those gorgeous green eyes were entirely concealed behind his long black lashes. When he spoke his voice was low and apathetic "You're dying."

I cringed at the words as realisation hit. I truly was dying.

I have never really been afraid of dying. It happens to everyone. It's natural. I used to believe that once you die you go someplace else, a beautiful place where the rocks are soft and the rivers run with honey. A childish dream perhaps, but a nice thought overall. Now I don't know what to think. I still don't fear death; it was the way Kieran portrayed me going that horrified me. Because of my father's–sorry, pretend father's-intolerant attitude towards flame, I had never been burnt before. That didn't mean, however, that I believed I would be immune *this* time. Could it happen, would I really just spontaneously set on fire, my flesh burning from within?

I knew the answer deep in my own heart. I just wouldn't accept it.

"Well," Kieran sighed, "I guess it's time for the horrible part." He frowned, his face crumpling into a deep and intense depression. I stared at him with wide eyes. God if Kieran looked gutted what did that mean? What could be worse than dying? Then he exhaled brokenly and bent down onto his knees before his bike, whispering, "I love you baby, that's why I have to let you go. I can't let anyone else have you."

I sighed irritably as he kissed his motorbike; then stood. To my surprise he then proceeded to push it over the cliff edge. I barely heard it plummet to the water over the sound of the crashing waves. Kieran gazed brokenheartedly where it had been.

"Goodbye," Kieran uttered softly to nothing, "You will forever be my only love."

I rolled my eyes at him. "You are an idiot," I muttered under my breath.

"We better get going. It's at least ten miles away yet," he said.

"How are we getting there? Wherever it is we're going. I can't walk that far right now." I admitted reluctantly, feeling sick again.

He smirked then gestured up at the sky. "I have unlimited Air Miles."

I followed his gaze dumbly; then gasped in understanding. "Fly there?"

"What did you expect?" he laughed cruelly, "A horse drawn carriage? Sorry to disappoint you Princess, but I'm far faster and more affordable; though I must admit baggage isn't included in the price."

"Please tell me you're joking," I begged, just the thought of being up there in the clouds, with only Kieran to catch me if I fell, made me shiver.

"Nope," he frowned "and the weight limit is fifteen kilos."

"But I'll fall," I protested, ignoring his comments.

He arched a perfect, dark eyebrow "Are you doubting my ability?"

"I said I'll fall. You've had more practice than me." *Lots more practice,* I added mentally. Yesterday I didn't know Phoenix existed and now I was going to ride one!

"True," he considered, "But you'll still be fine... as long as you don't give me any reason to drop you anyway." He didn't sound reassuring.

"I won't travel on or in anything without a seatbelt." I crossed my arms.

"You are strange," he frowned.

"I'm strange?" I scoffed almost hysterically, "You Change into a bird!"

He rolled his eyes, "Come on."

"No."

"What do you mean 'no'?"

"I mean 'no,' I won't do it," I stated, shaking my head and firmly planting my feet.

"You will." He waved me off, so absolute that it really irritated me.

"I will *not*," I argued stubbornly. "The others might let you boss them around but I certainly won't. I appreciate what you're doing but it doesn't mean you can boss me around." What makes him think he's so good anyway? Even if I'm dying, I still won't take any crap. I gulped, *dying...*

"Turn around." He commanded.

"No," I snapped rebelliously. I was determined I wouldn't do anything he just ordered me to do. I have my pride.

"Fine," he retorted.

He pulled his jacket off his shoulders, movements evidently aggressive, "Would you *please* hold this for me?" he asked with a pleasant, virtuous voice; contradicting the hostile set of his features. Before I replied he shoved his jacket into my hands.

I stared questioningly at him, wondering what he was doing as he unbuttoned the top of his shirt. I didn't move though; I was that stubborn. He continued downwards until his shirt draped open, displaying an immaculately toned body. My heart thumped unevenly as I remembered the image of him standing entirely naked on the edge of the cliff. A blush spread across my cheeks like wildfire. I hated it.

"What are you doing?" I demanded incredulously, trying to stare only at his face.

"Sorry, did you want a striptease?" he asked sarcastically.

I stared at him, bewildered "What?"

He rolled his brilliant eyes; they flickered brightly like fragments of stardust. "You know what a striptease is. And before you ask, no I'm not demonstrating."

"I don't want you to *demonstrate*," I said through gritted teeth, finally composing myself. "I mean, why are you taking your clothes off?" I asked as he kicked off his trainers, bending over to pull off his socks.

"Because I don't want to rip them," he answered, dumping his dirty shoes in my hands. "They're designer. Something you would know nothing about."

"Thanks," I muttered, equally sarcastic. Then I noticed the blood dribbling down his arm, "You're bleeding?" It came out as a confused question.

Kieran turned to look at his arm with a similarly confused expression, and then something clicked in his features,

"Oh yeah, I forgot about that. I got shot; again. Why must all the people I meet sooner or later try and shoot me?" he mused.

"Does that not..." I trailed off, looking closer at the wound; I could actually see a bullet winking at me. "Hurt?" I finished.

Kieran shrugged, "Probably. It would hurt a lot more if it was you."

"Why?" I wondered.

"I'm a Healer," he answered nonchalantly "My ability to heal others comes from my own strength, my own flesh. I need to be as intolerant as possible to pain."

I shook my head, "Nobody's intolerant to pain."

"I said as possible," he looked down at his arm, muttering to himself, "It's not that deep, I could pull it out..." he twisted his body then ungracefully probed his fingers into the bullet wound. Without even flinching he withdrew a gleaming silver bullet; dripping with hot blood. He threw it to the side distastefully. Then he did something utterly disgusting. He slowly pried apart the two sides of the wound, exposing the oozing red crater of flesh. Then, rather delicately, he spat into it.

I grimaced, revolted. "That's disgusting," I exclaimed, "What did you do that for?"

"Well I doubted you'd carry antiseptic," he looked up and down at the tattered remains of the clothes I was wearing, "although if you did, I would be interested to know where you'd kept it." He smirked, then turned back to his arm, "Nik will have a needle and thread. Let's hurry anyway, I'm cold."

"Okay," I said warily, "what do you want me to do?"

"Well you might want to turn away," he said arrogantly "I don't care if you see me naked but I don't want you to be overwhelmed with desire and embarrass yourself."

"I've already seen you naked," I said, for some unknown reason.

He looked back at me with a funny expression. I just turned away embarrassedly.

It was quiet; all I could hear was the wind and the sea, joining forces to demolish the crumbling cliff. The silence was unnerving. I waited, growing anxious.

"Kieran?" No response. I tried again a little louder and still nothing. Eventually I had to turn. There was no way of avoiding it. He wasn't there.

Immediately I was afraid. I scanned my surroundings with an eye for details, my heart hammering frantically, what if more men came? I was just beginning to panic when I heard the sound of beating wings. My head jerked up sharply.

The creature landed loudly but gracefully just a few feet away, digging his dark talons into the earth, demonstrating their throat-slashing sharpness as they cut deep. It was dark by now; his onyx plumage matched the sky. Carefully folding his immense black wings, he stared at me with round intelligent eyes.

That's how I knew; his eyes, Kieran's eyes, they never changed. Every part of him was this vicious monster with the cold calculating expression and merciless claws, except those eyes; they were undoubtedly human; full of hate, anger and emotion.

I cautiously edged closer, noticing the mostly concealed leather bands wrapped around both his wings so that a bag was perched at the top of his spine. I wondered idly where that had appeared from. Then I remembered the complicated strap thing that had been in the bag inside the car; it must be whatever that had been. A golden chain glinted around his neck.

"Kieran?" I asked. To my embarrassment my voice shook.

His eyes danced, like he was laughing silently. I took that as confirmation.

Remembering what he wanted me to do, I stepped back, clutching the remains of his clothes like I was protecting them. Suddenly he swept forwards, ducking his head and somehow, miraculously, I was on his back.

My stomach lurched as he leapt into the air. My scream was lost in the rush of wind. I grabbed Kieran's neck, thrusting my face into his dark feathers and squashing my eyes tightly shut. The folds of material, his clothes and trainers, pressed awkwardly against me. In a hysterically petrified and angry moment I contemplated throwing them, letting them plummet to the earth.

My heart pounded more erratically the higher Kieran ventured, adrenalin surged in my veins. The blasting air blew my hair back, gnawing at my flesh. In a weird way it made me feel better. It sharpened my hazy numbness, the biting chill drawing out the pain. Finally I opened my eyes.

And I was flying.

My fear evaporated immediately; this was spectacular. Honestly it wasn't that different to being on a motorbike, it was the same feeling of going incredibly fast, incredibly dangerously. I still had to rotate my body as Kieran jerked around invisible corners, clenching my thighs against the sides of his enormous body that I barely reached with my stubby legs. I listened to the beat of his wings, so steady like a sleeping heart. It was a very sedative sound.

The wind stung my eyes, filling them with brimming tears. I sunk down onto Kieran as he levelled out, pressing my head against the strange texture of his feathers. They weren't soft like I expected, they were as solid and impenetrable as plates of steel, more like armour than insulation. I closed my eyes exhaustedly, my head still throbbed; it was becoming worse. The cold crept underneath my skin like a virus, filling me with its malicious dose and I shivered; the quakes progressively becoming more violent as time ticked by. It was accompanied by a sweat that drenched my clothes. I glanced at my arms and they were so pale, snow white, my freckles had vanished, as if frostbitten by the cold.

My eyes closed to consciousness.

My body was losing the battle.

Chapter Seven

I could hear something through the deep water of unconsciousness. I didn't know what it was, it sounded like beating. Curiously I betrayed the ignorant part of my mind that was tempting me, compelling me to stay in the nice empty depths of nothingness. It was like space, almost deserted, until I started to kick my legs and thrust my arms out determinedly; then I began to see sparks of life, like stars. It became colder the higher I swam, and noisier.

Eventually I broke through the surface and my eyes darted open.

As my vision slowly adjusted to the dark surroundings, I realised in a terrified panic that the only things surrounding me were clouds and the piercing pinpricks of stars and planets. The vast skyline stretched into the distant night. I was in the air. Frantically bolting upright, the wind gnashed at my face like shards of scraping ice. I screamed but something hard clasped over my mouth. My heart thumped vigorously as I whirled my head around. I didn't feel relieved when I saw Adrian.

"Calm down," he ordered angrily, loosening his grip on my mouth so I could breathe; just. "It's alright." He didn't sound reassuring.

He released me. I looked down and saw feathers, dark brown feathers.

I gasped, a renewed fear igniting within me. I was on the back of a monster. Cautiously I leant over the monster's belly, shivering as the bitter wind clawed at my hair, acknowledging ocean far below me. I cringed, concentrating on gripping onto its armouring feathers so I didn't fall to a premature watery grave. Adrenalin pounded in my veins, fear pumping my heart erratically. I was a jumbled mess of blind terror and confusion. It slowly filtered into comprehension that I had been on a creature like this before I'd fallen unconscious. It was broader than Kieran, I guessed it was Nikolas.

"How did I get here? How long have I been asleep? Where's Kieran?" I yelled over the wind to Adrian who stubbornly ignored me. I turned to repeat my demanding questions. Eventually he responded with an ignorant shrug.

Looking around, I wondered where everyone was. Then I looked up and gasped. They were above me. I realised the two terrifying predators must have been the two girls. They seemed smaller than Nikolas underneath me, with slender, streamlined bodies covered over with dark feathers. They were beautiful, but terribly and deceitfully so. Their beauty hid their talons.

Then another monster swooped underneath Nikolas and I felt my perspective shift entirely into something of absorbed fascination. This monster was glorious; those emerald encrusted wingtips incandescent in the moonlight. It dived and twirled recklessly, slicing through the air with its cutting bladelike wings. I felt no longer afraid.

Then, to my utter astonishment, I heard a husky voice echo in my head, *How's your head, Princess, still not fully functional?*

I stared in shocked awe, *what the fu'-*

No swearing in my head, Kieran objected, to my utter astonishment, winking a rounded green and black eye. *I want to keep it clean from such vulgarity.*

How in the world? I thought bewilderedly.

His fantastic eyes brightened as he shrugged his feathers, *you're more Phoenix than human right now. How else do you think we communicate?*

Startled, I looked down at myself. No, I wasn't covered in feathers. I was a little redder though, like I was flushed. I didn't feel warm, I felt cold. The veins in my arms were raised, a dingy burnt red liquid pumping though them. My head was still hurting, a persistent and superfluous aching.

You can read my mind? I asked Kieran, horrified.

Yeah, he replied, *I know all your dirty secrets. Be prepared for future blackmail.*

Seriously? I thought frantically, my heart thumping. What a horrific thought.

No, he said *I can only hear what you want me to; when one of us is in this form.*

Does that mean I'm getting better? I inquired hopefully.

His mind-voice dropped, *No, It means you're Changing.*

I gulped; I really am going to Change. I can't believe my friends were right; I really am going to die a virgin. How depressing.

Kieran stared forwards as he uttered: *The darkest hour must pass before sunrise.*

I didn't have the time to think it over; Kieran had suddenly jerked his beak upwards, immediately serious, ostensibly sniffing the frigid air. Trying to be surreptitious, I mimicked his movements. I couldn't smell anything. I glanced around, watching as the others breathed in the scentless air. *Can you smell that?* Kieran asked generally. I shook my head, but the others made agreeing noises.

What is it? My mind-voice was disreputably impatient.

Home, they chorused simultaneously.

What...? I wondered just as Nik made a prodigious dive through the air, tipping almost vertical and falling at a blindingly fast speed. My eyes widened in shock but before I could do anything the others were copying him. I gasped in horrified astonishment as we cascaded towards the ocean waves, accelerating faster than I thought possible. I clutched tighter to Nikolas, my legs clenched tight, planting my face into his feathers and screaming profanities. I opened my eyes at the very last minute to see a ridiculously small-looking clump of rocks in the seemingly endless pool of salt water.

I braced myself for a rough landing and wasn't disappointed, jolting backwards violently and praying not to be catapulted into the ocean.

Getting off Nikolas seemed an even more daunting task, I realised as I looked down at the rock a couple of metres below. To my annoyance Adrian slid off Nikolas's side and landed perfectly. When I tried my legs buckled underneath me and I fell on my ass. I managed to straighten up after a couple seconds recovery; the intimidating Phoenix had already disappeared from sight. As I looked up searchingly Adrian shouted me over.

I stumbled over to him, suddenly very aware of the great expanse of water surrounding me. It made me anxious, to be on a tiny rock in the middle of the ocean, however as I ventured over to Adrian, I immediately became aware that he was standing in front of a fairly large hole in the rock that stood metres above my head. It was about the size of a child's paddling pool. I realised, as I clambered up the slippery rock, that its depth was unknown as the light only filtered down to the top layer. It rose much higher than the placid sea surrounding, though during severe storms I imagined it filled in; I guessed the bottom still contained sea water.

"Go on." Adrian snapped, "Get going."

"Down there," I said, "You're joking, right?"

I looked at his deadly serious face, avoiding those intensely black eyes, and thought that he wasn't the type to joke. Or have humour at all.

"Where have the others gone?" I wondered, eyeing the hole sceptically.

"Where do you think," Adrian spat, glaring at me.

I'd had enough, "What's your problem?" I demanded.

His glower intensified as he snarled, "You really have no idea what we are doing for you, do you? We left Kariak for a reason; who are you to make us go back?" he demanded, "You selfish bitch, you have no idea."

"I'm not making you do anything," I snapped, "I'm dying; your friends seem to think they can save me. They have compassion, but I didn't expect it."

He sighed with melodramatic hostility, and then proceeded to climb down the hole on his own. I watched him disappear, resisting the urge to kick him on his way down, then waited for a moment. I looked around for no reason, seeing what I knew I would see, water and night's sky, then sighed; I knew I would have to eventually go down the hole, it was either that or swim. Which I was pretty sure I couldn't do.

I gripped onto the ledge of the hole and slowly backed my way into it, my feet groping the slippery wall for a place to rest and balance.

"Come on Princess," Kieran called from below me in a voice so loud I jumped and nearly slipped. "We don't have all day. Well," he amended himself, "we do. But you don't have all day."

I gulped and cautiously edged my way down. As the light became weaker the further down I climbed, I became more and more dependent on my sense of touch, feeling for somewhere to grip onto. It wasn't too far down before I managed to touch something with my foot that definitely wasn't rock. Rock doesn't usually complain when you hit it, you see.

"Sorry," I muttered to which ever girl I'd kicked.

"Jump, I'll catch you," Nikolas said patiently. "I'm right underneath you."

Now, if it would have been Kieran or Adrian who'd have said that I would have laughed at the idea, but Nikolas had this calm steadying voice without a note of harshness or derision; it was impossible to believe he would do anything to hurt me. So I took a deep trusting breath and let go of the wall. There was a burst of air then hands immediately snagged on my waist and stopped my fall. He instantly put me down.

Complete darkness surrounded me. I was very aware of the bodies surrounding me. They radiated heat in the non-existent space. I accidentally brushed someone's side as I shuffled restlessly, realising I had touched bare skin. Those who had changed hadn't dressed. Kieran was once again butt naked and in close proximity; apparently it was a natural state for him.

"Anyone got a light?" Nikolas wondered.

"There's one in Ruby's bag," a girl, Chara I think, answered.

There was movement around me as I perked up, "Someone has my bag?"

"I got it for you at that party," someone offered; a pleasant female voice, Briseis. "I knew what would happen when I saw you in that bonfire; I thought you'd want it."

"Thank you," I said quietly. I felt oddly relieved that some of my things had survived despite the fact that I probably wouldn't end up needing them anyway; with my impending doom and all.

Someone lit the lighter and I just caught a flash of skin and curves before awkwardly glancing away towards the wall-which thankfully was the place where the lighter was being directed. That insignificantly little flame showed little of Kieran's body as he kneeled down before a large spherical boulder, barely flickering over the prominent muscles of his broad shoulders.

"Hold this there," he ordered to Briseis, gesturing at the lighter which she grasped accordingly and he proceeded to firmly grab the rock.

Nik turned to me. I just made out the side of his strong jaw and the fan of his eyelashes in the dimness. He began speaking. "When we move this rock there is going to be a gush of sea water flooding in here. What we want to do is to get through the water to the other side and swim up to the surface of the sea, which will hopefully be Kariak's shores. You see, this is a weakened spot in the Wards that protect the island, a fracture if you like. I won't go into details now on how it works, but do you understand what needs to be done?"

I nodded, but I had no clue what he was on about.

"There are too many of us to get through separately," Kieran stated, "There won't be enough time. Lads, help the ladies. Ruby, you're with me. I don't suppose you've ever swam before?"

I wracked my brain but I knew the answer was no. I'd always avoided swimming; it just never seemed something I'd be interested in. I muttered a 'no' and I could see the smile brighten the shadow of his face; it had an edge.

"Good," I heard Adrian grunt behind me, "That means at least for now she isn't conditioned against it." What did that mean? Of course I was terrified.

"Brace yourselves," Kieran instructed, "Ruby, get behind me. When I say go, grab onto my shoulders, close your eyes and take a deep breath. Once you feel you are out of the current kick your arms and legs until you reach the surface." His voice dropped then into a deep almost kind murmur, "If you're having trouble I will be there."

Kieran and the other men took hold of the boulder and nodded at each other. Then, with astonishing effort, they began to push the boulder away.

Instantly water gushed over my feet, flooding so powerfully I stumbled backwards against the rock wall. I barely managed to scramble over to Kieran, the liquid firing at us like shards of broken mirror, before he shouted "Now!"

I gasped a quick breath and practically threw myself onto Kieran, furiously shutting my eyes as he dived forwards into the watery onslaught.

The last thing I thought before I hit the water was: *I can't swim.*

We crashed through a wave of water, but its power was indomitable. I could feel Kieran's strange metal bag underneath me pull us back further with its weight. Though my eyes were squeezed tightly shut and my hands clasped desperately to Kieran, I could tell we were still travelling at a devastatingly slow pace. I could feel his muscles move as he stretched out his arms to claw at the walls of the rock, attempting to pull us through despite the battering force of the current.

The impact of it was so intense it was painful, but slowly I could feel myself come free of the full force of it. Slicing deeper into icy depths, my lungs began to itch longingly. Suddenly Kieran and I separated when my fingers accidentally slipped from his flesh.

I wanted to find him but I knew what I had to do. I kicked my legs and moved my arms, feeling myself move through the ridiculously cold water. The cold hadn't been so obvious until now, perhaps because I was too distracted by the force of the water cascading onto us. Now, however, it cut me like a thousand glass splinters. The pain was incredible. Unbelievable! I had never felt such cold; all I knew was that I wanted out of it.

As I swam in a direction I hoped was upwards the pressure of the water seemed to loosen and I knew I was nearing the surface. I lifted my arms to distinguish when I found air but to my horrified shock my hands touched something else. It was cold, freezing cold. As I ran my palms along the barrier that blocked my way to safety, it slowly came into comprehension that I was trapped under thick impenetrable ice.

Instinctively I opened my mouth to gasp but instead swallowed water. It was grimy and salty, thicker than normal; like blood. I coughed involuntarily, subsequently gulping more; searching frantically for none-existent air. A petrified panic exploded throughout me, I tried to feel my way for a crack in the ice, but I was deluded in thinking I could escape this watery fate. I was trapped. I bashed the ice with my fist, trying furiously and pointlessly to break it. The hope that I could succeed was the only thing I had left to cling on to. Behind my closed eyelids, where I was inevitably drifting away, my body too numb to feel the pain anymore, I saw a flash of sudden brightness.

The next thing I was really aware of was the sound of drumming.

Should drumming hurt? It was hitting me, I swear.

Then I realised. Someone was, quite literally, beating the life back into me.

My eyes burst open. I coughed up what felt like gallons of bitter water.

"Will you stop trying to die on me?!" Kieran yelled. His voice was saturated with a mixture of anger and relief. "Honestly, I have had enough of saving your ass," the angry part seemed to be dominating, "Once you burn, I refuse to play guardian angel anymore. " He babbled antagonistically as he pounded my back with his fist, causing me to throw up more ocean. I wasn't listening.

He could have warned me, stupid git. "You could have mentioned the ice." I half-coughed with a gravelly voice. I will never, *ever*, voluntarily go into water again; I was officially scarred for life.

"We didn't know," I heard Nik's voice admitting from a short distance; "We never anticipated that the sea would have frozen this early in the year."

"You'll be okay," Chara continued, "Your fever will burn off the cold soon, it won't affect you for long."

I shivered, attempting to swallow the throbbing pain in my throat. My lungs ached tremendously, I was heaving nothing now. I stared at sand and felt Kieran move away from me. Eventually I felt stable enough to look up. When I did, I realised that everyone else was putting on clothes. *Look away Ruby.*

I saw a movement next to me and glanced up. Kieran had now thrown on some dry(ish) trousers and was currently sitting back down in front of me. Roughly, he shoved on some chunky leather boots; like army boots. Pulling blades from a bag and sharpening them; they glinted dangerously.

"Salt is not good for my blades," he muttered irritably.

His bare shoulders dripped clammy ocean water. The pearls rolled over his sculpted collarbones, tracing the deep indentations between the plains of muscle like rivers in valleys. I looked at his emerald eyes, concentrating on the silver metal, and noticed his thick lashes held tiny beads of crystal too. As I watched in an almost mesmerised fashion, a droplet shimmered obliquely down his cheek, journeying over his perfect lips. I felt embarrassingly compelled to reach out and capture the drop. To hold it up to the light and see if he'd somehow turned it to diamond. I think I was dribbling, not good.

I'd never seen anyone so beautiful in my life. It was ridiculous.

With an effort I dragged my eyes from Kieran. I glanced around, we were in the arms of a curved beach; the sand was the dull gold of wheat grain. The ocean stretched out like a perpetual frozen blanket; how did we get here? I didn't ask; some things are better left to the imagination.

In front of me I saw random tufts of grass eventually leading up to a sprawling coniferous forest. The fresh vibrant green complemented the cool crisp air. Peaking over the tops of the trees I could see mountains that grazed the sky. It was absolutely gorgeous, a winter wonderland. The exact opposite of what I'd expected. It looked like Alaska.

"So this is it?" I asked, casting my gaze again on Kieran. He now wore a dark shirt and was currently strapping a thick belt around his hips. He then started adjusting the leather and metal straps on his bag thing, wrapping the straps around his biceps and hiding blades in secretive pouches.

I didn't know what to do. Everyone else seemed preoccupied with accessorising themselves with bizarre weapons. They all wore similar dark clothes made with an unrecognisable black material, thicker than leather. Anxiety started to crawl up my back.

"Are we going to war?" I asked nervously.

Briseis came closer, apparently fully prepared to raid the Bank of England. She grinned, "Nobody walks into those woods unarmed; they're not protected." She said it as if it were inevitable that we should meet something dark and dangerous -other than Adrian- in there. I shivered at the thought.

"Can I have a dagger or something?" I wondered.

"No," Kieran said absolutely without even looking up. "We don't have the time to delay our journey while I stitch your arm back together."

I frowned but didn't comment as I gaped at the numerous weapons, "Where did they all come from?" I wondered, more to myself than anyone else.

Chara regarded my sodden clothes with a frown, "You need to change."

"I know, that's why we're all here, right?" I joked lamely. There was an awkward silence; I guess they weren't impressed by my attempt at humour.

"Put these on," she handed me some clothes similar to everyone else's.

"Can I not just wear my own?" I asked, trying not to sound unappreciative.

"No," Nikolas interrupted firmly.

I surrendered, accepting the bundle of clothes. Chara waited and I stared at her, realising, "You want me to get dressed here?"

"You'll eventually get used to it," she sighed but pointed off to her side, "If it makes you feel any better you can go behind those rocks. Don't go far. If you're too long then I'll get Adrian to fetch you, and *that's* a warning."

Grudgingly I trudged off through the wet sand; my feet occasionally sinking completely in. I felt a sting of grief; my dog had loved the beach. Swallowing my sorrow I stumbled behind a boulder and peeled off my sodden jeans. They were being difficult. Finally I struggled into the given clothes. At closer inspection I discovered the material was not like leather at all. It consisted of an almost scaly substance. As I went back, I was surprised at how flexible and light the deceptive clothes were.

I linked myself into the circle of people. Kieran's face was an apathetic mask. Glancing around, I saw a similar expression on Adrian; though his was more emphasised. My vision flickered to Briseis and she was smiling, nearly affectionately at the land. Nikolas wound a comforting arm around Chara.

"No matter how long we've been gone; this place still…gets to you, doesn't it?" Chara sighed restlessly, surveying the impressive world like an old forgotten friend. I shivered lightly; she'd been right, the fire burning within me had already targeted the cold. My skin felt warm to the touch already.

"It's still our home," Nik murmured.

"It was the people in it who ruined it, not the place itself." Adrian spat sharply. Hate practically radiated from his pretty brown skin.

"I used to dream about it." Bris said.

I used to dream about it too. I just didn't realise at the time.

"Let's go," Kieran said.

Chapter Eight

As we edged closer to the forest it took me a moment to realise that Kieran hadn't followed. I paused uncertainly then slowly crept towards him. He had his back to me, the straight hard line of his jaw upraised as he gazed at the glistening ice.

"What happened to you here?" I asked quietly.

When he finally turned his face was angry.

"Nothing happened to me here." His voice was filled with bitter contempt. "*I* had a great life." He laughed humourlessly. "I was young, powerful and full of promise. I was a Son of the Ashes and I was an Ashaik." He breathed out then, shaking his hair, sprinkling little droplets from the glistening strands. "I was also ignorant. My blood was my pride. I never thought it would be my shame as well."

"What was the problem?" I wondered softly.

Kieran looked at me with those gorgeous emerald eyes; passion smouldered there like a constantly burning fire. I saw something else in him, a reason behind the anger. He hesitated for a long moment, his lips pursed as if calculating whether or not he could trust me with his secret. Eventually he sighed, looking away and murmuring, "My brother is human." I frowned in confusion, puzzled how this could even be possible. Kieran's voice was filled with a resentment that didn't seem aimed at me. "He never burnt."

Kieran returned those piercing hawk eyes to the ocean. He spoke like he was the only one listening. "Being human, to my father and my country, was like being a parasite. It is seen as the ultimate disgrace."

I spoke gently, "What did he do?"

Kieran met my eyes; there was a fierce protectiveness in his.

"Everything in the book: beat him, cursed him, tried to kill him frequently." Something flickered in his features, something morose and guilty. "I should have known," he whispered, "but Adrian's too proud, he never told me anything. I had no idea. But one day, I caught them both fighting; *really* fighting, there was blood everywhere. Adrian had defended himself for once. I didn't know what to do. In the end my mother found them and knocked my father out while he wasn't looking–she knew what was happening."

His eyes drained of emotion. "My mother turned to me and told me I had to leave with Adrian–not just the city but the whole island. She said to take him or he'd be killed. She said he needed me. I looked at his unconscious body and knew what I had to do. I made my plans to escape. I was seventeen."

I gaped at him, speechless. I never expected all that to spill out of him.

The thought of it was awful. I gazed at Adrian differently now, at the tense shoulders of his thick frame retreating into the woods. Noticing how his eyes flickered around suspiciously. Finally I understood.

"Your mother didn't come," it wasn't a question, but he answered it anyway.

"No," he said curtly, he deliberately avoided my eyes.

"You were seventeen? How long were you in England?"

"Two years."

"How did you escape? Through that rock again?" I probed cautiously.

"That isn't important," he said, his features conditioning back into a solid unapproachable stare. With that he turned and followed the others where they'd begun to walk off towards the coniferous forest.

***

The trek through the forest was long and precariously intense. The ambiance would shift so suddenly that it made my skin crawl. I still couldn't believe I was actually here. Not in my world anymore. It just seemed far too strange to believe, so I didn't even bother trying; to me this was just a long strange dream.

At first it seemed a nice place.

The surrounding pine trees swayed their spiky fur, festively filling the air with a refreshing scent. The ground was covered in intricate patterns of ice, natural complicated decorations, almost invisible like marks from ice-skates. It reminded me of Christmas with the scent of the trees and the cold chill.

"Why are we not flying there, wherever we are going?" I asked Nikolas. He was the closest to me. "Surely it's faster?"

"It's too dangerous, the forest isn't protected," Briseis interjected. "There are monsters living here that could swat us out of the sky like flies. At least we're out of sight in the trees. All we have to worry about down here is big bugs."

The thought of something so big and terrifying it made the Phoenix cautious was a very scary thought indeed. I watched my surroundings intently.

"And we're heading to Forenna, the Capital," Nik explained. "It's the only mixed city. All the others are segregated."

I frowned, confused, "What do you mean?"

"Our kind is divided into four Tribes. Earth, Air, Water and" he glanced at me as he spoke, "Fire. All you need to know is that Phoenix are like their element, in appearance and power. For example, a Phoenix of Air is very pale with almost clear hair and eyes; and they will have a certain amount of control over their element. This lets them evoke Air and do things with it."

"Like what?"

"Change the direction the wind blows," Chara suggested. "It's very useful when flying. If you can get a good wind behind you; you go faster."

"Are you an Air Phoenix?" I asked thoughtlessly.

Everybody laughed. I glanced down embarrassedly. What did I say?

"No, chick," Chara smiled, "the different Phoenix tribes are very distinctive. All of us here look similar because we're of Earth. You are of Fire, that's why you look nothing at all like us. Trust me; you'll be able to tell the difference."

Yeah, they did look nothing like me. They were all tall, tanned and mysterious. I was loud, stubby and ginger. Thanks for pointing that out.

Nik seemed surprised. "Surely you remember how badly the Tribes are prejudiced against each other? It's been that way for generations. Its only now, after seeing the way people behave in your country towards each other–blacks and whites together, all different races, colours, genders–that I realise how wrong it is here. Hedero is a city only populated by Earthbirds. And the Air Phoenix only live in Ciza and so on."

"That's really sad," I commented, frowning, "but why not Forenna?"

"Forenna used to be a human city, that's why it's so old. It's as old as your pyramids," He explained, patiently. "We are native to Kariak, our people were born here. Forenna is the city that the Original Mother lived in before she Changed. And after she Changed, eventually the humans who lived here died out; replaced by us because we are stronger and more adaptable."

"The Original Mother?" I questioned.

"Don't you remember anything about the Resurrection?" Nik was surprised.

"Of Jesus?" I said confusedly.

Adrian shook his head impatiently, "No, not of Jesus you moron, of the first Phoenix." When I shook my head he rolled his eyes.

"Well, our legends say there was a first Phoenix and she started out as a human woman." Nikolas informed me, "I'll tell you the story," he smiled.

"One day the sun shone so brightly and the air was so hot that the land became alight with flame. The woman tried to protect the people; she saved many lives but eventually the flames overwhelmed her; she died. She was only young and pregnant with her own children. Water, Earth and Air tried to help her for they saw what her bravery and sacrifice cost. But Fire would not be extinguished and eventually the woman turned to ash. Fire finally saw his wrongs and produced a spark of life again for the woman. Water mixed with Earth to rebuild her body and Wind sculpted her into shape. With all the elements working together, life arose from the Ashes in the form of a magnificent bird with the power of all four elements.

"What happened next?" I wondered, intrigued by the way he told this obviously beloved story.

"She wandered alone for a while, watching and missing her husband. That winter she laid four eggs. When they hatched, each chick had a gift from one element and also possessed the ability to transform into a human; for it was with their mother's humanity that the elements remade her. The four first Phoenix grew up as humans and eventually had children of their own who inherited the same affinities. These gifts were passed on again and again and eventually began the age of the Phoenix." He finished.

"What happened then?" I asked "Why did the tribes split up?"

Kieran appeared as if from nowhere; he'd ventured off ahead for a while to 'find something'–I didn't want to ask–and interrupted, "Jesus Ruby, he's not a bloody encyclopaedia; leave the poor man alone." He added, almost as an afterthought, "Oh and we might have a little problem."

"What is it?" Chara began, but stopped to listen. Everyone went silent.

I heard a patter, distant but progressively growing closer and louder. It sounded like the tapping of rain on a conservatory roof, thousands of points of pressure showering down restlessly on glass. Automatically Kieran reached for one of the blades dangling from his chunky belt. He withdrew it, effortlessly, sliding the steel from its scabbard in a way that seemed far too natural. This was something he was well accustomed to.

There was a loud rustling of leaves. Instantly I shifted my vision to the direction of the sound. From a smattering of thick brambles, a creature appeared. It was like a giant millipede. A millipede about the length of two park benches and as tall as my thigh while on all its legs. Its winding segmented body was armoured with a seemingly impenetrable outer layer. It didn't have any eyes, at least not that I could see, but I could clearly visualise the rest of its splintered teeth from the few spilling from a huge gaping mouth, which occasionally dripped foamy saliva. It seriously needed a napkin.

It hissed at me, as if guessing my thoughts.

"You've got to be kidding me," I said lowly, glancing at Briseis. "I didn't think you meant bugs *that* big."

Without hesitation it snapped forwards, startlingly fast. The thing would have snatched Briseis's leg if Kieran hadn't have sprung forwards, swinging the blade high and piercing where a shallow valley formulated between its head and its exoskeleton. The creature collapsed to the ground, screeching violently. Kieran slammed on top of it, stabbing it again.

I stood there for a moment, staring at the honey-like liquid now dripping from Kieran's blade as he stood. Did that really just happen?

"Is it dead?" Bris asked.

Kieran shook his head sharply. "Just stunned," he answered.

"Um," Briseis swallowed, uncharacteristically anxious, "He had friends."

With wide eyes she scanned the coniferous forest. I followed her gaze, flinching when I noticed another millipede-thing march into the clearing. As I watched in horrified astonishment, I counted at least half a dozen more surreptitiously surround us, one even crawling down a tree trunk. I swore under my breath. I hated bugs.

Kieran grabbed me, harshly yanking me against him. My breath caught.

The others took up defensive positions, gripping weapons in preparation. The creatures leapt forwards simultaneously; slashing at everyone with their razor-sharp teeth. Two came straight at me and Kieran.

With swift, precise movements Kieran swiped at the first one. It reared back and the otherwise crushing blow missed; glinting off its protective armour. Kieran dodged us out the way while I struggled to get free. A strong hand clasped unyielding around my waist.

"I can help," I insisted angrily as the second thing charged forwards.

With a swift lance of Kieran's blade the thing toppled to the ground; in half.

"How?" Kieran hissed; plunging the knife into the second thing.

It hissed like a rattle snake. Rearing back, it doubled my height. The blade was now embedded in the centre of its body, piercing part of its black shell. *That must have been a strong hit,* I thought. I watched as Kieran pulled out the blade and relocated it to a precise spot. It collapsed. Dust glittered up where it landed. Kieran released me unexpectedly; I stumbled forward but managed to catch myself before falling onto the remains of the dead thing. Its wounds oozed a dingy yellow liquid that filtered slowly to the earth. More dribbled from is drooping mouth. The fat droplets cast stringy threads that demolished boundaries between the carcass and the grass, like amber leaking from tree bark in long sticky strands. It was vile.

"I could have helped," I muttered stubbornly, to no one in particular.

I glanced around; only three creatures were still alive. Kieran automatically snatched another blade from one of the straps on his arm, spinning it he sent it hurtling through the air. It faultlessly penetrated the soft dip between the creature's head and body. That stunned it momentarily, giving sweet innocent Chara a chance to tear out its bowels. Kieran ran at the last two and everybody shuffled back. Fearlessly, with eyes of a predator, Kieran pulled anther blade from his belt so he had one in both hands.

Swinging them around his wrists, he smiled at the creatures, "Come on my beauties. I don't have all day." He was actually *enjoying* this.

One hissed and jumped at him, Kieran sliced at it but the other was coming too. He let one fall on him, and somehow rolled it over so that it was stuck on its back. In a fragment of a second, Kieran raised both blades high and slashed through the creature in a crossing motion just as the last thing came at him from behind. Without turning, he shoved the blade through the last thing. It fell towards his back and he spun, dislodging his sword, disgustingly spraying yellow blood everywhere, letting it fall.

What shocked me most, and will still shock me until the day I die, was the way everyone calmly picked up their bags and continued down the path like nothing even happened. I stood there, astonished, as they passed me.

After that I didn't even dare speak. I grew sufficiently paranoid, my suspicious eyes permanently scanning the forest. I stayed close to Kieran. No matter how much I hated to admit it, I felt safe with him.

Mostly I think I was imagining it, but I swore I caught formidable glimpses of movement in the trees. Though whenever I focused properly I only saw shadows. It kept me on edge, alert. It kept my heart beating erratically and my senses sharp and defined. Perhaps it was a good thing I was bricking it.

I don't know how long passed, minutes or hours, but with every second, I grew weaker. With every step my muscles flared with new aches and pains. With every breath I was closer to death.

Then, abruptly we arrived at the top of an extremely steep valley.

The rock crumbled away almost vertically beneath my feet, revealing at the pit of the slope a crystal-clear river carrying shards of floating ice from further north. I gulped as I contemplated the hazardous descent. The land stretched out everlastingly in frozen mountains, unhampered and undisturbed by human hands. We were still much further away than I had hoped.

"How are we going to get across?" I asked shakily.

No one was breathing as heavily as me, but Briseis collapsed inelegantly to the floor, her arms splaying out in melodramatic exhaustion. Kieran frowned at her. Nik perched on a rock and Chara joined him. He passed her a bottle of water from one of the bags he was carrying and she gulped it down gratefully. Before Nik could drain his bottle, Bris snatched it away and finished it off. He raised his eyebrows but she shrugged unapologetically, "I'm about dying."

Bris's gaze flickered to me, her eyes wide as she realised what she said. It took me a moment to understand why she looked so guilty.

Kieran, of course, spoke first, "We can't go anywhere until we find the Healer." He glanced over at Adrian. "I'm afraid that's your job, you'll know where she is more than anyone else. Briseis you'll have to take him." He looked over at Nik and Chara, "I guess I don't need to explain to you both what needs to be done."

Nik frowned, "No, unfortunately you don't."

"You're the most..." Briseis trailed off, searching for the right word, "...believable, Nik. If anyone can talk us out of something it's you."

Nik nodded, looked at Chara who shrugged and looked at me before they disappeared down the valley. "Good luck, fledgling." She said and Nik smiled hopefully.

"Come on then," Briseis gestured to Adrian, "No point waiting." She looked at me before they too went "See you on the other side." Adrian didn't speak.

I turned to Kieran "What now?" my voice had transformed into a breathless rasp. "Where do we go?"

"There's no point in leaving yet, not for a while, you might as well save your energy." He said as he shrank to the floor and pulled off his bag.

I carefully sat next to him, staring at the view of the mountains, thinking to myself about how I'd been here before but forgotten. I remember now, I remember the taste of the air. Sweet. Foreign. Exotic.

"Did you miss it here?" I asked him eventually, noticing him watching the mountains with a peculiar expression.

"I was born here, had friends and family here, didn't have to hide here and was practically *worshipped*; of course I miss it," He huffed irritably.

"You were worshipped." I repeated dubiously.

"Every day the peasant children would come and give me offerings of jewels they'd collected from the mountains." I turned around to look at him, eyebrows raised, but he continued nevertheless. "And the *women*. Well, I don't think you're old enough to hear what they gave me."

"Are you actually a compulsive liar?" I wondered seriously.

"If I said no, would you believe me?" he countered, eyes flashing.

"Probably not," I admitted, "but I really doubt that you were worshipped."

"Aye, you are right." Kieran admitted. "It was lustful adoration that I received from those beautiful women; and hatred from their husbands."

I laughed despite myself, "You're so full of crap, Kieran. I don't know how your neck manages to hold the weight of your head."

"It's a very good neck, I grew it myself," he assured me. He glanced down at my arm, "Your marks are starting to show."

I looked down. It was true. Those tattoo patterns Nik had made appear earlier were spreading faintly across my arms.

"They're pretty," Kieran admitted unwillingly, referring to the marks. "You know, in a girly fire-swirling kind of way."

"I think there's a compliment in there somewhere," I said. "I think you actually just called me pretty."

"I said your marks are," he agreed grumpily.

"Nah," I grinned jokingly, "Don't deny it; you think I'm pretty."

His face was suddenly terrifyingly serious. "Ruby, saying things like that could get you killed here."

"What?" I waved him off, "Don't be ridiculous."

"No Ruby," he continued, eyes deadly earnest, "If anyone in anyway thinks that we are closer than we should be, if they heard you say that and got the wrong idea," he shook his head, exhaling, "the consequences don't bear thinking about. You heard what Nik had said about the tribes. He was right."

I pulled a face, "It can't be that bad."

"Come with me," he said, "We're not far from the Wall. I'll show you."

I followed him, stumbling as I became more exhausted, for about twenty minutes, down the valley and around the base of a large chiseled mountain. After struggling my way around a sharp rocky bend, as I was just beginning to gasp with the pain of walking, I saw immediately what he meant by the Wall. I staggered back in shock and horror then slumped down onto my knees, gaping up at the fifty meter high wall with a sickening lurch in my stomach. I looked away, unable to continue looking.

"This is what I mean when I say the consequences are serious Ruby," Kieran said softy. I looked up at him, "I don't mean to scare you; I just need you to realise that in this world you have to play by the rules. I know you're used to being free to be with whoever you want, but here you have to stick to your own Tribe. Same goes for healing. A healer is not allowed to heal those from a different tribe. You're not Earth, you're Fire. Even worse, you're a Swartette and I'm an Ashaik and if anyone knew I'd healed you we'd be up there."

I turned back to the bodies on the Wall. Initially my eyes focused on the hundreds of severed wings impaled to the rock with iron stakes, reminding me of the butterflies you'd find pinned under glass in a museum. Dried dribbles of blood streamed down the walls like gruesome fingers from where the flesh and bone had been vigorously hacked through. There were so many, wings of gold, blue; even the pure white of angels had been smeared in blood and anguish. My eyes drifted to the bodies that were scattered occasionally underneath the wings. There were less of these and many were decaying. The stench of rotting flesh filled my nostrils. I counted nineteen bodies altogether, each branded with a symbol cut into their foreheads; ostensibly drawn with knives. The blood had been cleaned away so the symbol could be revealed but I couldn't decipher any of them.

The body that was most horrific seemed fairly new; it had yet to weather. She was a young woman, her skin must have once been a creamy colour and her hair was once the most beautiful strawberry blonde. I edged closer despite myself, transfixed by the enormous mound that still expanded her dead belly. She had been pregnant.

I wanted to cry, tears even brimmed. Her eyes remained open but dead, looking out at an impossible horizon, her face lapsed in an eternal sadness.

The mark on her forehead was different to all the others but one who had silver hair and who hung underneath a pair of disgustingly rotten grey wings.

"She was pregnant," I whispered, my voice a hollow shell of its normal self.

"Treason," Kieran read the mark on her forehead. "She went against Fire, and judging by her stomach, it must have been with a man. The only way they'd execute a pregnant woman is if the baby was mixed." He glanced over to the silver-haired young man, "This must have been her lover."

"How could they do that?" I felt sick. Why did he bring me here?

"It's here to stand as a warning," Kieran murmured apathetically. He turned to me, "Do you understand now? You must never tell anyone I healed you."

I opened my mouth to speak but my words choked in my throat.

A burst of agony rippled through me. Like a wave, the pain crashed everywhere, right down to my fingertips. I cried out involuntarily.

It was a million times worse than before; the extremity of it caused my head to spin nauseatingly and my limbs to convulse vigorously. Though I had never been burnt before, I could tell I was being now. A scalding pain in my lungs impulsively triggered me to gasp. The torture grew worse. I screamed.

It was time to die.

Chapter Nine

I doubled over, trying not to breathe.

I tried to concentrate on what Kieran was saying...something about flying through the streets...probably have to fight our way through. The monster in me was roaring ravenously. Boiling blood; charring flesh; growing stronger.

I looked up and saw Kieran's brilliant eyes staring sympathetically at me. I managed to nod, but struggled to turn my head. Everywhere was agony. By the time I next blinked Kieran was in bird form. Stretching his wings out, he completely blocked the horrible view of the mutilated bodies with his looming silhouette.

Then I screamed as the monstrous fire suddenly shifted into my heart. *The pain,* I cried to Kieran. *It's too much.*

Breathe shallowly, Kieran instructed, *it'll help.* He looked perplexed at my expression, *you're early! You shouldn't be burning for another two hours yet.*

Sorry, I'll try and die slower next time, I glared bitterly.

His advice didn't alleviate the pain, in fact it technically did nothing to quench the intensity of the fire; instead it gave me something to focus on other than the excruciation of my limbs. I furiously ignored the feeling that my veins were running with acid instead of blood, concentrating on the throbbing in my lungs as I tried to slow their expansion. Once my breathing was closer to normalcy, I eventually persuaded myself to stand. I shook violently as I struggled to clamber onto the gigantic monster that was Kieran.

Kieran suddenly leapt into the air and dived. His body was parallel to the steep decline of the valley, mere meters away. It was the weirdest rollercoaster I've ever been on.

We picked up speed, accelerating instantly like black lightning.

The scenery transformed from icy slopes to the tall majestic mountains that scraped the sky with their sharpened peaks. Trees coated the mountains, filling the air with a rich fresh fragrance. The highest peaks held dustings of snow probably hundreds of years old. We were moving so fast, a hundred times faster than Kieran had before. The sun was rising. I looked at it; the colours mirrored the fire that was dancing within me. I looked away. I barely seemed to blink before we were reaching the outskirts of the city.

Shifting my vision forward, straining my spine straighter with astonishing effort, I tried to see the city. It was located at the bottom of an enormous crater in one of the larger mountains, appearing to me like the inside of a perfectly rounded volcano. As we travelled closer I comprehended the sheer size of the valley. Its outskirts provided another steep descent through ice and rock, then forest, before finally revealing the glorious city surrounded by walls.

Sprawling in the middle of the city's magnificence was a building with a tower that, to my amazement, seemed to be forged from gemstones. It was a lot bigger than any other building, even the impressive palaces that perched higher up on the valleys walls. The gemstones twinkled translucently in the sunlight and a proud stone Phoenix, its wings outstretched as if in welcome, had more jewels dripping from its feathers. It had a crown of flowers and at the tips of its wings hovered glass orbs of incandescent firelight and droplets of shimmering water. It was superfluously radiant.

It terrified me that my eyesight was suddenly perfect; I knew what it meant.

Kieran continued at an impressive speed, I tried desperately to hold on. As we neared the buildings, Kieran swooped dangerously low to land before an impressive gate made of solid gold. The arch was decorated with various stones and ancient-looking runes in a foreign language that I recognised immediately. My mother's language; I hadn't forgotten it over the years.

The rough landing hurt me even more and I was gasping again. How much longer did I have to put up with this? How much longer until my body just surrenders to the fight? Kieran grudgingly forced his way forwards towards the gate, where we faced five exceedingly large guards and a woman sat at rectangular table. I couldn't decide if she was beautiful or just plain terrible.

She was like an ice sculpture; her skin luminously white - like she'd been locked in a windowless room since she was born, paler than me, even. She had wide grey eyes that turned coal black at the rim and hair which was shocking. It was absolutely transparent, like thin icicles that were convoluted in random directions. When her eyes narrowed, I realised she was as hard as ice too.

I need to get into the city, Kieran said urgently.

"Access rune," she demanded bitterly.

I don't have time for this; the girl here is dying; she needs a healer. He was obviously struggling to stay polite and dignified. I could feel the tension practically rolling off him like mist off mountains.

The woman's cool eyes regarded me briefly, her expression lazy and uncompassionate. *Sorry,* she apologised, not bothering to even try and sound sincere, *but everyone needs to show their access rune.*

Kieran leaned over, intimidating, his sharply curved beak close to her unfriendly face. Her eyes flashed hostilely. *Let me through,* he demanded, *can't you see she's helpless.*

Well if she's helpless, she countered, *there's no point us letting her in is there?*

Kieran glared down at her, and then with one impressive sweep of his wing he sent the long table flying. It crashed explosively, thick paper and cups of steaming drink spraying everywhere.

My name is Kierakai Ashaik, his mindvoice was undeniably authoritative and dominatingly powerful, *Second son of the Ashaik Elders, High-Protector and trained Assassin under the Fourteenth General. Let me through or, so help me, I will take action. This is my warning.*

You think you scare me, boy? The woman laughed. *I remember you all right, the younger of the Ashaik sons, the ones who disappeared.*

That's me, now let us through, he ordered.

Oh we will, the woman smiled vindictively, *but you're going straight to the tower. Guards!* She glanced back to the men.

Automatically the guards were coming at him, Kieran charged against them; battering their thick frames with his powerful wings. Obviously this approach was not profitable for the guards, within seconds they were on their backs. Changing their tactics they suddenly burst into dark terrifying Earthbirds. They clawed at him, snapping with their deadly beaks, tearing at him. There were too many. Abruptly I slipped to the floor. I struggled to stand up again, swaying, trying to take in the scenery but my body screamed in agony. The five massive guards were battering Kieran; he fought back determinedly, hitting one unconscious with an almighty kick to the head.

I looked around for help, but there was nobody nearby.

Then I felt the crystal eyes of the woman boring into my back. Cautiously I turned, feeling my agonised limbs ignite even further. It hurt so badly.

"Who are you," it wasn't a question, it was a demand.

I understood her instantly. I couldn't believe my mother had lied to me about her native language. I must have never been in a car crash. I must have never had to re-learn English. No, I had been a total novice.

"Nobody," I spluttered, wincing as my throat burned from the effort. I spoke in her language, it coming back to me with a surprising fluency.

"Well, nobody," she smiled eerily, "your friend is going to die."

I looked up, it was true Kieran was not winning, but he'd knocked down another two guards and was currently freefalling. I knew this trick; I'd seen him do it before, last time I was dying. He got so close to the earth, less than a meter away, before he pulled up. Another guard fortunately didn't anticipate that, and crashed to the floor. *Two more*, I thought.

At this point the woman frowned, irritated, muttering something about how she always has to do everything herself. I saw her forehead crinkle in concentration. Like a stake through my chest I saw what she was doing. My vision darted up to Kieran; he froze in midair. The others were hurtling towards him, another guard joining them as if from nowhere.

I remembered Nik saying something about Phoenix developing different gifts, could she be physic? It seemed so. Oh shit! A spark of intuition explained: that must be how she lets people into the city, she searches their minds for the chance of a threat.

Kieran controlled himself. I sighed in relief and he dived downwards. Using his advanced flying skills for protection, he was faster. The sky was black now, not a fragment of sunlight remained. The woman grunted unhappily, trying to get a better hold on Kieran. Before I could listen to my better judgement I punched her. She staggered back in surprise. Then her surprise transformed into infuriation.

"Stupid bitch, do you know what you just did?" she spat ferociously.

She righted herself, than I felt a wash of -*presence*- in my mind. However as soon as she entered my consciousness she felt the unbearable excruciation that my body was in. She screamed shrilly, releasing her mental hold. She hadn't expected that. She instantly leaped forwards, her hand bolting up to strike me hard across my face. The powerful blow sent me crashing to the ground. Sharp chips of gravel raked through my weakened fingers as I struggled to get up, scraping wiry red cuts. The pain was overwhelming. I collapsed into the dirt as her foot collided with my ribcage; knocking the air from my lungs.

The icy woman smirked once before lifting her pointed chin, closing her eyes in concentration. I was no longer a potential menace. The white skin above her eyes wrinkled into shallow lines; like cracks in concrete. I looked up; Kieran was caught between the remaining two Earthbirds. He kicked at one with his thick black talons, tearing its chest. Four more guards were coming. If he stopped fighting for even the briefest of moments he wouldn't be able to get out of that. In the end I had no choice. My instincts took over.

I opened my lips, unleashing a voice so powerful it didn't seem to belong to me. "Don't touch him. Close your mind."

My voice was beautiful, mesmerising, I held nothing back. It didn't hurt, surprisingly, not anymore than it already did. I felt the same strange energy trickle down my spine that I had in the pub only a few days ago, it mingled with the throbbing pain already residing there, but this time it was intentional. I had no idea what I was doing, really, but I continued to repeat that last sentence; my heartbeat drumming rhythmically as I spoke. The tingling sensation pulsated, coiling up my spine and spurting into my head like a fountain. It was impossible to ignore; impossible to control.

I was losing it. My instincts were overwhelming. "Close your mind."

The ice woman was clutching her ears desperately, her eyes wide and terrified as I drained her existence. Drawing out everything she had; her memories, her energy, her talents and numbing her mind to it all. I didn't want to do this, but I couldn't help myself. "Close your mind." My voice was angry. I was shouting before I knew it. A dominating, almost scary feeling took over me; this wasn't me. This was a dangerous thing I could do.

I had two choices now, either I stopped or I continued.

Glancing down at the pitiful woman, withering in an agony that maybe even matched mine; I stopped as my anger dimmed. She fell unconscious.

I glanced up at the sky, watching as Kieran tore and swiped at the warriors. He was phenomenal, furious. They were coming at him from different directions but he fought back with skill and confidence. Like everything with Kieran; he was brilliant at this. I waited only a few minutes until he landed beside me. I couldn't look at him. I didn't want to know what he was thinking as he stared down at the woman. I just didn't want to know.

The power I had felt was gone. The pain was worse. It kept getting worse.

You're bleeding, Kieran told me quietly.

I didn't care; it hurt too much to lift my hand for confirmation.

The fire was all I could think of. I'd had enough. I just wanted to lie down and let the flames come and get me. I just wanted not to feel it. I felt so ashamed of myself I couldn't bear to look at what I'd done to that woman. And I had enjoyed it; the power. It was sick. I was becoming a monster.

Finally looking at Kieran, I watched his beautiful feathers sway like grass in the wind. I watched as he stretched his strong wings; preparing to lift me. I watched those never-altering eyes as they blazed and bored into my soul. He knew I was giving up. I couldn't stand the pain anymore.

Kill me, I begged him, *please Kieran. Kill me quickly.*

He could see what I was going through. He could see how much I wanted the pain to end. I wanted to sleep, forever, if that's what it took.

He shook his head sadly. *If I do that, then I'll never see you again.* Then he scooped me up carefully, spreading me across his back. *Hold on,* he ordered firmly. I didn't. I couldn't. My hands wouldn't respond. *Damn it Ruby! If you don't hold on, all our efforts to save you would have been pointless. Do you not care about us? Do you realise what'll happen to us now for leaving? Your father will have us all executed. We'll need you. But first you need me to save you.*

I knew he was right. It wasn't fair. They'd done so much for me. Risking their future, their home, their lives, and I would not let them do it in vain. I cried out as I shifted my arms, wrapping them around Kieran's large form. The fire burned viciously in my wrist and the tattoos on my arms were glowing in pulses. The agony was intensifying still. I screamed helplessly as I wound my fingers through his reluctant feathers, clamping on with all I had.

My breath came in short shallow gasps. I felt the floor lift beneath me. I closed my eyes and tried to concentrate on my pathetic grip. I could tell we were moving fast. I will not die. Not after everything.

But still I wondered. *Do you believe in heaven?*

I believe, Kieran said firmly, *that you don't need to know what I believe, because you aren't going to see it for a very long time.*

All of a sudden I realised that we'd landed.

"Is this the girl?" said a business-like feminine voice. She spoke with calm authority.

My neck painfully shot up, startled. A woman sat on a roundish blanket woven with a complicated series of intertwining threads. We were in the centre of a small clearing, surrounded by ancient trees. The stars sparkled curiously above and millions of tiny black flowers grew around me.

Yes it is, mother, Kieran said respectfully, *her name is Ruby.*

The healer was his mother? Kieran's *mother* cursed me? Wow small world.

She was beautiful; obviously related to Kieran. Their eyes were identical, emerald and onyx, but her skin was lighter. The only part of her features that showed her age was the few strands of silver in her inky black hair.

Kieran gently lay me down. I relinquished my desperate hold. The pain exploded again. From the corner of my eye I saw a flash of emerald light. The woman told me that her name was Garnha and not to worry. I could feel the tears streaming down my face, hot and sticky; though I managed not to make a noise. This seemed like a great accomplishment.

The flames blazed uncontrollably and I knew I didn't have a lot of time.

Suddenly Kieran was there, human. He'd pulled his dark trousers on but hadn't bothered with anything else; his exposed skin was beautiful.

"What can I do?" he asked his mother, his face serious and professional.

"Sit her upright for a start," Garnha told him calmly. "Do you have the stone, Ruby?" she asked me, her voice kind and compassionate.

"What?" I wondered, confused.

Garnha seemed to notice something; the necklace around my neck. "Never mind," she uttered, and reached for my mother's necklace. I would have protested but I was too weak. She pulled off the small blood-red gemstone that had always hung from my chain though it never really matched. My eyes widened but she returned my chain and I put it on, watching her.

Another intense flare of pain ignited within me. I screamed uncontrollably, high-pitched agonised wails. I couldn't think. I tried to stop, only managing to reduce it to pitiful whimpers as my blood boiled; literally. I gasped, frantic.

Opening my eyes, which I hadn't realized I'd closed, I watched as Garnha put my jewel in a small wooden dish; quickly reciting something too complicated for me to understand. She held up a knife and slashed it across her palm; letting the blood drain onto the stone, then picked up my palm and did the same to me. The cut was clean and my blood fizzed and boiled as it filed the bowl. The crimson gem melted immediately. She picked up the bowl.

"Kieran you need to restrain her," she said and my eyes widened in fear. "You are going to have to lie flat on your stomach, Ruby. I'm going to make a small incision into the back of your neck."

I glanced at Kieran, terrified, but he nodded and I did as I was told.

I lay down, my body shaking. My arms were above my head and Kieran's knuckles clenched white as he wrapped his hand over them, his other hand becoming an inescapable snare on my lower back. I panicked as Garnha came closer, holding the substance that had miraculously transformed into a thick yellowish liquid. I shuffled back but Kieran stopped me.

I had no way out.

"Just try and relax," she cautioned.

Relax, I scoffed mentally. I closed my eyes tightly, preparing myself.

At least I couldn't see the knife as it came towards me; but damn I soon felt it. My breath came faster and faster, I balled my hands into tight fists. The blade she used must have sliced deep, travelling what I estimated to be at least six inches. The pain exploded. I screamed, trying to squirm from Kieran's grasp, but he held me tighter, pinning me to the floor.

"No more," I cried, "Please." I spluttered blood, my head going dizzy as my body starved of oxygen. I could feel the horrible metal instrument scrape down the bones of my neck, damaging my tissue all the way down. Then I felt something cold slop into my open wound, a squirming sludge that wriggled deep; wrapping around my vertebrae like a maggot. It hurt even more and I cringed, gritting my teeth so hard I bit my lip, drawing blood. I could also feel more hot liquid pouring down my neck, in hot sticky rivers. Carefully Garnha moved something over my neck. A cloth.

"It's done now." Garnha uttered softly.

I collapsed back into the ground. Kieran released me. Everything hurt.

No frigging difference there then. I turned and lay on my stomach, glancing up at the dusty night's sky.

It was like gravity was rotating and now I had the pressure of the universe thrust against my insignificant being. All the sorrow of the dying stars, the strength of the planets, and the pain of the people was crashing down on me harder than Niagara Falls. It was too much. It was obliterating me. The force of the fire continued increasing. I had mere minutes. I was clutching a delicate leaf on a dying autumn branch, at any moment it would snap. At any moment it would be winter and I'd be lost to eternity.

Anything is better than the pain, I tried to convince myself.

I wondered if I was going to see Mum at Heaven's gates. I imagined Max barking impatiently as I drifted closer to them. Would she be happy to see me, or upset that I'd hardly even lived yet? Was there even a Heaven? Was I just going to stop existing, lost to a vast nothingness for all time?

I turned my neck to look into Kieran's beautiful, sad eyes.

He slowly reached up his hand, gently helping me sit up so that my back leaned against his body and I was in his comforting arms. I winced but the pain was dying now, I was dying now; numbness was taking over. Kieran unexpectedly trailed his fingers across my cheek; so lightly my heart stopped momentarily. He cupped his hand against my face; cooling my blazing skin as he rubbed his thumb across my tears, erasing them; tying to comfort me.

"Sungha," he whispered softly, so low I knew only I could hear. Somehow that word had more significance than anything else in the world. It's what I had said to Max though I had no idea what it really meant. It's how Kieran knew what I was, even before I did.

It didn't calm the fire, but it calmed my soul.

Kieran stroked my hair soothingly. I painfully touched his hand which lay around my waist. He let me intertwine my fingers in his, so small in comparison, like a heart in a ribcage. He knew I was scared. I realised my hand was shaking. I remembered the Wall, I knew even this was a risk. Even then, I knew where we were heading. He smiled sadly, a heart-breaking smile.

For the shortest, most meaningful moment of my life I forgot everything.

I forgot where we were, I forgot I was dying, I even forgot my pain. All I could feel was Kieran's hand tenderly resting against mine. I felt him breathe unsteadily; I felt wetness against my cheek, I felt my skin tingle, I felt my heartbeat, I felt him shiver, I felt things too complicated for understanding.

There was nothing, nothing in the world except this moment.

Then flames rippled across my skin.

Kieran moved away from the fire and I was alone. I'd never been more alone in my entire life and without the comforting presence of my perfect stranger I finally gave in. Where I was going, I couldn't take anyone with me.

Everything dies eventually.

Chapter Ten

Fire hums. How strange it was, knowing I never even realised.

I followed the music, surrounding myself in its captivating power. I let it fill me, rejuvenate me, I let it rebuild me. I could feel the earth's warmth and incredible ability to make things grow. I could feel the water dripping intermittently through the rich soil, very slowing replenishing me and demolishing my thirst. I could feel the artistic fingers of wind moulding and sculpting; paying passionate attention to detail. It was bizarre, a tingling sensation, like pins and needles when your foot falls asleep. I wondered if I had a foot yet.

Whoa, that was a really weird thought.

It was a slow process, you know, resurrecting and stuff.

Or maybe it just *seemed* a slow process.

No, it definitely was a slow process.

Gradually my new limbs started completing; one by one. First a heart, then other organs, then muscles, and then eventually I had skin and...hair?

I've definitely waited long enough, I thought impatiently, finally opening my eyes. My vision blurred, like the interrupted debris at the bottom of a lake. When it settled I felt a spark of amazement. Everything had changed, as I had.

I rose up from the earth, feeling strangely elongated and stretched; my body fantastically alive. Looking down, my eyes widened, seeing vibrant red feathers. As I stretched my arms, I realised they weren't arms at all; they were wings. I had wings. Seriously; I had beautiful crimson wings that glowed iridescently. I watched in astonishment as the gold tips glistened brighter than burning embers. I also had claws as dark and dangerous as Kieran's.

Thinking this, I wondered where he was, but as I glanced around to search for him I got slightly distracted. Everything shone in these eyes. Like the soil wasn't brown anymore, it consisted of immeasurable quantities of rainbow fragments, so infinitesimal that even my new eyes had to concentrate. It was alive with colours I hadn't even imagined existed.

Scanning around with my new vision, everything gleamed with its own unique energy. There was so much I could finally *see*.

I could see the individual bristles at the very tops of the pine trees, the ants marching in armies towards sheltering pinecones. I saw a mouse shuffle restlessly under mountains of dried leaves and wooden splinters, surrounded by purple berries, as it hibernated for winter. I could zoom in on a droplet of water hanging precariously from a blade of grass miles in the distance and I could calculate the temperatures of living organisms just by looking at them.

I heard and smelt everything. Like my vision, I could focus in on weaker fragrances and sounds that would have previously been overpowered, such as the clean sharp tang of citrus fruits carried on a southern breeze.

I was so busy appreciating my new advances that the slow steady rhythm of breathing lungs escaped my notice. I soon noticed several pairs of eyes staring coldly down at me from within the trees. There were six Phoenix bathed in shadow within the branches, metal armour complicatedly attached to their wings and bodies. I gulped nervously. Shocked, I nearly gasped aloud when I turned to find half a dozen men in armoured uniform watching me.

The men came forwards. I meant to ask them who they were but it came out as a panicked squawk. Where were the others? Surely Nik wouldn't leave me alone? I didn't know what to do on my own. Had they been captured?

"We won't hurt you," assured one man, his face unidentifiable beneath a heavy metal helmet. "If you don't try anything, we won't hurt you," he promised, though a warning was in his part-concealed eyes. "Come with us."

I eyed him suspiciously. *Where?* I thought, only just remembering how to communicate when a bird; to use my mindvoice.

"To where your friends are," he answered informatively.

Where, I thought again, more firmly, regarding him with sharp eyes.

"They're with The High Council, of course," he said, surreptitiously edging closer. I tried to stand as tall as possible, attempting to look intimidating. Then I remembered Phoenix in the trees and thought; okay, maybe not.

I thought quickly, calculating and weighing out my options. I could be walking straight into a trap. But then again, what other choice did I have? I couldn't fight them. And I certainly couldn't, like, fly away or something. I didn't know how, and they'd only catch me anyway. I was lacking options.

Finally I surrendered, following them. They surrounded me, caging me above and around. God, these people really thought I was a threat if they wouldn't risk less than twelve Phoenix to capture me. I almost laughed.

I smelt the spicy scent of fear on their chests.

We'd reached the perimeter of the forest, where the trees thinned to become some sort of park. Following a winding, convoluted path made from a pale gold stone, eventually we discovered another gate. We walked under it, passing the guards effortlessly. It led us directly into the city. What's with all the gates? Then I remembered that the city was warded.

The city streets were eerily deserted, but I could feel inquisitive eyes watching me suspiciously, their sneaky gazes boring into my back. As we passed what looked like a school I noticed a group of small children playing outside. What struck me was that all their eyes were black; despite their different Tribes.

The guards wasted no time in ushering me towards the impressive gemstone building in the centre of the city. The guards seemed to knit their bodies closer. It wasn't a pleasant feeling. The doors at the front of the building were also guarded; however we were immediately gestured forward. Once inside, I was led up a spiral staircase. At the top were two opposing doors, I was forced towards the right. Looking inside, I shivered.

Before I could protest I was pushed into what looked like a cell, the door instantly shut behind me with a loud click. I glanced around; the room was dark with no windows and only a small lit torch on one wall. There was a wooden bench to my left, a dirty sink with a mirror above it, and nothing much else. I waited for a moment, my thoughts frantic.

It wasn't long before the door opened again and someone stepped through.

It was a man. As the light hit his familiar face a hundred memories gushed into my head, the most prominent being of fear and abuse. I remembered hiding under the staircase in a great palace, listening to see whether or not the screaming had stopped. I gasped in understanding. He was my father.

I didn't know what I'd expected, but I never thought he would look quite so much like me. His eyes were the identical to mine in shape, but where mine were solid black his were golden in the middle then turned black at the perimeter. We shared the same high prominent cheekbones and strong nose; though his skin was darker with more freckles; a deceptively innocent face. His hair wasn't like mine; rather his was so blonde it looked white.

I stared at him for what seemed a long time, unable to tear my eyes away. My heart was thumping uncomfortably, what was I supposed to do? He was the very reason my mother had fled in the first place. That must mean something. Now I was facing him. What do I do, what do I say?

He scrutinised me intently before frowning, "You *seem* familiar, but it's been a long time, you can't surely be my child." His voice was beautiful, but he wasn't talking to me. He was merely speaking his thoughts aloud. "Is it you?" he wondered, "Speak!" He demanded with a sudden deadly authority. Lynk, that was his name, I remembered.

My name is Ruby, I said slowly, my mindvoice quivering slightly.

"I don't believe you," he said, "Change."

How? I asked pathetically. I didn't know how to Change.

He spoke impatiently "You need to think of fire, your element. Feel it flicker inside you, and then use it to Change yourself. You'll know what to do."

I, on the other hand, wasn't quite so convinced.

I closed my eyes and did as I was told. I thought of fire. It didn't work.

"You're not doing it right," Lynk said.

Well, you tell me how, I snapped, my emotions everywhere at the sight of him and my frustration in my inability to Change.

"Try something different," He offered coldly. "I take it you're only just getting used to the idea of being a Phoenix so your element won't have much of an effect on you," he explained sharply. "Try thinking of something important to you; something that gives you a reason to be human again." He walked to the door "I'll give you a minute. There are clothes near the sink."

Once he was gone I tried to calm my nerves and focus. I closed my eyes again, thinking about the Ashaiks, of how much they'd helped me. Now I needed to be human to help them. With the strength of that in mind I felt a flicker of something. I needed to help them. I *could* help them. The flicker ignited into a spark. I followed the spark, drawing it up through my system, the way one might pull a tree root from the ground. The feeling of hot water trickled down my spine, filling me with wonderful heat and energy. I felt it tingling through me, almost painfully, like when you first get into a steaming shower on a freezing winter day.

A sudden blinding agony raced through me. I moaned in pain and shock, feeling my body shrink, muscles contracting into smaller fragments, squeezing together. The power disappeared. I opened my eyes, subsequently exhausted. The pain slowly ebbed away. My body shook uncontrollably.

I staggered awkwardly over to the sink, pulling on a plain shapeless dress made of a hideous black material that itched and hung, miles too big, away from my body. I looked up, just catching a glimpse of myself in the mirror.

I stopped, looked again and drew a sharp surprised breath.

I'd always looked young for my age. Now though, I seemed to have aged five years since yesterday. My face had changed shape, my cheekbones growing higher underneath long framing eyelashes. My eyes had completely transformed in colour. They weren't coal black anymore, rather they were identical to Lynks; golden yellow iris fringed with ebony. It was shocking, but that wasn't all that had changed. My hair had brightened to a startling red, streaked with highlights; it looked dyed, no natural hair surely was so crimson? Golden freckles now coated every single plain of my skin, like fallen autumn leaves; I was glowing-an incandescent incarnation of fire.

My body had matured too; I had a more voluptuous shape now. My hips had widened slightly, my waist narrowing and legs lengthening. And, for the first time in my entire life I actually had a decent set of boobs. My tattoos had appeared again too, those strange miraculous marks that had first appeared as I began the Change. I could see the full extent of them now, spiralling patterns that began at the base of my back, up to my neck, across my shoulders and down my right arm. They were darker than I remembered, definitely black, but shimmering with gold dust only if they caught the light. I was surprised how much I liked them, the design, my design was beautiful.

The sound of knocking brought me back to reality, Lynk didn't wait for an answer. Returning my gaze to him, standing in the doorway, he was examining my face like an artist. "Come with me," he finally uttered.

I followed him out of the tiny room, my bare feet treading carefully over the freezing wooden flooring. He took me through another door and I breathed a sigh of relief. Briseis, Adrian, Nik, Chara and Kieran were inside.

Then my stomach dropped, that was a bad thing.

They stood together in the middle of the room, encircled by guards and important-looking people on big high-backed chairs, one of which Lynk immediately sat on. Everyone stared at me, but I only saw my friend's hands; chained together in large metal cuffs.

"About time," I head Kieran's voice grumble in my head. "I'm so very bored."

"Is this the girl you speak of?" said an ancient, powerful voice. I turned towards the direction of the voice and saw an old man with white hair and eyes so blue you could drown in them.

"That's her, Lord," Nikolas told him, his face alight with relief.

"I'm Ruby," I confirmed; the foreign words tumbling off my tongue impulsively. I walked quietly over to the others. Looking at the trapping metal shackles, I noticed swirling symbols that glowed fiercely. I shuddered.

"Well Lynk, is that her?" the old man asked.

Without shifting those topaz eyes from my topaz eyes, he spoke. "She's my daughter, Declan," he told the old man apathetically. "Those eyes are mine."

I stared at the floor, hearing sharp intakes of breath. I fiddled nervously with the edge of the oversized dress, yanking it down.

"Well," said the old man, Declan, grudgingly and involuntarily, "that changes things. You can go." He nodded at Chara, Adrian, Bris and Nik. They were roughly shoved aside by the Warriors who'd brought me here. "Because, as Kieran rightly pointed out, there isn't actually a law about leaving the Island, only about breaking the wards and then leaving the Island. And since you didn't actually break any wards; I guess we can't prove you actually left."

Kieran leaned over to whisper with an annoying grin, "He says 'actually' a lot doesn't he?"

"You two, however, attacked guards." Declan turned on us. "Do you know what the consequence of that is?" his eyes darted mercurially to Kieran, "You should remember from last time, Kierakai, and the time before."

Kieran smiled darkly, "Fine and punishment, or confinement."

The man nodded, "That's right, and what would you prefer?" he spoke patronisingly, like he was talking down to a child. Kieran needed to stay calm, or we'd just end up in worse trouble.

"Option three." He decided, eyebrows rising hopefully.

Declan's eyes narrowed marginally, "And what's that?" Declan inquired.

"That you let us go because, obviously, we had no choice but to do what we did." He glanced meaningfully at Lynk, "Otherwise Ruby would have died at your gates and you would have been responsible for the death of a Fledgling." *I did die*, I thought, *I just didn't stay dead*. "A Royal Fledgling as well," he emphasised. I glanced over at him in surprise; Royal? What? "Plus I didn't kill anyone and that white bitch had it coming." He smirked mischievously and I was tempted to stand on his foot.

"That white bitch," snapped another Air Elder, his hair as transparent as his irises, "is my daughter."

Kieran just seemed amused, "That's your misfortune."

Another man, around fifty with salt and pepper hair, leant forwards. His skin was brown with that everlasting tan only acquired hereditably. His eyes were so dark green they looked as black as Adrian's. "How about you stop smiling, Kierakai," – he almost spat the word - "and pick an option or I will."

"But a smile makes you look more attractive," Kieran objected, grinning happily. Then he frowned, his forehead creasing, "though, judging by your face, you didn't know that, did you?"

The man gritted his teeth, "I would have thought that after all these years, Kierakai; you might have learnt some manners."

"Manners are for people who deserve them," Kieran snapped. I turned and looked at him in horror but he continued, "And I'm not going to the jail," he confirmed with clarity. "I'm too pretty to go to jail; I'd like to keep my anal virginity intact, thank you."

I nodded in agreement; the other option didn't seem *that* bad.

"The fine will be three hundred half-sapphires. Each," spoke up someone.

Kieran paused, "And if we can't pay that?" he smiled, "I doubt my lovely father will bail me out."

There was a brief, intense silence.

"We could take it in feathers," the old Earthbird smiled sadistically.

"I don't think even *I* could pull off the bald look." Kieran said thoughtfully.

Luckily someone else suggested, "You could work it off?" It was a woman with blue and silver hair. "We need an ice sculptor for the Winter Festival. I remember your work from childhood Kierakai; and you are certainly qualified," she added meaningfully, her blue eyes sparkling.

"What about the girl?" someone else asked.

The woman turned to me. "She has a voice gift, why not use her at the Winter Festival as well? Our singer pulled out yesterday; it's perfect."

Before I could respond Lynk interrupted, "She needs to learn to control herself anyway, or we'll have even more catastrophes. We might as well start immediately," he told the lady, his voice was spectacularly persuasive.

The woman smiled in agreement, shooting an almost smug look at the dark man with salt-and-pepper hair. "So it's settled then, you shall both be involved in the Winter Festival and therefore repay your fines."

Great. Before I could respectably protest, Kieran said silkily to the woman, "Thank you Lady, we accept your generous offer." He smiled flirtatiously.

"But I can't..."I began hastily.

"Shut up," Kieran hissed under his breath. "Do you want your feathers pulled out? We aren't pigeons; our feathers grow from the bone."

Kieran grumbled. "So," he wondered curiously, "what's on the punishment agenda today?"

It was the dark Earthbird's turn to smirk, "Surely you remember Tulbeck?"

Kieran smiled in mock joy, "How could I forget."

My skin prickled anxiously. I was confused.

The man with greying black hair clicked his fingers expectantly, a mean almost-sadistic smile creeping onto his lips.

"How deep?" Kieran asked indifferently. What was happening?

The Council Members talked briefly among themselves, and when they turned back to us, Declan answered, "Three each."

Kieran hesitated calculatingly, his eyes shifting from person to person.

"Three what?" I muttered to him.

Kieran ignored me completely. "I take it that it doesn't matter who takes it, as long as the punishment has been fulfilled?" His voice was way too nonchalant. What was he planning? Why wasn't he explaining anything?

Declan's eyebrows furrowed suspiciously. "What are you getting at?"

Kieran shrugged casually, "I'm making an offer," he slowly took a fraction of a step towards Lynk. Their eyes locked, "To take hers. None of this is her fault, and she doesn't deserve it," he explained factually.

Without the briefest hesitation Lynk responded, "And what do you benefit from this, Kierakai?" he inquired sceptically.

"Peace of mind. And that's not my name."

"Done," Lynk confirmed, and seemed to relax slightly.

I frowned incomprehensively at Kieran. Not understanding any of the arrangement. "What did you just do?" I wondered bewilderedly.

Kieran avoided my eyes as a warrior came forwards, laying down a large sheet made from a coarse red material. Kieran kneeled on the fabric, facing the only open window in the room; it was more a balcony than a window.

"Kieran," I called demandingly. What was he doing?

It was only then that I noticed a man on the balcony. He turned and walked with an unnecessary slowness towards Kieran. He was absolutely gigantic, way over six feet tall, at least. He had hair that was diaphanously silver, cold grey eyes and an unfathomable expression.

"Hello, my psycho friend," Kieran greeted cheerfully, "guess who came to visit you?"

The man appraised Kieran with an intrigued, almost lascivious study, but said nothing. My vision then directed itself to the strange curved device grasped in the man's right hand. It was black but had the texture of bone and it took me a few seconds to realise that it was the sharp blade-like bone from the tip of a skeletal Phoenix wing. The bone appeared to be polished to a dangerous point that I knew could cut glass. Suddenly I knew what was about to happen and I sprang forwards.

Hands roughly grabbed me, yanking my wrists back and forcing them through imprisoning shackles. I pulled and wrestled against the chains. The symbols on the handcuffs glowed electrically when I moved, slowly starting to burn, charring my skin. More arms held me back now in an unbreakable restraint. I kicked out ineffectively, screaming until somebody gagged me.

"I missed these special moments with you," Kieran smiled.

Two guards came forwards carrying a piece of wood. The man brought up the wing bone, slashing once at the wood. It snapped in half.

"There's no need to show off," Kieran muttered.

I couldn't believe this was a punishment. I missed England. What century did these people live in? Hadn't they heard of ethical punishment?

Wordlessly the man moved behind him...

I screamed again with renewed force, almost choking on the cloth in my mouth, battering against the arms that contained me. I tried desperately to break the lock chaining me. Eventually I cried in frustration, I couldn't stop it.

I clamped my eyes tightly. I winced at the sound, the brutal slicing of flesh, feeling revolted as the scent of metallic blood wafted to my nostrils. I couldn't open my eyes. I was afraid to look but I knew what was happening. That vindictive monster was slicing the deadly wing bone down Kieran's back in a swift motion; digging inches deep.

Kieran made no noise as the wing-blade gouged though his skin with a professional precision- probably drawing a symbol that represented his crime. I held my breath, my heart hammering.

I felt sick when I couldn't keep my eyes closed any longer. I didn't look at the blood pouring from the fresh crevices on Kieran's back, splattering across his shredded shirt and streaming down to the red sheet.

I saw Kieran's vacant eyes and was suddenly even more scared.

Chapter Eleven

"You will receive all the information about your work placements by messenger. I assume you'll have a place to stay," Declan stated, his voice slower now, lazier; apparently the exciting part had finished.

Kieran shakily stood up, wincing in pain he staggered slightly; Kieran who never trips or falls and is constantly graceful, staggered. He straightened up, precariously tilted, nodding sharply.

"Well," continued Declan indifferently, "we'll expect notifications on your living arrangements as soon as possible. If you don't inform us within the next twenty-four hours we won't be letting you off so lightly again." He warned. I scoffed mentally, glancing at the indignant stripes across Kieran's back, immersed in blood. *That* was light?

"You can go," Declan dismissed authoritatively.

Silently the guards released me. Unlocking the fiercely glowing shackles; my wrists had blistering sores from where I'd attempted to wrench free. I rubbed the charred skin, feeling the ribbed scabs already forming. God I healed fast now, or maybe it was just an effect from the handcuffs.

Walking over to Kieran, he met my eyes. A look passed between us, a glance that told me we needed to go, now.

"Wait," I heard a voice behind us command, "You don't think you'll get away that easily do you?" We froze in synchrony. It was Lynk.

I turned around, looking at Lynk; my father. God, that was weird to think. He was smiling, but it had a distinct edge, "Now you've Changed we shall have to have a little celebration, won't we?" I glanced over at Kieran in confusion but Lynk continued, "It's tradition that a High Daughter of the Ashes should provide a great celebration for her First Fledged Flight. Don't worry though," he added with that suspicious smile, "I shall arrange everything; after all, you are my daughter."

I stared at him uncomfortably; the look in his eyes frightened me.

"Tomorrow night," he concluded. "We'll have it then." He looked over at me one last unnerving time before dismissing us.

We sluggishly made our way to the spiral staircase, carefully trudging our way down. Eventually we exited the building. I breathed in the cold, crisp air which wound up my bare legs. It was at that point that I remembered I had no shoes. Today was just getting better and better. Kieran was staring at me, amused at my appearance; focussing on my hideous ill-fitting dress no doubt.

"Sexy," he smirked sarcastically, despite everything.

I demanded to see his back. He shrugged and turned, taking off his shirt. When I realised the extent of the wounds I gasped. It was horrible; how could he even stand up? I had been right. Like the marks on the foreheads of the bodies on the Wall, it had been two identical symbols that they'd cut into Kieran's flesh. I couldn't decipher the gruesome marks but I knew that one had been meant for me. I knew they were deep enough to need tough stitches.

"Does it hurt?" I asked, knowing it was a stupid question.

He frowned at me as if I was mentally incompetent, "Obviously."

"Well, it was a stupid thing to do," I told him seriously. "I could have taken my own. You know I could have." I scolded him, suddenly angry. "You don't always have to play hero."

His eyes narrowed, "I don't *play* anything. I'm just naturally this selfless."

I was definitely annoyed now. "Why did you have to do that? Was it to make me feel worse?" I interrogated him furiously, "because if you did then congratulations because it worked."

He glared at me. "I can't believe you're yelling at me for doing something to help you," he said bitterly.

"It didn't help me," I stated, "It just made me feel awful."

"Not everything's about you, you know." He was annoyed.

"Not everything's about you either." I countered.

"What's *wrong* with you?"

I glared right back, "Nothing's wrong with me," I retorted, "I just hate it when people underestimate me. I should have taken my own punishment. I knew what I was doing when I attacked that woman. I'm not a child."

I was remembering things now. Horrible memories flooded back, of arrogant Elders and children throwing rocks at me in the street, trying to provoke me to see what I would do. Everyone thought I couldn't control myself. That my determination was in vain because inevitably I would fail just like my dead siblings. My mother certainly thought that; she took me away from this place, away from my *home*, just because she thought I couldn't handle the Change. I was stronger then, stronger than I had been yesterday, and I still managed to Rise. I *was* strong... but nobody believed me.

Kieran's expression softened in understanding. "I didn't want you to go through that for something that was my fault."

I frowned, "But it wasn't your fault. You had no choice but to fight them."

His brilliant green eyes dimmed in shadow, his face abruptly hardening again. "That wasn't what I meant."

So what did he mean? Oh my God, is it a natural phenomenon that all men are idiots; even the supernatural ones? If it weren't for the threat of extinction, we could survive far better without them. Kieran stomped off.

I flinched as I caught a glimpse of his scathed back, but quickly followed him, carefully avoiding rocks and uneven surfaces. After about five minutes of tiptoeing over pebbled road with bare feet, we reached a shallow river which we followed to the top of the valley, mostly through large farming fields filled with crop.

"Oh," Kieran remembered suddenly, reaching into the pocket of his jeans, withdrawing my mother's gold chain, "I forgot to give you this, it survived the flames. Found it on top of your Ashes."

What a weird thought. I was once Ashes. I took the chain gratefully, thanking him. It was the same as it was before, the same individual links decorated with ancient runes that I couldn't decipher. They looked burnt into the metal. I put it around my neck, it felt lighter, no longer bearing the weight of the red stone; or what I thought had been a red stone.

"What did Lynk mean?" I asked Kieran "When he said about organising me a celebration or something?"

Kieran slowed his fast pace, sighing and dropping back beside me. "It's a tradition," he explained, "that Royalty have a big celebration when they've Changed and invite everyone. It's a public event-"

"Wait," I interrupted, "Royalty?" I demanded, "You never told me that."

"Well it's the equivalent I guess. The word 'High' here essentially means Royal," he explained. "There's a Royal family for each Tribe. The Ashaiks are Earth." As he said this I remembered with a spark of surprise what his name was. "The Falton's are Water, Carbeck's are Air. And the Swartettes are Fire." His eyes shifted to me in that instant. "That's you."

My mouth gaped open in shock as he stared-very seriously-at me. "M*e*?" I asked incredulously, the thought just seemed ludicrous. I'm not even sure I am a Phoenix, never mind a *Royal* one.

"Yeah," he said bitterly, "hence why Lynk's on the High Council."

Eventually we arrived before a massive house high up on the valley ledge, the main city glowed beneath me. It was a very eccentric Palace, something straight from a Tim Burton film. Complete with black marble columns, gothic twisted roof and arched looming windows with velvet curtains, it was all spires and points; reminding me of the Sagrada Familia in Barcelona.

"This place is creepy," I commented as Kieran appeared beside me.

"Try living here," he muttered. I noticed for the first time, past the long porch boarded with a wood so dark it appeared black; the name Ashaik was inscribed in swirling Karisian symbols–in the common language.

"You lived *here*? But it's…well, creepy." I protested and he laughed, wincing when the movement hurt him. I hastily asked, "Why are we here? Is this where we're staying?" I shuddered at the thought.

"No," he answered curtly, walking forward with hurried steps. "And keep quiet; you're not technically welcome here."

I followed him up some creaking wooden steps, they groaned miserably as my weight disturbed them. Kieran knocked on the door and almost instantaneously a woman appeared. Before she could say anything, Garnha shuffled her aside, telling her to stay in the other room. She called her 'slave' and it shocked me at how casually she pronounced the word.

Garnha was wearing an elegant silk dress that seemed too fine and expensive to wear during the day. Her shimmering straight locks were pulled into a high plait, emphasising her prominent cheekbones. Her sparkling emerald eyes looked tired. I think I even saw a few fine wrinkles fanning shallowly from the corner of her eyes now that the sunlight allowed me to see her properly. Other than the obvious exhaustion, she looked incredible for her age. Not that I could guess accurately what it was.

She hurriedly rushed us inside, leading us down a long, dimly illuminated corridor and into a room. It was plain except for a wooden table in the centre, surrounded by various cupboards.

Garnha pulled out a chair and gestured for Kieran to sit down, he did, reluctantly. Then she rummaged in a cupboard and brought down some white cloths; handing me one. "Would you remove some of the excess blood from his wounds?" she asked calmly. "I just need to fetch my equipment."

I nodded, "Do you want me to wet it?" I asked. It felt weird. Last time I met her I'd been much in need of medical intervention and Kieran had automatically become helper. Now it was the other way around.

Picking up a glass bottle with a cork lid and no label, she handed it to me. "Just pour a little of this on it. It'll sterilise the cuts."

She walked out of the room and sighing. I made my way over to Kieran.

He grinned mischievously at me, those white teeth flashing unexpectedly. "I would say, Miss Ruby, that you should be wearing a naughty little nurse uniform, but considering how little you already have on, I'd rather you stay like that." He was trying to irritate me.

"Watch it," I warned as I opened the bottle and pressed the cloth against it, allowing the liquid to momentarily absorb into the soft white fabric, like nail varnish remover on cotton wool, without the nasty smell.

"I will," he answered, his gaze sweeping intimately up my bared legs.

I blushed uncontrollably, shuddering under his gaze. This he noticed and smirked arrogantly. "I think the blood loss has gone to your head," I muttered; he was actually *flirting* with me. Going round behind him, I told him to take off his shirt.

"You've been waiting to say that, haven't you?" He said, slowly tearing off the shredded remnants of his shirt, all teasing evaporating from his features.

As gently as I could, I began to dab at the deep wounds. He winced a lot, his muscles contracting and making the pain worse. But he never complained. My sore wrists throbbed as I delicately dabbed at the gruesome wounds. It was a good thing I wasn't squeamish. His back was really damaged, it would scar. At least it had stopped bleeding.

"How bad is it?" he asked breathlessly, like he'd just run a marathon.

I frowned; the truth was it was really, really bad. His back was swelling and patchy, the skin around his deepest marks upraised and inflamed bright red. "It's just a little scratch," I lied unconvincingly, "barely noticeable."

Kieran glanced at me, a strange flicker in his eyes.

At that point Garnha returned, carrying more bottles and bandages. I quickly moved out of her way and leaned against the wall. I watched, bizarrely intrigued, as Garnha edged closer to Kieran. She deposited the bottles on the table, and then professionally finished cleaning up the wounds.

"Kierakai, why are there two marks?" She wondered suspiciously. Then her face quickly sparked in comprehension. She glanced pointedly at me. "You took hers."

"I did." He agreed, "Hence the lack of wounds on *Ruby's* back."

Garnha let out a frustrated breath. "Well that was stupid," she scolded angrily, "Now they'll think that there's something going on between you two. That isn't making this situation any easier," she sighed exasperatedly, her eyes darting from the two of us, then they narrowed, "There *isn't* anything going on, is there?"

Automatically Kieran responded, "Of course there isn't," I felt my stomach drop at the resentment in his voice. "I know what happens to those who break the Laws of the High Covenant." The image of the mutilated pregnant woman on the Wall flooded into my head with a painful flair.

She spoke with a calm dignity, "But does she?" she wondered philosophically, "This isn't her world, Kierakai."

Kieran opened his mouth to speak but I quickly intercepted him, "I know the Law too," I told her honestly, then shuddered. "I've seen the Wall."

She nodded finally, accepting my words more than her son's.

"We need to hurry," she said, quickly smearing some more blue liquid onto Kieran's back, "your father will be home from the High Council soon."

"That stings," he grumbled moodily.

"Good. Maybe you'll think twice next time." Garnha retorted.

"Your Dad's with the Council?" I asked.

They both looked up at me.

Kieran answered slowly, "No he's *in* the High Council."

My heart quivered as I remembered the salt-and-pepper haired man with those hostile eyes that had reminded me of Adrian. His brown skin was like Kieran's. I gaped in understanding. "The one who told the warriors to get Tulbeck," I realised, horrified. No wonder he and Adrian had wanted to leave.

"That's the one," Kieran confirmed savagely.

Garnha laughed humourlessly, "Be grateful you're not married to him."

I wondered why the hell *was* she married him. I guessed she had no choice.

Garnha warned Kieran, "There will be no exercise for at least a week. I will only heal the top layer; it'll split if you're not careful. That means no running, no flying, and no fighting-"

"-And no fun," he finished, nodding reluctantly.

I watched as Garnha rhythmically muttered words and swept her hands across Kieran's broad back without actually touching him. I gasped as the raw indentations slowly began to glow. Garnha's palms, as I observed, slowly became covered in spiralling tattoos that glowed darkly and gradually closed the wounds. Eventually the wound subsided into mere glistening scars.

"Wow," I breathed, "That's incredible! Is that what you did to me?" I blurted unthinkingly to Kieran.

"You did what?" Garnha exploded, her eyes darting to Kieran's guilty face.

Oh shit. I'd forgotten healing was High Treason too.

He frowned at me, "Sometimes, I really do want to seal you inside a shipping container."

I pulled an apologetic face, muttering oops. Garnha looked as if she was going to blow up. She opened her mouth but the creaking of heavy feet on the porch steps halted her words. We all froze. Then in a blindingly fast movement Garnha swooped up the bottles on the table and hastily shoved them in a cupboard. Shuffling us desperately out the room, she ordered, "Go out the back way and take some horses from the stables or something; no flying. I'll distract him. No riding after this, watch your back, and don't think that this means you're getting out of anything Kierakai." She frowned before rushing in the opposite direction. No goodbyes. No affection. Nothing.

My heart was pounding louder than my footsteps as I followed Kieran through intricately designed corridors. There were so many, like the bewildering hallways in a large hospital or Pan's labyrinth.

We came to an abrupt dead end.

Kieran swore under his breath. I looked, terrified, at him. What would his father do if he found us here? I knew that he was a violent revengeful man, and now we were all alone, without any witnesses, who knew what he would do. I could tell from Kieran's reaction it wouldn't be to throw a party.

We heard footsteps down the hall.

Kieran shoved me into the nearest room. Luckily there was nobody inside and there was a window. Yanking it open he gestured for me to go first. My eyes widened at the tiny gap. Without hesitation Kieran lifted me into his strong arms, unceremoniously shoving me through the small space. My arms scraped against the wooden frame.

I landed ungracefully on my bum, quickly shoving down the hideous dress as it had ridden up, exposing a little too much. In any other situation I would have felt extremely embarrassed but we didn't have time. I quickly stood up as Kieran forced himself through. Running, we headed towards a large out building which I guessed was the stables. Entering I was shocked to discover half a dozen stalls all filled with horses. Phoenix rode horses?

Kieran spotted a particular horse, a chestnut mare.

"Hey sugar," he greeted, "how have you been?" She recognised him instantly, braying and snorting excitedly. He looked over his shoulder, pointing to a misty-grey horse, "Take Shadow, he was Adrian's but he didn't want him after he got Amber."

I hurried over to the horse. He was a beautiful creature; his coat a light grey freckled with a darker colour. As I got closer he stepped eagerly forward, letting me stroke his long pretty face. How something so obviously gentle and caring could not be wanted, I had no idea.

"He's lovely," I observed, "Why didn't Adrian want him?"

Kieran was handing me a saddle and various other riding equipment, "Do you know what to do?" he asked and I nodded, instantly beginning to saddle the waiting horse. I was glad I had volunteered to help out my friend Abby with her horses when she went on holiday; otherwise I would have been absolutely clueless. As Kieran prepared his own horse he explained, "He's not a war horse, he was built for endurance rather than strength."

"Oh," I said and after a few intense moments we were ready.

Climbing onto Shadows back I petted his groomed neck, tentatively encouraging him forward. Kieran was on his mare already, his horse was quite a bit larger than mine, obviously built for battle, but mine had the speed and freeness of a young stallion. We rode out of the stables and galloped off. Following Kieran up the garden, I realised that my apparel was not suited for horse-riding. My bare legs slipped continually and I was extremely uncomfortable, my lack of pants and a good sports bra to blame.

We rode our way towards a forest, following a path. Now we had reached camouflage I felt safer and we slowed to a trot. I petted my lovely horse admiringly, "Thank you, gorgeous, it's much appreciated."

"Any time," Kieran said.

"I was talking to the horse."

"Don't say that. I'm allergic to bullshit."

"That's strange, because that's all that seems to come from your mouth."

"Okay, I've changed my mind, keep talking to the horse."

Once we were through the trees we slowly made our way down the valley, every now and then spotting houses amongst the beautiful scenery. About twenty minutes later we crossed a couple of fields filled with caramel-colour crops that danced in the breeze. It must have been late afternoon because the sun was dipping low in the sky. In the distance I spotted a cottage just past a field of grape vines. We waded through the vineyard carefully, trying not to stand on blooming plants, heading towards the little building nestled deep in a sea of green. It was adorable.

It was like Anne Hathaway's cottage in Stratford-upon-Avon, except this roof was tiled and not thatched. It was all cream walls coated in intertwining ivy, tasteful wooden beams, bright tulips in patches with other fragrant flowers, and general cuteness. It wasn't a massive place, but it had charm and a welcome feel to the air. Kieran led the horses to the side of the building, to a fenced off area which I soon realised was a field with a little stable. It looked nothing at all like I expected a Phoenix home to look.

"Where are we?" I wondered.

Kieran smiled unexpectedly, "This is Ebony's place."

"Whose?" I asked.

"Ebony's," Kieran repeated. I frowned.

Leaving the horses, we rounded the side of the home, stopping at a wooden door. There were flowers carved expertly into the wood, interlacing vines that curled artistically with pointed leaves, adorning the simple entrance. Kieran lifted his hand to knock but before his fist touched the door it burst open. A small woman charged through, throwing her arms around Kieran.

I had to admit, I was a little surprised.

"Kierakai!" she rejoiced, squeezing him tightly, "I missed you so much."

He grinned, a little startled, "You too, Ebbs."

More people were tumbling out of the door, I recognised Chara and Briseis, but then a man stepped through and crossed his hands over his forehead, then his heart. Somehow Kieran was mimicking his movements while the girl clung fiercely to him. The man's gaze shifted to me with a cold ferocity and instant suspicion, I fidgeted uncomfortably.

"Let him breathe." Nik shuffled outside to see the source of the commotion.

Ebony finally released Kieran. She was quite small, about an inch shorter than me and she had a pretty, rounded face and moss-green eyes. She was as cute as her house and bounced energetically up and down. When she saw me she smiled carefully but kept her distance.

The girl bounded off to stand next to Chara, her face alight as she chattered loquaciously. Then I noticed someone else, a little girl around four years old. She was gazing quizzically at Kieran with shining black eyes. Kieran's face lit up in wonder as he kneeled down before the little girl.

"Libby, say hello to your uncle Kierakai," Ebony said.

"Libby," Kieran smiled proudly. "You've grown so much."

She smiled sweetly, shyly hiding until Kieran offered his hand, which the little girl took and Kieran lifted her protectively into his arms.

That meant that Kieran had another brother or sister he hadn't told me about. Was he related to Ebony or her husband? I looked at Ebony with her shiny black hair and her moss-green eyes and knew for definite. He had a sister. I almost felt a little betrayed that he hadn't told me.

I shuffled awkwardly, suddenly remembering how much undressed and incongruous I was. Ebony seemed to notice this, instantly bounding over.

"Of course, you need your things," she remembered. "Follow me this way."

She led me into her little home; the others eventually following. The hallway was decorated with vibrantly hectic tapestries, hanging from the walls by curved metal hooks. A soft yellowish light emitted from strange crystal balls looming above. The stone floor was unexpectedly warm against my feet. There were weatherworn boots muddily laid atop a straw-woven mat and keys jangled from a hook on the back of the door. It was a complete contrast to the Palace I'd just been in.

Ebony directed me into a homely living room. Mistreated sofas sat around a low wooden table, on which were plates of bread, cheese and meats. Seeing the food, my stomach grumbled hungrily and to my embarrassment Ebony heard. She gestured compassionately for me to sit, offering me a plate. I took some bread and cheese, gratefully thanking her as everyone sat down.

"Your things are upstairs when you're ready. I'm afraid you and Briseis will have to share a room," she admitted nervously.

"You mean I can stay? Here?" I asked in bewilderment. I thought we were just stopping here and then I would have to find a local inn or something. Not that I had any money or anything of worth.

She frowned. "Of course you can. I don't care what anyone thinks," she suddenly decided in a loud determined voice. "You brought my family home, and if they say you're okay then I believe them."

"Thank you," I said genuinely, feeling relieved.

Chapter Twelve

The soft yellow light escaping through the thin curtains eventually awoke me the next morning, that and the wonderful scent of frying bacon. I was spread out across the bed comfortably. My arm, recklessly throw out in my forgotten dreams, dangled over the edge of the mattress. My cupped palm caught the sun's welcoming rays, warming my fingertips. My eyes slowly fluttered open. For a while I thought I was at home, until I realised that Max wouldn't come to lick my hand to wake me properly. It was a sad thought. I missed him so much; he was often the only constant happy figure in my life.

Last night had flown by. I had a bath, ate dinner and spent most of the night talking with everyone about nothing and everything. It was nice, relaxed. For the first time in what seemed like weeks I felt truly okay.

Sighing, I sleepily tumbled out of bed, throwing on whatever clothes my hands could find. The room was empty, I slowly realised; Briseis must already be up. Opening the door, I journeyed quietly downstairs. There was no one in the living room so I went into the kitchen. My stomach growled as the overwhelming smell of bacon smacked into me with renewed force.

Kieran was standing at the stove, brandishing a metal frying pan like it was a deadly weapon, apparently providing a one-man show for little Libby; who was clapping enthusiastically on a seat at the stone counter. She was wearing pink cotton pyjamas. Kieran wore only a pair of grey joggers and no shirt. I hung back for a moment, unable to help myself as I ogled over his perfect naked torso. I wasn't normally the type of girl that gets all hot and bothered when she sees a fit guy, but Kieran was different.

The rippling muscles coated his body like armouring and his tanned skin was the gorgeous colour of cinnamon, tarnished only with battle scars. A dark gold chain, almost identical to mine but with different symbols, hung perpetually around his neck. But it wasn't just his appearance that sent butterflies flittering in my stomach, it was the way he carried himself, with such an air of confidence it bordered on conceit. Every step he took was calculated, every movement assured and purposeful; graceful with the same stealth and precision as a hunting animal. I soon fussed over the chaotic mess of my hair.

Kieran looked up when I entered; speaking to Libby. "See," he said, "I told you she would come when she smelt this. This one's a right little carnivore."

"Carnivore," Libby repeated happily, her black eyes shining. I wondered in that moment whether or not black eyes had something to do with not only being a child, but also if it was just someone who hadn't burned in general; like Adrian.

"Little," I repeated, raising my eyebrows, while smoothing down my tangled mop of 'hair'.

He finished frying the bacon, proceeding to pile it up onto thick slices of crusty white bread. Then he put the pan back down and came to stand over me with his towering, muscular frame. Jeez, his biceps were as big as my head. He didn't need to say anything else; the challenge was in his eyes.

"I'm not short," I protested eventually, shoving him from my personal space like he'd bitten me, not that I'd mind… *quit it Ruby,* I battered myself. "You're just big. Where is everybody?" I asked as I groggily clambered up onto the available chair next to Libby. I smiled when she waved.

Kieran served up breakfast, handing a bacon sandwich to Libby with the crusts delicately sliced off; meanwhile I attempted to keep my eyes away from Kieran's chiselled body. Libby snatched the sandwich up hungrily.

"Bris is in Adrian's room, probably fornicating." My eyes widened in surprise at this but he continued nevertheless, "Chara is in her room being antisocial. Will and Nik are hunting but of course I'm not allowed to go as its too straining on my poor frail back." he said bitterly, "And Ebbs went for food, leaving me in charge," he added with an intentionally superior tone.

"Does Ebony have house insurance?" I asked innocently, "or does she *want* it to burn down?"

"Why?" he retorted, "are you planning to sing?"

"It's too early in the morning to deal with idiots," I muttered grumpily.

"So go outside then," Kieran suggested. "I'm sure at least one of your personalities would appreciate it."

"Shut up."

"Or what?" he smirked arrogantly. A flicker of irritation fluttered in my stomach; which was still persistently complaining about my lack of morning-food. I'm grouchier when I'm hungry.

"I'll kick your ass." You never know, maybe I could.

"Pah!" he scoffed, "You sure you can even reach it?" he looked down at me from his superior height and smiled.

"I'm *not* short," I said then thought curiously, "Is that really where Bris is?"

"Probably," he shrugged, "It wouldn't be the first time."

"Really?" I wondered, perplexed at the thought of anyone being able to like Adrian enough to want a relationship. He was just so cold and…angry.

"Yeah," Kieran frowned, "The only problem is, I think Adrian actually likes her, whereas she just wants him because she thinks it annoys me."

"Why would she think that?" I asked.

"We used to mess about a bit," he said nonchalantly, "But she wanted something more. I don't think she ever got over it."

"Oh Kieran," I sighed, looking out of the window, seeing rolling grey clouds hovering above the mountains in the distance, dropping millions of snowflakes "Must every girl you meet fall in love with you?"

"Afraid so," he laughed, and then his expression dimmed and softened unexpectedly, "Though none so far have counted for much."

I looked at him with a quizzical stare, but then my attention wavered as the intriguing scent of bacon wafted to me again. My stomach moaned. Kieran smirked. As the strips sizzled in the pan he casually asked, "Want some?"

I nodded eagerly, "That'd be nice."

How come things take so much longer to cook when you're really hungry? Kieran picked up the pan finally, bacon cooked, and started carelessly tossing the yummy stuff up on a thick hunk of homemade bread. I swear my mouth watered as he laid it on a plate and slowly sliced it in half Jamie Oliver/M&S style. Coming around the side of the table, carefully emphasizing his movements, he carried the diet-ruining, hangover-curing breakfast. My belly rumbled ravenously again as he picked up the sandwich, offering...and abruptly ripped a bite from it. Smiling arrogantly through a mouthful of pig, he said, "You know where the pan is."

Growling, I plonked off the chair and went to fetch my own damn breakfast.

"A gentleman would have made it for me," I grumbled, more annoyed by his teasing than anything else. There was more uncooked bacon wrapped in a brown sheet of paper, like an old-fashioned butcher had packaged it. I took two slices and carefully laid them in the centre of the spitting-hot pan. Kieran had the nerve to plonk into my chair and smirk.

"I'm not gentle, princess, I'm rough and ignorant like a real man," he informed me, tearing into his sandwich and licking his lips irritatingly. "We were waiting for you to wake up. Or slither from your lair; whichever it is that you do."

I was instantly suspicious, "Why?"

I finished frying off the bacon, found the loaf of white bread and hacked off a thin slice, then assembled my sandwich. I then began to devour it.

"You eat like such a lady," Kieran frowned.

"So do you." I smiled attractively, displaying most of my sandwich.

"But yeah, as I was saying, we were waiting for you to get up because Chara and Ebbs need to take you to Temardra."

Before I could say anything, Ebony literally danced into the room. "Morning," she greeted cheerfully.

"Morning," I said politely.

"Mummy," Libby rejoiced, throwing up her arms so Ebony could scoop her up. Ebony hugged her close for a moment before sitting her back down.

"How are you?" she asked me as she lifted a canvas bag onto the table and began emptying the contents, mostly vegetables. "Did you sleep well?"

"Fine thank you," I answered courteously.

"Has Kieran told you about us taking you to Temardra?" She wondered. "You need to buy some things for tonight. And get inked, if you want to."

"Inked?" I asked.

"Do you want to keep your marks?" She wondered, gesturing towards the gorgeous spiralling patterns that covered my right arm and slowly made their way over my new body. "If you do, you need them to be inked over with Tabya ink; otherwise they'll be gone in a few weeks. Of course you'll still only be able to see them before or after a Change and while you're using your gift, but most people choose to keep them anyway."

I never even thought that I would lose my marks. I felt like they represented the new me, a fresh start, I didn't want them to just disappear.

"Does it hurt?" I asked.

"It's done with a needle and ink," Kieran said. "Of course it hurts. Any tattoo does."

I glowered at him but then heard someone coming down the stairs. It was Chara and she'd overheard the end of our conversation. She was fully dressed and added when she entered the kitchen, "You also need a wing brace."

"What's a wing brace?"

"You know the leather bags that wrap around wings?" Ebony asked.

"Yeah."

"You need to have one of those, only you need a proper one."

"A proper one?"

"Here," Kieran gestured for me to follow him. "I'll show you."

Nodding to Ebony, Kieran lead me outside into a massive pavilion-type building which I first assumed was a garage–except now I think about it they don't actually have cars here. Opening the door, I realised that it was really a room filled with weapons, equipment and other dangerous Phoenix devices. Opened doors lead outside to a gravelled tennis-court sized pitch. Weird markings were painted onto the floor in bizarre curling circles.

"Here," Kieran said, walking towards me while carrying something dark and heavy-looking, "this is a wing brace."

He lifted up a massive lump of heaving material. It opened out as a series of complicated straps made of a strong black material and metal links that laced together in protective columns, like chain mail. I frowned at it, trying to picture how it would fit on a Phoenix. It just looked like a heavy mess.

I said eventually, "How the hell does that work?"

"Complicatedly," Kieran replied. He stretched it out and the muscles in his arms stood out like thick cords; it must have been seriously heavy. "This one's mine from when I used to guard."

"You were a guard?" I wondered, but he was, seventeen when he left here. How young was he when he was a guard?!

"A second protector actually, for the Lady Delia," he answered. "As soon as I Changed she said she wanted me. To be fair, who could resist?"

"But you must have been like fourteen or something!" I protested. How could he have the responsibility to protect someone's life at that age?

"I was twelve," he corrected, "and a little advanced for my age. Soon got bored though; everyone seemed to like Delia, hardly anyone tried to kill her."

"How boring for you," I muttered to myself. I walked over to Kieran and held up my hands, palms upraised, "Can I look?" I wondered.

"You won't be able to hold it," Kieran stated.

"I'll be fine," I assured him, reaching for it. Instinctively he moved back.

"No seriously," he said, "you won't be able to hold it."

I gritted my teeth irritably. I can do what I damn well want. "I can do it."

Kieran shrugged, his expression was filled with lazy contempt; like he wasn't really that bothered what I did anyway. He dropped it into my hands.

And I collapsed under the weight of it.

Bloody hell, what was it *made* of?

Kieran reached out as I stumbled over, gravity pulling me unyieldingly. He moved as if to grab me to stop me falling over but instead just took hold of the brace and let me fall. I landed roughly on my backside.

"Careful," Kieran warned, picking a piece of dirt off a silver buckle on the wing brace. "You might break it."

Embarrassedly, with a face brighter than a strawberry, I staggered back up again as Kieran hung the wing brace back up on the wall where it joined several others.

"But why do I need one?" I asked finally as we were re-entering the house.

"Because you're a Swartette, therefore you need to look like one, be trained like one and be as deadly as one. And anyway," he added, "it'll strengthen your wings."

We were back in the kitchen now; Ebony was still in there, sweeping Libby up into her arms, saying to me as she left the room, "We'll get going in about half an hour."

"Okay," I called, but she'd disappeared.

"She's gone." Kieran said.

"I know."

My first visit to the massive city centre flew by. As soon as we left the house we walked through the fields down into the main city, and it wasn't long before I was led to the biggest high-street I had ever seen.

It was basically the Karisian version of Paris's Champs Elysées, only larger and somehow more spectacular. The buildings were all tall, artistically constructed and blatantly old. The avenue stretched for miles it seemed. It wasn't snowing here like it was in the mountains; it was still bright and sunny despite the chilling wind. A paved road ran down the centre with impressive black streetlamps and shops running parallel on both sides.

People walked down the pavements. Groups of teenage girls wandered with linked arms, chattering away with smiling faces. Men walked with their girlfriends, clutching burdening shopping bags by their fingertips. Sharp business-types marched purposefully with stern, distant faces. I even saw people who acted suspiciously like tourists, pointing at the ancient buildings in parties-generally being annoying and in the way.

Scattered on the long cobbled road were thriving market stalls selling everything imaginable; produce ranging from dried fruits to weird elemental equipment which I was clueless as to their function. Shows of dance, music and astonishing flight displays occurred constantly, surrounded by eagerly watching crowds. It was vibrant, it was exciting, and...well, very noisy.

The girls automatically steered me towards the largest building on my right. I had been curiously edging closer to a man who was doing fantastic acrobatics as a bird, bending his body convolutedly into ridiculous positions.

"First we need to sort out your brace," Ebony explained, her voice loud as she struggled to be heard over the conventional sounds of a busy city day.

We entered into what I imagined Tiffany's would be like. The floors were covered in expensive patterned carpets, the walls decorated with fine art, and all around me were hundreds of glass cabinets, only instead of jewellery these cabinets contained very expensive looking weapons; some encrusted with jewels the size of my fist. The ceilings were high and the walls covered in gigantic metal wing braces and armour. I was too busy ogling, my mouth unattractively gaping open, to notice when a man stepped forwards.

His voice eventually filtered through my bewildered mind. "Welcome. Can I help you with anything?" I heard him greet decorously.

I looked towards the voice and saw a handsome man, around twenty, with hair brighter than a poppy and wearing a dignified suit. Chara answered him automatically. "We are looking for a full-plated wing brace," she stated, business-like, "for Ruby Swartette. It needs to be suitable for the High Flight."

"Ah," he nodded knowingly, "This way."

He gestured for us to follow him and he led us towards the left hand side of the huge room, towards a blond woman behind another glass cabinet. She was fiddling with an emerald coated dagger that she must have stolen from the Tower of London. She smiled warmly, flashing a set of small white teeth.

"These ladies are after the Swartette wing brace," the man told her seriously.

"Swartette?" she raised her eyebrows, scrutinising our ordinary appearances with assessing eyes, probably wondering why a Swartette would be hanging around with two Ashaiks. Then she shook her head, her face dissolving into friendliness. "Oh good, we did wonder whether or not it would be completed in time when we got the order yesterday."

I glanced over at Chara and Ebony in confusion, who shared identical expressions. I spoke up, "Order?"

She frowned at our puzzled faces, "Yes, High Lynk Swartette placed the order in yesterday for a gold full-plated wing brace fitted for a medium build female. All measurement alterations can be completed tomorrow after it has been displayed tonight. Ah," she said, "Here it is."

I glanced over to where she was looking as two men carried over a gigantic gold wing brace, similar to Kieran's earlier with its heavy chainmail links and long blade-like plates of armouring. Kieran's was nothing in comparison to this one; it was overwhelmingly beautiful and expensive with its ruby and diamond encrusted chains and plates. It was apparently a traditional one; which basically meant you couldn't fit extra blades in it –though why the hell a Phoenix would need blades as well as talons and sharp wings, I had no idea.

"It is set to be sent straight to the High Flight tonight, so there is no need to take it now," said the woman, nodding at the men, who removed the brace.

"So has this already been paid for?" Chara asked.

"Of course," she nodded.

"Oh," I said, looking at the other two, "well that's sorted then."

As we left the building Chara said, "Well that was strange, that Lynk paid for everything."

"Well I'm not complaining," I said, "I don't know how I would have paid for one anyway to be honest. How much is it to be inked?"

"Nothing for you, you're Royalty," Ebony said. "To be honest that's why we brought you, we thought you wouldn't have to pay for a wing brace either. It would be payment enough in advertisement for the shop."

"Why is my brace gold though," I wondered, remembering a little about metals from school lessons. "Gold is soft. Why use it for armouring?"

Ebony smiled, "It's mostly for show, not for fighting but the gold is treated to strengthen it."

"Oh," I said.

We next made our way to where I would be tattooed. The building was older, but kept in good condition. There were large paintings on the walls, more mark-like patterns in different styles, and there were three rows of occupied seats where people were being tattooed with sharp needle-like instruments and bowls of diaphanous ink. I wasn't really nervous at all to be honest. I knew that if I'd decided to have a tattoo a month ago I would have been a nervous wreck before going, but now that I'd gone through the pain of the Change, the thought of a measly little tattoo didn't bother me at all.

In the end it wasn't really that exciting. Ebony had been right as well, I didn't have to pay to be inked and it didn't take very long either, considering the size of the mark I had. The woman who did it seemed ancient, deep wrinkles cracking her face, but she was obviously the most experienced professional in the place. It did hurt, but it wasn't unbearable and every prick of the needle was fast and precise. The transparent ink was strange. I didn't know why it made the marks permanent but if it worked...

It took the better part of an hour. I definitely appreciated it when Ebony suggested lunch at a nice little restaurant on the way back. She recommended 'Taleni' and since I didn't know what anything else on the menu was, I ordered it. It turned out to be a spicy rice-based dish which came with tasty cracker things and strangely textured vegetables I had never tasted before. After drinking an ominous sparkling beverage which faintly tasted of strawberry-quite obviously laced with some form of alcohol-we headed off to the other side of the main street to get the others clothes for tonight.

By now the afternoon was growing late and my feet ached. Chara and Ebony talked as we walked, while I watched the acrobat from earlier. I was so caught up in the image of his twisted body that when somebody abruptly exploded into me, I didn't have time to react as I was shoved towards one of the alleyways that branched out from the main street.

I screamed as hands yanked my hair, forcing me quickly down the street. A knife was immediately at my neck. I swallowed, feeling the blade delicately flutter over my skin. The main street had vanished instantaneously, along with the bustling crowd. My heartbeat pounded erratically. Everything changed suddenly. A moment ago I was happily watching the acrobat and next I was struggling against the rough hands that held me, absolutely terrified. How long till the others noticed I'd gone? I closed my eyes, praying.

When I breathed the icy frigid air, opening my eyes, I was somewhere else. I'd been pulled down another alley.

With wide panicking eyes I screamed again. It was darker here; I didn't know where I'd been taken. A sweaty hand covered my mouth and lifted me forwards. I struggled desperately, kicking out. I couldn't breathe properly. I heard words being mumbled behind me and I felt my throat swell as fingers wrapped around my neck. I could barely see as I was carried down the alley. I didn't know who was attacking me, but suddenly I was shoved against a wall.

A man's body pressed securely against me, my back against the wall. I had no room to escape. There was no way out.

The hands released my neck. I gasped. I could breathe again, but my body was now frozen into involuntary immobility.

It was too dark. Too deserted. Where was everybody? I saw the flash of red, red eyes and then something cold and sharp was pressing against my throat.

The knife.

Chapter Thirteen

"If you use Chyun'ju, I'll cut out your damned throat," said the man. His voice was deep and eerily calm. "I know who you are," he spoke as if he were talking to a lover, low and passionate. A tremor rocketed violently though me as his other hand slid to my back, lasciviously tracing the lower area of my spine. Pain flared where my marks had been permanently tattooed. His eyes were simultaneously malicious and hungry and his sharp nails scratched my skin like a scalpel. "I know what you can do." He pressed the blade deeper into the soft flesh at my throat. I forced my neck up, trying to stop it digging in. Pain exploded into me; I tasted blood. "And I know exactly what I'll do if you don't comply."

I pleaded with my eyes. I didn't know what he was talking about. I couldn't speak. I could feel hot sticky blood leak down my neck. He removed his hand from my patterns to join it with his other hand as the blade slowly moved forward. I needed to be brave; surely Chara and Ebony would find me. What if they couldn't get through the crowd? What if they thought I was lost or something? Actually, did I want them to find me? Then they'd have to fight.

"I know your father's formed alliances with the Barlayic. I have seen his army of them in the mountains," he said. "What is he doing?" he pressed the blade harder and hissed "Tell me".

I tried to shake my head. I didn't know anything, especially about my father. I wanted to scream that I didn't know. He sliced the knife deeper, the blade sinking as easily as if it were cutting soft cheese. Pain throbbed in my neck; I could feel my throat bleed. I wanted to cough. Then faintly I heard the wonderful melody of Chara's voice. I looked out towards the end of the alley, subsequently tearing my skin further. The man ignored the sounds.

From the corner of my vision I noticed a rock on the floor glint as it caught the light when the man accidentally nudged it. I had a plan, sort-of.

"Perhaps," he wondered silkily, "I'll cut out your voice and send it to Lynk in a pretty envelope. He can't use you then, little weapon."

"I don't know anything," I tried to say. As the words spurted out excruciatingly, flecks of my own blood spat into his crimson eyes, the only part of him I could identify; he blinked.

In the instant he blinked the blade on my neck relented slightly. I used all my strength to push him back. Startled, he staggered. Sweeping down, I picked up the rock and slammed it down onto his skull. There was a loud crack, but I'd only caught him; he'd twisted his head at the last moment. He groaned in pain and flung his blade. I heard it coming, flinching to the side.

The blade struck the wall next to me, just clipping my ear.

I gasped again. I swear the darkness was creeping closer to me. My heart drummed. I heard Chara call my name again. The man growled, hostile and animalistic, then I heard the clang of a dagger hitting the ground. The sound was loud enough for Chara to hear. Her calls were growing closer.

"I'll come back for you," the man promised belligerently.

Then those vicious bloody eyes turned from me. Footsteps sounded down the alley in both directions now. I collapsed against the cold floor. I could barely breathe. It was like I'd tried to swallow a wire brush.

"Ruby!" Chara said my name, panicked. Then I was being lifted up, in surprisingly strong arms. I was beyond caring about being heavy, my throat was screaming silently. Suddenly light blinded me.

"Oh my God," I heard Ebony gasp, "look at her throat."

I struggled to remain conscious.

"She needs a healer; get her to the infirmary."

"She needs Kieran." Chara stated firmly.

There was a brief pause before I heard Ebony mutter swearwords lowly.

Suddenly I was being lifted onto something big and soft. My fingertips barely recognised the silky feathers in the unbearable pain. I dipped in and out of dreams, horrible nightmares. Crimson eyes were watching me; pain stalked me, I heard the bark of a dog. A cool wind was only felt when it left. Then I heard the most beautiful voice in the world.

It swore words too awful to repeat then continued, "Why does she always have to get into sodding trouble? She's been here less than a day."

Slowly I opened my eyes; Kieran was glowering down at me. His eyes are so beautiful when he's angry, I thought dazedly.

An abrupt and very painful pressure was against my throat. I gasped, feeling bloody bile rising up my throat like toxic poison. My head swam, but very slowly the pain was reducing. A bizarre sensation was knitting my broken cells back together. I became aware of words being muttered, chanted against the skin of my neck. I could see the very top of Kieran's head and nothing else. I felt his hot breath sending shivers across me while his hands gradually mended my wound, allowing the pain to fade into bleak nothingness. When he was done he sat up, his body looming over me. Eventually I became aware that I was on the ground outside Ebony's house and I struggled to sit up. As I moved my throat burned and I coughed up blood. I struggled to breathe, spitting more red; red like my attackers eyes.

I opened my mouth to thank him but no words came out. Seeing my panicked eyes Kieran said, "You won't be able to talk for at least a couple of hours... Serves you right," he added antagonistically, obviously extremely angry with me.

I staggered up and looked at him meaningfully; he didn't have to bloody save me. He understood my expression completely, standing up too.

"It's not like I have a lot of choice in the matter. You could at least try not to walk into danger. I'm sick of saving your stupid ungrateful ass."

He was infuriated and so was I. Why the hell was he being like this? It wasn't my fault I was attacked. I wanted to scream at him not to bother saving me next time but my words wouldn't come out.

He smirked arrogantly as I mouthed soundlessly, "Still, at least there's a bright side to everything."

"Kieran, stop it," Chara scolded, suddenly wrapping her arm through mine and coming to my defence. "It wasn't her fault; somebody must have dragged her down an alley at knife-point."

"What did they look like?" Kieran asked briskly, his jaw clenched.

She shook her head, "I never saw them, it all happened too fast."

"So wait, we don't know who attacked Ruby or why," he concluded bitterly. "Well that's brilliant, Ruby," he said sarcastically, "now we're all in danger."

He might as well have smacked me in the face.

"Kieran," Ebony shot, "don't speak to her like that."

"Why? At least I can speak," He countered; his expression hostile. I had never seen him this angry before. He turned to look sharply at Ebony. "You know the truth now. I healed her in England, but not only that, I brought her back from the Depths. There's no point denying it anymore. I'm her healer and I goddamn hate it."

It was like I was a balloon which he'd deflated. He couldn't have said anything that would have made me feel any worse. I felt the tears form but I furiously forced them back. It was the most horrible thing he'd ever said to me but I wouldn't cry. I couldn't look at him. I couldn't bear to see the resentment in his eyes which reflected in his voice.

"You don't get it Ruby," he snarled at my expression, "It's not just the Wall we have to think of. Every time I heal you our bodies become connected on a level nobody understands. If I keep doing it sod knows what will happen."

I stared at him incomprehensibly, unable to say anything.

"Arhh," he exploded, "I'm going to fly. Take her inside and for God's sake don't let her eat anything." Without another word he stormed off, tearing at his clothes as he went.

"He didn't mean it," Chara assured me as she led me upstairs and into mine and Bris's bedroom–she still wasn't back. Ebony went to check on Libby.

I looked into her kind sincere eyes but knew she was wrong. Kieran hated me. I'm just a burden to him; I endanger his friends and family, and I constantly land him in trouble. I am really just a nuisance. I wouldn't want me if I were him. He was right.

Chara understood, "Kieran's just upset," she said softly.

I shook my head pathetically.

Chara smiled sadly, "Get some rest. Just put on something comfy and stay in bed, okay? Do you want me to get Kieran to come up when he's cooled off a little?" I shook my head miserably. "Okay, I'll come back in a little while."

As soon as the door shut quietly behind her I buried my face in my pillow and suddenly wanted my dog more than I thought possible. I cried, and it hurt. I was scared of that man, afraid he'd return as promised. I was angry and hurt by Kieran. And I just wanted to go home, but didn't even have a home anymore. I had nothing left of my old life, my old self, to depend on.

The hours dragged by slowly. Kieran didn't come to see me. Bris didn't return at all. I lay awake for a very long time, knowing that soon I would have to go and Change. I had no idea what was even going to happen at my own celebration. I kept remembering those blood-red eyes. I snuggled deep under my protective covers, squeezing my eyes tightly shut. Eventually I drifted off.

A child was standing in a paved courtyard. An atmosphere of warm sunlight was streaming down onto her upraised face. She wore a long red dress that matched her glorious hair, curling in mesmerising ringlets around her waist. She consumed the sunlight greedily, taking it all in and twirling her little hands, palms upward, to catch the scintillating air. She turned slowly at the sound of footsteps.

"Light will not make you powerful," said her father, stepping into the magnificent yellow air. He gestured towards the corner of the courtyard, towards a caged white tiger that growled when he looked at it.

"But it is pretty," the young girl objected and her father gave her a look which made her think he disapproved of her observation.

"Beauty is an optical illusion. Alas, it is useful for deception, but you don't need to know that right now. Lets practice your

voice, shall we?" he encouraged, and the girl seemed pleased that he wasn't mad at her.

Her father spoke to two slaves who pulled up the latch of the wooden cage holding the tiger. The furious beast charged out towards the little girl. She stood very calmly, smiling, then opened her mouth and began to sing. She sung so beautifully that the animal stopped in its tracks, seemingly fascinated and hypnotised by her voice. She willed it closer, letting it sit before her. Then she looked expectantly at her father for further instruction.

"What else can you make it do?" he asked.

The child smiled sweetly again, and brought up her freckled hands meaningfully. The tiger instantly obeyed and stood on its hind legs, clapping its front two paws together. She beamed excitedly at her father, waiting for his approval but he frowned disappointedly and her face fell.

"Anyone can teach a tiger to do that," he told her seriously, "make it do something it normally wouldn't."

The little girl looked confused, "Like what, father?"

"Make it walk back into the cage," he suggested indifferently. He turned to the slaves and nodded. The slaves instantly brought forwards lit torches and set the wooden cage on fire, furious flames shot up instantly.

"Now," her father continued, "make it burn."

"Won't that hurt it?" asked the little girl, around four years old.

"Of course it will," he replied, "but pain is a good thing, it makes you see clearer."

The child looked at her father who gave her an encouraging nod. She began singing again, louder now, persuading the tiger forward at her father's command. The white tiger walked into the flame without hesitation, completely infected by the monstrous power of her voice, it sat immobile as the sparks slowly ate away its fur.

Only its eyes were screaming.

The little girl watched the tiger die because of her. She was crying. Then her father made all her doubts and fears disappear as he touched her on the shoulder.

"Very good," he smiled and she beamed because he was proud of her. His enchanting voice let her know that she had done the right thing.

"Very good," he repeated quietly, looking out at the burning animal with flickers in his own golden eyes, "my child."

My disgustingly sweaty body jerked bolt-upright. My eyes darted open. Breathing heavily, the blood gushed to my head, making me dizzy. I was shivering in uncontrollable convulsions. It had just been a dream.

"Ruby?"

I screamed automatically, flinching back from the noise so fast that I smacked my head on the wall behind me. *Ouch.*

A hand clamped across my mouth and an image of that alley flooded into my mind. Terrified, I kicked out at the person who was restraining me. The darkness was closing in on me again. I couldn't see my attacker. My heart was hammering a million times a minute, at least that's how it felt, and I punched the shadow clean across his jaw.

He swore angrily as he held me down. Muscled arms restrained me inescapably as I squirmed like a worm on a hook.

"Ruby, calm down," I slowly realised that I recognised the voice. I looked up to see Nik. He released me, then sighed, "What am I going to do with you?" He rubbed his jaw where I'd punched him. "I heard what happened."

I nodded, and then said shakily, "I'm sorry... I didn't know it was you." My voice worked thankfully, but it did crack and throb painfully.

He just smiled with kindness, "Don't worry about it, you've had a rough few hours. It's time for us to go."

I slowly sat up; my body ached tremendously, "Where?" then I remembered. "Oh God; the Flight," I swallowed with sudden terror, "Where is it at?"

"Has nobody told you yet?" he rolled his eyes exasperatedly, "Jeez, Chara's been out with you all day and not spoken to you about it?"

I looked at him expectantly, taking his question rhetorically.

He sighed, leaning forwards and speaking calmly, "What will happen is you'll have to climb up to the top of the north mountain cliff. That's where the celebrations will be. There'll be a lot of people. When you get up there you'll have to do a couple of things to do with your element, I'm not quite sure because I'm of Earth, but you'll probably have to walk through fire. Then you'll have to dive off the cliff. The adrenaline should make you Change."

"Should," I repeated nervously, "Does that mean some people don't?"

"Sometimes," he answered honestly.

"You've got to be joking. Why is everything in this place so dangerous?"

"Why do you think we left," he muttered quietly.

I glanced over at him, "Why did you?" I wondered softly.

"You'll have to ask Chara that, not me," he answered, and then assured me with that calming gentle smile "You'll be fine anyway, tonight, you're a natural."

I took a deep shaky breath, "Thank you Nik."

"Are you ready?" he asked, standing up and offering me a hand.

"Not even close," I admitted, staggering up, my nerves jittering already.

"Come on," he grinned. "Just think, after you've jumped off a cliff in front of thousands of people, achieved your First Flight, been the perfect party host, then you might even be able sit down for ten, maybe even fifteen whole minutes."

"Really? That long," I laughed exhaustedly, "In that case let's get going."

When we went downstairs everyone was standing by the door except Kieran, who was nowhere in sight. Good, I thought, though felt secretly stung. It was dark outside, the storm clouds from the mountains earlier had dissipated and the sky glittered with golden stars. It seemed cold too, though my body didn't feel the temperature like it had before. It was rare that I felt truly cold now.

"We'll take you up to the bottom of the north cliff," Chara said, "But you'll have to climb it yourself."

I frowned "On my own? I don't know where I'm going."

Chara smiled patiently, "Someone will be with you; it just can't be us. To be honest this is quite an important event. I wouldn't blame you if you wanted to stay clear of us for tonight; for suspicion's sake."

I frowned, waving this suggestion off; still feeling unbelievably anxious. Briseis noticed this, smiling, "You look terrified. What you worried about?"

It was time for me to laugh, "Just the whole jumping off a cliff thing."

"Your body will know what to do," Nik promised, "Even if you don't."

I took a deep breath and nodded. The others went off to Change and while I waited for them to return I gazed up at the sky, suddenly wondering whether or not my mum was watching me. Would she be annoyed that all her hard work to keep me from this place had been inevitably unsuccessful?

The others returned and I climbed onto Chara's feathery back when she offered. We leaped off into the air for what I hoped was my last piggyback ride. The flight was quick and we soon landed, separated from the others, at the base of the north side of the valley, where the wall was so steep it was a vertical ledge. The others had continued straight up to the top of the mountain ledge, where I could just make out the orange light polluting the sky from blazing bonfires.

I jumped down off Chara, my knees buckling as I landed. I was so exhausted, I felt like time was zooming ahead of me, faster every second.

There was a young man standing in front of me.

He was golden and angelic; the first male blonde Phoenix I had seen, other than Lynk of course. His skin was dusted in pale gold tan, no freckles and absolutely flawless. His eyes were amber, tinted slightly orange which was in some way both mysterious and alluring. He was tall and athletic, built like a runner but not quite as muscular as an Ashaik. As I neared I realised he was Kieran's exact opposite.

He was light; Kieran was dark; soft and hard, fire and Earth.

Good luck chick, Chara said encouragingly, before sweeping off into the air.

"Jayson," the guy smiled warmly, offering his hand to shake. I took it, his grip was strong, his skin startlingly hot.

"So you must be the Swartette."

"That's me," I said tiredly.

"You excited?" he wondered as we began walking up the side of the cliff, where the rocks tumbled from the top in a steep slope.

"Nervous," I admitted.

"Why?" he inquired, grinning excitedly, "It's the best feeling in the world."

"Falling?" I laughed.

He shook his head with a light easy-going laugh. "Flying."

"What's it like?" I questioned.

"Do you want to know the soppy truth?" he asked and I nodded interestedly, "It's beautiful." He sighed, glancing over at me with those strange amber eyes, "The whole word disappears underneath you and suddenly you're free. Everyone does it the same way: over the edge. The fear and adrenalin apparently draw out your instincts." I listened quietly, trying to picture what he was saying, imagining the drop. "I remember my First Flight was a summer's day. The sun was brilliant. I flew above everything, through the clouds; they're kind of soft, you know, like a damp blanket. But the sun kept me dry and warm and the wind lifted me...it's hard to explain," he sighed distantly, "but it was the best."

"It sounds it," I agreed, noticing the glacial foothills that were beginning to peak into my view as we climbed higher up the slope; the sparkling folds of rock were sharpened impressively. I tried to imagine what it'd be like to fly but I couldn't. It was like a blank wall stopped me. Perhaps I wasn't meant to experience such a wonderful-sounding thing.

"What's it like up there?" I asked as the climb grew steeper. To my surprise, I felt instantly comfortable with Jayson. He reminded me a lot of Alex back at home.

"There are a lot of people," he answered, "and, of course, a lot of fire displays. There's a tent on the right where you can get undressed."

I stopped in my tracks, staring at Jayson with wide surprised eyes, "What do you mean, undressed?" I demanded.

"Well you aren't exactly going to be diving over the edge fully clothed are you?" he laughed.

"I'm not doing it naked if that's what you're thinking," I said sternly.

"No, no," he waved me off, "you'll have the ceremonial cloak; of course."

The last section of rock was nearly vertical; it took all my concentration to climb. I gripped my hands tightly into available cracks, following Jayson's capable lead, thankful that I was used to tackling such mobile rock faces because of living in the Lake District. When I clawed my way over the last section of rock I saw that a massive sheet of red material, painted over with golden spiralling patterns, covered my view of the celebrations on the other side. There was a great amount of noise propelling from the other side of the sheet, sounds of talking and metal clashing and the bang of tribal drums.

To the right was a tall wide tent that I assumed was where I was supposed to get dressed. I turned to Jayson, my eyebrows raised. "So you're telling me I have to go out in front of thousands of people, *in nothing but a cloth?!*"

"Cloak," he corrected light-heartedly, "yeah, here it is." He went off into the tent and brought out a long cloak shimmering with gold thread woven into beautiful intertwining patterns. "It's not that bad, get going." He shoved the cloth into my hands and half-pushed me into the tent.

I reluctantly surrendered, grudgingly stripping off. There was another outfit hung up in the tent and I was under no illusion that I could wear my own clothes: I guessed that the gold halter neck dress before me would also be forced onto my skin. It was a gorgeous dress, corseted and made of fine silk, but I was more of a jeans and t-shirt kind of girl; personally. How did they know it would even fit? I wondered.

I wrapped the cloak around my body, finding no way of tying it. I looked around for something to tie it with, having no intention of wearing it open, if that's what they expected they were kidding themselves. In the end I used the rope that tied the curtain of the tent, wrapping it round my waist and wearing the cloth as a wraparound makeshift dress. I took off my mother's chain, placing it safely on the side so it wouldn't snap when I Changed; if I did.

When I came back out the tent Jayson laughed at my appearance, but it was a genuine humorous laugh, not in any way nasty. "Well that's different."

His smile was quite infectious. "Look, I'm wearing it like this. If you try to stop me I'll yell pervert *really* loudly."

He grinned manically, "No, don't. I can't wait to see Lynk's face."

We walked over to the curtain. "Ready?" Jayson asked.

I nodded and he pulled back the gap in the curtains. I heard a crowd roar.

Chapter Fourteen

The moment I stepped under the curtain, light burned down onto me. Thousands of glass spheres floated above my head from strings attached a net roof, bright candles burned encased within the orbs. Fountains of flame ran around a startlingly large audience, amazing displays of fireworks boomed in the starry night's sky and bonfires lit a gigantic dance floor. Behind that were rows of various tribal drums and strange musical instruments I'd never seen before in my life. To the right, dug into the ground at a lower level were rings of cushioned seats and to the left, nearer the cliff ledge, was a bar pouring out cocktails at an unhealthy rate. I was standing at the highest level, the VIP section. Surrounding me were the entertainers; acrobats on ropes, fire-eaters, sword jugglers and dancers in ridiculously skimpy outfits, their Phoenix wings somehow displayed while the rest of their body remained human; like angels. Except angels wouldn't dance like that; in a way that mocked their virtuous appearance.

The atmosphere was hot, electric and intense. I glanced back uncomfortably, searching for Jayson and luckily he was at my side. The instant people started to realise I was there a thunderous applause erupted. It surprised me, these people didn't know me; it was like being a celebrity. As it quieted I noticed Lynk stalking across the main platform towards me. As he approached I saw him note my appearance with a twitch of his otherwise indifferent expression. He wasn't happy about it. I almost smiled. As he faced the crowd, there was an eerie silence.

He opened his mouth and addressed them. "Tonight we celebrate my daughter coming of age. It's been a long wait," he glanced back at me and I looked away, feeling the power of his gaze too much to bear. I hated that he called me his daughter. I wasn't his daughter. He continued, "But tonight she will take her First Flight. Let her Change be swift, her wings strong and her journey true."

Everyone stared at Lynk, seemingly transfixed by his presence; it was strange how someone could be so influential even among others of equal status, though I knew it was nothing to do with his sparkling personality. It was that voice, that evil beautiful voice that would make you feel happy to drown just to hear some more of its words; its notes and textures. It didn't work on everyone, not when he wasn't concentrating, only the weaker Phoenix felt the fascination, but it was still difficult not to be enraptured by such a perfect sound. It was a dangerous drug to indulge in. A drug I also dealt in.

He turned to me. "Follow me to the flames, Ruby." It was all an act. Past the voice and those golden eyes, identical to mine, past that smile, was the same cold vindictive man calculating how best to use me to his advantage.

I had no choice but to follow him, thousands of eyes on me, through the crowd. They parted like the red sea as we came closer and made our way down steps, no longer covered by the lit net roof. On the other side of the main section of the crowd was a path covered in golden petals. On either side of the path were beautiful flower arrangements meant to look like fire; red, yellow and orange buds bursting with sweet fragrances. One particular blossom that captured my attention had electric-orange petals with streaks of yellow running down them like buttercup paint.

The path led to an archway made of what looked like wooden reeds. Underneath it was more wood and behind it was about a metre of rock before the sheer drop of the cliff. I took a deep breath as we neared it. Lynk edged closer to me.

"You have to take the cloak off before entering the arch," he hissed petulantly. "Don't you dare embarrass me or burn that two hundred year old ceremonial cloak."

That's why it smelt so musty, it was a museum relic.

I knew they'd make me do something like this. I would just have to take it off the moment before I step through the arch. I assumed it was going to be lit. I guess people won't be able to see me properly through the flames. I'd just have to be quick. God, Phoenix really didn't seem to have any shame whatsoever. They seemed far too pro-nudity.

"Fine," I growled back. "But I am not your daughter."

"You are mine," his snaring eyes flickered to me, his voice quiet but intense, "You'll learn your place, Ruby. You'll soon learn."

"I am not the child I was when my mother took me," I said. "Don't underestimate me."

He looked back at the crowd, who'd edged closer. Jayson was suddenly beside me again holding a lit torch. Lynk nodded and took the torch.

"As High Fire Elder," Lynk said, raising his voice to the audience "I will light the Ceremonial Arch." As he spoke he lowered the torch to the wooden base.

The arch sparked up instantaneously, it was blatantly coated in something flammable. The fire spread up each side of the arch and across the top, creating almost a door of flames. I stared at the blaze and my human instincts, drilled into me when I lived in England, were screaming not to walk closer. The fear of burn was dominant for a moment, until my deep rooted Phoenix instincts took over. I could feel the warmth from the fire tickle over my skin, encouraging me forwards, giving me an unexpected bout of confidence. I glanced over to Lynk, waiting for my cue.

"Be blessed by the Flames." Lynk said loudly.

With that the drums began a slow beat, which soon picked up the pace into a chaotic rhythm. People cheered and clapped. The drums were too loud, their tune too boisterous and obtrusive. I blocked the sound out. I took a deep calming breath and ignored the world, forgetting the crowd, forgetting my father. All that I focused on was me and the flames. One more breath and I moved my hand to the curtain tie that held my makeshift dress together. Facing the flames, I opened up the material, feeling instantly naked and exposed; even though I knew no one could see me yet. Then I thought what the hell, lifted the cloak from behind me so it still covered my body before letting it drop. I felt a rush of excitement. My heart was pounding as I stepped confidently–if not a little quickly-through the flames as the cloak fell.

My eyes were tightly shut but there was no pain. It was an uncomfortable feeling, too much heat; it made me feel light headed, but I was soon free of it. I was standing at the edge of the cliff, my toes practically hanging off the side, and before I could even think about it, before I could even take a breath or hesitate as I saw the 400ft+ drop; I bent my knees, raised my arms, and dived over the edge.

There was no fear, only freedom and adrenalin.

I fell through the sky, wind flooding up from underneath me. I somehow managed to think of Changing, of becoming a bird, realising how much I actually wanted this. It was exciting. I was thrilled to be doing this. It was an unexpected shock that drove my muscles to tingle and convulse violently. I could feel my body stretching and shaping. It was a bizarre feeling, something indescribable to anyone who's never felt it. It all happened so fast. The reforming of my body increased like the tempo of a song, ending in a sudden burst of heat. An excruciating wave of pain echoed across me and I knew two things for certain. One: my body had transformed into a Phoenix and two: I belonged in medical science.

Slowly I opened my eyes and saw through that spectacular impeccable vision. The beauty of the earth took my breath away; though it was unnervingly close, if I'd took just a few seconds longer I wouldn't have made it. I let this thought go. All my previous terror drained away. I opened my wings confidently, the air immediately lifting me. It took a few beats of my wings before I got into the rhythm of it and instinct took over. I felt so powerful and free, everything came so naturally. I loved every moment; dipping through the air and willing the chilling wind to run refreshingly though my feathers. I wasn't cold. I was exhilarated. I was born for this.

I was flying; I couldn't get over the fact. Me, I was in the air, soaring above the world without the assistance of an aeroplane. I was flying, I was a bird and I was flying. *Flying!* It was unbelievable. At one point I came low enough to realise there was a lake at the bottom of the valley ledge. I headed towards it, dipping lower, pausing my wings so that I could glide and slice through the air and catch my reflection in the water.

A beautiful crimson Phoenix followed me like a shadow in her watery parallel world. Her body was short but slender, coated in feathers burning like wild untameable flame. She had enormous wings splashed at the tips in sparkling gold. Her gold and black eyes were wide, framed by dramatic ashen lashes. On the crest of her head were two long gold feathers. Her talons were sharp and deadly.

This was really me. Oh my God, if my friends could see me now.

Everyone dreams and fantasises about being able to fly; I was living the dream.

Ignoring the party, I headed towards the surrounding mountains, leaving Forenna behind, flying up across the undisturbed land. Sometimes I would see flickers of colour in the moonlight which I soon decided were precious stones–though they weren't that precious here as they were used as currency. Flying closer I realised they were crystals; uncut and unhampered, growing in piecing shards that thrust up towards the heavens. I saw pine trees, smelled them. I watched animals scurry into their hiding places. A pack of grey wolves even howled in chorus as I passed.

As brilliant as it was, I knew I had to head back. I didn't want to, not in the slightest, but I knew they'd be waiting for me to return. I flew under the stars, almost swimming through the air, back the way I came. As the cliff and the celebration came into view I swooped elegantly over their heads. When they saw me they cheered again. I meant to land where the tent was but my landing was rough and I skidded across the ground, painfully scraped my wings across the rock.

I might have to work on landings. Once I stopped I headed towards the tent and attempted to Change. It took longer than it had before, as I'd forgotten how to do it, and in the end I heard someone on the other side of the tent asking if I was okay.

Luckily it was Chara's voice I heard.

Just struggling a bit, I admitted.

Here, I heard Ebony say and something was passed through the curtain and onto the floor of the large tent. It was one of those glass spheres that hung from the net roof; within it was a tiny burning candle. *Use this, it'll help you concentrate. Listen to the flame.*

I concentrated on the little light, feeling it flicker near my skin. I tried to block out everything else. Eventually I listened hard enough that I heard the almost inaudible hum of flame. Closing my eyes I followed the sound specifically, imagining I could join it. The warmth intensified to heat which spread like a shooting star up my arm, across my collarbones to my spine. Automatically my own trickle of energy intermingled with it. My back was throbbing, almost painfully. I focused on the sensation; willing it to intensify.

I vaguely heard Chara warn, *Just make sure you're actually thinking of Changing; otherwise it could be a total disaster.*

There was the stretching and shrinking of skin and the sudden excruciation. I opened my eyes and I was me again. I was shaking with immediate exhaustion.

"You okay?" Ebony wondered.

"Fine," I said, frowning exhaustedly. "I take it I have to wear this dress."

"Probably," she called back through the curtain.

I huffed and struggled into the damn thing. Suitably uncomfortable, the girls helped tie up the corseted back. The skirt of the dress fell just below my knees and the silk material felt soft to my touch. It was ever so slightly too tight but who needed to breathe anyway? I had a choice of shoes, in a range of sizes, but I stuck to the heelless sandals, ignoring the fact that they were the ones that matched the least because I didn't work well in heels. Once I'd finished, the girls fiddled about with my hair for a minute before we finally exited the tent. Now I could finally relax.

We went to the bar and ordered drinks, which came immediately in the form of large fruit cocktails. The drums behind us were beating loudly, complicated impressive rhythms that corresponded with a strange bass instrument and higher string instruments. It was fast, electric and exciting. It made me want to dance. As we made our way down, people were approaching me and congratulating me. They called me Lady, it was bizarre. I was well-known in my little town in the Lake District, but then again the town was so small everyone knew everyone. I couldn't believe it, everyone seemed to know me, seemed to know my story better than I did.

It was then that I spotted Kieran. He was down on the lower level on one of the circular seating arrangements. He was drowning deep in a sea of people; partly-concealed by heaving brown bodies, but what covered him most was the gorgeous pair of tanned legs sprawled across his lap. My relief soon turned to annoyance.

Those legs belonged to the most beautiful girl I had ever seen. Her hair was darker than onyx, flowing like shimmering water down to her narrow waist. Her skin had a brilliant Arabian glow. Her eyes were like milk chocolate, sparkling and framed by the longest damn lashes I'd ever seen. Her lips were full, curved into a sexy twist as she whispered something in his ear, giggling and touching his chest.

Have you ever hated anyone for no reason except that they had something you didn't? Well she was that girl, and she had everything. I hated her.

"Ruby!" Kieran called me over, interrupting my thoughts.

I slowly walked forwards and stood before him. I raised my eyebrows expectantly. He seemed to understand.

"This is Sofia," he explained, okay he did not understand. I didn't want to know her stupid name; I wanted her to get her stupid long legs off of him.

"Nice to meet you," I lied between my teeth, not removing my furious eyes from an oblivious Kieran. I was still extremely pissy at him for shouting at me earlier and storming off without another word.

"Sofia, Ethan, Cole, this is Ruby; I told you she'd come find me." The girl and the two other men nodded. The men were big and very scary-looking.

The girl sat forwards, finally taking her legs off him and smiling beautifully at me. She was so gorgeous I could have been sick. "Aww, she's so cute, Kieran, you never told me how cute she was." She patted him all giggly and girly on his chest. It made me furious.

Who did she think she was? I can't believe she just called me cute, like I was five or something. I hated her. Maybe I should hold her still with my voice and cut her lovely hair until I thought it was 'cute'. I stopped myself, why was I so irritated? Was it purely just because she was so beautiful? Or was it that arrogant look on Kieran's face and the fact I was still annoyed at him?"

Kieran smirked, knowing my face well enough to see just how angry I was. I shoved everything back down; I would not let him have one up on me.

"What did you want?" I asked.

"What are you offering?" he wondered, "I could use a beer."

"I ain't offering nothing except a slap in the face." I muttered.

He slowly shrugged himself upright, "See you later," he winked at Sofia. Then he came closer, casually nudging me forwards, "Come on, Princess."

"I'm not going anywhere with you until you apologise to me," I snapped, yanking away from his touch, not caring who saw. I was so mad at him, how dare he look at me like that, treat me like that, show off with that gorgeous stupid girl, after everything earlier.

He rolled his eyes, "You'll be waiting a while for that to happen," he said. God, is he really that proud that he can't admit that he did something wrong?

"I'd rather your response to be something like, 'I'm sorry'," I told him coldly.

"Come on," he said, completely ignoring my comment, "I've got you a present."

"No," I stood my ground. "I don't care. Apologise."

He stared at me for a moment, those gorgeous emerald eyes boring deep into me. I couldn't look away. He released his gaze and turned away calling, "You can either come with me without an apology, or stand there, still without an apology. Up to you."

I wanted to scream he was so infuriating, but I followed him anyway. Storming in front of him, I knocked him with my shoulder as I passed. He looked over at me with a quizzical expression, like he was unsure why I'd done that. I just looked away, my chin jutting out petulantly. He led me away from the main celebrations, past all the seats and over the normal undisturbed land. In the distance I could see a small bonfire surrounded by people about two-hundred yards from the main party.

As we got closer I realised there were only seven or so people, of mixed Tribes. There were three Earthbirds, an Airbird, a Firebird and two Waterbirds, all in human form, lying on the ground or propped up against a long wooden log. Some were chattering quietly, other's smoking something that stunk like crushed pine leaves and dirt.

There was only one girl, with long nearly diaphanous silver hair that had clumped together in spindly dreadlocks. She was speaking to an older guy with fiery eyes that sent shivers to my spine; even though I knew the shade was slightly off to be my attacker.

"Kierakai," he said his voice deep and gravelly, he stood up and clapped his hand together with Kieran's, "It's been a long time. Not long enough, though," he considered, "to remember exactly how much you owe me; in kills or cash."

Kieran laughed, "You'll get it, my friend, after-" But he was interrupted.

"After the next hit," the other guy finished, smiling. "You've not changed." They both sat down, I followed suit. "What's it like on the other side?" the man questioned.

"Shush," Kieran pulled his finger to his lips mockingly, "You know I never left these shores." He leaned in close to the other guy though, whispering loud enough so everyone could here, "Its shit. Rains all the time."

"Ah," the guy said, and then turned to me. "You must be the one they brought back. I would guess you've been through a lot too."

"She's exactly why I'm here," Kieran said, "I need someone to train her. A lot of people want to kill her, including me at times, and she's a bit pathetic."

"Isn't she supposed to be able to do Chyun'ju?" the man frowned.

"Yeah, but she's crap at that as well."

I glared at Kieran, irritated, but before I could say anything the man spoke again, "Why can't you train her?" his expression was openly calculating.

Kieran answered, "I've got some other things to take care of."

I didn't like the way Kieran said 'take care of' and felt it was time I spoke up. "Who says I need training?" I demanded, "So far I've been perfectly capable of not dying."

"Elegantly put," Kieran commented.

The man's eyes flashed from me to Kieran, "And how are you going to pay for this? If you're demanding the time of one of my best assassins I'll need a replacement." My eyes widened as I finally grasped what they were talking about.

"I'll be perfectly capable of filling that void, on one condition," Kieran said.

"What's that?" the man asked, then guessed, "You want some Leaf don't you?"

Kieran nodded.

"You know the deal," the man said, "kill first, Leaf later."

"I know," he said. "I need it."

"Alright," the man said, "Deal. Jayson," he called loudly, "I've got you a job."

I looked over to where he directed his voice and saw the same Jayson from earlier. I hadn't noticed him before as he was perched right on the lower ledge of the cliff. He got up, walked into the light and smiled at me, "Hello again, gorgeous."

My cheeks burned brightly, for some unknown reason. Nobody had ever called me gorgeous just like that. I guessed he did that with everyone. He really was quite attractive, I thought as he stepped into the light of the fire, the gleam off the embers making his blonde tendrils shine gold.

Then he froze as he glanced over at Kieran. Kieran froze also beside me.

"You," Kieran snarled.

I glanced over at him and his eyes were black, his pupils dilated so much in anger that they devoured the vibrant colour of his iris. His breathing quickened and the expression on his face was positively murderous. Before anyone could react, Kieran, in a blindingly fast motion, took two steps; simultaneously reaching inside his clothes for a sharpened blade. He moved swiftly to Jayson, who staggered backwards, inches from the ledge. Kieran was immediately upon him. It happened so quickly. I barely seemed to blink before the knife was at Jayson's throat as he dangled over the cliff ledge, held up only by the Kieran's fist as it clutched his shirt.

Chapter Fifteen

"Kieran," I screamed, racing towards him, "Don't!"

He wasn't looking at me; he didn't even glance my way. His eyes were cold, black and full of an animalistic fury. He bared his teeth, practically growling. There were no other emotions in him except anger and hate, it radiated from him, from the upraised veins in his clenched fist and the stiff unmoving muscles of his shoulders.

"Give me one good reason why I shouldn't slit your throat," he demanded. His voice was low but smooth, perfectly calm; contrasting the hostile set of his features.

Jayson didn't speak, only stared unyieldingly back at Kieran.

Kieran moved the knife forward, just piercing the flesh of his neck a millimetre deep. I didn't recognise him in that instant; he could have been mistaken for Adrian.

"Kieran," I said slowly, trying to reason with him. I didn't like this Kieran, for the first time since our initial interaction I truly comprehended just how dangerous he was. An assassin, they'd said; a cold blooded killer. "Kieran," I said again, "let him go." Kieran flinched at the sound of my voice, but he ultimately ignored me.

"Do you have any idea what you did to us?" Kieran snarled. "He sent hundreds after us. So many people were killed, innocent people, because of you."

"I have my reasons," Jayson replied, utterly apathetic.

"What reasons?" he said, leaning forwards, forcing Jayson lower off the edge of the cliff. Nobody around me spoke or even moved; the air was so tense. Kieran took a breath then shouted, screaming at Jayson infuriately, "What reasons?!"

"Kieran, come on," I said warily, edging closer.

"Ruby," Kieran glared at me, "Stay back. This is nothing to do with you."

"Kieran," it was another voice, similar to Kieran's but deeper and rougher. "Leave him, I'll deal with him." It was Adrian, suddenly looming behind me. His expression was stern, his eyes indecipherable; his motive incomprehensible.

Kieran stopped momentarily, glancing back at his brother. "You sure?" He'd calmed down dramatically at the sight of his brother, I could see the emerald colour of his iris again, but he was still dangling Jayson off the edge of a cliff.

Adrian nodded. I looked at Adrian, really looked at him, and for the first time noticed the slightly off look in his skin, the startling paleness of his cheeks. Was it the heat of the bonfire making him uncomfortable? Why was he all of a sudden stricken and ill-looking, despite doing a credible job of trying to disguise it?

"Well you're going to have to give him a minute," Kieran said, and I saw the glint in his eyes, "he's got a long way to climb."

Then to my astonishment Kieran looked back at Jayson, smiled, and abruptly let him go. I dashed forwards but it was too late, Kieran had already dropped him. He was already falling. I stared at Kieran completely gobsmacked, but he just grinned sadistically and I eventually remembered that Jayson should be alright...if he Changed before he hit the earth. The cliff's height was shorter here and my concern showed through in my features. Kieran shrugged nonchalantly and continued forwards, his face once again a mask of quiet fury.

I followed him in amazement, dumbfounded that he'd actually just dropped someone off the edge of a cliff and not even glanced back. I heard it then, the piercing cry of a Phoenix. As I turned around I saw an impressive golden

Phoenix bound towards us through the air. It skidded furiously across the floor as it landed in front of Kieran, hissing maliciously and digging its massive sharpened talons into the soil.

Kieran didn't flinch, didn't make a move to turn and continued arrogantly stalking away, his back confidently to the monster. It spread its wings, a four meter wingspan, and snapped forwards to attack but Adrian slipped in front of Kieran. The beast halted momentarily, to my surprise, and there was silence.

Kieran walked over to the older man he was talking to earlier, his face unreadable but his voice rough and firm. "You'll get your kill. Where's my Leaf?" he demanded.

The man stared quizzically up at Kieran, unfazed by everything that had just happened, "I'm not switching Jayson," he said, "it's him or no one."

"I don't care," Kieran growled, power practically streaming off him, radiating from his pores. He towered over the man dominatingly. "Just give me my Leaf."

The man shrugged and handed over some small pieces of extraordinary thin paper, almost transparent, and an open box the size of a small matchbox, filled with a strange greenish moss-like substance. Kieran snatched it from him, snapping the tiny wooden box shut, and continued walking away from the bonfire and the celebrations. He made his way away from the cliff ledge, walking directly to where the trees began in numbers. I followed him uncertainly.

"Kieran," I called and his pace eventually slowed, then stopped as he sat down on a large boulder. He opened the little box, took a tiny amount of the substance onto his hand and pushed the box back into his pocket. I stared at him, confused and a little frightened, "Kieran, what are you doing?"

"What does it look like?" he muttered. Taking a piece of the thin paper he filled it with line of the mossy substance, proceeding to roll the paper around it like tobacco. Once he was finished he looked at me, wondering, "You can't snap-fire can you?"

I frowned at him in confusion, "What?"

"You know," he said impatiently, "Snap your fingers and spark a flame."

I just stared at him.

"Right," he sighed, "You are a seriously crap Firebird."

He felt around in all his pockets looking, I assumed for some sort of lighter. He seemed surprised to find a match in his pocket, but he shrugged and struck it against the boulder, lighting the rollup. He raised it to his lips, breathing in the smoke deeply then opening his mouth slightly to let the smoke play about his lips.

He seemed to relax almost immediately. He exhaled, seeming to shrink into himself.

"What is that?" I asked, frowning.

He looked at me but didn't seem to focus actually on me, "A drug."

"Well I gathered that," I glared. "I didn't know you took drugs."

"Well why do you think I had such a problem being chased after by drug lords in Manchester?" he laughed arrogantly, like I was foolish not to have known.

"You told me it was because you slept with one of their wives," I said irritably.

"I did," he answered, taking another drag. The smoke smelt of dirt and ice. It was a strange combination of scents. "But that was only because one of them shot me. I was going to pay them eventually. People have no patience these days."

"What is it?" I asked warily.

"A bit like cannabis but much stronger; it helps me relax," he explained. "That's why I got in trouble; I was trying to find something strong enough for my body."

I didn't know what to think, I was too exhausted to question it now. Instead I sat down on the floor next to the boulder. The ground was damp but soft and I leaned back into the rock; closing my eyes. When I opened them Kieran had finished smoking and sank down beside me. His whole body was relaxed, his breathing low and steady, such a contrast to earlier. It was a shame that it took a drug to make him feel so comfortable. Though to be fair, I couldn't say much about it, I knew absolutely nothing about it or why he took it. I wouldn't say anything for now. Not if it didn't seem to harm him. He was watching the night sky.

"I'm sorry about earlier," he uttered eventually, still not removing his eyes from the incandescent heavens. "I just hate feeling like I do when I see you, your blood pouring onto my hands, knowing I need to save you. And knowing I shouldn't."

I looked at him in shock, "Surely it's a good thing you want to save my life?"

He looked at me. "Not here. It's classed as High Treason. You've seen the Wall..." he shuddered, "but if I was there when you were attacked I could have prevented it; there's no law against that."

"You couldn't have helped, Kieran, even if you were there. It happened too fast."

He placed a large hand against the boulder, blocking a flash of green lichen with his long, slender fingers. "I wouldn't have let him walk away," he muttered darkly; his lovely face suddenly volatile. "Crawl away maybe; but not walk."

"He said he'd come back for me." I cringed.

He turned to look at me seriously, "You need to tell me exactly what happened." The chips of emerald in his eyes flickered with something deep and impenetrable.

I grimaced, but knew he needed to know. He would know what to do. I fidgeted uncomfortably, running my hands through my tangled red locks, all plastered unattractively to my head with sweat from the heat of the bonfire. Kieran didn't even seem to notice. My eyes were fully accustomed to the scarce light now and I saw everything as perfectly as I would normally.

Finally, I began to describe what happened this afternoon. He instantaneously adopted that serious business-like demeanour and shot questions at me like *I* was being interrogated for attacking someone. He wanted to know what the man looked like, getting stroppy when all I could tell him was that he had red eyes. Then he asked me what he had said. I told him about what he'd said about my father, about an army or something in the mountains. He didn't sound happy about that either.

"Lynk's planning something?" Kieran murmured, more to himself than me, as he vigorously paced in front of me. "But what? He practically controls the whole of Forenna with the High Council backing him."

I shrugged unhelpfully.

"We need to find out more," he continued, suddenly turning to look at me with realisation. "You."

"What about me?" I croaked wearily.

"He's going to train your voice, isn't he? So you're ready for the Festival."

I nodded slowly, unwilling to know the direction of his thoughts.

"You could get him to talk."

"Yeah, right, "I scoffed.

"I think you could."

My eyes widened, "I don't even know him," I protested. "Plus he doesn't trust me. It was only earlier when he was saying how I 'must learn my place'." I frowned.

Kieran shook his head, eyes calculating, "True, but he's still your father whether you like it or not." Then his expression became sad. "And he doesn't want you badly injured because he thinks he may still be able to use you; it was obvious by the way he agreed to let me take your punishment. That's why he made that Council member ask you to sing at the Winter Festival; he wants to see how powerful you are.

"If you could convince him that it was your mother who stole you away from him, and that you never wanted to leave, you could get him to trust you. Then, once he trusts you, he'll tell you things..." he trailed off thoughtfully.

My mouth was gaping open, "Kieran..." I spoke with my eyes, I couldn't do this.

Suddenly he stopped pacing and swiftly sat on the edge of the rock.

His emerald eyes were intense and uncharacteristically serious. "Ruby," he pronounced my name with a purposeful clarity. "This is important, if he's forming an army it's really bad news. It means he's planning something. He already has the High Council pretty much in his control; just imagine what he could do with an army. We need your help," then his voice lowered roughly, "*I* need your help."

"I can't..." I began.

"Ruby, I remember what he was like; a true believer in Fire superiority. If he's planning on war, it'll be pro-segregation. I know that for definite. You'll be my enemy, and you won't see Chara, Nik, Ebony or anyone of Earth.

You don't want that do you? You don't want to be responsible for separating my kind even further; of having people killed, just because you were too afraid to lie to your father?"

I looked down at the ground. He was right.

"I'll think of something," I surrendered eventually.

"Don't worry, my plans always work." He assured me boastfully. "And even if they don't, I'm incredibly adaptable."

I rolled my eyes and he took that as confirmation.

"So what's the deal with Jayson then," I wondered.

Kieran glanced at me, his face automatically shutting off. "Like I said earlier it's nothing to do with you."

That irritated me, so I continued questioning, "But you were..."

He interrupted me before I finished, "Drop it Ruby."

I pulled a face, was quiet for a moment, and then continued nevertheless, "But what about those people? Who were they?"

"The older guy used to be my boss," Kieran muttered, closing his eyes.

"Were you really an assassin?" I asked curiously, unsure how I felt about that.

Kieran opened his fierce eyes, glaring at me, "You're not going to let this go are you?" When I shook my head and smiled, he sighed again; more exasperated. "Yes, I used to kill for money or drugs. It's what I'm good at. It's not an uncommon or even illegal practice here. That guy I hit for indirectly works for Council Members. I killed mostly criminals, rapists, murderers; generally really bad people."

I picked up on the word 'generally' and grimaced, "But not always?"

"No," he answered, his eyes suddenly haunted, "not always."

"So I'm going to be trained like an assassin." I said, bemused at the thought.

"No," Kieran said. "You are going to be trained so it's less likely you'll be killed by an assassin."

"Why aren't you training me?"

"I've split open those scars on my back when I flew earlier. I need to wait for them to heal as much as I can," he informed me. "But that will take longer than it will for you to be attacked again."

I took a deep breath, "Is it always like this here? So violent; so dangerous?"

"The most beautiful time to be alive is during the height of war and death," Kieran quoted. I'd never heard the quote before but it made sense; in a way. He glanced at me, "How's your neck?"

"Hurts," I admitted.

"Can I look?" he asked.

I nodded, lifting my chin so he could see the long ugly scar that cut across my neck; just another mark to join the other's I'd gained over the past few days. His fingers gently probed along; he was very close. Too close for comfort. The fever on my skin intensified dramatically as I felt his hot breath flutter against my neck, I shivered. His silky hair tickled. I winced at a sensitive spot.

He looked up and told me it was looking good, though I didn't believe him. He met my eyes and held them in his, mesmerising me into immobility. God, I hate it when he looks at me like that. The whole world seems to stop spinning for a perfect moment. I felt a strange sensation that I had never felt before, a sudden rush of warmth spread through me. My heart picked up speed almost instantaneously as I looked at Kieran. His nose nearly touched mine. I couldn't breathe. I couldn't think.

Then he suddenly stood up and backed away from me.

"We better head back," he muttered awkwardly.

"Yeah," I murmured, equally uncomfortable.

We headed back in silence, a good few feet distancing us as we walked. I felt confused by my own body. What had that been all about?

We headed back over to the main party, which was now in full swing, despite its lack of supposed host. Lynk was nowhere to be seen however Chara, Bris and Ebony were right in the middle of the dance floor. I smiled at them and they waved, gesturing me over. After a brief hesitation I did, but Kieran carried on. To be honest I was glad to get away from the awkward tension.

They were standing under an unroofed area. The stars twinkled above; the moon was huge and silvery. Intermittently, soundless fireworks exploded in the sky like a shower of vibrant colour. Powerful lights filtered through large gemstones above us, casting multi-coloured spotlights over a swarm of bodies. People moved together like shoals of fish, perfectly in time to the music. The music here was completely different, almost tribal from the booming drums.

Impulsively, I drew towards the crowd, soon becoming part of it. Somebody passed me a shot of something ominous, the girls took one each too and I downed it thoughtlessly; the nasty concoction burned my throat. Okay, maybe I shouldn't have drunk whatever it was in that glass. It was hot here, the air unavoidably thick and sweaty, but the atmosphere eclectic and alive. It was too loud to talk, only dance, which we did, though we received confused or suspicious glances. I assumed they were wondering why we were dancing together as members of opposing tribes. I ignored them. They should mind their own business.

It wasn't long before I had to sit down; the other's joined me, sitting on one of those circular seating areas. I lay down, my head resting on a pillow. The others were talking immediately; girlish giggling conversations obviously provoked by lashings of alcohol. They talked about men, hotly discussing sex and who I should be paired up with. I laughed as they pointed out people in the crowd, choosing mostly gingers.

"Nope," I said as they guessed my 'type'. I actually didn't think I had one.

Briseis was grinning manically, "I bet you like the blonde ones, I saw you chatting with that one earlier."

"You mean Jayson?" I asked, feeling a little too giggly,

"I'm not sure, he looks a bit surfer-ish. I think I prefer someone a little edgier. What's the deal with him and Kieran, anyway?"

Chara took a swig of what looked like champagne then frowned, over animatedly, "It's not just Kieran; it's Adrian too. All three of them used to be good friends."

"So what happened?" I wondered curiously.

"I'm not sure," Chara answered, "I knew Jayson told Lynk that we were planning to leave the Island, but I never understood why. I don't get it either," she pondered, "why the Council didn't punish us for those deaths. I hardly think they could have forgotten." She frowned, puzzled.

"Is that why so many people were after us the night we left?" Briseis wondered, "Because some boy told on us? Aw, man; that sucks; loads were killed that night."

"There's more to it than that though," Ebony said. "Something happened way before that, between Jayson and Adrian, I remember when Adrian came to me the night before you left. He was in a right state; never seen him so upset."

"I don't think even Kieran knows what happened that night," Chara said thoughtfully, swirling around her champagne in her glass. "I remember too," she said to Ebony. "They must have had a really massive fight or something."

"Maybe that's why Jayson did it," I said, "Just in a moment of anger."

"Humm," Briseis mused, "Who knows?"

"Hey, speaking of..." Chara said, glancing over to her right where, sure enough Jayson was standing talking with some friends, acting completely normal. Like nothing had happened earlier with Kieran.

"What do you make of him?" I wondered to the girls, I still wasn't certain.

"I don't know," Chara replied. "But he's sure good-looking! You know, if you're into blondes." She winked at me.

I frowned, feeling slightly dizzy after I took another swig of my own sparkling drink.

"Aren't you bothered about what he did?"

"I don't know the whole story," she shrugged. "I can't make any judgment until we know why. We've all made mistakes." She had a point, to be fair.

"Of course," Briseis sighed "No one could beat the divinity of Kieran's ass."

I sputtered as I laughed, Chara too, but Ebony pulled a face, "That's my brother you're talking about."

Chara grinned cheekily, shaking out her long dark brown hair, "Which one?" she said jokingly. "She's had both."

I stared at Briseis, but her face was unreadable except a smug twist of her lips, "What can I say? Ashaiks do it and do it well."

Ebony clapped her hands over her ears, grimacing, "I don't want to hear this."

Chara laughed, "Careful Ebbs; she'll be after you next."

I noticed Jayson looking my way as we all laughed. He smiled cutely. I retaliated with a dopey grin; to be honest mostly influenced by the alcohol bubbling in my veins. He broke away from his friends and gestured towards the dancing, a question in his eyes. Chara nudged me forwards, noticing my distraction.

"Go on," she urged, grinning.

I shrugged and got up, heading back into the electricity of the dance floor, to the beat of drums, walking with Jayson. The alcohol buzzed in my body, making me dizzy. I could smell it on him too; he'd obviously had more than me.

But soon Jayson was getting too close for comfort, his hands running along my exposed body invasively. Jayson pulled me closer when I didn't protest, moving his hands down my bare thighs. I looked up, but he misconstrued my response, thinking that I'd lifted my chin to kiss him–which I definitely didn't. He pressed his hot lips against mine roughly. I moved to shove him back, but my hands got caught in between our bodies. I tried to pull back but his hold tightened. I tried to tell him to get the hell off, but my words were muffled and unrecognisable.

Then, to my relief, he was yanked off me and I could breathe again.

My rescuer came in the form of Nik.

I looked gratefully at him, and he nodded to his right. I followed his line of vision, to see Kieran leaning against the wall, watching me. His expression was terrifying; he was glaring poisonously at Jayson. His broad shoulders rose and fell rapidly. I could only imagine what he was thinking. He turned and started walking away with great effort.

Chapter Sixteen

The celebrations ended pretty soon after that, well for us at least. Chara had soon consumed far too much to drink and was extremely ill, all over poor unsuspecting Nik. We headed home quickly after that. The party had lost its exciting edge and I still didn't see Lynk again. Kieran had mysteriously disappeared.

Back at Ebony's I couldn't sleep. I didn't know why. Briseis seemed to have drifted off almost immediately. As I waited for sleep, the great obsidian atmosphere of night swelled closer, suffocating any light that attempted to filter through the curtains. My mind was drifting in a dreamy haze, but my body was frantically awake.

Suddenly I heard an angry shout outside.

Something triggered deep in my cells, compelling me to look through the cloaked glass windows that concealed the outside world. I struggled with my blankets trapping layers, then stumbled to my feet, idly wondering why I wasn't still tucked up in bed, other than the nagging feeling that my attacker had returned.

Pulling back the curtain, I was almost disappointed when I didn't see anything. But the feeling grew stronger still and instinctively I fumbled with the lock, carefully sliding open the glass window doors which lead to the tiny balcony.

Instantly the icy wind hit me, blowing my freshly washed hair across my face, whipping at my bare arms. Blinded momentarily, I wrapped my arms around myself as if protection from the plummeting temperature. I jerked my head sideways to resurrect my vision. Then I noticed Kieran.

My heart sputtered dramatically as I swept my eyes over him. He was in that strange courtyard I'd noticed when he'd shown me his wing brace before, next to the pavilion filled with weapons and training equipment. Now I understood it was a practice ring. He was standing in the middle of the centre training circle, brandishing a double set of knives and practicing slow graceful movements followed by swift pivots and throws of the blades into various targets. He shouted every time as he struck the target. He also wore no shirt and as he moved I watched in fascination the way the muscles of his back stretched and contorted. The way, as the tempo of his training heightened with more intense exercises and weights, the sweat dripped down his naked torso, following the indentations of his abdomen, like the artists fingers had pressed a little too hard as they sculpted his immaculate body.

There was pure concentration on his face; no other emotion except perhaps fatigue or pain. I understood the pain. When his shirt was off I couldn't help but see those deep, sometimes bleeding lacerations carved into his back. They didn't look red or particularly inflamed, but they looked painful. Why the hell was he training with those split open? He didn't even have any bandages on. It made no sense, especially after his reluctance to train me himself. My first day of training was tomorrow morning with Jayson, who he absolutely hates.

After a while Kieran sat down on a bench, breathing deep and glancing up at the sky. He was completely oblivious to me watching, slightly perversely, from a distance. He rummaged around in his pocket, withdrawing that small wooden box.

I heard a shuffle of footsteps behind me. I glanced back, surprised, to see Briseis awake. I smiled at her, pretending I hadn't been staring at Kieran, but she knew.

"He does it every night," she commented quietly, walking beside me. "He'll go for a long run later too."

Well that explained the abs. "But why?"

"He doesn't sleep otherwise," she murmured apathetically. "This is his way of tiring himself out. I think his dreams haunt him. When we used to sleep together he used to move in his sleep, always restless, sometimes he even used to say things."

I looked at her curiously, asking gently as she gazed at Kieran, "Do you love him?"

She glanced over at me with a half-smile, "I used to, but he broke my heart. I can't ever forgive him for that. I can pretend but," she sighed, "I can't."

I looked at her again, seeing an invisible scar as visible as light in her eyes. I went to bed with what she'd said in mind. I kept those words close to my heart.

I still couldn't sleep though. When I eventually I did, my own dreams haunted me, dreams of attack and deep blood-red eyes. When I woke up it was obvious I'd barely slept more than an hour. Sighing irritably, I got up.

Tiptoeing across the bare floor I left Briseis sleeping in her bed, then carefully made my way downstairs, lacking a plan. On my way past the bathroom I noticed feet dangling over the threshold. I looked closer, seeing a familiar scene to what I'd witnessed at my last party–one of Alex's back home. Chara had collapsed onto the floor of the bathroom, her head awkwardly twisted on the side of the toilet seat. It smelt a bit grim in there, but when I tried to wake her up and gently move her she growled at me and mumbled something about staying there. I assumed a similar interaction had happened with her and Nik so I left her there.

Travelling downstairs, I headed outside. I knew what I was going to do, I wanted to fly again. I wanted to feel that miraculous wind through my feathers, breathe in ultimate freedom and, hopefully, tire myself out. As I stepped through the door I realised that the storm that had been brewing earlier had finally struck. Slushy cold rain soaked my hair instantly, sending a deep chill straight to my bones. I glanced about the sky, seeing rolling grey clouds and intermittent strikes of lightning. The rain fell in sheets from above, pattering the grass in a way that made it dance to and fro. The sound was relaxing; a contrast to the almighty claps of thunder.

I was about to head back inside when a voice stopped me. "I wouldn't go back inside on a night like this if I were you."

I glanced over to the source of the voice, noticing Kieran walking towards me. Briseis had been right; he had gone for a run. He had thrown a shirt on since last time I saw him, but it hadn't done him much good. The rain had soaked him through, saturating his clothes to the point where the material couldn't possibly hold anymore. It dripped off him in rivers. His white shirt stuck to his skin, clinging so intimately he might as well have not worn one. I could see the hard ridges of his chest; the striking tattoos that were displayed because of his exhaustion.

He ran a hand through the drenched strands of his hair, shaking out orbs of water like glistening bubbles in a bathtub. The colour was beyond black now, so dark it shined almost blue, making his skin appear pale and luminous in the moonlight and his full lips a warm enticing shade darker than usual.

I stared at him, confused and irritated at the thumping in my chest.

"Are you kidding?" I wondered, "The weather's awful."

He shook his head, "Can I show you something?"

"Depends what it is," I replied cautiously.

"Are you in a brave mood?" Kieran asked.

"Always," I nodded.

"Good, because where I'm taking you, isn't for the fainthearted," he warned.

I was curious now. "Where are we going?" I asked automatically, making my way over to him. I was already soaked anyway.

Kieran put his finger to his lips and gestured for me to follow him. He quietly led me forwards, "Chara will try to kill me if she finds me doing this again."

"I doubt it," I muttered, thinking of her passed out in the bathroom. "What are we doing?" I asked, seeing lightning flashing through the surrounding conifers.

"Go and Change. I'll find you."

"Are you sure you're not just going to leave me to freeze out here?" I asked; I wouldn't be that surprised.

Kieran snorted, "Don't be ridiculous. My diabolical plans are far more intricate and clever than that."

I did what he said and walked into the sheltering trees, hiding myself between the largest, eventually managing to Change. It was as strange and excruciating as before, and it was made worse by the cold–it was hard to think of fire and spark a flame within you when the temperature was plummeting. I left my clothes under a low branch, hopefully shielding them from the snowy rain. I clambered out of the trees, my tail feathers clumsily catching pine needles, and then finally Kieran's dark shadow appeared. He gazed at me with those intelligent rounded eyes then took off into the air, and into the lightning.

I opened my powerful wings, feeling high. With an almighty flap I was in the air. I panicked immediately, stopping my wings from beating again and landing on the ground. I grumbled in frustration at my own foolishness and leapt into the air, frantically moving my wings to gain altitude.

You don't have to do that, he said as I rushed after him *think of flying as a rhythm, find the beat that fits you. If you keep doing that you'll tire too quickly.* Kieran instructed, then added, *and don't get struck by the lightning, I'm told it hurts.*

You think? I wailed over the thunder, *Kieran this is completely reckless.*

You can go back if you're scared, Kieran offered challengingly.

No, I'd never hear the end of it.

We headed north, closer to the lightning, actually following it. It was beautiful and terrifying and we caught up with it as we flew into the mountains. Kieran instantly ordered that I should stay directly behind him as he dashed off into the bolting electricity, darting between the currents extraordinarily fast. I struggled to keep up, my heart racing as a hot blast nearly caught me. It was so mad, insane; we could have died at any moment. My instincts were taking their time to kick in too, I felt more wobbly and inexperienced now than during my First Flight. Adrenalin surged in my wings. We dived and swirled our way up, the pressure gradually creating a crushing feeling against my ribs, making it slightly uncomfortable to breathe. Eventually we reached the clouds, tumbling through them at an alarming rate.

And then it was clear.

Stars twinkled in their nothingness like pearls at the bottom of the ocean. The heavens were vibrantly alive with millions and millions of stars. The moon was huge; a perfectly balanced silver disk. Up here the world was as sparkling, yet clear as an innocent mind. Below was a thick cotton floor, hiding the underworld.

Look down, Kieran said. I glanced down at the grey rolling clouds again, seeing the lightning flash across their foamy texture. It was magnificent, so bright. *It's called ripple lightning,* Kieran explained. *You see the way it explodes out across the clouds like a pebble thrown into water?*

It's amazing, I sighed.

Nobody ever dares to come up here and see it.

We're here, I said.

I heard the smile in Kieran's voice. *We are.*

We swam through the skies until the lightning moved on, grumbling as it went. I never thought I could have seen anything so spectacular and was surprised that it had been Kieran who'd shown it me. Every strike was obvious and powerful, to a terrifying extent, lighting up the clouds like they were being zapped into life. Eventually it had to end though and we flew back down to the boring safety of the house. It wasn't sleeting there anymore; in fact the air was so cold now that it had been snowing. The clouds had vanished too, revealing the incandescent stars and striking moonlight which made the fresh snow glitter.

Me and Kieran Changed separately, and then went upstairs. Kieran turned to watch me go towards my room and I was suddenly frightened. Once Kieran and his reassuringly-confident presence were gone I would be unsafe again, awake to await those dreams of bloody eyes. My eyes, wide and frightened, glanced towards the window: only the stars were there to watch if my attacker returned. I couldn't believe how scared I was, I just flew through lightning for God's sake.

Kieran saw the fear in my eyes, glanced at the scar that I now touched with my fingertips, the one freshly made by my attacker's hand only this morning. He understood almost instantly. "He won't come back tonight," he promised.

"How do you know?" I asked.

"You stabbed him."

"He also stabbed me and I'm miraculously alright." Well, sort of.

"I'm only in the other room," he said, "I might not be of Fire, but us Earth Assassins can throw a mean pollen attack."

"Really?" I wondered.

"No," he said, "I'm a Phoenix, Ruby, not a Pokemon." I made a face and he sighed. "Come on, I'll get you something that'll make you feel better."

He led me into his room. There was nothing much really in there except a bed, wardrobe and a desk piled high with various weapons. It was a small room, but extremely tidy and dominated by a comparatively disproportionate window. It dwarfed the tiny room, letting in an extraordinary amount of light that reflected off the snow outside. His bed was made and he sat me on the edge of it as he rummaged in one of his draws. I tugged my fingers through my knotted wet hair.

As he turned around his soaked grey joggers hung low on his hips, displaying the deep indentations of muscles above the cotton through his damp shirt. The pale light washed out the fantastic tan of his skin, making it seem mysteriously luminous. I trembled; suddenly a hot fever erupted across my skin. My stomach fluttered unbearably. He still wore that strange gold chain that glinted over his collarbones. I'd left my own in my room before bed, how come it hadn't snapped when he Changed? Then I saw what he carried; a small deadly knife. As he stepped directly under the window a star of light ran down the blade like a drip of liquid metal.

Eventually he interrupted the silence as he passed it over to me. I grasped it cautiously by the pommel; unsure of how to hold it, surprised at the weight. "Keep it with you," he said. "Even if you don't want to use it you'll know it's there."

"Thank you," I said appreciatively, trying not to cut myself on the sharpened edge as I placed it down on the bedside table. I glanced up at him, "really, thanks."

"You're welcome," he uttered silkily.

"Kieran," I wondered, "Why can't you sleep?"

He sat down beside me, glancing seriously my way, "Why haven't you tonight?"

"I'm too keyed up tonight," I explained, then nudged him encouragingly. He seemed different now, a softer more relaxed Kieran. There were distinctive shadows under his eyes though; I knew he was exhausted. I could smell that strange drug on him too; the smoke had recently been absorbed into his clothes.

He nodded, "Same reason; only every night."

I knew he was lying, after what Briseis told me earlier but I wasn't really surprised.

There was a strange dancing light in his eyes. I couldn't look away all of a sudden.

He slowly leaned down, getting closer, almost unconsciously. "You shouldn't be here." His voice dipped to that low, seductive murmur, "In my room; alone."

My eyes never left his. "Do you want me to go?" I whispered; something strange pulling me in closer to him.

The power of those mesmerising eyes was ten times as strong as my siren's voice. I wanted him to get closer.

He shook his head, "No, I don't want you to go, Ruby."

That was it, the way he said my name; it was that that made bumps rise on the back of my arms and a shiver tremble through me. The way he pronounced the R with such clarity, rolling it very slightly, accentuating an exotic edge that I was previously unaware of. It was a verbal caress the way his tongue formed the word, leaving those gorgeous lips parted slightly as he finished it; unintentionally showing his white bottom teeth. And it was *my* name he was saying. Me.

There was a strange heat in the air, an electric vibe that formed a fine shine on my palms. The way Kieran was looking at me was startling; a look I'd never received before from anyone. His expression softened and all of a sudden he looked his age. The youthful skin of his face relaxed infinitesimally, smoothing out the hard lines of fatigue and stress. Without a warning he lifted his hand towards me.

He trailed his fingers over the scar across my neck tentatively, barely touching me. He smelled deliciously of rich earthy spice and smoke. I couldn't help myself. I could feel my body doing it before my mind gave it permission. My instincts took over as I leaned forwards, pressed my face against his cinnamon skin, inhaling deeply before leaning back and waiting for him to ask what the hell I was doing. He drew back to gaze seriously into my eyes, as if trying to understand something complicated.

He didn't speak; instead his words flowed through his hands as they hesitantly began sweeping my hair back, gently intertwining his fingers in its damp crimson curls. His eyes never once left mine. He smiled so beautifully I could have cried. It was my favourite smile; a soft, barely noticeable curve of his lips with no trace of bitterness or arrogant humour; a secret smile.

I smiled back, feeling his chest press against mine as he bent forwards. His heart met mine through our clothes, our rhythms matching in perfect synchrony. My lips quivered as he moved his hand from my hair to cup it against my cheek. His hand was hot like a live wire; his palms covered in those inked tribal tattoos that were so damn sexy when they appeared.

Lightly, his thumb traced the curve of my lips.

My trembling hands rose thoughtlessly, wrapping around his shoulders as he drew closer; catching the rough scars on his back. My insides seemed to leap from my body and disappear somewhere else, leaving my body to take control. His lips were millimetres from mine. My eyelids began to close instinctively. I could feel his uncertain breath as he removed his thumb from my mouth...

But then an awesome current of energy burst from his fingers.

Kieran pulled back abruptly, still just centimetres from me. I was breathing too fast, feeling high, ecstatic, and strangely...healed.

My hands flew to my throat; it no longer hurt at all, no remnants of that constant nagging feeling I'd had all day. "You healed me," I said with blank astonishment.

He grinned that mischievous grin of his that set my mind on fire. "Cool," he said lazily, his eyes watching my face with an absorbed, hungry look that tightened the muscles in the pit of my stomach.

His next movement astounded me. He sprang forwards, his lips immediately crushing mine in a wild hot kiss that left me gasping. I responded automatically, my stomach doing a bizarre flip. I yanked him down onto me, our bodies in line. I could feel the weight of his hard muscular form pressing down on me. The kiss grew rough, desperate. His hand ran down the side of my body, following the curves. His fingers were hot, gripping me tightly with such ferocity. I moaned against his mouth with pleasure. His tongue ran deliciously across my bottom lip; then bit it lightly. My heart leapt, sensations bubbling across me.

"Ruby," he muttered my name against my mouth and I gasped; my body fantastically awake and alive, and hot...very hot.

He stopped suddenly, his eyes widened and his expression transformed as he seemingly caught up with what had happened, heard that it was my name he'd been saying. "Holy shit," he swore, scrambling off me faster than if I had leprosy. "Mistake, big mistake. Bad-word! Double bad-word."

I just looked at him, hurt. "That was a mistake?"

He nodded vigorously as he paced across the room again.

I could feel my heart tear in my chest, my face fell. I whispered, "Why?"

He turned sharply to face me, "Because we aren't supposed to be together. We can't be. It's impossible. That shouldn't have happened."

He might as well have punched me. I looked down at my hands, feeling the tears of rejection forming as I furiously tried to contain them. I didn't dare look up when Kieran said my name. I couldn't make myself do it. I picked at my ragged nails, not realising how much my hands were shaking. For the first time in my life I actually felt something for someone and this happened? Why did it have to be this monster?

"Ruby, look at me," Kieran ordered severely, but my disengaged mind didn't respond.

"Ruby, look at me," he repeated again and I couldn't ignore the ferocity of his tone. He was closer than I thought, less than a step away. He stared with seeking eyes.

"You understand why we can't, don't you?"

I didn't say anything, I just returned my gaze to my nails.

He reached forward but I jerked back from his hands before they could touch me. I stared unfocusedly at the quilt, clutching my tears. I stood up, unable to bear the pain in my chest anymore. From the corner of my eyes I saw him reach out again. Then he paused and let his arm fall limply to his side.

I walked unsteadily towards the door. Now my back was turned the tears finally fell. The soft click of the door was that loudest thing I had ever heard. Back in my own room I buried myself in my sheets and cried silently until I was too exhausted to continue. I was an emotional wreck. Feelings I barely knew I had spilled out of me in waves of flooding tears. Was it because I'd felt dependent on Kieran ever since I'd left? Is it just that I'd latched onto him because I had no one else? Did I even like him really, underneath it? I couldn't decide but either way Briseis had been right.

Chapter Seventeen

It was while I was getting dressed the next morning, when I glanced into the mirror that I realised that I was missing the long jagged scar that cut across my neck. It had completely vanished. What the hell?

Rushing, I quickly shoved on my jeans, and then raced back over to the mirror. The small scars on my forehead and palms had disappeared also. As I examined the rest of my body, I realised with shock that every little disfigurement that had flawed my skin had disappeared. Like nothing had even been there.

This must have been Kieran, somehow. What else it could possibly be?

Heading over to the bathroom, knowing already that he was the reason I wasn't having a nice hot shower right now; I thumped heavily on the door.

"What, Ruby?" came the gruff response.

How did he know it was me? "I want to talk to you."

"Everyone *wants* to talk to me, " he grumbled irritably, "but it doesn't mean everyone gets the pleasure,".

I was not in the mood to be messed with. "Now, Kieran," I ordered severely.

"Never, Ruby," he answered, mimicking me.

I sighed angrily, "It's important."

"So is my morning routine, which in case you haven't noticed, you're not part of." He snapped, but the door swung abruptly open.

I stumbled back, not thinking he would have given in so quickly. His dark hair was glistening with beads of water that dripped down his tanned shoulders. He must have literally just tumbled out the shower. His expression was so hostile I cringed back automatically. "Go on then," he said, green eyes flashing, "I don't have all morning to listen to you complain."

I was suddenly infuriated. "I have no scars."

"Brilliant," he said sarcastically.

My eyes narrowed, "I'm serious; they're gone."

"Well, that's interesting." Kieran mused thoughtfully, "Why don't you stay here, and I'll think it over while I finish my shower."

"What did you do?" I scolded accusingly.

He glared at me ferociously. "*I* didn't do anything."

"You must have done something." I glared right back. "Scars don't magically disappear." I raised my eyebrows sceptically, "Plus, you're the healer."

He whirled around to show me his naked back; the cinnamon skin stretched flawlessly across his shoulders; no longer bearing marks of substantial damage. No deep inflamed lacerations. No puckered scars. He turned again, meeting my angrily confused eyes.

"My back begs to differ," he snapped. "It's a shame. I like my scars; they show that I live in the arms of danger."

"Or the arms of reckless idiocy," I muttered.

"Better than wasting my life in fear and ignorance," he retorted.

"How could this have happened?" I still sounded like I was accusing him.

He scowled again, "I don't know."

"I thought you knew everything," I shot bitterly. God I hated him so much.

"I know it's you not me," he snarled. "I warned you that every time I heal you our bodies become more closely interlinked. It's happened before, the more you heal one person and no other, the closer you get physically. Nobody can predict what will happen to us if we carry on, especially because we're of different Tribes." I stared at him blankly and he growled in frustration. "I've had enough of this conversation." Starting to return to the bathroom, I stomped after him. The shower was still running, steam wafted up in spiralling circles.

"Well I didn't ask you to heal me, did I?" I demanded indignantly.

"I think this definitely counts as an invasion of my privacy," he said lazily, looking at his hair in the mirror. Then he glared at me, "It's not like I had a choice. I didn't want to heal you; it's you who doesn't seem to understand the severity of it."

"You're the one who did it. You're the one who told me to go into your room," I retaliated.

"Because you were fussing over some guy who attacked you," he pointed out, eyes returning to me like blazing emerald flame. "An overreaction if you ask me."

"Overreaction," I repeated, my voice consciously raising a few octaves.

He towered over me dominatingly, with that arrogant superior look.

"You're always overreacting. I'm surprised you're not bored of it by now."

"I'm bored of arguing with you."

"Go away then. I'm in a really bad mood and I know you'll be very upset if I rain on your glorious little parade." he spat sardonically.

"Why are you being such an asshole," I snapped. "Sometimes I really wish you'd just act like a normal human being."

"But I'm not human," Kieran smirked, leaning forward, "and let me tell you something you probably didn't even realise when you were Changing into a massive red Phoenix; neither are you."

"We are human, or at least part-human."

"Stop holding onto the past Ruby, nothing can change you back." He smiled cruelly, knowing that he was being harsh.

I was so angry. "I think you're scared, scared of being human because then you would have to have an emotional capacity greater than a wet mop."

"And that's something you're an expert on now, is it?" he raised his eyebrows, but his voice was infuriatingly composed.

I wanted to scream. I was about to say something else when I heard footsteps on the stairs. We both froze like a rabbit in headlights. I glanced at the stairs, panicked, hoping nobody had heard our...um, conversation.

"Get away from the door," Kieran hissed sharply, pushing me out of the bathroom before slamming the door closed in my face.

Trying to be nonchalant as I walked towards my room, my legs felt stiff and awkward. I heard Ebony call from behind me, "Ruby, are you okay?"

I turned around, clutching my hands nervously, feeling like I'd just been caught doing something naughty-like being alone in the bathroom with a half-naked boy. "I'm fine," I answered too brightly.

She looked suspicious, "I thought I heard yelling."

"Not from me," I said, quickly changing the subject. "Is it okay if I get some breakfast?"

Instantaneously her expression softened, suspicion forgotten. "Oh, of course, chick, you've got a big day today anyway."

I laughed, hearing how off it sounded. "Every day recently seems to be a big day."

She frowned at me but then shook her head. "There's bread and jam on the table. Just get what you want."

I smiled awkwardly, shuffling off downstairs. I knew what Ebony had meant about the big day thing: it was my first training session with Jayson. Now that would be awkward after his attempts to kiss me last night, plus Kieran would have to take me as no one else knows where it is. Yes, what a big exciting morning it would be. Just when I finished my breakfast and thought things couldn't possibly get any worse there was a knock at the front door. It was a messenger. This afternoon at twenty past two, at the Old Hall, wherever that is, Lynk wanted to meet me to assess the 'damage' done to my voice. Great. Bloody fantastic.

I wasn't disappointed.

The walk was as quiet and uncomfortable as I expected. We didn't speak once as we made our way into the city centre. Kieran walked stubbornly ahead of me, ignoring me furiously but leading the way. After a while I started to get the feeling that we were heading to the bad side of town. When I eventually asked him where we were going he answered with the words: The Underworld.

I saw what he meant. The whole area seemed dirty and ominous. As we walked the streets were oddly silent despite the fact that there were people about. They appeared very withdrawn, keeping their coats covering their bodies and hoods over their mercurial shifty eyes. They only walked in small groups, speaking in whispers. I felt a cold chill in my spine being here, but we turned a corner and the next street was slightly livelier with more people.

The depressed cobbled road needed work, but there were what looked like shops on either side of it; selling God-knows what. There was a dodgy-looking pub on the right, people drinking steaming liquid from pitchers even at this time. Next to that was what looked like a brothel, judging by the scantily clad women sat outside, smoking unattractively from large pipes and eyeing Kieran up as he ambled past. Hatted merchants tried to sell us things, but Kieran ignored them and I followed him quietly, frightened that I'd be robbed, raped or murdered at any minute. He headed down a side road to a narrower street then through a door.

Inside there was smoke everywhere, clinging to the walls and my skin like cellophane. It stunk of something indescribable, laced faintly with human sweat and urine. There were people buried within the smoke, but few, and most looked paralytic, lying on what looked like hospital stretchers on the floor, their eyes glazed over with a misty film. They twitched occasionally, lifting a tube of smoke to their mouths at intermittent occasions, inhaling deeply before going back to the dreams their intoxicated minds created. I held my breath as we past the dirty figures, to a woman in the back who stood dealing what looked like a fine white powder to a small man with electric blue hair and skin a waxy pale colour.

All I could think was: where the hell had Kieran taken me?

I stayed close at Kieran's side, nervously attached to his shadow. He spoke a few words in the woman's stretched ear. She pulled away, nodding with a toothy smile. Kieran continued through a door, up narrow stairs. Away from the smoke my heart calmed as we ascended the staircase. At the top was a door, which he opened.

Inside was a large room about the size of a basketball court; as tall as it was wide with springy wooden floors and partly mirrored walls. The mirrors were flecked with blackened dirt. It reminded me of an old barn house or factory room. It was built entirely of wood and supportive rafters speared the walls up high. Lining the walls were weapons on shelves and metal hooks. These instruments weren't for decoration, I realised anxiously; across the wooden floor were mats, weights and benches, followed by painful looking exercise equipment that I was uncertain of its function. In the middle of the room Jayson was fighting with another Firebird, both brandishing live blades and in the corner of the room was the older man Kieran had been talking to last night. He sat at a makeshift desk sorting through paper.

"Wait here," Kieran instructed, going over to speak to the man. He returned a moment later carrying a brown envelope, "Right, I'm off."

I stared at him in horror, "You're just leaving me here?" I demanded.

Jayson and the other Firebird had stopped fighting now. The other Firebird, a woman, approached the older guy, speaking to him. Jayson made his way over.

Before Jayson neared me Kieran grinned cruelly. "You'll be fine. I know you're well enough acquainted with Jayson to ask if he'll bring you back." Before I could argue Kieran turned his back on me and left the way we had come.

"Hey," Jayson smiled. "Listen before we start, I'm sorry about last night. I was really very drunk and probably did a good job of making myself look like an idiot."

"You did," I agreed, but half-heartedly.

"Well," he said cheerfully, "despite having a massive hangover, I'm going to try and make up for it."

I smiled carefully, "Good."

"Well for a start, it's not really a problem today," Jayson said, "but tomorrow you should wear something more suitable for fighting."

"Okay," I nodded. Nik had offered me some of Chara's fighting gear, the trousers made from that strange flexible material that looked like leather but was actually scaly. I'd said no, not wanting to look like a vampire slayer on my first day.

"Right," Jayson clapped his hands together, "to start with I'll just walk you through some basic blocks, because you should always know how to block before you know how to attack." Then he added, when I glanced at the weapons apprehensively, "and don't worry, we won't be working with any weapons just yet."

I breathed a sigh of relief. "I'm glad."

Now, if it was Kieran he would have laughed and said some sarcastic remark, but Jayson just smiled sweetly. "They can seem a little daunting to beginners," he agreed honestly, "but pretty soon you'll be fine with them. If you work with weapons long enough they become like an extension of your own body."

I frowned, "I doubt that. I've not picked up a knife in my life, except to chop carrots."

He laughed a nice relaxing laugh. "Then this must seem weird to you."

I nodded; feeling slightly less uncomfortable, "Very."

"Well," he smiled brightly, flashing a set of amazingly white teeth, "I'll change that," he promised. "Let's begin."

He was very patient, I was glad to discover. First he did a quick warm up–joining in so I didn't feel like too much of an idiot as my boobs jiggled about while I embarrassedly did star-jumps. He taught me some simple blocks, their names, and how I would use them in an emergency situation. Then he showed me how to punch and strike correctly. Next he got me to practice on some hard round pads, like they use in martial arts, until he thought I was good enough to move on. And for the last ten minutes of my session he showed me some self-defence. Learning how to get out of grabs was quite amusing, mostly because it involved a lot of kicking to his 'sensitive' area-apparently to distract the attacker. Then I had to disengage and damage; which I failed epically at. I soon discovered that, despite the environment and previous situation, I actually had fun kicking the crap out of someone. I soon tired though, last night's leftover exhaustion weighing me down.

"That's enough for today, Ruby," Jayson said eventually.

"We're done already?" I asked, surprised.

"For that part yeah," he smiled. "But I thought you might want to test your affinity for Fire. You know, practice some skills."

"What do you mean?" I wondered, confused.

He continued patiently, "Well you're a Swartette, right? That means you'll have the potential to be really good at manipulating fire, maybe even sparking it."

"I can do that?" I asked, bewildered.

Jayson smiled, "Yeah, of course."

Okay, maybe it wasn't so bad here after all, though I still wasn't looking forward to walking back through that horrible smoky drug den or even the streets later. I hoped Jayson would come with me.

The first thing he did was explain the principles of sparking fire. It really wasn't as exciting as he made it out to be. It just reminded me of things I'd unconsciously known all along–that my father had already taught me at a far too young age-and that just seemed so strangely obvious. Like where fire comes from in the body-from the tiniest space between your spine and brain, so that thought and action are connected-or why it stops flowing as you get older-because it uses your own energy to spark it, and otherwise you'd be drained of energy and get health problems. He explained all the rules about controlling fire too.

Finally he went through the basics.

"To spark a flame is something done unconsciously," he explained. "If you think about it too much then you'll just get all wound up and never be able to do it. It's like Changing, it comes naturally. Most people associate sparking with doing something physical, for example, snapping your fingers. Actually sparking the flame is the most difficult thing to do. Once you've done that you'll find it relatively easy to manipulate."

I nodded listening carefully, nodding.

"First you need to clear your mind and listen," he said. "There is a flame inside every Firebird, but each hums differently. To be able to unleash that flame you first need to hear it. It's exactly the same as Changing. Find the energy then ignite it."

He went silent to let me listen. I knew it was there, I'd heard it before. It was surprisingly easy to hear, a faint but real hum, barely a flicker inside me.

He smiled when I nodded. "Concentrate... now snap your fingers."

I did as he said. I snapped my fingers and to my astonishment it worked first time. My mouth dropped open at the tiny light flickering between my thumb and forefinger. My face lit up, and I bounced up and down with excitement gleaming from my golden eyes, "I did it! Oh my God, look!"

He laughed, "Well done," Jayson congratulated. Then I heard his stomach rumble. "Man I'm starving." He lifted his voice to the older guy in the corner, "What time is it Jack?"

"Two," he replied.

The flame in my hand extinguished immediately. "Oh crap, I'm supposed to be meeting Lynk in twenty minutes!" I was panicking, "I don't even know where I'm going." I stood up immediately, gathering my stuff without a clue what to do or which way to go. Where had the time gone?

Jayson stood up instantly, standing in front of me with a serious expression. "Calm down, it's okay, I'll take you. Where is it at?"

"The Old Hall," I said.

"Right," he nodded, "that's not that far. I'll show you."

"Are you sure?" I asked.

He pulled a face, "Trust me, after last night it's the least I can do."

He walked over to the other side of the room, opening a door and taking me down a flight of steps that was outside the building. It took us down to ground behind the dodgy street that I was led here from. We took a left down the alleyway, then a right at the next street and I recognised the outskirts of Temardra, the centre, instantly.

I huffed an angry noise as we quickly passed through the streets. That arsehole Kieran had taken me the other way just to scare me, the stupid git. *Maybe that was how he got introduced into those drugs,* I thought suddenly. If he was an assassin training in that room above that drug den; that woman did seem to recognise him.

Within ten minutes we arrived. I didn't expect it to look like a college. The main building was long and made of basic grey stone, nothing spectacular but surrounded by various outbuildings and courts. Jayson swept me inside instantly, past a main reception and down a long corridor into a massive windowed hall.

It was completely empty. "Is this it?" I wondered.

"Yeah," he said. "I'll be off then. You're still early. I'll see you tomorrow."

I thanked him appreciatively and he smiled before he shut the door.

I waited a long time for Lynk to arrive. I couldn't believe he was late. When the door finally swung open I flinched. It slammed violently into the wall as Lynk strode though aggressively.

Forget formal greetings, the first thing Lynk said–well, yelled in an explosive kind of way-was, "You're living with the Ashaiks!"

Suddenly, memories of his destructive rages flashed before my eyes. Though they were never actually aimed at me–usually a slave or my mother-I remembered the terrible fury that would echo through the entire building, making me shake in fear. He needed to calm down. I knew that for certain. He can be devastatingly powerful when his control slips.

I spoke more calmly than I felt; in all honesty I was petrified. "I had nowhere else to go."

His familiar face was so consumed with rage, he represented fire perfectly: its savageness and brutality.

"You won't be staying there any longer. Do you have any idea just how much it would cost me if the High Council found out? If my daughter–a Swartette-was living with Ashaiks! It's disgraceful. It's disgusting!"

"I don't see how." I said quietly, realising it was the worst thing I could have said.

The topaz in his eyes was devoured by the black of his pupil, making him look even scarier. "You have lied to me."

Then, before I could respond he struck me hard across my face. I flinched, eyes wide, my cheek stinging underneath my palm.

I decided to play the role of guilty teenager who'd come home drunk from a Friday-night house party. "I'm sorry. I have disappointed you."

"Yes you have," he agreed hostilely, though his face flickered in surprise.

"I do not remember much of here. Please forgive me," I said, staring pleadingly into my father's cold angry eyes, like I gave a damn.

He only seemed slightly suspicious. "You shall be immediately relocated to Fire Palace. I refuse to let you make a fool of me by living with them. You will go without a fuss, do you hear me?!" he was shouting again, recalling his infuriation from fiery depths, the beauty of his voice was distorted by the malicious volume.

No, I couldn't possibly live with him, no way.

"That's not fair!" I complained, this could not be happening. *Shut up, shut up, shut up,* the sensible part of my mind screamed.

His dark pupils expanded again. "You belong to me, Ruby; everything of yours belongs to me until you are eighteen or married."

"I can't live with you," I uttered, deflated. He was really going to make me do this wasn't he? I stepped away from him, terrified suddenly.

"You can and you will," he snarled.

There was a short silence as I struggled to digest what had just happened. So what, I was now being forced to live with Lynk? If I didn't know better, I knew I should have fought and refused, but I did know better. I knew that there were benefits to this. Not necessarily benefits for me, but benefits for this country if I just did what I was told. I needed to find out if anything was going on with Lynk; if my attacker had spoken the truth about him forming an army. And if so, what was he planning, when, and how could I stop it? I knew how vindictive he could be.

Lynk was visibly attempting to control himself. The rapid rising and falling of his shoulders eventually slowed until stopping entirely.

"After this, I expect you to go to that *Ashaik's*"–he practically spat the word–"house and pack your things. I will send for guards to escort you through the city." His tone was still sharp and demanding but at least he wasn't shouting. "You have permission to fly as much as you want, as long as you are accompanied by a Guard." He said it as if he thought he was being reasonable; which he wasn't, at all.

"Yes father," I said respectfully, nodding my head remorsefully like I gave a crap what he thought about me.

"You will learn, Daughter," he spoke slowly, his voice as dangerous as poison, "even if I have to teach you all over again."

Chapter Eighteen

"Now that everything's all nicely straightened out, I shall remind you of the art of Chyun'ju," Lynk said, his voice suddenly calm and polite. Jeeze it was just one thing after another with this guy.

"Chyun'ju?" I asked. My attacker had mentioned that word.

He came closer so he was little over a metre away. He was speaking slowly and cautiously now, as if careful not to get too angry again. "The voice gift is called Chyun'ju. It means 'Siren' in the old language. Don't you remember anything at all from my teachings?"

Yes I did. I remembered sore throats, long hours and animal cruelty. Instead of saying that, I just answered, "Not much."

He released a composing breath, obviously fighting not to be frustrated. Through gritted teeth he spoke, "I guess we'll just have to start all over again then, won't we?" He walked gracefully across the room with the cunning poise of a stalking cheetah. He loomed over me, eyes sharp and instructive; examining my face to see if I was listening attentively. His presence was really quite unnerving.

He started. "Positioning is vital, otherwise you could damage yourself. Your feet should be shoulder-width apart, your spine straight,"–I shifted my posture accordingly, as balanced as a yoga instructor-"Chin up," he ordered, snapping it up himself with pale slender fingers, then he squared my shoulders with a rough jerk and I swayed precariously. "Breathe deeply...that's right. Now, copy me so I can see the extent of the damage."

He began with a simple scale but his voice was absolutely spectacular, transforming into startling loveliness. So impossibly beautiful, captivating and intriguing; like the call of a lover, so hard to refuse...

I shook my head, trying to focus my suddenly clouded mind. I was determined not to be affected by the hypnotic power of his voice. Not that I could be really, if there was one thing I remembered about Lynk, it was that his voice didn't work on me like it did on others. The force of it had just caught me unprepared. I wouldn't let it happen again.

Copying his scale, I heard how weak I sounded.

This didn't escape Lynk's notice.

He shook his head irritably, "Release your voice; you're restraining it."

"Am I?" I asked innocently.

He nodded. "There is a reason we are called Sirens," he said, his dangerously exquisite voice radiating its unsuppressed capacity. He continued, "We reach into souls with our sweet songs and voices, capturing their very essence and therefore commanding control of that person; just like those human stories of the sailors and the ships. That was us. We can do whatever we want with that person once we hold their souls. Just imagine the chaos we can cause, the devastation..." His eyes had burned brightly with some eccentric excitement, but now they dimmed as they saw my face. "How do you expect to do that if you won't release your voice?"

I didn't *want* to control people. I didn't *want* to cause destruction and devastation. God, this guy's even more nuts than I'd given him credit for.

"Again," Lynk ordered severely.

When I'd finished repeating the notes he frowned a little, showing some thin creases in his marble forehead. No streaks of grey were in his peroxide blonde hair. Like Kieran's mother it was hard to judge how old Lynk was. He had sort of an ageless appearance, like time didn't affect him. It suddenly occurred to me that I didn't know how long Phoenix lived for. Is it the same as humans, or were the myths correct? Is a Phoenix reborn every time he or she dies? Surely not, this place would be infested with them, *us;* whatever.

I realised I'd drifted off and concentrated on what Lynk was saying. "Slightly better," it didn't sound like a compliment, "but you're still not loosening everything. You probably don't realize but trust me, you aren't."

I didn't trust him. I didn't trust him even a little bit. But I did understand what he meant, I *did* hold back on what would make me unbelievably powerful, like a child clutching the string of a balloon. If bad things happened when I tried to control my voice, then God knows what would happen if I unleash it. It could either be amazing or catastrophic.

Lynk made me do more scales as a warm up. Each time shouting corrections at me when I'd didn't hit the notes exactly perfectly and each time letting the notes have a broader range. So high that humans couldn't hear, and so low the floor trembled at the sound.

My voice seemed sad. I could hear it, no matter how brightly I tried to sing. I sounded sorrowful, like the violin. It was the kind of pure, virtuous sadness that left people weeping. My music was opposite to Lynks; his was violent and harsh in its divine beauty, whereas mine was mournfully lovely.

After we'd finished scales, Lynk had me practice certain songs as another warm up. I remembered one my mother had written; she used to sing it all the time before she died. Then I couldn't understand the lyrics because they were in the old language, now I sang it with actual comprehension.

The funny thing was, it didn't sound any different, like I'd already known the song's meanings just from listening to the music itself. I was trying to make Lynk relax, that was the idea of the song, but I doubt it was working.

Next came actually speaking, and he brought in some wild animals for this, getting me to practice controlling them. It was easier, the smaller the animal, but they soon increased in size until the last one was a massive grey wolf brought in from the mountains.

Guards dragged it in snared with chains. The beast was huge, larger than my German Shepherd by far, and he had weighed an impressive eight stone. This creature was angry, it snarled viciously under its muzzle. Two large men chained it to a large metal ring attached to the middle of the floor. They snatched the muzzle off it and scurried back instantly. The creature growled, maliciously baring its huge sharp teeth.

Its eyes were frightened though, underneath the exterior. I pitied the poor thing. Its dirty grey fur had been messed up, scruffily neglected and covered in flecks of dried blood. It looked starved too; far too thin for a wolf that size.

Lynk watched me, his eyes hard and calculating. I knew what he wanted me to do. He wanted me to approach the vicious beast. My stomach flipped nervously as I stepped forwards. The wolf glanced over at me, snarling another warning for me to stay back. I continued forwards, stepping within its reach and speaking softly, dipping my voice into a low calming tone.

"Hey," I said, lulling softness oozing from my voice with a hypnotic edge, the wolf noticed me immediately, growling lower and more ferociously. "It's okay boy," I held my hands up, palms facing it. My voice was beautiful to even my own ears, the transfixing power outstanding. "Calm down."

The wolf's ears twitched and it growled again with renewed aggression. It bared its teeth but eventually stepped backwards.

"It's okay," I continued persuasively, going down onto my knees before it. The creature stilled then sat down on its hind legs, looking at me with a dazed fascinated gleam in its grey eyes. "There you go," I smiled, reaching out to stroke the tamed wolf, "nobody's going to hurt you."

Lynk stepped forwards, "Well done Ruby. I see you haven't forgotten everything. You can finish for the day." He turned to the two men. "Kill the wolf," he instructed firmly, "It's no use to me now."

I stood up immediately. "No! Don't touch him."

Lynk eyed me dismissively, then glanced at the two men who hesitated, grasping sharpened blades, "I said kill it."

I stood in front of the wolf protectively. There was no reason to kill him. I felt a connection with this poor creature. He was taken from his home, snared in chains only to be attacked and injured. There was no way I was letting anyone ruthlessly kill him. I would keep him. I lowered my voice, all my passion and my power streaming out over my tongue.

"Stop," I ordered the men as they came forwards. The strength of my command was impossible to defy. I put everything I had into it. Fiery energy burned along my back. They halted. "Drop your weapons," I insisted and they listened. Lynk stood watching with hawk eyes. "Now, unchain the wolf." They walked over and did as they were told. The rush I got from seeing them do what I said was amazing; I had complete and utter control of them. I glanced at Lynk, but he was silent. It never occurred to me that this was a test.

Once they unchained him, I called the wolf over and he followed instantly, tottering over like a puppy. I walked towards the door. I glared at Lynk. "I will take the animal." I was gasping for oxygen like it was an addictive drug. Truthfully I felt like I'd swallowed a knife.

By now, my throat blistering, Lynk smiled vindictively, "Be my guest," he gestured. He looked down at me, those calculating topaz eyes cool and unfathomable. "Go straight to the Ashaik's and pack your things." He dismissed me, "I shall see you again later." *That sounds like a threat*, I thought grudgingly but quickly scrambled back to escape the room. I needed fresh air, uncontaminated by the noise-fog that still lingered.

I couldn't believe I just did that.

And by that, I meant everything I'd just done.

I'd released my voice on those men without thinking and it had actually worked. The wolf trailed along beside me unconditionally. I'd also survived a session with my father; somehow securing myself a place at the Fire Palace.

Shaking my head, I stumbled blindly through corridors, trying to suppress all that. I eventually wandered outside. I had no idea where I was going. I headed out of the front of the building, to my surprise spotting Kieran. He was by the entrance, leaning on a brick wall; waiting.

I headed over to him, irritation bubbling in my chest already.

"What are you doing here?" I demanded.

"Alright, Arsey," he said, raising his hands. "I was waiting for you, like a nice person I am, to take you back." He glanced down at the gigantic wolf that followed me, who was now eyeing up Kieran with deep suspicion.

"What's with the stray?"

"A nice person!" I scoffed, ignoring his second question. "You took me through that dodgy area this morning just to terrify me. You utter arsehole!"

He laughed, stood up straight and started walking, ignoring what I'd said and acting like it was perfectly normal that a huge wild wolf was following me around.

"So, what happened? Chara said that you've been to see Lynk." He glanced down at my new friend, frowning. "That mutt's not him is it? You didn't, like, kiss him or something and turn him into that did you Princess?"

"I'm moving to the Swartette Palace," I told him, my vision stayed stubbornly planted on the snow-covered streets surrounding me. If I let my imagination wander I could almost pretend I was at home; that the mountains that watched me protectively from a distance were British, that the wolf was a German Shepherd–but it wasn't raining so the notion died instantly. Plus this was a massive city, complete with skyscrapers and bustling people. I'd never been to a city.

"What?" Kieran bellowed unexpectedly.

I glanced at him, realising he was astonished and infuriated. It confused me, I hadn't anticipated his anger. To be fair, I probably should have; Kieran's always angry, at least with me. We headed at a reasonable pace down the paved streets, quickly taking the fastest route out of the city. We were already in the outskirts; luckily the Old Hall wasn't that close to the centre.

"I thought you wanted me to do this," I said unevenly.

"I wanted you to *talk* with Lynk, *talk* to him, not *live* with him." He began ranting melodramatically. "You don't even know him. And you don't know anything about living in a place like that. You don't know the courtesy required; the stupid little conventional things that must be done, the things that absolutely cannot be condoned. There are a million rules in a house like that. I know; I've been there. You'll have guards at your door; a protector constantly at your side, slaves everywhere. And you won't be able to..."

Interrupting his ramblings, I cut him off, "You told me this was important. You were right. If Lynk is up to something, he's been planning it for years, probably before my mother even took me-"

"You aren't going," he stated unambiguously. "It's too..." His words halted abruptly when he saw my expression.

"Too what, Kieran?" I snapped, "Too dangerous?" I probed bitterly. "Since when have you given a damn about my safety?"

His face was so unapologetic that it made me even angrier. "It's too dangerous for you." His angelic face was smooth and expressionless, confident that he was right in his arrogant superior way.

"I just tamed a damn wild wolf," I snapped. "I'd like to see you do that."

We were almost out of the main city now, heading east towards Ebony's. The forest we had to cut through to get to there was nearly upon us. Grand coniferous trees soon loomed ahead. As we travelled deeper into the trees the convoluted path thinned and dissipated.

"I can handle Lynk just fine. He is my father."

"You don't know everything." Kieran shot back irritably. "You don't know that after you ran away, Lynk slaughtered everyone in his house."

That silenced me. "What?" I said eventually.

"A Palace usually has around two-hundred souls in it, including Swartettes. He killed most of your cousins and your grandparents."

"That's how most of the Swartettes were wiped out," I murmured softly to myself. "Wasn't he arrested?"

Kieran was gazing forwards distantly again, as if his mind was elsewhere.

"Most who were murdered were slaves, and they don't really matter because they're not technically Phoenix. It's the people that haven't Changed who become slaves. It's sad but true. This is why no one can know about Adrian. But yes, he should have been punished for his actions, probably executed. When he went to the Council he convinced them of his innocence and blamed it on someone else." He glowered menacingly at the sky. "Despite the blood on his hands they believed him and, because he'd killed one of the two Swartette Elders on the High Council, he was given that position."

I gasped in shock. They gave Lynk even more authority because he'd murdered half of his family? How twisted is that? Kieran nodded. "Most say that Sirens are cursed, not gifted."

I shuddered at that. Trying not to think about it, but I couldn't help myself.

"What happened to the person he blamed it on?" I asked finally.

"He was executed."

"I'm sorry," I said determinedly, "But I still have to go. I have no choice."

I was now even more terrified about it. Knowing what Kieran had just said to me. I heard a snap of a branch somewhere behind me, I turned, eyeing my surroundings suspiciously then, satisfied we were alone, continued forwards. The wolf growled suddenly, frightened, then dashed off into the trees. I stared after it, confused.

"Don't be stupid," Kieran hissed harshly, oblivious, "you have a choice."

He was angry again when I glanced across at him. Why was he being so stubborn? He was the one who'd convinced me to try and get information on Lynk in the first place. Obviously it didn't quite go according to plan, but still, I would be a lot more help where I was going.

"I'm not being stupid," I objected. "I'm being responsible. You were the one who told me to find out what my attacker was talking about. Can't you see this is the best way?" Another rustle of leaves; I frowned sceptically as I turned. Am I being paranoid? Kieran was too busy moaning to notice.

"Not like this. You'll go mad over there."

Purposefully not meeting those influential persuasive eyes; I said, "I'll be fine."

"No, you won't," Kieran argued antagonistically, "you aren't going."

I was about to say something else but my lips paused. Kieran had stopped suddenly. Becoming totally immobile, he listened attentively. I heard a whistling sound coming very close. Before my slow mind could register what was happening, an arrow was shooting towards my chest, whistling as it flew…I flinched back immediately.

Kieran's reactions were faster than mine; he unleashed a long knife from his belt immediately, in a flash knocking it from its course with the blade.

"Run!" he commanded.

Adrenalin pulsed erratically in my veins, my heart hammering loudly. An instinct triggering in my spine, compelling me to Change and to fly away for protection. But I knew that wouldn't help, I'd just be a bigger target. Plus I'd never get through the trees alive.

More whistling noises pierced my ears. Arrows showered down around me. I panted as I ran, struggling for oxygen. My stomach churned; the muscles there tightened with unexpected pain, aching already. I pushed my legs faster. An arrow whirled through the air, cutting shallowly across my arm. Pain throbbed in my arm, making it difficult to concentrate. The arrows were shooting from the trees, how many people were there?

"You're hurt." Kieran shouted, his voice rising over the heavy thumping of my feet over rocky mud. His steps were light and agile; quicker by far.

"Just a scratch," I called back breathlessly.

"Well, oh mighty wolf-tamer," he glared. "You picked the wrong wolf. It's bloody disappeared; useless bastard."

Another arrow missed us by inches, thudding to the frosted ground beside Kieran. I tried to look behind me but was afraid that if I did I'd stumble over my clumsy feet. We ran faster, my breath coming in rapid gasps. God I was so unfit. I felt like I was breathing in an ice mist, it clung to my lungs, freezing and burning simultaneously. My foot slipped and I nearly fell, but caught myself again in the nick of time. Fear pounded in my head, screaming.

Eventually the arrows stopped falling, to my relief.

We didn't slow down though. We raced out of the trees, feeling safer in the open. I soon recognised the familiar fields drizzled in snow like white icing sugar sieved onto a cake. Kieran's breath came in fast shallow huffs. My breath was verging on hyperventilating. *Calm down,* I ordered myself. But I knew who'd shot at us, who nearly killed me.

My attacker was back. And he was pissed.

"It was my attacker," I gasped as we climbed the white slanted land.

"What, you mean the guy who was shooting arrows at us? Never," Kieran said sarcastically. "God everyone really *does* want to kill you."

I gulped anxiously, ignoring him until we finally arrived at Ebony's house. Then a thought occurred to me. Slowing as we travelled closer, I asked nervously, "Won't he be able to track us here?"

"Yeah," Kieran answered certainly, "but I doubt it matters anyway. Both times this person's attacked you– assuming it's the same guy–you've been fairly alone. My thought is that if he wants to kill you, he'll wait until you're not in a house full of Ashaiks."

"Lucky me. You're probably right though," I admitted reluctantly.

"I'm always right. Jeez this guy doesn't give up." I didn't bother to respond as we rounded the side of the house.

I turned to Kieran. "Are you alright?" I asked insistently, though he looked perfect as normal, miraculously even his hair wasn't messed up.

He just snorted arrogantly, "Of course, Princess, I'm not dumb enough to be shot by an arrow." He pointed to the shallow trench in my skin from where the arrow had sliced through; blood was rapidly pouring from the gash but I dismissed the pain. It wasn't too deep, but it stung badly in the frigid air.

My eyes narrowed into glaring slits. "Don't be nasty. I was just checking."

"What, because you're so worried about me?"

"Just because you don't care what people think doesn't mean you can be so obnoxious." I scolded, annoyed. "I just wanted to know if you were alright."

"Well I'm not all right," he answered petulantly, stopping to glare at me with those beautiful ferocious eyes, a darker shade than usual. "I'm with you."

"If you feel like that then why don't you want me to go to the Fire Palace?" I responded frostily, glowering right back.

"Because I don't like being apart from you any more than I like being with you," he answered in a rush, confusing me.

"That doesn't make sense, Kieran," I complained. "You talk crap."

"I speak the truth and nothing more," he retorted, storming off and swearing violently under his breath. I followed him grudgingly.

We rounded the cute homey cottage, passing blooming red and white flowers drizzled in snowflakes. Roughly yanking the front door open, Kieran let the wood slam dramatically against the side of the house. I rushed to catch it before it could swing back and hit me.

"Kieran," I snarled his name.

He turned around, his expression honestly innocent. "Oh, didn't know you were there Ruby. Next time you stalk me make it more obvious."

Sighing exhaustedly, I went into the living room. Everybody was conveniently together, squashed around the sprawling coffee table; even Briseis was clustered against Adrian. Then I realised why the room seemed significantly more crowded than usual. We had visitors. And judging by everyone's faces; unwanted visitors.

Two of the biggest men I'd ever seen were positioned in a dominating, military stance in the centre of the small room. They both had shortly cropped hair the colour of cheese puffs–nothing like mine, before I even go there-and were both surprisingly attractive considering they were built like rugby players and subsequently had Orc-ish tendencies. They were identical twins.

I'd seen the Earth Warriors before, but I had no idea that the Fire Warriors could be just as terrifying. They certainly wouldn't be picked on for being ginger. To be honest they would probably eat whoever tried.

"Who the hell are you?" Kieran demanded, breaking the silence. Kieran never, ever seemed vulnerable with that overconfident attitude of his, but these guys even made Adrian look small. They must have been at least seven foot tall. I felt like a midget.

"I am Kian; this is Finn," grunted one of the twins, in curt, clipped sentences. "We are here to escort Lady Ruby to the Fire Palace."

Oh my God. It was happening already.

Chapter Nineteen

"Try and take her," Kieran growled challengingly. "I'll break all of your fingers if you lay just one on her."

I glanced at Kieran, unable to hide my astonishment. Now he wanted to protect me? After everything he said last night. I shook my head. I knew these guys would resort to violence if necessary so I reluctantly volunteered, "I'll go, but I'll need my things."

Glancing purposefully at Chara and Nik I asked, "Could I have some help?" Kieran glared furiously at me, fire smouldering in his emerald eyes.

Nik's kind, handsome features were nodding understandingly as he nudged Chara forwards. "We'll help," he offered.

Then one of the guards held up his hand, palm forward like he was stopping traffic, "Wait; the Lady has an injury that needs attending to." I looked down in surprise; having forgotten the skin-deep wound on my arm from the arrow's slicing tip. It had stopped bleeding and the pain was fading into a drunken numbness; though healing it without Kieran would require stitches. Before I could protest a warrior stepped forwards, reaching up behind him to retrieve something from his metal wing brace. I shook my head decidedly. "It's just a scrape. I'll be fine until we reach the Palace." The man grunted but reluctantly agreed; I guess I kinda had some authority.

Nik, Chara and I went upstairs, leaving the intimidating company. We didn't speak until my bedroom door shut. I noted with surprise that the knife Kieran had given me last night, which I'd left in his room, was sitting shining on my bed. I frowned at it, confused but oddly touched. Then

Chara's patience burst and questions exploded out of her frantically.

"What happened? What did you do? Why are strange men here to take you away? Do you want to go? Don't you like us anymore?" Her lovely hazel eyes were wide and very upset.

"Don't be ridiculous, of course I don't want to leave." I quickly assured her then dropped my voice because I knew just how brilliantly Phoenix can hear when they concentrate–even from downstairs. "Remember what I told you about my attacker, that he knew Lynk was forming alliances or something..."

She nodded, and I continued. "This afternoon Lynk found out that I'm living with you guys and was pretty mad. He said he lawfully owned me until I'm married or eighteen or something."

"Here, that's true, actually," Nik admitted. "Did he take anything from you?"

"My freedom; he's demanding that I move into the Fire Palace with him, but it's probably going to be the easiest way of getting information, so..." my tone twisted bitterly, "I'm going to go and find out as much as I can."

"But Ruby, what if your attacker was lying?" Chara asked worriedly. "I mean. Then you'll be stuck with Lynk for no reason."

I hadn't even thought of that.

Eventually I shrugged, "I don't know. I guess I'll just deal with it, but to be honest I don't think this guy was lying. And oh," I'd almost forgotten, "me and Kieran were just ambushed by–we think–him again. He shot arrows at us on the way here."

Chara's eyes went wide again. "That explains your arm." Then slowly she said, "I don't like this; surely there must be another way?"

She seemed honestly concerned. I withdrew an uneasy breath, "I'm not running away again. I need to do this."

She still didn't seem convinced but Nik said, "I don't like this anymore than you Chara, but I think Ruby is right. We need to know what Lynk is up to; I mean, the High Council isn't exactly going to do anything about it."

I went over to my bed, only just realising that I actually needed to pack. Chara saw my hesitation and instinctively pulled out my heavy gold wing brace from last night and began stuffing all my important things in its numerous hidden pockets, including my new weapon. She explained she'd send my clothes and stuff over in the morning. She packed enough clothes for two days though and my mother's necklace.

"Okay," I said when Chara finally finished. I was straining under the leaden bulk of the wing brace Nik had hauled over my shoulders; it weighed me down like chain-mail underwater. "How am I going to carry all this?" I could barely stand and the brace wasn't even full.

Chara carefully clutched my other bag. "You'll probably be flying to the Fire Palace. You'll be stronger once you Change."

I cautiously arranged the heaving brace, attempting to straighten up and gulping anxiously. "You mean I have to Change in front of them?" I asked.

She frowned, "I guess so. Is that a problem? Don't you remember how?"

"No, no," I assured her quickly, "it's just I don't particularly want to run around in the snow completely naked until I turn into a bird." Now that is a sentence I never thought I'd have to say.

"It's the whole naked thing, isn't it?" Chara asked.

I nodded, "Yep, it's the naked thing."

She sighed, almost frustrated; but not quite because Chara was far too dignified and patient to get annoyed. Then she said, "If you're that bothered you'll just have to sacrifice some clothes. But it is ridiculous and impractical. You need to learn to embrace this way of life, Ruby, and part of that involves being naked in front of people from time to time."

I rolled my eyes, "Well, it's a good job these jeans are old."

It was only at that point when I realised Nik was laughing.

Chara frowned, "What's up with you?"

He shook his head, "You two just make me laugh."

"Nikolas Ashaik," Chara warned, "now is not the time."

He stopped chuckling but still couldn't demolish his cheeky smile. I couldn't help it, smiles were infectious, and I grinned too.

Chara sighed maternally. "Come on you too, we need to go."

Though, as I clambered back down the stairs, nearly falling under the incredibly straining mass on my back, I thought I saw Chara smile.

Downstairs, it didn't surprise me that Kieran was having a rant. What did puzzle me, however, was that he stopped as soon as he saw me return.

The ambiance abruptly turned awkward and uncomfortable.

Then thankfully Chara came to my rescue. "She's ready," she announced, purposefully turning to hug me goodbye and whispering in my ear, "Good luck, Chick; keep your head. We'll see you soon."

Ebony bounded forward, fiercely wrapping her arms around me. It was so easy to love Ebony. "If you don't come visit very soon," she warned, "I will personally come and fetch you." She released me.

"I'll come see you as soon as Lynk lets me," I said, glancing at the apparently oblivious twins. They were both starring off in different directions, their strong sharp features looking vaguely bored.

Nik smiled, "See you soon," and gave me a quick hug.

I got a hug from Briseis and an indifferent nod from Adrian. A glare from Ebony's annoying husband whom I've barely seen, and then I finally turned to Kieran, feeling nervous.

"Bye Kieran," I whispered.

He smirked arrogantly, "I hate to ruin your meaningful sentimental goodbye before you even begin, but it isn't my thing, Princess."

Then he turned, and walked off.

I waved to everyone else as the men led me outside. It was snowing again, but it wasn't pretty flakes that were falling now, it was almost a blizzard. One of the twins said to me, "Are you alright with flying?"

I wanted to scream, no I bloody wasn't okay with flying! There's a storm brewing and I don't want to rip this top! Instead I just nodded, "That's fine."

As soon as I thought they weren't looking–they were busily Changing their pale muscular bodies into Phoenix- I regretfully thought of fire.

The familiar energy gushed instantaneously up my spine while my limbs stretched and contracted to correspond with the ill-fitting wing brace. I heard my clothes rip. When I once again opened my eyes, I had that brilliantly focused vision. I stretched my wings, dripping in bulky metal links, taking in the wonderful atmosphere only visible in this bizarre body.

This way, said one of the twins in my head. He wasn't exactly ordering me and he sounded polite and respectful, but still, didn't any Phoenix here know how to say please?

The huge twins pushed off the ground. I followed them up into the lashing snow.

I think I'd forgotten how wonderful flying is. Even with the weight of an elephant stretched across your wings. We climbed though the air effortlessly; snow swelled around me like a shoal of fish. My mind was sharp enough to identify each individual flake. The view was breathtaking, the blanketed fields, the magnificent city arches, the gemstone tower, the piercing skyscrapers. *This scene belongs on a Christmas card,* I thought.

I flapped my immense wings, feeling spectacular and elegant. Beating the air rhythmically, I laughed ecstatically at the joy of flying. I didn't care that that my guards were watching me with peculiar expressions. I loved the feeling of the biting wind running through my waterproof feathers. It came so naturally, finding the right wind currents to glide me faster, like riding an ocean wave. I was so high I didn't even complain about the significant weight increase that joined forces with gravity to drag me down.

Then I noticed the house.

From above, I saw a sprawling Palace with courtyards and gardens, structured from a strange whitish stone. The rock was chalky-looking, like alabaster. Great bonfire-torches lit the Palace walls and ancient swirling symbols adorned the striking supportive columns. This strange, almost Grecian Palace was nestled high on the mountain valley ledge, directly opposite the Earth Palace miles in the distance.

We landed in the biggest of the three courtyards. I recognised it from previous dreams. I shivered involuntarily. This place held bad experiences.

I remembered instantly the giant fountain in the middle of the courtyard. A memory sprung back to me. Pictures flooded into my mind. Lynk was shouting at a slave next to this fountain, oblivious to me perched high up in the tree in the corner of the courtyard, camouflaged by leaves and brambles. I wasn't alone either, a boy sat with me. I told the boy to hush.

Then a block in my head sprung up and I couldn't remember anymore.

"Welcome, Lady," said a female voice. I turned towards the sound and saw a little woman with white-blond hair that curled beautifully to her waist. She was standing on a raised patio that was sheltered from the brutal weather.

On one side of her was expensive outdoor furniture made of artistic metal ringlets, linked together to form fire. On her other side was my mother's swing, carved from a rare white wood and perfect for the blistering summer months. It was where my mother would regain her sanity after a long day.

The small woman spoke again. It was difficult to estimate her age, she had no lines creasing her face, nor any teenage blemishes. Her skin was pale and luminous but her face was plain.

"My name is Evelyn. I am the High-Slave of this Palace," she explained coming closer. She had a blanket in her delicate arms, "Please, come in, the weather is awful."

I stepped under the protection of the sheltered roof. The dainty woman then turned towards the Fire Warriors and they gave a brisk nod before flying off.

Why aren't you just thinking to me? I asked inquisitively, abandoning trying to distinguish her age. She was very beautiful.

She seemed genuinely surprised by my question, "I am not worthy to enter a Lady's mind, or any Phoenix mind of higher authority." She answered hesitantly, cautiously, as if she wasn't sure if I was playing a trick on her.

That's ridiculous, who told you that? I wondered. I had a pretty good guess.

She shook her head incredulously. "The High Council decides the law for the Slaves. It's the way things are."

Oh, now I get it. Then I felt sympathy for the girl; there probably were a lot more things she can and cannot do. How did people become Slaves again? I think Kieran had told me that those who didn't Change automatically became slaves; the old fledglings like Adrian. There must be a surprising amount of people that don't Change then, surely?

"My Lady..." The girl began politely but I quickly interrupted her.

Please, call me Ruby.

"Begging your pardon," she replied quietly, unable to hide the shock in her black eyes, "but I do not believe that would be appropriate."

I waved her off by moving one of my long wings, accidentally hitting a nearby chair. I frowned at it, then insisted, *It's Ruby...sorry what's your name again?* I asked, feeling discourteous.

"It's Evelyn, my Lady," she replied politely.

I shook my big head, *Ruby, it's Ruby.* I insisted.

"Ruby," she amended, still uncertainly. "Your father is in a meeting, he will not be back for hours. Would you like to Change so you can come in?"

I nodded; pleased that at least she wasn't calling me 'my Lady' anymore. I mean, come on, I wasn't the Queen. I swear and complain too much and I really do not like little dogs, especially corgis. Proper dogs have a minimum height standard; if it's below the knee it's a mutated rat, or a confused ferret.

I was losing focus again.

Thinking of fire, its harshness and brutality and its contrasting warmth, I listened for my own flame's hum. Eventually I heard it, feeling it ignite deep inside me, slowly winding up and down my spine…

A minute or so later I was standing on the cool wooden patio with two feet, two legs and two arms. I was human again. I shook from the Change. I dropped my brace onto the floor, my weak human muscles unable to carry it. Automatically Evelyn came forwards, wrapping a thick blanket around me.

I thanked her then followed her into the massive house.

It really was a Fire Palace.

Everything looked expensively decorated. The crystal chandeliers looked suspiciously like diamond and ruby and they twinkled brightly with unique burning flames. The walls and ceilings were painted with Firebirds and absolutely everything was draped in gold. Gold was everywhere, framing the huge glass windows, the threads in the drapes, covering the seats, *everywhere*. The floor was made from dark red stone and it was polished to perfection. There was a grand table in the centre of the massive ballroom we entered, the kind you only see on films during an important celebratory banquet.

I whistled lowly, "This room is beautiful."

Evelyn smiled, appreciating my comment, "We try to preserve the Grand Hall as best we can. We spend many hours trying to keep it as it is now."

I nodded, agreeing. I bet it did take a very long time to dust in here; especially the tremendous balcony and magnificent stone stairs on the far side of the room. As I remembered my nakedness I thought perhaps I should continue touring *after* my butt is properly concealed.

"Do I have a room?" I asked Evelyn.

"Yes Lady. Follow me please."

"It's Ruby," I insisted as I followed her through a large set of double doors.

Turning a corner I realised this place wasn't quite as empty as I'd first anticipated. There were people moving around everywhere. I clutched my blanket self-consciously as servants-I wouldn't call them slaves-trailed behind business types and posh snooty people; visitors I guessed. They scurried past silently; none even glancing at me.

We wound up a spiral staircase, stopping at a door at the very top. Carefully Evelyn pulled open the door, gesturing for me to enter.

It was my old room.

It was painted a soft orangey red colour, straw-stuffed toys perched on my four-poster bed; vast collections of children's books were still piled up on shelves and a desk with quills, ink and paint was in my 'creative' area. A personally drawn picture of a scarlet Phoenix–presumably my mother-was still pinned up on the wall next to my east-facing balcony.

It was like the room had been frozen in time. It was quite creepy.

"Does this not please you, Lady Ruby?" Evelyn asked, seeing the tears in my eyes. I quickly forced them back. Why was I crying? Get a grip.

"No, its fine," I assured her quickly, then realising something I asked, "Oh crap, I left my clothes outside in my brace."

Evelyn walked across the room to show me a small wooden table made from a reddish brown wood, on top of it was my wing brace. How the hell had it gotten there so quickly?

Then I heard a quiet, polite knock on the door. Expecting that Evelyn would answer; I waited. Evelyn was looking at me strangely until I understood that I was the one who was supposed to respond and stuff.

"Come in," I called awkwardly; the door opened. In walked two pretty girls, both with long braided hair and pinafore-type clothes.

"These are your Slaves," Evelyn announced and they both did silly little curtsies. I felt like I should be wearing a wig and a corset, prancing around complaining about cucumber sandwiches and waiting for Mr. Darcy to arrive on a white horse. This was ridiculous.

Evelyn continued, "Lord Lynk has made it very clear that you should not be left alone. There are guards positioned outside your room and around the Palace. Your Slaves will always be near you while you're here and you'll have Protectors if you wish to leave."

It sounded like a prison.

"You shall always be safe here, Lady Ruby."

I bet, I thought bitterly. "When is Lynk coming back?"

Evelyn answered, "A couple of hours."

So I had plenty of time to snoop around while he was gone. Then I glanced at my new 'maids'. I wouldn't be left alone, I realised suddenly. How could I?

"Unless there is anything else you need, I shall attend to my other duties," said Evelyn respectfully.

"Of course," I smiled. "Thank you," I added before she shut the door.

One of the little maids came forwards, "Would you like to unpack, Lady?"

I nodded gratefully, thinking that packing and unpacking seemed to be the only thing I did recently; that and being attacked and healed again.

She smiled warmly, "I shall unpack while you are dressing."

"But all my stuff is in my brace and the rest is at Ebony's," I protested.

"Lord Lynk had some things already sent to you," explained the other maid, gesturing for me to walk forwards into a dressing room.

Grudgingly I followed her while my other little maid unpacked my things. This to me seemed silly; how could I know where my things were if I didn't know where she'd unpacked them? Either way, I had no choice. In the dressing room, my first tiny maid scurried off into a wooden wardrobe to retrieve a dress. Me and dresses do not happily mix.

Realising I didn't know her name I quickly asked and she answered that it was Ellie. Though it translated as Ellie in English, it had a funny accent which was quite amusing. I didn't point it out.

"Well, Ellie, let me tell you now, I am not a big fan of dresses," I warned her, trying to remain polite and dignified.

"My Lady," she answered, a fraction of a frown creasing her forehead, "it is expected that you should always be dressed accordingly."

"According to what?"

"Your High Name, of course," she answered quietly.

I sighed; she would probably get into trouble if I didn't do exactly what was expected of me. I cringed but said reluctantly, "Alright but I am not wearing a corset, or a wig."

"That is fine, my Lady," she seemed confused.

Trying not to think about how strange it was being helped to dress, I said, "Call me Ruby."

"I do not think that would be appropriate, Lady."

It was going to be a long night. I huffed.

"Can I have a look around?" I asked Ellie once I was dressed.

"Yes my Lady, I'll just fetch your Protector," answered Ellie, moving swiftly towards the door.

"I don't need a..." I objected automatically, but she was already gone.

"It is for your safety," said the other girl apologetically.

"It's punishment," I muttered. These girls were lovely; don't get me wrong, but I didn't need to be escorted everywhere and have everything done for me. I'm a big girl. I can wipe my own ass.

When the door opened one of the scarily big twins stepped through. My stomach dropped disobediently. Not this guy, anyone but this guy.

"This is Kian," announced Ellie, "your Protector."

A deep irritated moan bubbled in my throat; I managed to restrain it before it unleashed. Annoyance panged in my stomach like cramp. My head was already beginning to ache. I'm never going to be alone. *Never.*

Chapter Twenty

I wandered aimlessly with my silent company, frequently getting lost then having to ask Kian directions. He would respond with a grunt and a point in an opposing direction so very politely-like a caveman. My petulance about having to be escorted around like a child had not yet dimmed.

I discovered many rooms, including dining rooms, greenhouses with the roofs covered in snow, glass rooms and big ceiling-painted rooms filled with occupied chairs. Unfortunately those chairs were filled by people who also blatantly ignored me. I tried talking to a young girl with bright red hair almost identical to mine, but as soon as I approached her she walked off.

There were lots of places I was forbidden to enter. Mostly these were visitor's rooms, which I understood, but some just seemed silly. Like I wasn't allowed to go down to see the Slave's quarters or I wasn't allowed in the kitchen. The most intriguing thing I was denied access to was the entire third floor.

"You can't go there," said Kian gruffly.

We were climbing upstairs after exploring the second level when I'd noticed another staircase. I'd attempted to climb it but was abruptly yanked back.

"Why not?" I asked curiously, glancing up the stairs. If I stretched my neck around at an awkward angle I could just see a closed door at the very top.

"It is Lord Lynk's chambers."

"He has a whole floor?" I wondered incredulously, "Why?" What could he possibly be doing up there that would take up an entire floor? Housing an army? Well, *that* was an unnerving possibility.

Kian grunted indifferently. "He has many floors," he answered trying to lead me back down the stairs. I followed reluctantly.

I almost smirked, "You don't know, do you?"

His closed face seemed to flicker ever so slightly, "I am not permitted such information."

I think that was the longest sentence he'd said so far.

"You must be invited up there." he explained briskly.

We'll see about that, I thought, feeling the challenge trigger an instinctive response in my mind. Whatever was up there, I would find out.

Eventually I stumbled upon a library and found momentary contentment. My warrior-guy sat in a chair while I searched the room. It was a beautiful circular room, stacked to the painted ceiling with books, scrolls and coloured strips of parchment that held maps. I studied some of the maps for a long time, thinking it might be useful one day.

Everything was icy mountains here until you reached the southern area of the island where the foothills gradually sloped into hills, then 'summer' forests, then deserts. The biggest desert was called Trigate-about the size of Britain-and that was where the Fire City–Ephizon–burned on the horizon.

I must have spent hours in there, but soon my rumbling stomach became overwhelming and I headed back to my room. When I arrived my maids suddenly appeared beside me.

"Would you like supper in your room, Lady?" asked one of them.

I nodded appreciatively.

Both girls scurried off to the door and by the time I'd put down the few books I'd borrowed, servants were streaming into my room carrying plates of steaming food. Not expecting dinner would come quite so fast, I slowly made my way towards the little wooden dining table. Sitting down, my suddenly ravenous stomach growled. The servants went out again, leaving jugs of red liquid, cold salads, various meats and hunks of thick farmhouse bread smothered deliciously in creamy melting butter. There was far too much but I dug into my food, feeling alone.

Once I'd politely excused my maids and all the food had been cleared away, I finally tiptoed over to my balcony to check if anyone was out there. Unfortunately there were more guards below my window. Damn. I knew that my lovely Protector Kian was outside the other door. I went back to plonk grumpily onto my massive curtained bed.

I sighed, glancing above me at the ceiling; it was a pleasant colour, the delicious orangey-red of ripened peaches. A sweet, innocent shade it was, unsubstantial from a distance until you examined really closely, finding intermittent accidental splutters of gold from the painter's clumsy brush. It was a blank canvas for my thoughts, which soon turned to Kieran. I still felt stung by his reaction to me the other night, the way he'd looked at me, so undeniably horrified. It made me cringe just thinking about it.

Suddenly I heard a loud intrusive knock on the door. My body froze. I carefully sat up and spun around just as the door creaked open.

Lynk was home.

He walked forwards with that familiar feline stride, his face unreadable. His luminous skin was dotted with pale gold freckles that somehow made him look even more dangerous; it was an innocent danger.

"You're here," he stated, almost suspiciously.

Trying to calm my fragile nerves, I pulled on my poker face. "I am," I answered, nodding my head and impulsively straightening to my feet.

He glanced around the room in a way that made me think he hadn't been in here in a long time. "Your room is what you expected, I take it?"

I nodded, though it was an absolute lie. "It is how I remember it," I answered, skilfully calm and composed while my head was spinning.

"Have you eaten?" he asked.

"Yes." *This isn't at all awkward*, I thought sarcastically. Then a question flooded into my mind. "I need to go out tomorrow morning. I have a friend who's teaching me some defence."

He looked sceptical, obviously not liking that idea. "You can go, but with your Protector. If he informs me it's in anyway unsuitable you won't go again."

My eyes widened involuntarily, my cool demeanour wavering. "I have to have a Protector with me? To go to a *lesson?*"

It wasn't the best thing to say, I realised. His face contorted in anger, I should have known how capricious his moods were, as volatile and ever-changing as the tide. So easily influenced…

"Yes," he burst, making me flinch. "You will have one every single time you leave this room. I do not trust you. Do not think me stupid, Daughter."

"Don't call me that," I blurted unthinkingly "I'm not your Daughter."

Lynk didn't speak for a long time. His flat black stare frightened me; his pupils seemed to devour his entire iris. He towered over me; intimidating enough to make me shrink back, coil away like a frightened snake.

"I will call you whatever I please," he bellowed, his face tearing apart, "I made you." He roughly came forwards, yanking me by my hair, speaking furiously into my ear with a hissing cutting tone, "You belong to me."

"Get off me," I yelled. My hands trembled as I felt my hair ripping out. I tried to get him off. Bloody hell, where was my Protector now?

Eventually his tight grip loosened enough so that I could pull free. I guessed it wasn't just my attitude that had made him so suddenly infuriated, that outburst had been building over time. My hate for him rose in my throat like bile, coming up in bitter premeditated words.

I glared at him, all pretences demolished. "I am not your weapon." My voice was deadly cold and serious. "I am what I choose to be and what I choose is anything but what you are," I said slowly, sounding much braver than I felt. I couldn't allow him to see my fear; he fed off fear like some vindictive parasite. I shielded my eyes from his.

He was breathing heavily. He brought his hand up to smack it hard across my face. Despite the dizzying pain I somehow managed to stay upright. Ouch, that would bruise. He came forwards again, I staggered back out of the way but he pushed me down onto the bed, grabbing my throat and pressing his thumb hard into my windpipe. I choked, coughing as my airways cut off. I struggled under his grasp, fighting to get away. I couldn't breathe, I was trapped. I kicked at him in feeble desperation, just clipping his knee. He didn't like that. He reared back, releasing my throat and before I even managed to gasp a shaky breath he was punching me. His fist connected with my eye, just above my cheekbone; blinding me momentarily. I screamed in pain, trying to get away. I shuffled back impulsively but he grabbed me in a vicious snare and hit me again, this time just lower on my cheekbone.

I'd had enough. The pain and adrenaline forced out my instincts, and when I spoke I unleashed the full potential of my voice on him. "You're a monster," I told him darkly, feeling the waves of immense power saturating my voice "but I am not afraid of you. Get off me, Lynk." I felt the sound search him, locking onto him like target. It stunned him momentarily, but he was too strong to allow such feeble access.

When he recovered, he spoke silkily with no traces of the hereditary *Chyun'ju* I'd just used at all. "You haven't seen anything yet," he told me, a serious warning glinting in his eyes. He walked across the room to leave. "And you won't be having any more lessons from me. If you want training, they'll be brought here, to our courtyard. You are not to leave the house." He snapped before slammed the door like an overreacting teenager.

The world went silent.

Then I sunk down onto my bed.

I could feel myself beginning to panic, my lungs hyperventilating uncontrollably. Everything just caught up with me. Furious tears rolled down my cheek. Frantically scrambling around, I searched for my old jewellery box. Opening it, sweet melodies twinkled in the air. I knew music was the best way to keep my head under control; to keep my spine from imploding in a fury of dangerous energy. The gentle rhythm and soft chiming sounds relaxed my muscles immediately. Music was my drug.

I fell asleep listening to it.

Two children sat high in a tree at the side of the great courtyard.

"I told you I could beat you up here," boasted the little girl. Her curling crimson hair was wrapped in a messy braid, some of the bright ringlets had escaped during the climb but her smile remained untouched.

The little boy was slightly older than the girl, by a couple of years. His face was rounded and cute, his hair a mop of tight brown springs, and he had a lovely grin that seemed to stretch endlessly. His ragged clothes suggested he was the son of a slave. He poked the girl with a twig and objected, "Only because you kicked me!"

The girl shook her head, those freeing curls falling across her little birdlike face like a lion's mane. "I did not," she protested absolutely, snapping off thin branch to poke her only friend back, "You must have mistaken a branch for my foot."

Now the boy was shaking his head, "Don't be silly, trees don't move."

"Some do," she answered, gleaming. "I read it."

"Where?" inquired the boy. He wasn't privileged enough to learn to read. His mother was a slave, and those directly descended from the Unchanged automatically become Slaves too; until their first fledged flight; if they Change; which is rare.

"In a book," she said. "Mother says there are all sorts of creatures past the mountains."

"We should go see them!" enthused the boy.

"Yes," agreed the girl excitedly. "We should-"

But her words halted as the courtyard doors opened. The girl heard her father's voice, sounding angry. Instantly she told the boy to be very quiet. He was.

"What do you mean, 'we have no time to get more slaves!'" he yelled at a slave who was obviously shaking with fear. The girl froze; she knew what father could be like when he was mad. She scrambled further back to conceal herself in leaves.

The slave cowered backwards towards the fountain. "We cannot receive any more slaves to replace those we already have *lost, my Lord. The High Council have not permitted it." He shuddered apprehensively.*

Lynk looked down at the pitiful slave, speaking dangerously. "Find a way."

The slave looked terrified, he stuttered. "It is impossible, my Lord. What with all the slaves you send as messengers to the Barlayic soldiers," he swallowed nervously, "and them being…eaten. Of course the High Council doesn't know about… "

But the Lord had had enough. In a burst of fury he ripped his blade from his belt and plunged it into the slave. The man cried out; falling into the fountain. Blood gushed into the water, turning it a gruesome red. The slave screamed in agony until Lynk brought up his sword again. This time the blade streaked across the slave's neck, slicing mercilessly, severing his head from his body to silence his disturbing wails. The fountain ran with diluted blood.

The boy in the tree couldn't help it; he screamed.

The girl instantly clasped her tiny hands across his mouth but it was too late.

Lynk had heard.

"Who's there? Show yourself!" he shouted angrily, his powerful voice ringing out in a way that made the terrified boy start climbing down the tree. The girl wasn't affected by her father's voice, she never had been, but that didn't stop the boy from automatically being mesmerised.

She tried to yank him back but he'd already gone, in body and soul. The girl waited desperately as her friend edged towards her father. She prayed to the Mother.

Her father gazed down at the little boy; knowing he'd heard too much. Raising the blade high, Lynk stabbed through the boy's heart. The girl in the tree felt sick but she knew she couldn't move; she couldn't make a sound.

Or she'd be next.

I woke up gasping, tears streaming down my cheeks.

Running my shaking hands across my face, I felt my head spin.

The boy's name was Reuben; I remembered now. He'd been my best and only friend for three years before that had happened. The other children had hated me, calling me only by the name 'Siren'. They avoided me like the plague. I recalled that Lynk had later come to tell me, deceivingly apologetic, that Reuben had been killed by a mountain bear attack, though I'd known the truth. That was when I finally started to see Lynk for what he was, no longer deluded by a childish image that he was my father and I had to love him.

There were some memories I'd rather remain forgotten.

Getting out of the warm comfort of my bed, I stretched. If there was one good thing that came from that real nightmare, it was that I knew something. Barlayic Soldiers? Who were they, a different kind of Phoenix? I didn't suppose it mattered very much. Kieran would know.

I cringed, my heart thumping heavily at the thought of Kieran. I stared up at the ceiling, feeling utterly alone. It must have been early in the morning by now. Outside it was still dark; perhaps it was three, maybe four o'clock? I lay awake for a while, painfully thinking about Kieran and the way he had looked at me. Those beautiful, heart-breaking eyes staring straight at me in a way no one ever had. In that moment I'd felt nothing but pure elation. In all honestly it had been a surprise to me that it was Kieran I was feeling these emotions for, the most arrogant messed-up boy I know. My own brain had been hiding it from me. My body had known for ages. He barely looks at me and I shiver. The way he'd touched me, his fingers skimming my lips so delicately it was like a dragonfly over water, oh, and when he spoke my name; *my* name.

I wanted to cry. Kieran didn't want me and my father wants to abuse me. I was trapped in a Palace surrounded by guards and a Protector intent on keeping me incarcerated. My only friends were miles away, and they weren't even supposed to be friends with me. They wouldn't be allowed to visit me here of course. I was completely alone. I missed my friends, my mother, my dog and most of all I missed Kieran. I needed his confident presence to make me feel safe, even if he didn't want me. I was stupid to think he ever would, a short ginger thing like me; with him, the incarnation of Adonis? No way. I've seen the girls he can get. I didn't have a prayer.

A slow deep depression fell over me like a mist. I'd never felt so awful. I knew I had to get out of here, even if it was just to fly to clear my head. I just wanted to be alone; even from my own thoughts.

I carefully stumbled out of bed; I was still wearing my clothes from earlier. I stretched, my spine twingeing in protest. My face ached, a constant nagging sore that would intensify dramatically if touched. I glanced in the mirror on my way to the door. My eye was severely swollen, my cheek puffy on one side and already a shadow of a bruise was formulating. My neck was a horrid pinkish colour, purple finger-shaped marks already covering my throat. I exhaled painfully then tiptoed over to the door.

Pressing my ear against the dark wood, I listened attentively, concentrating. I heard continuous breathing on the other side, two sets of lungs exhaling and inhaling in perfect synchrony; two awake guards. Damn. Then, thinking this, I wondered about the word awake. Perhaps I could put them to sleep. I think I'd read something like that in one of my borrowed books from the Library…

I padded quietly to the desk where I'd left the old tattered books I'd borrowed. I checked a particular book, carefully separating the crinkled pages until I found what I was after. Scan-reading the page, I realised that yes, Chyun'ju could be used as a sedative, but no, it did not explain how.

I paused again. Wait, I had done this before hadn't I? Back home I'd sedated a whole pub of people. They'd been human; but it must count for something.

Well, it was worth a shot. My mother used to sing a song if I couldn't sleep, a lullaby in an ancient language I still don't recognise. I'd always drifted off immediately. Perhaps if I sung that it would do the same for me?

Once again tiptoeing towards the door, I quietly began to sing my mother's lullaby. The beautiful melody drifted through the door surreptitiously, slowly capturing the guard's attention. I continued, my voice deep and soothing, until I heard their breathing slow even more. It was actually working. By the time I'd uttered the last lyric I was absolutely certain my guards were unconscious. Their chainsaw snores echoed loudly in the hall.

I was still cautious as I turned the doorknob. Very slowly, the door creaked open. I glanced down to find my guards drunkenly sprawled across the floor. Cool, at least now I knew how to get out of my room at night. I didn't know how long they would stay asleep so I quickly hurried. Clinging to the shadows, my worries were in vain; the halls were eerily silent and deserted.

Heading out the back way into the gardens I noticed more guards in the distance. They were facing the opposite direction to me, searching for danger that attempted to enter; not escape. I crept silently around them, behind a trimmed hedge and down some stone steps. I was more concealed as I entered the wood-like garden. When I decided I was far enough away I Changed, leaving my clothes under a pile of rocks. I took off into the air, relief flooding into me. I'd actually made it.

I flew in a dreamy state through the air. It was a cold night, a grey overcast hanging in anticipation above me, waiting for the perfect moment to scatter its frozen dust onto the earth. I headed thoughtlessly towards the mountains, my body impulsively taking me in directions my brain was unaware of.

It wasn't long until I realised I'd been unconsciously flying towards the Wall. I spotted it from a height then uncertainly landed before it. I edged closer nervously, and then kicked myself mentally, my subconscious voice reminding me that you shouldn't fear the dead; it's the living you need to watch out for. I still stayed a good few foot from the bodies though.

The pregnant girl was still there, her body slightly more decayed but not as much as you would think because of the preserving icy weather. She must have once been so beautiful, was it really worth it? I wondered if she thought so. Staring at her I acquired a new mind set. If this was the consequence of being in a secret relationship with someone of a different Tribe then I doubt it was something I wanted. After all you can't love anyone when you're dead.

Whatever happened with Kieran would have to be forgotten. He was right, we weren't meant to be together. I don't want to end up on that Wall beside her, my head marked eternally with my crime, despite how ridiculous a crime it seems to me. My life was dangerous enough as it was without making things even more complicated for myself. Yes, I would just have to try and forget my feelings for him. That couldn't be that difficult surely?

With that in mind I headed back. I Changed and dressed when I returned, knowing that I would have to sneak back in. I froze when I heard someone coming my way and ducked behind a tree. I waited a moment, glancing back as they walked past.

And my heart stopped beating. All I saw was the back of the person and I knew immediately that something was very wrong. I saw wings, but not beautiful feathered wings, no, these were all wrong. Huge deformed wings they were, with grey skin like wet leather draped over twisted bony structures. The creature disappeared almost instantly into the forest, leaving me gaping, petrified, behind. What the hell was that?

Scrambling up I rushed back, goose bumps coating my body now. I was terrified, what *was* that? I crept past the guards around the back of the Palace, ducking in through an open window when one of them nearly spotted me.

Instead of even bothering to look for any more excitement tonight, I followed the shadows quickly back to my room.

The guards were still sound asleep on the floor when I got back so I slipped into my room, instantly immersing myself deep in my bed sheets. I wrapped the material walls around me again, but it was no use, I was too damn keyed up to sleep. I was, quite frankly, freaked out. I think I drifted to sleep twice and then woke up again, my heart hammering dramatically and sweat clinging to me like frog slime.

I was still awake when it was time to get up the next morning.

Chapter Twenty-One

The maids came in very early to wake me. I would have normally been extremely aggravated and grumpy at being made to get up before eleven, but they brought food with them, so it was more acceptable.

"Is Lynk in today?" I wondered through a mouth of egg and toast.

Ellie, the smallest and younger of the two, shook her head, "No Lady, he is with the High Council today. Would you like some orange juice?"

I nodded, smiling appreciatively as she poured me some from a crystal jug. The other maid, whose name I've forgotten already, was laying out clothes on the bed. I glanced at them. Strong black trousers made from that scaly leather material and a loose shirt underneath a structured corset-like thing. The corset looked surprisingly comfortable, its function closer to armour as opposed to suffocating.

I frowned at the clothes, swallowed a mouthful then asked politely, "What are those clothes for?" I gestured towards them with a pointed finger.

"You are training today, Lady," the other maid answered respectfully. This whole 'Lady' thing was starting to do my head in. "Jayson Wanowa is expected in half an hour. Your father made contact last night."

I frowned again, utterly confused. Why would Lynk contact Jayson to come over here to train me? I knew he wouldn't allow me out of the Palace any time soon, and I know he said that if I wanted training my trainer would have to come over here, but I never in a million years expected him to go out of his way to make it happen. Was it guilt after last night's onslaught? I doubt it; there must be something in it for him.

"Would you like a bath now, my Lady?" Ellie asked, abruptly dragging me from my thoughts, her black eyes carefully avoiding the bruises on my face.

I shook my head, "I might as well wait till after training. I'm only going to get all hot and sweaty anyway."

"Would you like assistance getting dressed, my Lady?" wondered the other maid.

"No, I'm fine," I said, quite irritably. "And stop calling me 'my Lady'. I am just the same as both of you. I don't want to be treated any differently. Ignore Lynk and his superiority bullshit. With me you can do and say what you want."

The girls looked astounded, frozen in disbelief. I nodded in satisfaction. Good, at least they're finally listening to me.

Jayson wasn't late. When I arrived at the surprisingly large training courtyard with my stupid ignorant Protector, Jayson was already there, smiling brilliantly.

"Ruby," Jayson greeted, "I'm glad to see you're dressed more sensibly today." Then he saw my face properly and gasped.

"What happened?" he asked; his amber eyes wide with shock.

I didn't realise that I needed an excuse. I stammered under pressure, trying to think of a reason to have a bruised face. "Umm, I fell," I lied lamely.

"You fell," he repeated doubtingly.

"Um, yes, on a door knob." Did I really just say that? God, cliché or what?

"Ruby, you don't have to lie to me," he assured me, stepping closer and examining my face more carefully. He noticed my arm, cut by my attackers arrow; now neatly stitched up. He frowned in genuine concern, "Did Lynk do this to you?"

I stared at his soft amber eyes uncertainly. Could I trust him? I'd felt before that we'd had an immediate connection, but after what happened at the party...

"You can trust me," he said honestly, speaking low so my Protector couldn't hear, not that he was noticeably paying any attention anyway. "I know we had a bad start, but I am a good guy really. I am sorry."

He seemed so earnest and I went with my heart and said, "Lynk did part of it," I surrendered eventually, "Someone with an arrow did that to my arm yesterday."

Jayson withdrew a shaky breath, then went deadly serious, "Okay, tell me what happened with Lynk first."

"Nothing," I shrugged, "He just wants to assert his control over me I guess."

"He's like that," Jayson muttered. "I mean, I'm fairly well known here, hence I was the one to escort you to your First Flight. But even when he asked me to do that, it was scary. Almost like if I said no, he'd cut my head off." Then he smirked unexpectedly, "If he could."

"Yeah," I agreed, staring down at the floor feeling weak and shaken, not only from my problems with Lynk but also what I'd seen last night. Was it all my imagination? I didn't really want to tell Jayson in case I was wrong, but who else did I have to talk to? It's not like I could just stroll out of here and go and see my friends.

"What about your arm?" Jayson asked gently.

"No idea," I answered, feeling deflated, "It's just this guy, he's out to get me. He nearly killed me in the street the other day then just yesterday he shot arrows at me on my way back from being with you."

Jayson frowned, biting his bottom lip, "What does he look like?"

I shook my head, "I only saw his eyes. They were red."

His face lit up in comprehension suddenly, "Red? There's a guy on our hit-list with red eyes. And it's quite rare."

"Where did the hit-list come from?" I asked sceptically. Who would want to kill the guy trying to kill me? (Unless they want him dead for another reason.) Could it be Lynk? If my attacker had really known information on Lynk and is trying to get more through me, then surely Lynk would be the one to want him dead? Maybe.

Jayson pursed his lips, shaking his head slightly so the golden tendrils of his hair fell over his eyes, "We're never told the source. Most of us don't want to know. It's our job; I don't want to make it more complicated. But the Boss will know, I could ask."

I nodded gratefully. Actually, his words were the first helpful things I'd heard for days. Maybe I really could trust him. "Please. Are you coming tomorrow morning?"

"Yeah," he smiled suddenly, "For the rest of the week too." He glanced over to my Protector and whispered, "We probably ought to start, don't want your friend getting all suspicious." He winked. I smiled, feeling my body physically relaxing.

I dropped the bag I was carrying to the side, hesitating to remove the small blade that Kieran had left for me. Kian walked to the other end of the courtyard, instantly resuming his usual hands-at-sides--stick-up-arse position. He watched silently.

"You want to learn how to use that?" Jayson asked, gesturing towards the blade which I was still eyeing uncertainly from its position in the top of my open bag.

"Yesterday you didn't even want to look at those on the wall."

I glanced over at the longer scarier blades hung up high on the wall of this training courtyard. Yes, they looked daunting, but having survived last night I wanted to know exactly how to defend myself in case something happens again. There is no way I am ever going to let that horrible, vindictive man, strangle me, again.

"Change of perspective," I answered eventually.

Jayson smiled that good-natured smile and said, "Well, first let's warm up."

We did a series of cardio exercises to begin with, to get my heart pumping. I realised just how unfit I was. I was doubled-over gasping after twenty minutes of sprinting, jumping and sit-ups. Despite the new exciting transformation of my body, making it leaner and more developed after my death; it still didn't tolerate exercise.

Apparently Jayson was going to ask Lynk if he could take me flying properly, teaching me techniques in the air. The only problem was that I'd probably be forced to have a guard with me. And that was even more humiliating.

"I'll send a message to Lynk," Jayson offered. "After all, he must want you fit and trained otherwise he wouldn't have sent for me today."

I never thought of it like that, "But why would he want me trained?" I wondered, more to myself than Jayson.

Jayson shrugged. "Maybe it's just for practical reasons; I mean what use are you if you've been butchered alive by some idiot you wouldn't let buy you a drink?"

I laughed, "I doubt anyone would kill me for that."

"You never know," he grinned then grew thoughtful. "Is it very different here from where you're from?"

"Very," I nodded unnecessarily, "at home all you need to walk outside with, weapon-wise, is an umbrella."

His laugh was light and pleasant, "Does it rain a lot there?"

"Jayson," I informed him seriously, "in England, it never stops."

We practiced a few of the blocks and attacks he'd showed me yesterday, and then finally I was allowed to get my blade out. Using some of the strikes and defences I'd already been taught, Jayson transferred the basic techniques into weapon-combat moves. Most were pretty similar only you had a knife in your hand. He was extremely helpful, explaining everything in acute detail.

Thirty minutes before the double-lesson was finished he passed me another blade and said, "Now let's apply it in a real circumstance. These blades are specifically blunted for sparring, but they will still hurt if you swing them about hard enough. Just warning you," he smiled, "if you hit me, I'll hit you back."

"Okay," I agreed warily, taking what he'd called a Gaborah blade; a type I'd seen Kieran using. It was longer, thinner and curved at the end, unlike a normal blade.

He swung forwards with his blade and automatically my reflexes kicked in. I blocked it high and swung over the top, he grinned excitedly, bashing the blunted sword to the side. He swung forwards again, this time low, and with a flick of my wrist I knocked it away. Just when I thought I was getting the hang of it, I had a blade at my throat.

"That was actually really good," Jayson sounded surprised, releasing me.

"Is that a compliment?" I asked.

"Maybe," he returned the friendly smile, "if you can do it again. You never know, it could just have been beginner's luck."

"I hope not."

We sparred for a long time, while my reactions slowed in exhaustion and I continued ending up on the floor. I didn't win, but did corner him a few times and I was getting better...slowly. When the lesson eventually ended I threw myself dramatically to the floor and chucked down a whole bottle of water to try and replace that which I'd sweated out. He agreed that I was probably too shattered to practice sparking any fires today. Thank God.

"Well," Jayson said, "I guess I better get going."

"Wait," I said suddenly, standing up and leading him over to the other side of the courtyard, away from Kian, who now had his back to us at the entrance but was probably still listening. Once I decided he was out of earshot I looked at Jayson. "I can trust you, can't I?" I said slowly, glazing sternly and seriously at his angelic face.

He hesitated for a moment, thinking what to say. Then carefully spoke in low hushed tones, "I can't make you trust me, Ruby. But I hope you can."

I took a deep breath and made a quick instinctive decision that came from my gut.

"Alright," I said, "I saw something last night."

Jayson listened curiously, leaning closer. "Go on," he urged.

"Right, this is going to sound crazy but I was out in the woods last night, behind the Palace, when I saw something strange. I'm not even sure if it was just my imagination or what, but," I took another steadying breath, "it didn't look normal. I only saw the back of it, but it had wings like a bat; all leathery and crooked."

Jayson stared at me apathetically and I prayed in that moment for him to do anything but laugh. Fortunately he didn't. He was incredibly serious; more so than I'd ever seen him before, "Are you certain?"

I nodded, "I am. I wasn't supposed to be outside but I couldn't sleep and wanted to fly. Then I saw it. I'm sorry," I apologised, feeling I'd inflicted all my potential craziness onto him, "but I'm trapped here. I had no one else to tell."

"No," Jayson's voice was darker now, saturated with a serious intensity. "I'm glad you did. And you're not crazy. It might be the Barlayic. But if it is, then that's not good. Not good at all."

"The Barlayic?" why did that word keep coming up?

"Daemons," Jayson answered, his amber eyes glancing at me. "In the ancient times that's what they called them. Back when people thought we were Angels."

I withdrew a shaky breath, so it hadn't just been my fatigue-induced imagination. Daemons! Could that be possible? I battered myself internally, snubbing myself: *You're a bloody Phoenix, you idiot. You Change into a massive red bird and have a siren's voice and you're questioning the existence of other creatures, Biblical, mythical or whatever?* I felt so overwhelmed. Is anything impossible anymore?

"Okay," Jayson had steadied himself, "This is serious. If you're telling the truth, then I have no idea what that means. A stray Daemon in the City just doesn't happen." He took a deep breath, "I'll have to meet you tonight, at the same time and place as last night. Don't say another word to anyone until we know for certain."

I nodded, suddenly terrified.

"Look, I have to go. What time and where?"

I explained as much as I could then he left. I stumbled back to my room, confused and utterly terrified. Daemons,

Barlayic; whatever they were. What were they doing here, in the Palace grounds? I knew I needed to tell Kieran and the others but I had no way of leaving the Palace. There were too many guards during the day and Kian would certainly not let me go. I spent the rest of the day thinking it over and trying to look it up in the library. Nothing was ever of any use.

Lynk didn't find me when he arrived back. I was glad. I didn't want another abusive night. I went to bed early in the afternoon then stayed up until it was time to once again sneak out. I put on the same outfit I wore for training, even wearing a weapons belt, containing the only small blade I had. Then I edged to the door, singing my sweet sedative lullaby in the darkness. My voice was quite scary to behold. It was like I wasn't even there. It was a ghost of a voice, so quiet but deadly, childlike in a creepy horror-movie kind of way. It did the trick though.

I followed the shadows through the building, tracing them with my fingers and hiding at heart-pounding intervals. When I finally made it outside, into the camouflage of the trees, I waited anxiously for Jayson. My heart drummed in my chest, surely people could hear it? Then all of a sudden, I spotted him in the darkness.

"Jayson," I whispered my heart thumping.

He was crouched down behind some thick brambles and when he heard me he put a finger to his lips, immediately gesturing me over. Nodding understandingly I crept over with cautious steps. I kneeled down on the damp earth next to him, he pointed forwards instantly. I glanced in the direction and my whole body froze in horror.

Jayson leaned closer to me with a worried expression and deeply disturbed amber eyes. He whispered so quietly I had to strain to listen. "That's not a Daemon," he shivered visibly, "I don't know what it is."

There were two of the things tonight, scarily not that far away. I lowered myself down, deeper into the concealing thorns, a cold sheen of sweat developing on my forehead. The things seemed larger tonight, taller than a full grown man, maybe seven foot tall? All I saw was those strange mutilated wings and shivered, a freeze descending to my core. You could see the crooked bones through the diaphanous membrane of their wings. As my eyes adjusted to the darkness I noticed something else. Though the membrane appeared to be like wet leather draped over the deformed skeletal frame, a thick skin like the webbing of a frogs feet, the wings also had the occasional underdeveloped feather piercing up through the flesh. These intermittent feathers were a dirty black/brown and looked like insulating down feathers except there was only ever one, alone; like they were falling out.

One of the creatures hesitated abruptly, I stopped breathing. It paused, seemingly sniffing the air. It turned around and I cringed, swallowing a petrified breath.

It was all sharp edges. It had long jagged claws on its bare feet and hands. Those ugly bat-like wings sprouted from its crooked back. Its skin had a waxy yellow tinge over a dirty brown base and it barely stretched over its flattened skull. Jutting from that skull were two massive curling horns approximately thirty inches long, nearly catching its wings. Its eyeballs were purple with yellow slits instead of irises.

One stepped closer, its lipless mouth expanding all the way to its pointed ears, revealing rows of needle thin teeth. I swear I could see something squirming between the gaps, like trapped insects. I felt a swift overpowering urge to be sick churning in my stomach. It glanced upwards suspiciously, into the branching rafters of the trees, sticking out a long forked tongue like that of a snake. Its body was wrong, coated in blackened scar-like marks. It seemed to be crouched down but actually was stood with an arched spine sticking up through its flesh. It looked starved, the way its ribcage jutted out of position, but I could guarantee it was well fed.

The thing's hideous slitted eyes scanned the environment one more time before it continued forwards. Jayson glanced at me, hinting that we should follow them. I nodded a reluctant agreement, my hands shaking violently. We carefully stood up, following surreptitiously from a distance for a long time, through the forest and up the steady decline of the southern valley wall. I followed Jayson's silent, assuring lead; you could tell he was used to this kind of thing, though perhaps not following these kinds of *things.*

The trees eventually broke away to reveal a steep rock incline. We waited in silence behind a large cluster of boulders. The creatures entered what looked like a huge cavity in the rocky wall above us.

I turned to Jayson, my breath coming in shallow rapid rasps now that the *things* were out of sight. "Do you see what I mean?" I said in hushed, panic tones.

"Yeah," he said back, his eyes constantly flickering around for danger. "But those things aren't Daemons, at least not fully." His face was pulled taught with strain and fear, "This is weird, really weird."

"What do you mean when you say they're not fully Daemons," I asked anxiously.

He shook his head. "I don't know. But I've seen Daemons, they're smaller stupider creatures. They've got scales and tails and live alone with lesser Daemons which they eat on occasion. These things," he shivered involuntary, "these things look almost intelligent. They look, I can't believe I'm saying this; like half breeds."

My mind clicked on immediately, "You mean..." I trailed off, choking back my words, "They're part, what...us?"

Jayson shrugged. "I don't know. But that would mean someone would have to have sex with a Daemon, surely nobody's that disgusting?" he cringed, pulling a disgusted face. He stilled, glancing back at the rocky cave.

The creatures were emerging again. I watched silently, my stomach churning again, my muscles clenching with unreleased adrenalin. The creatures stalked off, back into the woods in the direction we were hiding. We shuffled around carefully, adopting a better position. They walked straight by us in the darkness, disappearing into the forest as a chill ran over me.

"Right," Jayson whispered, "We need to go inside."

I gulped, my voice shaky but serious, "Okay, let's go."

Chapter Twenty-Two

As we quickly climbed the sloping ascent, our eyes flickered nervously around, sceptical of danger. We entered the huge rocky cavity in the valley wall, a trapping darkness descending upon us. Our feet were slow, hesitant on the icy surface. Obviously it had not snowed inside, but the ice had still wriggled its way in, lacing the entrance with hazardous patterns invisible in the blackness. It was like a fog, the dark, a thick suffocating mass that surrounded you so tightly it was like drowning. Even my sensitive eyes were finding it difficult to adjust.

The freezing air burnt my lungs. I had a seriously bad feeling about this. My anxiety showed in my clumsy footsteps as I slipped intermittently on the ice. Jayson grabbed my arm when I tripped badly. He caught me instantly, whispering that it was okay. My heart was pounding erratically, sweat drenching my clothes. I was terrified. I ran my hand down Jayson's arm, firmly grasping his hand not just for physical support. He squeezed it reassuringly then I felt him lifting his other hand. I heard a distinct snap echo against the walls, amplifying the snap of Jayson's fingers as he sparked a light. Pulling his fingers apart like retracting magnets the small flicker of flame expanded, casting a weak but warm glow on the rocks around me. We glanced around, scanning for anything of significance, my vision concentrating on some stone steps at the other end of the cave.

I pointed over to them and Jayson nodded; we walked forwards. I realised they were cut into the rock and went down into the ground like a cellar in an old house. We edged closer uncertainly, Jayson taking the lead. We carefully climbed our way down the steps, realising that here we were in the most danger; if someone came now we had nowhere to hide. I held onto Jayson's hand tightly, ignoring the sweatiness between our fingers. I was scared, there was no denying that. I was also paranoid; I kept glancing back behind me, into the deceptive darkness, thinking I'd heard something other than the rapid beating of my own heart.

There weren't many steps and we soon discovered what must have been a much larger room. I shivered in the stagnant air, following Jayson's light as it licked the walls. I could hear something, a faint disturbing scratching, almost like nails against metal. My fear picked up again. Jayson immediately pointed the light in the direction of the source. It was silent again, all we saw before us was rocky floor then the more distant bottom half of table legs. We edged closer cautiously. The sudden eerie silence was worse than the darkness.

Then abruptly Jayson lifted the light, urging me forwards as I reluctantly tugged against his hand, wanting to leave. The firelight spread up a high table, filtering across the bottom of what looked like a metal cage. He took a deep steadying breath then lifted the light one more time to reveal what lurked, scratching inside the cage. I yanked free of Jayson's grasp like lightning, shuffling back instinctively. Jayson flinched as the light settled on a pair of purple, slitted eyes and a terrifying screech filled the air. It was loud, horrifyingly so and the creature grasped the bars of the cage it was contained in, its clawed hands tugging at the bars as if it was in extreme pain. Its fingers were too long, all bony and crooked.

My hands pulled over my ears at the second assault of screeching. I tried to shield out the shrill piercing noise. The creature thrashed about wildly in the large cage. It had a flattened head and long horns. Its body was deformed, its limbs oddly contorted and short, thick brown leather-like skin stretching over prominent bone. As it scrambled back to the other side of the cage and I gained the courage to venture forwards–slightly, I noticed it was about my size. Its legs were unnaturally long, the flesh on them rigid and hard and its feet were like its hands. But what I focused on most was a huge rounded stomach that protruded unnaturally far from its body.

My only guess could have been that it was heavily pregnant.

I glanced over at Jayson with a horrified expression. When he looked back his face mirrored mine, "You see," he uttered, his voice saturated with a worried confusion, "that's a Daemon. Those things outside were not Daemons."

I swallowed anxiously as Jayson walked, parallel to the table, downwards, lifting the light to reveal cage after cage of the screaming creatures. Judging by their reaction I guessed that they didn't like the light. We kept going, counting twenty, thirty cages just in one row. All had the same unnaturally gigantic stomachs.

As we came to the last cage in the row, I whispered, "Jayson, I want to leave."

He nodded uncertainly, his eyes completely distracted, his thoughts elsewhere. Gingerly we crept back towards the steps, but then Jayson extinguished the light suddenly, grabbing a rough hold of my hand and pushing me back behind a narrow section of rock. My heart thumping dramatically again, I held my breath and listened. Scratching footsteps stomped down the steps, followed by the sounds of grunts and heavy breathing. My limbs froze, feeling a powerful impulse to curl up tighter. Jayson was frozen too, his body so still, it morphed into the rock.

We waited. Adrenalin pumped in my veins. We only had two choices now, one: try to sneak out the cave in the darkness, or two: wait until they go, which could be never. I decided not to risk it, buckling myself down for a long, intense wait. Jayson followed suit. There was rattling in the darkness, every now and then a short shrill screech of the Daemons. I cringed at every sound, flinching at every footstep that came closer than the previous one. My back began to ache in the awkward position I'd been put in. We waited, unable to see or understand what was happening. My body shook, the adrenalin preparing me to kick-start at the opportune moment.

It slowly went silent. A long gap of silence, where had they gone? When had I last heard them, how long ago was it? I couldn't think. Jayson nudged me uncertainly; I guessed he was wondering the same thing as me. I shrugged in the darkness, my shoulders touching his so he knew. Do we go? In the end he made the decision, he touched my hand slightly, urging me forwards. Extremely slowly, I straightened out on my hands and knees on the cold uneven floor. Jayson followed behind me. Crawling as silently as possible, we cautiously edged towards the only feeble light source, coming from the top of the stone steps at the other end of the room.

I barely breathed. The atmosphere was so intense. A pebble rolled across the floor; I flinched, stilling, but Jayson forced me forwards. We were nearly at the door; we'd have to make a run for it. All of a sudden a monster screamed in the cage above me and that was it, we exploded into action, racing forwards. We scrambled up the steps, hearing a commotion behind us, the sound of claws scratching the surface of the rock coming our way. My heart was flying now. I couldn't move fast enough. I was trapped in my own weak body. Low roaring screams bellowed behind me.

We'd reached the top of the steps, racing through the rock cavity. Before I knew it my body was reacting. I could feel a fiery energy building in my body before I even gave it permission. As we raced outside, the adrenalin was causing my body to Change. I could feel it. The fear was overwhelming and before I knew it I was leaping into the air, my clothes tearing underneath me. I was flying instantly.

Vital moments later, I noticed Jayson beside me. In bird form he was glorious; a beautiful golden colour with long slicing wings. I barely had time to register this; my mind voice came out in a panicked shout, *I'm sorry Jayson, I didn't mean to Change.*

No worries, Ruby, he said back, *just fly faster, I don't know if those things can fly and I don't want them following us.*

We raced through the skies, my wings beating faster and faster, exhaustion already plaguing me. My breath came fast and hard, my body was not used to this.

Do you know anywhere that's safe? Jayson wondered, realising that we weren't being followed but that we were heading nowhere.

No, I replied, even my mind voice seemed breathless, *but we need to go see the Ashaiks. Head west, we'll go to Ebony's.*

I can't go there. If you remember me and Kierakai do not get on.

Well for tonight you'll have to, I snapped, *this is important.*

He didn't argue, instead continued in a sulky silence. We flew, slowing, straight to Ebony's homely cottage. Landing outside, realising it was ridiculously late and I had no clothes. I frowned irritably then distanced myself from Jayson to Change, telling him to meet me in a minute on the right hand side of the house, where the training courtyard was. Once back in human form I looked around for something to cover myself with. I headed to the training courtyard, slipping inside the weapon's pavilion, looking for anything other than blades to clothe myself with. On the wall was a large leather wing brace, similar to the one Jayson had worn tonight–I bet he had a spare set of clothes. I lay the straps and buckles against my skin, there was not enough material to cover me in the slightest; it looked more like a restraint suit.

"Well I'm up for a bit of bondage if you are." A voice said from the other side of the room, it was deep and full of an amused arrogance.

I turned around, dropping the brace and trying desperately to hide myself. My cheeks burned brilliantly as Kieran sat on the other side of the room, on a bench, smoking God knows what from a fat roll up. I'd never even seen him as I came in. His eyes swooped up and down my body naughtily, an amused twist at his lips. I shivered feverously, feeling his gaze like it was his fingers he was running over my naked body. Suddenly Jayson walked in from the other side of the room, he had no shoes, but was wearing jeans and a shirt. My face burned even redder. Bloody hell, why don't Nik and Chara come in and see the show as well while we're at it?

Kieran frowned at Jayson, taking another relaxing drag, his voice perfectly calm. "I am not, however, up for a threesome. Two girls?" he considered, "Yes, that's always fun. But I do not cross swords with another man."

Jayson just stood there too, staring at me. For God's sake: *men*. "Are either of you going to give me your shirt," I said through clenched teeth, "Or are you just going to carry on staring."

"I'm going to carry on staring," Kieran said, smirking. He was really enjoying the embarrassment on my face.

Jayson tugged his shirt over his head, throwing it at me immediately. He at least had the decency to look ashamed of himself. I put it on instantly. It was massive on me, concealing down to the tops of my thighs. Kieran however, was still looking at me as if I was naked. Why the hell was he still up? Stupid insomniac freak.

"Kieran we came because we need to tell you something," I said seriously.

"If it's that you two are shagging, I really couldn't care less," he offered. I glanced at Jayson, cheeks flaring but Jayson just shrugged good-naturedly. He was used to Kieran's manners.

"Look, mate," Jayson began calmly, "Here's the thing-"but was interrupted.

Kieran whirled on him furiously, his voice suddenly dangerous, "I am not your mate. Don't insult me you piece of crap. I don't give a shit what you have to say."

"How many times can I say I'm sorry?" Jayson snapped angrily.

"At least one more," Kieran glared, "This time on your hands and knees."

"You can't keep pretending I don't exist to you," Jayson warned.

Kieran laughed, "I'm not pretending you don't exist. I'm pretending you exist somewhere else; like in the bottom of a well or on the end of my boot."

"You still hate me, don't you Kieran? Even after all this time." I heard a twist in Jayson's voice I'd never heard before.

"Okay," Kieran said, "I changed my mind. I *am* going to pretend you don't exist."

I stepped forwards, my anger still dominating my body from Kieran's unashamed staring. "Kieran shut up and listen," I practically growled, staring straight into those devilish green eyes. "Yesterday, I snuck out of the Palace at night. I was alone and thought I saw something in the forest, something strange. The next morning I told Jayson what I saw and he said to meet me at the same time and place again that night. This time there were two of them."

Kieran, despite himself, looked interested, "Go on." He instructed patronisingly.

"They were, we think, Daemon half-breeds," I said nervously.

Kieran just laughed arrogantly, taking one last drag then stubbing the end. He threw it out the window.

"We're being serious Kieran," Jayson said honestly. "They were taller than Daemons, very intelligent, with wings, horns and talons. I was shocked, but what's more, we followed them underground where there were hundreds of cages of real Daemons; pregnant real Daemons. We got trapped and had to run out, they nearly caught us."

Jayson gestured down at his ankle, where I suddenly realised there was blood soaking into the denim of his jeans. My eyes widened, but already Kieran had a serious expression and was waving us to follow him into the house.

At the foot of the stairs, he shouted obnoxiously at the top of his voice, "Wake up every one; get your lazy asses out of bed! Our dear friend Ruby is here and she's brought her girlfriend."

Eventually everyone stumbled awake and grudgingly came downstairs, hair a mess, sleep in their eyes, to see what the commotion was all about. Grumpily they piled onto the sofas in the living room. I realised that someone was missing.

"Where's Briseis?" I wondered.

Chara, yawning wildly in a dressing gown, rubbing her face as she spoke, said, "She didn't say she was going out tonight."

Ebony frowned, "She was in bed last thing I knew. But she wasn't in her room."

Everyone looked to Adrian, all thinking the same as me, but he shook his head. "She wasn't with me."

Nik shrugged, he looked, for once, grumpy. "Why the hell have you woken us up, Kieran?" He glanced suspiciously at Jayson, who sat uncomfortably beside me.

"Sorry," I apologised, "it was me who came over." I quickly explained what happened to us and everyone stared back at me dumbly, disbelieving.

"You're being serious?" Chara said slowly and when I nodded she took a deep calming breath, "Oh my God. What does this mean?"

"I don't know," I frowned, "But it ain't good. My attacker had been right."

"Speaking of," Kieran interjected, "Did you know that Lynk's called a hit on him."

I stared at Kieran in confusion. "What?"

"Yeah, my hit has red eyes. Red eyes are not common. And Lynk's the source. I looked through the files on the Boss's desk," he answered.

I frowned then remembered that Jayson had mentioned something about that; I doubted he had time to look into it further. I asked "Did it say the reason why?"

Kieran shook his head, "Nah, I doubt the Boss even knows that. The only reason I guessed that the source was Lynk was because it was from a Slave who used to work at my Palace but got called over to yours before we left; Evelyn or something."

The name sparked a flash of memory. *She is the High Slave of the Fire Palace.*

"What happened to your face?" Chara said warily, her eyes settling on the prominent bruises on my upper cheekbone and eye.

"Just my father going on a power-rant," I sighed.

"Bloody hell, Ruby," she came forward, lifting her hands to my face with delicate precision to get a better look. She examined me thoroughly, then let go. "Didn't you try and stop him?"

"Of course I did," I frowned. "I actually used my voice on him a little."

"Did it work?" Nik wondered.

My frown deepened embarrassedly, "Well, it stunned him I think; but ultimately no." Kieran smirked and I whirled on him with a vengeful fury still brewing from earlier. "Don't you dare smirk Kierakai; my gift is a lot more powerful than you think; I can sedate two full grown guards with just a few notes so shut the hell up."

Even Nik looked dubious, "Really?"

I tried very hard not to be irritated by Nik; after all I really did like him. "Yes," I said slowly, "that's how I can sneak out of my room at night."

"Are you sure you didn't just kill them?" Kieran wondered ignorantly.

I glared, "Yes. They were both wide awake this morning."

"I think I hear a hint of hostility in your voice, princess," Kieran noted innocently. "Life at your Palace not as fun as you thought it would be?" he smirked. "Did someone put vegetables under your mattress again?"

"I'm only hostile now I'm with you and your lovely attitude," I smiled charmingly.

"Wow," Nik breathed, looking thoughtful and ignoring us both completely. "Do you think Lynk can sedate people?"

"Probably," I admitted reluctantly, "though it was my mother who taught me; I just didn't realise at the time." I cupped my hands, intertwining my fingers.

"Can you show us this place then?" Nik asked seriously.

I glanced over at Jayson, who appeared very uncomfortable. "I can, but I'm not going back in," he said finally.

"And I'm not going at all," I said, shivering at the memory of waiting in the dark.

Nik took a deep breath, knowing that he would have to be the one to go; there was no way Kieran or Adrian would go with Jayson. Then, to my surprise, as Jayson and Nik got up, both brothers stood too. My nervousness showed in my expression. As they made their way to the door, Jayson smiled a reassuring smile.

"You look worried," he commented.

"Well, it was a bit dangerous, if you remember," I said.

He smiled, a relaxed look coming across his laid-back face. "I'll be fine, but maybe we should give training a miss tomorrow. I'm sure you need to head back anyway."

I nodded, "Yeah, but I'll probably stay the night here, if I'm allowed." I glanced at Ebony who nodded consentingly, "I really don't want to go back alone tonight."

"Okay then," Jayson smiled one last time. "See you then. And hey, maybe you can practice your voice on me some time," he winked. "Be a fun experiment."

I shook my head, grinning. "Go on."

He continued out the door followed quickly by Nik and Adrian. As Kieran cockily strode by I raised my hand to stop him momentarily. I turned on him, my smile dissolving rapidly under his intense stare. "Be good to Jayson." I warned. "He's my friend. Don't drop him off the edge of a cliff again."

Kieran raised his eyebrows, uttering under his breath "Friend." He scoffed. "I know why you like him, and it's got nothing to do with friendship."

I glared at him. "Why would you care why I like him?"

"I wouldn't."

"Good." I snapped.

"Good." He repeated then continued on down the hallway. God he was so infuriating. I wanted to scream.

"Try not to get eaten by a Daemon," I called after him, "You'll give it indigestion."

He turned around and winked, "Don't worry, if it's hungry, I'll make sure I offer it your girlfriend first; just to save its stomach, of course."

I turned around and stomped off in a huff. The girls were already going upstairs, probably going back to bed. I followed suit; irritated. In that moment I wanted Kieran to get eaten; just a little, maybe a leg or something. At least.

The next morning after breakfast I stumbled outside, finding the house utterly empty. Briseis hadn't been in her bed; Nik, Chara and Adrian were nowhere to be seen and Ebony had left to go to town, taking Libby, after we'd eaten. I found Kieran outside, bizarrely hauling a massive hunk of ice across the training courtyard.

I stared at him in confusion, "Kieran, what are you doing?"

He didn't flinch at the sudden sound of my voice. "Hauling ice," he answered.

I rolled my eyes, but decided to save that conversation for later; there were more pressing matters to discuss. "So, what happened last night?"

Kieran shrugged noncommittally, "Nothing much. I saw the Daemons in the cages but no half-breeds."

"But what do you think?" I said anxiously.

He didn't turn as he continued to push the heavy ice one last time, positioning it correctly. It was massive, about as tall as me and triple my width. Then he spoke, finally glancing at me, "I think it needs looking into."

"Another thing," I remembered, "Lynk has an entire floor that no one is allowed access to, there must be something going on up there."

Kieran didn't answer. He seemed really distant.

I thought for a moment, "Maybe I could find out more." I had an idea, "I'll sneak upstairs tonight and..."

Kieran's beautiful face was abruptly furious, the distance in his eyes shattering as he whirled on me, "No way."

"What?" I thought he wanted me to find out information.

"This is worse than I thought it would be. You don't know what's happening up there; you don't have experience with this kind of thing, and, quite frankly, you're about as subtle as a bull in a china shop."

My eyes narrowed, "You think you're more *qualified* than me?"

Kieran stared at me for a long, seemingly everlasting moment, looking as if he wanted to say something but was unsure. Then he sighed, and obviously said the total opposite. "Yes," he answered, squaring his shoulders firmly. I noticed the glint of his golden marked chain, "you are not allowed to go anywhere near that floor; nor anywhere near those Daemons."

"And that's an order, from who?" I questioned maliciously. Once again he was attempting to boss me around. Well, screw him.

"Your real protector." His eyes smouldered ferociously, burrowing into my very soul. "I am your healer and I am telling you. There is no point arguing. If it means chaining you to the goddamn floor, you're going to be safe."

You know, if he hadn't had said that, I probably would have listened to him.

Chapter Twenty-Three

I tried, petulantly, to ignore Kieran. I folded my arms across my chest irritably, my bottom lip jutting out like a sulky teenager. I stared unyieldingly at the massive chunk of sparkling glacier ice.

To be honest though, I lost my concentration when he took his shirt off.

My body instantly went rigid, tingling sensations exploded across my skin. I heard the material drop to the floor and held my ground, determined to ignore him and not stare at his body. I fixed my eyes firmly on the ice.

I jumped, startled, when the sudden sound of tearing flesh pieced my ears.

My neck snapped up at the horrible noise. I gasped as Kieran's deadly black wings gouged from his shoulders like cutting blades. His tattoos rippled across his arms, dancing over his biceps like waves. Those devilish wings spread from his muscular back while simultaneously he kept his human body intact. How he did it, I had no idea. His shadowy wings seemed even more gigantic now, dwarfing his mortal frame, hell, dwarfing the courtyard.

"How are you doing that?" I asked, sounding falsely uninterested. Blood dribbled down his back from the fresh indignant wounds.

"It's been a while since I've done it, not since England," Kieran grunted nonchalantly–like he didn't even feel the pain, "that's why I'm bleeding."

"But why are you doing it?" I demanded, stunned.

He smirked "Don't look too horrified Princess; you'll have to do this too."

My eyes widened in shock, "Why?"

His expression told me I was annoying him. "Ask Google, I'm busy."

"No wonder people thought we were Angels," I murmured under my breath. I could only imagine how breath-taking Jayson would be with his golden wings displayed like that; a perfect Angel incarnate. Kieran was the opposite, his wings so stunningly black, cuttingly deadly and dangerous. Complete with the smug defiant twist of his gorgeous lips, the only angel I could picture him being was Lucifer as he was cast out of Heaven.

I watched silently as Kieran folded his majestic wings forwards, wrapping them around the hunk of jagged diaphanous ice, smoothing over the uneven surface. He was polishing the ice with the flat side of his blade-like wings. Slowly the ice became a frictionless shape. Then Kieran used the tips of his wings–so dangerously sharp–to furrow deeper gashes. The ice artfully chiselled away to reveal what soon became identifiable as a snowflake.

I was so enthralled by Kieran's developing masterpiece that I found myself lost in his work. Fascinated, I digested the concentration on his gorgeous face, the way his shimmering black feathers confidently sliced and carved. It was flawless; a beautifully intricate snowflake chiselled perfectly from the ice. It rose incredibly, just above my head. Light filtered through it, casting sprinklings of colourful spectrums, it was as if it were carved from diamond. I couldn't believe how detailed it was, so many polished facets...I gaped at the sculpture in absolute astonishment.

Once he had finished, half an hour or so later, I was abruptly snared from my trance by Ebony returning from town.

"Ruby?" she called from the kitchen, her eyes wide, "What are you still doing here? Lynk will kill you if you stay much longer."

"Yeah," I called back grudgingly, "I'll go. Don't worry"

I felt something tickle the back of my neck as I got up to leave. The silky texture was unmistakeable, the soft side of Kieran's feathers. I didn't look back. His touch whispered one thing; be responsible. I ignored the gesture stubbornly. I was going upstairs tonight. I had to know what was up there.

My maids were gone. I was finally alone.

Once I'd arrived at the Palace it became apparent that the Slaves–to my astonishment–had actually covered for me. My maids, Evelyn and even the two guards from last night had promised to keep it quiet. I guessed it would be their necks on the line too if Lynk had discovered the truth. He'd left early this morning, before anyone had even realised I was gone. Evelyn particularly was angry at me, making me promise not to sneak out again, but overall I was quite happy with the result.

The day dragged by slowly. I had little to do, but as night came, I felt it had flown by. I converted my plan of action into a few simple steps as the opportune time approached.

Step one; get dressed again.

I pulled on my dark Phoenix Gear–my second set as the first, unfortunately, had been ripped last night–and rummaged around for a plain black shirt, scraping back my conspicuous red hair.

Step two; make sure I'm completely awake and prepared.

I hurried into the bathroom, refreshing my face with chillingly cold water. *Must wake up, must wake up,* I thought repeatedly. I needed an energy drink, the kind filled with caffeine, sugar and everything bad for you. *Shut up,* I battered myself, *I can do this without Redbull.* After all, I already have wings.

I was a little hysterical in my nervousness.

Step three; wait for the appropriate time.

I sat down on my bed, reading so I would stay awake, then I waited. Time slowly trudged past. After two hours had dragged by-and the whole building was apparently asleep-I emerged again.

Step four: remove the guards.

I crept over to the door leading to my balcony but halted when a dangerous glint caught my eye. Impulsively I followed the light, discovering one of Jayson's live training blades sitting innocently on my desktop; he'd forgotten it yesterday morning. Deliberating, I wondered was it best to take a weapon…

Maybe I was being stupid, maybe this really wasn't a good idea. I mean, Kieran was probably right, I wasn't trained and I didn't really know what I was doing. I shuddered at the consequences if I were caught.

I shook my head furiously. I'm not going back now. I picked up the blade.

Shuffling out onto my balcony as quietly as physically possible, I slowly crouched down onto the cool stone floor. My eyes searched the darkness, discovering guarding warriors directly below my balcony.

Instantaneously I opened my mouth, feeling the icy wind trickle straight down my throat like I'd just swallowed an ice cube.

My lullaby echoed over the wind, distorting the atmosphere; the breeze carried the soft enchanting melody. I felt it gently touch the guards below, so tentatively encouraging them to listen that they barely even noticed.

They slipped into a dreamless slumber. I turned and walked down towards the other end of the balcony. This seemed far too easy.

Step five: get onto the top floor.

Swallowing, I carefully pulled myself up onto the railing that ran the perimeter of my balcony, gravitating myself, grasping the edge of the wall. Praying it was stable enough, I climbed on top of the large wooden swing that perched patiently at one end of the balcony. Standing up straight, my balance wavered as the swing shuddered under my weight.

I glanced around for something to grab onto and luckily spotted a stone pattern that was carved up the building. My heart was beating fast now. I roughly wedged my foot into a small crevice in the stonework. Pausing momentarily as I searched for another suitable hole, I quickly found a piece of rock shaped like a flower. I grabbed onto it, hauling my body up. Finding another indentation I climbed up further, fiercely clinging on. Using the stonework I eventually scrambled into a position where I was next to the railing of the balcony above mine.

Stretching my neck I glanced into the room. Fortunately it was deserted. I swung myself up and over, landing professionally onto the stone floor. Staying cautiously crouched, I double-checked the room was empty. It appeared to be, so I carefully slid the glass doors aside.

The room was almost the same shape as mine, though no ornaments lay on the furniture. The large plain bed was made perfectly with hospital corners and obviously hadn't been slept in. Carefully, I tiptoed across the floor, pressing my ear against the door. Focusing my sensitive hearing, I listened for movement on the other side. Nothing. Nothing at all. For some reason this unnerved me. Fear is good, I tried to persuade myself, it makes you react faster. Then it hit me; I hadn't thought about what I would do once I actually got up here. I didn't have a step six. I'm such an idiot.

Instead of waiting for a full-blown panic-attack I delicately let the door creak open a crack. It was an empty hallway. Reassured, I slipped out into the dark corridor. Unlit lamps proceeded all the way down the hallway, corresponding between heavy wooden doors. The whole place was empty, dark and lifeless; like a lonely planet.

My mind was buzzing, electrically alive; every nerve in my body was charged, perhaps if I clicked my fingers sparks would fly.

Surreptitiously creeping down the shadowed corridor, I peeked into the occasional door. Predominantly they were identical to the first, empty untouched bedrooms. However, when I glanced into the last room, right at the very end of the hallway, I stopped.

No lamps or incandescent orbs lined the walls, but it wasn't the dreary darkness that made me pause initially. It was the smell. The walls were dripping with the rancid stench of inhumane living conditions. I gagged automatically, but as my nostrils adjusted I noticed things.

The one thick circular window at the far side of the room let an insignificant amount of moonlight struggle through, casting down like a gothic special effect in a horror movie, catching the sharp edges of mortal instruments. Knives, shackles, whips and various other lethal weapons were scattered across the scathed surface of a table. Crude-looking torture devices were stained with crusty reddish liquid. Edging closer, there was no mistaking that sickening metallic scent; Blood. I gagged again, bile rising in my throat as I breathed in the revolting odour. Losing my balance as I coughed, I stumbled forwards. It was what I imagined a slave ship would have smelt like. My legs bashed into something heavy on the floor, it rang like metal.

I'd had enough of the creepy darkness. It was as if it were sticking to my skin, wrapping itself around me with suffocating tightness, like a choking poisonous fog. I snapped my fingers with the charged energy in my system to evoke fire, relieved when the light burnt comfortingly above my palms.

I'd stood on some old-fashioned iron clamps that hold prisoners down by their waists and legs. The kind you see preserved in ancient castles. Smeared gruesome hand prints stretched out towards me in blood on the floor; as if reaching out for help. Shredded feathers were nestled into the liquid.

The worst part was that this blood was fresh.

I heard a quiet creak behind me, like the shift of feet on a wooden surface. Instantly I turned to the source, but found nothing. *Maybe it was just a rat or something,* I thought optimistically.

The hair rose on the back of my neck. I knew something was wrong. I listened intently, my heart pounding against my ribcage. A cool sweat broke across my forehead, formulating beads. The adrenalin that gushed through my veins told me one thing; get the hell out of here, now!

Then I felt a small breeze blow out my light.

As my eyes desperately adjusted to the darkness, I saw a flicker in the corner of my eye. Then, when I looked back at the table something was missing. Straining my eyes closer, I realised it was a knife. A terrified shudder rocketed through my stomach. I moved to clutch the blade at my belt to grasp it protectively. Immediately it was knocked from my hands, flying from my grip. I heard it smack into a wall loudly.

I was breathing heavily now, shaking.

I glimpsed another shadow. My heart felt like it was going to explode from my chest. I turned when the iron shackles made a noise as somebody–or something-caught the chains. Then so quickly I couldn't have even attempted to stop it, my legs were thrown from beneath me. I tried not to scream as I fell backwards, wincing in preparation for the crash but I landed on something hard and obviously human. Immediately a knife was at my heart.

The hot blade sunk slightly into my skin. Then in that millisecond, I felt the hands that grasped my shoulders and recognition hit. I knew those hands.

"Stop," I spluttered. The blade dropped.

The horrified surprise was blatant in his voice, "Ruby?"

Gasping slightly, I pulled my sleeve up to my chest to try and stop the bleeding; luckily the knife was one from the table and was blunted from over-use. I shivered. I nodded furiously, half-relieved and half-furious.

Kieran looked astounded, like he couldn't comprehend what he'd just done. Automatically he reached out, removed my hands, gently placing his fingers over the stabbed area. I felt warmth, saw a flash of black tattoos and when I checked I found my injury was completely healed. He released me. The pain dissolved into nothingness.

"Thanks," I muttered.

Kieran seemed to have decided how to handle the situation. Very predictably, he was mad. Well maybe 'mad' was a slight understatement.

"What the hell are you doing here?" he exploded ferociously, attempting to be quiet and failing epically. "I could have killed you."

"Really," I snapped sarcastically, "I hadn't noticed."

I swear to God he growled at me. "What are you doing here?"

"I could ask you that," I retorted angrily.

He ignored my comment, "It's dangerous, Ruby, go back."

"So far, the only thing that's been a danger to me is you." I retaliated bitterly, trying to keep my voice hushed.

"I'm only asking you one more time and then I'm going to throw you off a balcony myself. Go to your room, Ruby," he ordered.

"You go back, I'm not leaving."

He made a frustrated sound in the back of his throat, "Every second we spend here the bigger the chance we're going to be caught."

"Then stop trying to push me away and start actually listening to me." I whispered seriously. "I'm not leaving, so if you want to protect me then you're just going to have to come with me."

He exhaled sharply, but after a few intense moments he said, "You do *exactly* what I say." He emphasised, "No second chances."

I stared at him evenly for a long time, and then eventually nodded.

I watched as he bent down, inspecting the floor. The recent hand prints and scuff marks were still drying. Kieran frowned thoughtfully, stood then made his way over to the door. He closed his eyes, laying his ear against the door, listening. When he gave me a signal I padded over to him, silently going out.

I followed Kieran as we crept down the empty hallway, leading to a sort of waiting area type thing, with unoccupied chairs and dead neglected flowers in pots. Kieran touched the flowers as we passed, they sprang back to life.

Why was this place so empty? I know it should have been a good thing, but it was damn well spooking me out. There should have been terrifying monsters wandering about for me to sneak past; like in the movies.

Kieran found a door and pointed at it. I nodded comprehensively, waiting for him to listen for anyone on the other side. He shook his head and we made our way to another door. This time he gave a nod. I gently pried it open. Inside was a staircase, the kind you see leading up to balconies at theatres and football stadiums.

"Quickly," Kieran whispered and we hurriedly made our way up.

Kieran stopped just before we reached the top, turning completely immobile as he listened. I tried not to breathe.

Lifting his hand, Kieran gestured for me to come closer.

"There's someone about five metres away to our right," he murmured into my ear. "More than one person I think, guards most likely."

I pulled a face. "You got all that just from listening for two seconds?"

He rolled his eyes, "We're not in a good position here, if someone comes, we're trapped both ways."

He twisted his neck to the side, searching. All I could see was a banister draped in rich purple fabric and an ancient-looking ceiling painted with Fire Phoenix. Kieran turned back to me, recapturing my attention. "There's another set of stairs just to the side of us, but we need a distraction."

I thought for a moment, noticing that the lights running along the banisters were lit with burning torches. "I have an idea," I announced softly.

Kieran gestured for me to go for it and I took a breath, unsure that it would even work. I remembered what Jayson had said about manipulating evoked fire–once it was there it was easily manoeuvred. I followed my instincts, focussing on those flames, finding the power within me to make them bigger. Shaping my hands accordingly, the burning embers expanded so much that the flames caught on the material draped over the banister. Pretty soon the whole banister was burning.

I heard a shuffle of footsteps and some annoyed grumblings from down the corridor. Kieran waited, checking, then nodded and we both ran for the stairs.

Clambering up the narrow carpeted steps as quietly as possible we hesitated at another door. Kieran listened intently for a millisecond then swung it open. We entered what seemed to be another theatre balcony. Most importantly, there were no guards.

I paused to catch my breath, but abruptly Kieran yanked me down to the floor. Crouching low, he looked purposefully through a gap between the golden but grubby banister. I followed his line of vision, shuddering.

Down at the very bottom of the room-this floor must have an extension of the roof or something-was a circle of about twenty old-looking chairs. Sat in the chairs were a mixture of human Phoenix and those terrifying Daemon half-breeds. I shivered as I recognised the monsters. Their bat-like wings were leathery, their white skulls and purple eyes were even more piecing then before. Barlayic, Daemons, or half-breeds, whatever you called them they were horrifying. Even Kieran had frozen into stunned immobility.

I soon realised why. His voice was bitterly low, "My father's down there."

I glanced over at the men and sure enough noticed Kieran's salt-and-pepper haired father. I glanced at Kieran, his face was darkly apathetic.

I watched as a group of guards entered below, dragging a screaming woman and belligerently throwing her to the ground before Lynk.

She was stripped of her clothes, her entire body covered in dirty marks, burns, bruises and unhealed injuries; some still bleeding and oozing grimy yellow pus. Her long red hair had been repeatedly ripped from her head; intermittent patches of her scalp were visible, inflamed with bright swollen blisters. As she struggled to sit up, I saw the frail exposed bones move in her back. She was dangerously thin, most likely starved; reminding me in that moment of the wolf Lynk had once brought me to break.

The worst thing about her was her face. Her eyes had been taken. The sockets were empty; gruesomely black and rotting from neglect.

What had they done to her?

Lynk suddenly spoke up. I didn't think I could possibly hate him any more than I now did. He said calmly, "This is the last time I am going to ask you. What have you done with the Ephizon Metovah key?"

The poor woman trembled at the sound of his voice, swayed weakly, but she spat with honourable bravery, "I'd rather die than let you have it."

Lynk sighed impatiently; grumbling, "That can be arranged." He turned to the guards and nodded. Automatically they sprung forwards, grabbing her bony shoulders. Lynk got up and walked towards her, his golden eyes cold and calculating. "Eventually your walls will crumble," he warned the woman. "You're weak now; you won't be able to ignore my power for much longer. I suggest you just get it over and done with and tell me now."

Her head was bent forwards but I heard her response, "Kill me."

Lynk laughed humourlessly, "Why would I kill you? I still need you."

She didn't answer; she looked too exhausted to try.

One of the men in the chairs spoke with an annoyed, hostile voice. "Lynk, we won't be a part of your alliance and your plans unless we get something in return. We want access to the Eternal Light. If you cannot get it, then we shall leave." He glared, "You are wasting our time."

"You forget that once we get to the Eternal Light," he glanced over at the man poisonously, "we still need to unlock it."

"I'll be dead before I give it to you," screamed the woman suddenly.

Lynk smiled in a frightening sadistic way, "Who said anything about giving?"

His voice changed then, dipping in a way that was terrible to hear.

He was like a force of nature. I could hear the complexity of the tones he was using, so subtle to normal ears. Because I shared his destructive ability, I could feel it as the barriers protecting her mind and soul gradually weakened, losing the battle, as he spoke. The sirens call always wins in the end.

"Isn't there anything we can do?" I asked Kieran quietly, hearing the sadness in my voice. He shook his head; we both knew the inevitable.

I tried to block my ears, but the sound was too much, too beautiful, too obtrusive. Vigorously foreign words spilled from Lynk's lips, jabbing at the pitifully defending girl. The sound cut through her feeble shields, finally slipping into her weakened system. It was too late now. My heart sank. That one significant lapse in concentration cost her the one thing she'd kept safely behind her careful barriers. She was too weak to continue struggling. They'd literally beaten the will–and the life-out of her.

Lynk viciously grasped tighter; effortlessly now. It was nearly over. I could hear her answer as clearly as if she were screaming it.

She whispered brokenly, "I swallowed it."

The guards released her roughly. I watched as she bent over, gasping. The look on her ruined face confirmed what I'd already gathered; she'd surrendered. And Lynk was going to cut the key out of her.

Chapter Twenty-Four

I hated Lynk. I hated what he did with his voice. I hated what he did to that woman, and hated that she wasn't his first victim. But most of all, I hated knowing I could do exactly what he could. I made a promise to myself in that moment. From that point on, I would never use my voice to influence or control another person without their permission. Whether just to make them sleep, or just to get information. I would not become my father.

"Bane," Lynk called. One of the hunched, winged monsters stepped forwards with an evil animalistic grin across its Daemon face.

"Yes?" Its voice was gruff and intemperate; barely understandable.

"The Metovah key is inside our little friend here," he explained nonchalantly, gesturing towards the woman on the floor, quaking with terrified convulsions. "Would you extract if for me?"

The beast's raking nails scuffed the floor as it purposefully made its way over to the petrified girl. "Yes," it growled.

I knew what was going to happen, but I couldn't keep from looking.

I watched in horror as the creature snarled with a mouthful of razor-sharp blood-stained teeth. The woman screamed. My insides squirmed, revolted, my blood curdling in sickened anticipation. The monster growled menacingly, bolting forwards in a blur of brown flesh and scraggily deformed wings.

I looked away, scared and disgusted, a sick feeling sloshing in my stomach. I closed my eyes tightly as the girl

was brutally shredded apart. Her anguished wails soon
subsided, silence fell like nightfall.

The girl's pale, starved body was still and lifeless. A
gaping hole severed the flesh of her stomach, pooling
crimson blood around her body like a gruesome halo. I felt
absolutely disgusted. They'd savagely murdered her: *for a
key*.

When I heard Lynk say a smooth thank you, I wanted to
jump down there and rip his head off. I was so angry. I
couldn't believe I was related to this...to this...*monster*. But
Kieran roughly yanked me back down.

"What are you doing," he hissed furiously, "Look at
that." He pointed to the dead, disembowelled woman. She
was now being examined by the other half-breeds with
sickly hungry eyes. I gagged. "Do you want to end up like
that?"

Something flickered in the corner of my vision,
instantaneously capturing my attention. Whirling my neck
around, I caught a glimpse of Kieran making as if to stand-
but it was happening too quickly. The only thing my
hesitant brain registered was the six pairs of cold fierce eyes
that surrounded me.

My reactions eventually kicked in.

A hand roughly grabbed my shoulder. Instinctively I
swiped it away and ducked under another man's arm,
blindingly fast, to scramble out of reach of the restraining
arms. Somehow I was on the far side of the room, staring at
six Fire warriors. How did I manage to get out of that?

I glanced to my side-to where I expected Kieran to be-but
he wasn't there. Mercurially my eyes darted around until I
spotted him. My heart sunk in my chest, mortal panic
seizing my senses. He was handcuffed with those marked

wrist clamps to the dusty brass banister. They'd targeted the main threat first–that's how I'd gotten away.

"How did this happen?" he wondered confusedly to himself. Amazed, he twisted his captured wrist but the runes on the shackles glowed, burning. He frowned, crinkling his forehead.

All the while the guards were shuffling forwards, malevolence glinting like flint in their eyes. At any moment they would spring forwards and I would either fight or surrender. And it wasn't in me to quit.

"Never mind that," I answered Kieran sharply, "what do I do?"

Kieran was yanking unsuccessfully at the chains with a lazy, composed expression. Like this was merely annoying him. He shrugged casually, "Make sure they don't go running off and telling Lynk we're here. And be quiet about it; they're not exactly out of earshot."

"Okay. Sure," I muttered, gulping. "Thanks for the help."

Quickly reaching down to grasp Jayson's blade, I realised with another flourish of panic that it wasn't there. It was still in the torture chamber.

Many things happened at once then; Kieran sighed impatiently, the warriors pulled their blades from their belts, two ran forwards at me. Acting on pure instinct alone, I dodged back. From the corner of my eye I saw Kieran flick his free wrist. The whistling sound of metal flying through the air penetrated my terrified system. Suddenly the two warriors running dropped to the floor limply. Instantly I bent down to retrieve their curved Gaborah blades, clutching them tightly in both hands.

Trying not to look at the metal embedded in the men's throats, shaped like half a yin and yang symbol, I breathed deeply as more warriors sprung closer.

"There," I heard Kieran say, "Don't ever say I don't help you."

The tallest warrior swept forwards. He was fast but clumsy as he thrust his sword. I turned to the side. The blade missed me–the strike was slightly off centre. I pulled one of the heavy blades up and slashed it across his throat in a motion astonishingly natural. He staggered as I kicked him in his stomach forcefully, blood immediately spilling from his injury. He coughed flecks of red, his face turning purple as he struggled to breathe.

I didn't have time to feel shocked or disgusted at myself because three more men were running at me. Once again, my instincts worked for me. I blocked the first blade, knocking it hard to the side. The second one was aimed high and I swept my arm up to protect my head. The clash of metal rang loud. I knew that if we didn't quieten down, soon more guards–and subsequently Lynk and his fellow monsters-would hear.

The first and third guards moved in synchrony, both aiming for my heart. I whirled around to get out of range. Ducking slightly I reached out to swipe at one of the guards; they blocked effortlessly and attacked again. One of the Gaborah blades was knocked from my grasp. Swords were flying at me from all different angles. I was struggling to keep going. They were too fast, I was too inexperienced–or too out of practice.

Suddenly one man broke off from the fight, running towards the door, presumably to fetch assistance. That wasn't good. I did the only thing I could, I threw my only defence. Fortunately–by some impossible miracle-it aimed true and stuck him in his back. I had no idea how it hit him, but it did, and he tumbled to the floor. Panicked, I glanced back at the remaining warriors.

Shit, now I had no weapon.

"That was clever," Kieran said sarcastically, leaning casually against the railing. "Why don't you just use Chyun'ju, if you're so amazing at it?"

"I can't," I said, backing as far away as possible. The warriors slowly crept after me. Soon my back was pressed tightly against a wall. I had no escape. I couldn't even think. I didn't know what to do.

"Do I have to do everything?" Kieran murmured, stretching across to a dead warrior's body, grasping a stainless sword. I didn't see as he raised it high with his free left hand–I was a little occupied-but I certainly heard as he sent the weapon hurtling through the golden railing he was shackled to.

Lynk would have heard that.

But Kieran was free now and running over to the last two warriors as I fought desperately in the corner. One man turned as he approached, giving me the opportunity to lash at him. The man quickly blocked but now Kieran was upon us. Swiftly slashing, stabbing; his face an unimpressionable mask.

Relief flooded into me as the last man fell under Kieran's graceful lances, but fear soon returned when I heard the sound of footsteps running up the stairs.

The door was opening. Kieran and I looked at each other then bolted to the other set of stairs. We ran so fast I nearly fell. We came out into that empty hallway. Angry shouts echoed behind me. They were following. Slamming the door behind me, we crashed down the deserted corridor like lightning.

My heart was pounding so fast. I could hear running footsteps behind us, not too distantly either. Adrenalin gushed through my veins like rapids, pumping blood too fast and making my head spin. When I saw the open door that lead into that dark, creepy torture chamber, I realised I'd needed my blade. If Lynk saw it he might recognise it. Without hesitation I bolted in there, grabbed it and ran out again. Charging down the hallway we came to the right door. We needed to get the hell out of there, fast.

Kieran threw something at the glass balcony door and it smashed instantly, providing us with an easily accessible exit. We both ran through the hole, recklessly leaping off the balcony. In the milliseconds it took to fall, I grabbed on to the ledge of my own balcony, feeling the force of gravity wrenching my arms painfully. A blinding burst of pain shot through me, I'd possibly dislocated my shoulder. Luckily a familiar hand was there, hauling me over the railing an instant before I heard startled activity above.

Kieran dragged me into my room, gently sliding the glass door behind him. Voices faded outside but footsteps still creaked the floorboards above me. I felt it when my guards outside awoke from the noise.

"Kieran you need to hide, Lynk will probably check on me." I whispered urgently. He nodded in understanding, automatically crawling under my four poster bed; shielding himself under the lacy material.

I dressed in my nightclothes frantically, hiding the bloody evidence, and then jumped into bed underneath the sheets with my heart pounding. Drawing the semi-sheer curtains around my bed so the scene looked normal, I waited silently. I heard more creaks of the floorboards above me, and I closed my terrified eyes, my pulse still thumping erratically. Eventually the noises died down, but I heard movement outside my door.

Pretending I was sound asleep-while I was actually more alive than I ever had been before-I heard the sound of

Lynk's voice filtering through my door. He was talking to my guards, asking if I'd left the room at all. Lynk sounded unbelievably suspicious. My heart skipped a beat. Sweat pearls formed on the back of my neck, grossly mingling in the strands of my tied hair.

I didn't hear Kian's grunt of a response, but I heard when the door quietly pulled open. My eyes stayed firmly shut. I tried desperately to keep my breathing slow and even. Eventually I heard the door softly click shut and Lynk murmuring to Kian to watch me. I waited five minutes, still pretending to be unconscious, before I cautiously peeped through my eyelashes. I sighed inaudibly in relief.

I reached down to grab a handful of the material that scrunched up around the bottom of my bed, pulling it up so Kieran could climb out from under the mattress. Only when I caught the sight of my fingernails did I realise that they were crusted with dry blood; blood that wasn't my own.

Reality whacked into me like a ton of bricks across the stomach. I had killed people. I had killed men with families. Their blood still clung to my fingers. Lynk would find out. Somehow he would know it was me. He was already suspicious; he knows but doesn't have any proof. He could find evidence.

All I could think of was those warriors' dead faces; that woman's excruciated screams, those terrible creatures, and the fact that Phoenix were probably trying to track us right now. My head was a mixture of incomprehensible images, of sounds I didn't want to hear and yet were recurring over and over; screams, shouts, songs.

Lynk knows and he will kill me.

Or he would get his monsters to do it for him.

I could feel my body violently shaking in panicked, frightened convulsion. I had killed innocent people. I was no better than Lynk.

Distantly I felt hands on my face, warm hands, but they couldn't bring me back from the nightmare inside my own head. I was vaguely aware Kieran was speaking, his lips moving meaninglessly, but I couldn't understand. I looked down at my hands, still stained with red, realising that they were cold, extremely cold. My entire body felt icy and empty.

Arms were suddenly wrapped around me, lifting me to the bathroom. I didn't respond. Kieran sat me down carefully so I was leaning with my back pressed against the bath. Watching numbly as he turned on the sink tap, I saw water spill out, filling the bowl. Swirling clouds of steam wafted up. Kieran grabbed a cloth, dipped it into the pool of water, then cautiously dabbed the material against my hands, wiping away the blood and grime tenderly, like I was a child who'd accidentally grazed my hands. I felt dirty and disgusting, utterly revolted by myself. Sweat matted my hair in a horrid repulsive mess.

Through the foggy haze orbiting my head, I felt Kieran smooth the damp flannel up my arms, cleaning the dirt away as he went. He scrubbed and cleansed while I stayed still and incomprehensive. I knew I shouldn't have just sat there, but what else could I have done? I was a killer now, and nothing could ever change that.

Somehow I was back under my bed sheets. I felt as if this was a dream, like I was watching it happen from far away and I couldn't do anything about it. I just sat there while Kieran came and shuffled in next to me; pulling me closer to his secure warmth, wrapping his arms around me.

I didn't want anyone to know what I'd done. I felt so ashamed.

Momentarily, I may have drifted off to sleep. But when my eyes opened again, it seemed like time had passed. Looking up, I realised that Kieran was still there, watching me. I felt a bit calmer than I had before. I could smell smoke on him, his pupils were dilated and there was a slight dimness in his eyes; he'd taken some more of that drug; it was obvious.

"Hey," he smiled sweetly, making my bones crumble. He was so relaxed, it was nice. I didn't even care that it took drugs to make him like this. A small part of my brain remained stubborn though, reminding me that this wasn't the real Kieran. This was someone that drug had created; nicer though he maybe. This wasn't him; his real self.

"Hi," I said quietly. "Thanks, by the way," I knew he understood what I meant. "You didn't have to do that."

Kieran nodded smoothly, it was a good thing I could see in the darkness, my eyes adjusted already. "You were in shock."

I shook my head, my heart falling. "I'm a killer, Kieran. I murdered up there," I told him, trying to keep my voice down.

He looked down at me with a peculiar expression distorting his marvellous, shadowed features, "No Ruby, if you hadn't had fought back; then it would have been murder. Those guards would have been ordered to kill on sight. The stakes were too high in that place."

"That doesn't change the fact that I've now killed." I disagreed.

Kieran moved his other hand a fraction, the one that was draped over my shoulder, so that one of his fingers could lift my chin; forcing me look into his gorgeous emerald eyes.

They were impossible to decipher; too many ambiguous, complicated emotions in there. It was like looking into a mirror.

"Do you think I'm bad?" he questioned emotionlessly.

I gazed at him carefully. "I think you're complicated, sometimes too complicated for me to understand."

Kieran continued indifferently, "I have killed people, a lot more than you'd think and a lot more than you'd want to," he shook his head. "Blood, death, destruction, it's what haunts and motivates us all."

I struggled now. Kieran wasn't a murderer, I knew that. But everything he said made sense. When I didn't answer for a while, he explained, "I don't kill for pleasure, I don't enjoy it. It was my job," he stated certainly. "I've done things I regret, but for the majority I don't have regrets. There have been times when I've had to kill in numbers to protect my friends, my family; it is slaughter then, cold hard massacre. That surely makes me bad?"

I shook my head, "No, Kieran" I sighed finally, "I refuse to think you are bad; if it's to protect others."

"But that's not always been the case," he reminded me. "It was my job, still is really. Jayson's too. It's what we're good at. That's why we do it."

I struggled, thinking, "I don't know; I guess it's just something you've always known. I know it's a different world here too. Death follows us here."

"But it doesn't need to," he said. "It doesn't have to. I chose this life, I chose to be trained and I chose to kill. What I am now is because of what I've done."

He looked away from me then, his face uncertain. The seconds ticked by.

"It's not really that though that bothers me," I whispered eventually, "it's knowing I'm no better than my father."

Kieran sharply turned towards me in shock and anger, staring fiercely into my eyes. "Don't ever say that," he ordered. "You are nothing like him."

"I am though," I murmured sadly. "You know what he did to that girl, the way he forced the information out of her? I can do that too."

He shook his head wildly, backing away so he was sat up about a foot away.

"Just because you *can* do something, doesn't mean you're going to." He snapped, his eyes blatantly telling me I was being ridiculous. "I can take away pain *and* give it, but it doesn't mean I'm going to. Your voice is powerful, and it can do horrible things, but it's also a gift."

"I don't see how it's a gift," I argued doubtfully. "I can control people's minds. I can control their actions, their words, even their *thoughts.* How can that be good?"

"You're being stupid. If a man was walking across a road and you saw a car coming which he didn't notice, you could make him move out of the way before it hit him; saving his life."

"There aren't any cars in Kariak."

"Stop trying to be clever, you know what I mean," he huffed irritably.

I sat in silence for a while, digesting all his words. Kieran was right, again. My voice was a gift if I used it for good. Neglecting it would not help anyone, but using it properly might.

"What's a Metovah key?" I asked.

He didn't look at me as he answered, "A Metovah key is one of five keys that unlock the top of the gem towers. As well as being the wards that protects the island, we keep sacred objects in the very top of the towers."

"So what's the Eternal Light?"

"The Original Mother captured what we call 'pure elements' and gave them to her four children. The Eternal Light was the gift she gave her Fire child. It's a hollowed out diamond about the size of a football, inside is a glowing light that never burns out, or at least hasn't for six thousand years."

"I remember somebody mentioning pure elements," I realised, "I can't remember where from though."

Kieran nodded, "It's held in Ephizon, the Fire City, but I guess Lynk is going to try and get his hands on it." He added, and then frowned, "I don't know why he's giving it to those men; nobody can open it. Either he knows something we don't or he's actually a moron."

"Nobody can open it?" I repeated questionably.

Kieran shrugged. "No. And nobody knows what it does—except blind people when they stare at it for too long."

"Why would Lynk want that? If he wanted to blind people it'd be easier just to take out their eyes." I shuddered at the thought; remembering the woman.

"I don't know." Kieran answered.

"What about the rest of the pure elements? What do they do?" I wondered.

He glanced warily around my room for a second, "The Eternal Light is the only pure element we have. The rest were lost over the centuries."

I grimaced.

"I think Lynk must want the rest of them," Kieran told me; "I bet he's trying to find them, like every other person on this God-damned island. He'll never find them, nobody has, nobody will."

I stared down at my hands for a moment, thinking that through.

"Lynk wants too much," I sighed eventually, and I could tell that Kieran realised he'd gotten through to me.

"He wants what all men want," Kieran said, "what they can't have."

I looked up at him, surprised.

"Do you want what you can't have?" I asked, wondering what the hell Kieran would want. He had absolutely everything.

He smiled softly, carefully reaching forwards to gently trail a finger down my cheek. My skin burned and tickled where he touched me. I trembled, and tried not to think about how much this contact would hurt me tomorrow.

"Every day," he answered.

Then he pulled his hand back, his eyes going strangely blank as he stepped towards the balcony, ostensibly ready to leave.

"Are you sure it's safe?" I asked anxiously.

Kieran frowned, "Of course it's not safe. That's what makes it interesting."

I rolled my eyes, "Don't you worry about the guards? Lynk would have put more guards out now as well."

He snorted quietly, "No guards can get past me. I hold the record for the fastest air-dive in Kariak."

"Really?" I asked, raising my eyebrows dubiously.

"I do, actually," he answered sincerely, "I even beat your little girlfriend Jayson; what a shame. Nobody thought the sun shone out of his ass *that* day," he added sarcastically, a mean twist in his lovely lips.

"It's probably because of your enormous head," I told him. "Its weight is bound to make you fall faster."

"No because if that's true, Jayson would have definitely beaten me." He soundlessly slid open the glass door and the cool night air whipped at my face. He turned, pulling off his jacket to prepare for the Change.

"Can't you just Change down there where I can't see you?" I grunted antagonistically, knowing what he was going to do.

Kieran grinned disobediently, flashing those white teeth. "I was just giving you something nice to dream about," he answered innocently as he tugged his shirt over his head. My skin fluttered as I saw his lovely, lovely body. Damn that boy was hot. I felt the blood gush to my face.

"I want nice dreams," I retorted, "not nightmares." And ignoring my lesser judgement I turned over under my covers, the material muffling his reply.

I didn't see him fly off, but I felt it.

Chapter Twenty-Five

Reluctantly I dragged myself from my nice warm bed. My little maids were watching me moan and swear as I stretched; my muscles felt as tight as stretched elastic. Note to self: *never* fight anyone again.

Ellie shook her head, frowning, "I have never heard anyone swear quite as much as you in the morning, Ruby."

I laughed, glad she was finally talking to me like an actual person rather than a Lady; Trixy wasn't as easily persuaded. "Sorry," I grinned.

"Jayson's here, by the way," she announced. "You slept in."

My eyes widened as I bit into my toast and jam. "Oh crap," I muttered through a mouthful of bread. "Has he been here long?"

"Five minutes," Ellie answered, "He wishes to take you out flying."

"Can I go?" I asked, "Is Lynk in?"

"He's out for the day but you have to be back by four; Evelyn says no later," Trixy said, packing my golden wing brace with training gear and attaching a blunted blade onto one of the straps. "If you are out then we'd all get in trouble, Lady," she continued. "You must take your Protector though," she added.

I grumbled, but reluctantly agreed. At least they were covering for me.

"Where is he?" I wondered.

"Waiting in the gardens with Kian," Ellie smiled.

"Right," I said, taking one last bite of my breakfast.

I stripped naked except for a silky cloth that I wrapped around me, and then hauled on my ridiculously heavy brace. I loosely tugged it over my shoulders, my back arching painfully from the weight. On my balcony, I welcomed the fiery energy that cascaded down my back as I Changed, the silky material pooling to the ground underneath me. The pain was sudden and excruciating, but it soon wore off. I was getting accustomed to it now. I took off into the air, discovering Jayson by the fountain, waiting with my big terrifying protector.

Ready? He asked and when I nodded we took off into the air. I followed him with effort, my muscles weak and strained from yesterday's assault. He noticed this, *Are you okay?*

Kian stayed quite a distance behind us and was obviously blocking out our thoughts for privacy, but I still kept my mindvoice down.

Yeah, I guess, just tired. I haven't had a proper night's sleep in a long time.

His neck twisted as he hitched his head to the side, *Why not last night?*

Well he knew everything else; I might as well tell him what had happened. I explained quickly and his eyes were focussed and calculating. He agreed that something really wrong was happening, but didn't know what to do. When I mentioned seeing Kieran there he frowned in puzzlement.

I'm surprised he went; to be honest, it's not like him.

I think he knew I was going to go, to be honest, I admitted.

We were heading to a large field. Positioned in the middle of it was what looked like an obstacle course, only in the air. As we landed I prepared myself for a long morning.

I was breathing heavily, sweat clung in the spaces between my feathers and my heart was racing. The past hour and a half had been more vigorously exerting than anything I'd ever done in my life. I felt like I'd been thrown in a washing machine and been left to tumble.

I didn't like Jayson anymore; I think he'd tried to indirectly kill me.

Forced against my will, I'd been dragged and deceitfully persuaded to fly through hoops, dodge between pointy stick things-which should go die-and practice immense dives from phenomenal heights over and over again until I got what classified as a 'decent' time. I had to try and be fast enough to catch weights when Jayson threw them from a hundred metres away, ten foot off the ground; which he assured me *wasn't* impossible; all the time wearing my million-ton gold wing-brace.

I learnt tricks to make dives faster, to change direction in split seconds, and went over the art of accelerating and gliding.

My wings hurt, I hurt. I was still shit-scared about the monsters that were living–and plotting with my evil father-above my bedroom. I needed to find out what Chara, Nik and everyone had told Kieran. And I'd spent all morning tackling ridiculously-difficult, exhausting obstacles like I was a bloody Peregrine falcon. Well I wasn't a bloody Peregrine falcon. I was a Phoenix. And not only am I a Phoenix, I am also English. And the English are good at two things: queuing and complaining; and I was going to do the latter.

Decided; I did the flying equivalent of marching over to Jayson. I hovered in the air, moving my wings persistently to make sure I didn't lose altitude. I stared sternly at him. He was perched atop a large stone column and was apparently recording something by scratching his gigantic sharp talons into the stone-which I'm sure he's not allowed to do-as this was a public place; part of a local training centre for new flyers.

Jayson, I began fiercely, preparing to tell him that there was no way in hell I was catching any more weights, but he interrupted me.

You're all done Ruby, he said, finally looking up, *you can go now if you want*.

I'm done? I asked hopefully, hearing the relief in my voice, *no more hoops?*

There was laughter in his eyes; *I take it that you don't like agility drills?*

I shook my massive feathery head; *It's too much like hard work.*

It is hard work. He chuckled in my head.

That's the point. I grumbled tiredly. *I need to go over to the Ashaiks. I don't know if you want to come. I need to talk about last night.*

He thought for a moment, deliberating whether it was important enough to put up with seeing the Ashaik brothers again: eventually he surrendered.

It didn't take long to arrive at Ebony's. I was grateful that I actually had clothes to dress into this time. Kian followed silently behind us. Once suitably clothed, we made our way over to the small training courtyard where, sure enough, Kieran was, hauling out another hunk of ice. When he saw me, he smirked, "So, is this going to be a regular thing now?"

I went closer and as he noticed Jayson behind me his face went blank and impenetrable. Then he saw my huge fierce protector and frowned, Kian stood at the other end of the courtyard by the exit, waiting patiently. Plonking down onto the floor exhaustedly, I wrapped my arms inside my clothes for warmth against the icy floor. "Yes," I said, feeling provoked.

"You just want to watch me work." Kieran stated arrogantly.

"Kieran, grow up," I told him, irritated; Jayson stood awkwardly next to me.

"I can't," he told me petulantly; "it's not my birthday."

I rolled my eyes at his immaturity, "What did everyone say about yesterday?"

"To leave it," he answered seriously, turning so I couldn't see his expression, beginning to examine the glacier ice with his sharp eyes.

"Leave it," I repeated incredulous, utterly shocked. It was the last thing I had expected Kieran to say. "What do you mean, leave it?"

"I mean, don't do anything," he answered moodily. "There is nothing we can do. My mother was there when I got back yesterday; she knew everything already. You remember how my father was in that little group? Well, he's not very good at hiding it, apparently."

"Oh," was all I could say. Kieran persevered.

"My mother said that there are special networks that are also suspicious of Lynk. They know how he is controlling the Council and are looking into what he's up to. We have to leave them to do their jobs."

"So that's it?" Jayson spoke up, questioning bitterly, "We're just going to give up and let Lynk do what he likes?"

"No, we're going to let the people who are supposed to stop him, stop him." He snapped, bitingly harsh.

"But you're Kierakai Ashaik! You're a warrior." I protested, feeling almost betrayed. "How can you just say that?"

He turned to look at me, but his eyes were unreadable, "I have no choice."

"There are always choices," I argued frantically, "*always*. You saw it Kieran. You saw what Lynk did to that woman, you know about those...*things*, and you know what he did to me." I pointed at the bruises that still covered my face. "He can do much worse. And you're just going to let him get on with it?"

"You don't understand, Ruby, I can't do anything. My mother made us swear the Sacred Oath." Even though he was harsh and defensive, I knew he was hoping I'd understand. "I can't break it. It's impossible."

Jayson looked just as horrified as I felt when we realised Kieran was telling the truth. "Why would she...?" Jayson murmured, trailing off.

I knew what the Sacred Oath was. My mum did it to the slave who had pretended to be my father. It can only be broken by death or allowance from the person it was given by.

Kieran looked down at his hands; they were clenched into tight fists as he glared viciously at Jayson, "Because Lynk has already taken her husband from her. She doesn't want him to take her children too."

Suddenly I felt empathy for Garnha. Lynk had destroyed her entire family; probably turning his father into the monster that nearly killed Adrian.

"Okay?" he demanded, "Just leave it." He finally turned back to his lump of ice. "Now, are you going to stay there and watch me, or are you going to do something?" he wondered, "Because I find it hard to concentrate when you're staring at my ass."

I felt a tingle of colour blush my cheeks rosy. Then I heard someone walking behind me. I turned around in surprise, my jaw dropping open as I saw that beautiful girl from my First Flight celebration; the one who had been all over Kieran. Her long gorgeous legs were barely covered in a tiny skirt; her vest top was low and revealing a voluptuous cleavage. Her skin was a flawless cinnamon colour and she seemed to glow with a radiant luminosity. She was so perfect I felt myself retch with jealousy.

She ignored me and Jayson, strutting straight up to Kieran as I watched in painful astonishment, my eyes wide as she stretched up her amazing body, wrapping her arms around Kieran's neck and pressing herself *right* against him. She kissed his cheek, her stupid fat head covering the expression on Kieran's face; then she moved her face around to kiss his neck intimately, whispering something inaudible in his ear. I glanced away, my anger flashing across my face but I knew I couldn't get angry, not with witnesses around.

"Right, I'm off," she smiled, pulling back. "Thanks for this morning."

She winked at Kieran, with a naughty twist on her pouty lips then walked away, shaking her stupid skinny ass as she went. I gazed after her, ever single hair on my body raised in fury. I turned back to Kieran, who had distinctly apathetic features.

"What's she been doing here?" I demanded slowly through gritted teeth, forgetting momentarily that Jayson was next to me.

"You're too young to know," he smirked and my anger flared dramatically. I physically had to stop myself from charging at him. "Don't you have something to do? I've got sculptures to make." He was avoiding my eyes. I suppose I did need to distract myself from my sadistic thoughts of castrating Kieran.

"Well," I decided, "I'm supposed to be singing at this festival thing, aren't I? But no one's contacted me yet so I don't have any music to practice with, but I could use a guinea pig."

I glanced at Jayson and he smiled, relaxed, "What do you need me to do?"

"Not much," I admitted, "just try not to get hypnotised by me."

Kieran laughed, "You aren't that good Princess."

I whirled on him, "I am," I snarled. "Why don't you believe me, do you want me to prove it?"

Kieran folded his arms across his chest, "Go on then."

I turned around, hearing footsteps; it was Briseis. She sat beside me. "Thank God that evil bitch is gone," she uttered under her breath to me. I assumed she could only mean Sofia. "What's going on?" she asked loudly.

"Ruby's giving us a demonstration of her gift," Kieran smirked.

"Cool," she turned to me, "How?" I shrugged. Then she giggled suddenly and whispered in my ear, "You should make them strip." She suggested.

"I can't do that," I objected, spurting into laughter.

"Of course you can," she winked, continuing to whisper. "Serves them both right for being arseholes. More Kieran than Jayson, but I do remember Jayson the other night at your Flight..." she trailed off suggestively.

I glanced at the cheeky excitement on her face and a slow agreeing smile crept on my features. "All right," I turned to the boys, both now stood in front of us. "Do you both give me permission to use my voice on you?" I asked, arching my eyebrows challengingly.

They both agreed but uncertainly. I stood up. Walking slowly around them with an unnerving stare, I took a deep breath, feeling excited energy bubbling in my chest; up my windpipe and flowing over my tongue as I spoke. My voice came in a deep mesmerising lilt, a rare seductiveness escaping from my mouth in a soft hum that entranced the hearts of the men before me. *I'll show them what I can do,* I thought confidently. I glanced up from underneath my eyelashes as I swept past them, knowing that eye contact emphasised my grasp on people. I stopped in-between them; both had their eyes hooked on me.

"Listen to my voice," I said softly, practically purring, visibly seeing their body's tense as they fought me. Kieran, in particular, struggled, trying to look away. I continued, my voice faintly hypnotic, cautiously easing them in. "You can hear me. You are in my control," I smiled, unleashing my voice with a sudden exciting force. "First, what I want you to do is..." I trailed off, then dipped my voice lower, "Take you're shirts off: slowly," I said mischievously.

Kieran struggled. Jayson was hooked. I repeated myself until they both did as I said; obviously fighting me but unable to stop. Behind me Briseis was giggling like a school girl, as they brought up their hands to their shirts. I smirked; impressed at my own power and glad I was getting my own back for them both staring at me naked the other day.

"Drop them to the floor," I commanded; they followed my orders impulsively. I continued with my voice low and dangerously hypnotic. I had to concentrate now, so as not to go too far and break my hold over them, or worse, damage them. I glanced back at Briseis who grinned encouragingly, "Okay," I continued, "Shoes and socks off." They complied instantly. I smiled, "And now your trousers." Briseis was hysterical behind me now as the boys slowly, in complete synchronisation, stripped outside in the freezing weather; until they stood in just their boxers.

They both had beautiful athletic bodies, lean muscle building them up. They were so different; dark and light, black and blonde, Fire and Earth, and yet both were equally gorgeous.

"Turn around," I continued.

Irritation flickered in me as I noticed the scratches across Kieran's back; long like nail marks. An overwhelming anger saturated my voice as I realised what exactly he'd been doing with Sofia. Those marks were because of her. I was initially going to stop there but I didn't now, because of that. "And the rest of it," I demanded and they did, revealing a narrow strip of ass, thigh, then everything. I turned to Bris. "I think I've made my point."

The energy had gone from my voice, a sudden exhaustion pinned me where I stood, but it was definitely worth it for the looks on Kieran and Jayson's faces as they slowly came into realisation what had happened.

Jayson looked down in astonishment, his cheeks turning crimson and I laughed humorously as he pulled his boxers up. Kieran picked up his clothes with a blank stern face, "Okay, point taken."

"Ruby that was amazing," Jayson said excitedly. "A little depraving…" He considered as he put his trousers back on, "but amazing never the less. I had no control at all over what I was doing."

"Speaking of depravity," Briseis turned to me, "Have you got your outfit for the Winter Festival yet?"

I shook my head. To be honest I'd purposely thought as little as I possibly could about the damn thing, which some idiot had offered me to sing in.

"Have you practiced Half-Changing yet?" she wondered.

I stared at her in blank incomprehension. "What?"

"Like Kieran does," she explained, "When he sculpts."

So *that's* what Kieran meant. "Why have I got to do that? It looks painful."

"It's a display of physical strength," Jayson explained, "You're a Swartette, you have a High Name; it's compulsory. Just like Kieran and Nik will have their wings out to shows their high status."

"Do you have your wings out too?" I asked anxiously. He nodded.

"Ebony does as well," Briseis volunteered, "and because she's female she'll have to have her tail feathers out too."

"I have to have my tail feathers out too! How am I supposed to wear clothes if I have bloody great feathers sticking out of my ass?" I was flustered.

Bris bit her lip, as if unwilling to tell me something, so Jayson intercepted calmly. "You won't be wearing many," he admitted composedly. "You'll wear *Brellusk*, the traditional Phoenix wear for events like this."

"Which consist of…?" I trailed off.

"Well, your tail should be covering most of your bottom half and the rest you'll wear kind of a draping skirt and sandal-like shoes," Briseis said.

"And on the top half?"

"It's difficult to explain, but kind of like a halter-neck bikini top. Only fancier."

"Wait, wait, wait," I gasped, horrified, "I have to sing in front of a massive audience wearing the equivalent of my underwear!"

Briseis shrugged, "It's traditional. I'll be wearing something like it too, though perhaps less dramatic."

Well that makes me feel a million times better, I thought grudgingly.

"I'm hungry anyway," Briseis announced, getting up. "I'm in the kitchen if anyone wants me." With that she bounded off into the house.

"I better head off too," Jayson said, "I have a hit to track."

I nodded, "Okay, see you in the morning?"

"Yeah," he agreed, then stopped as he was about to leave. "One more thing," he walked over to me. "I was just wondering if you want to go with me; to the Festival, I mean."

I looked at him, startled, and wondered, "What, like a date?"

"If you want, or we could just go as friends. It's up to you." He explained casually, "There probably won't be many people you know there; I thought familiar company might be appreciated."

Automatically my thoughts went to Kieran, who was ignoring us from a distance. What would he think? I know he'd be angry, but to be honest he had no right to be. He's bad for me, he messes with my head. The image of those nail marks popped into my head with a renewed surge of anger, why shouldn't I go with Jayson, if Kieran had already moved on?

I smiled, realising that he was waiting for an answer. "Sure," I grinned eventually, feeling like I'd betrayed my own heart, "Of course I'll go."

Jayson smiled brilliantly and he really was handsome, all gold and angelic.

"Great," he said. He bent down to slowly touch my hand to his face, touching his lips to my skin. I felt nothing. No sparks, no flush, not even a skip of my heartbeat; nothing. Kieran could make me shiver with just a look. *Shut up Ruby*, I thought furiously, *stop thinking about him*.

Jayson was still smiling as he walked away.

Kieran was facing away from me, his velvety-black wings suddenly sprouting from his shoulders. He hacked at the ice maliciously with the blades of his wings, sprinkling diaphanous shards across the floor like fragments of a shattered mirror. He was angry.

You haven't done anything wrong.

"Um," I gulped anxiously, "Is it okay if I..."

I saw the prominent muscles of his back twitch under his magnificent wings. Staring fiercely at his work, he stated, clipped and biting, "Just one question." The hard line of his jaw clenched sternly, "Why him?" His eyes reflected anger but his exterior was as composed as a poker player. "You could have anyone you want, and yet you choose him, why?" I could see his knuckles were strained white as they gripped the frozen surface.

Why did he think I could have anyone I want? Did he mean because of my voice? Okay, now I was mad. Jayson was *not* under my influence...well, not anymore. Kieran had no right to be angry at me. He was the one who had said he didn't want me. He *didn't* want me. So why can nobody else have me?

"It doesn't matter why," I told him viciously, feeling my head start to pressurize painfully as I struggled to fight away angry tears, "not to you."

"Of course it matters," he snapped, whirling around to glare at me.

"Tell me why then, Kieran," I demanded icily. "Why would you care? What's the hell has it got to do with you?"

"It's got everything to do with me-" He began furiously.

"*Why?*" I wailed suddenly; my voice rising a few octaves. My head was screaming, my heartbeat pounded like a drum. I turned to Kian, my voice so strong and authoritative he did exactly what I said, "Kian go to the front of the house and wait for me there. I won't be long." He obliged immediately.

"Do you think this is easy for me," he yelled right back, glaring into my eyes with a fierce intensity; he looked deranged and possessed with anger. "Do you think it's easy for me to just stand there and watch him steal you away?" *From me,* his eyes added.

"You can't steal something that doesn't belong to you," I screeched, furiously battling the tears that burned my eyes. "It was *you* who didn't want me. *You* who said it's impossible for us to be together."

"It *is* impossible, but that doesn't make me want it any less." His voice dropped then, he stepped forwards almost unconsciously.

"Kieran," I cried, shoving him roughly back. "You can't just say that and then go running off with that girl like I know you will. You can't. What were you even doing with her?" I demanded. "I've seen the scratches on your back."

"She came to me," he snapped. "What was I meant to do?"

"Tell her to sod off," I glared.

"Don't you understand? I'm *meant* to be with Sofia," he explained, his voice rising again in bitter frustration. "She's of Earth. I'm of Earth. No matter what I want, I can't change that. "

My hands dropped lifelessly to my sides. Ouch, that hurt. He might as well have stabbed me with those brutal, dark wings of his. "I know that," I said "but in that case I'm meant to be with Jayson too. Or someone else like him."

"I don't want this," he told me weakly, like his lungs had been deflated. He reached out to touch my forehead with those soft, shimmering feathers; removing the pain there. He was close; his glorious angel wings near.

I looked up into those eyes and they were sad, filled with a lifetime of war and pain. "It doesn't matter what you want," I said, "not in this world."

His lovely wings closed around me like a soft blanket. "I know," he uttered.

I smiled, looked down at his wings where they delicately tickled my skin. These wings, I thought, they really are amazing. How could something that can slice through ice like a knife, embrace so carefully as well? He looked down too and his expression automatically transformed, like he'd just realised what he was doing. Impulsively he released me and backed off, returning to his work while rubbing his forehead as if it were sore.

"Lady," Kian said, returning. "We have to go, Lynk will be back soon."

I nodded, "I'm coming." I took one last painful glance at Kieran then followed Kian.

Chapter Twenty-Six

I closed my eyes and thought of fire.

Instantaneously the energy pulsated down my spine, zapping into my susceptible nervous system; subsequently possessing every compliant cell in my body. I made myself focus on the development, concentrating as the vigorous energy recoiled again, dominating the muscles in my back. Encouraging my cells to expand and multiply, I felt my wings sprout painfully from my shoulders. My closed eyelids twitched as the appropriate time arose. Seizing the opportunity, the vibrating sensation obediently halted, but as the milliseconds passed my Phoenix body struggled, wanting to continue the Change while my mind rejected the notion.

I was gasping now, blood churning in throbbing veins. The energy fanned through my entire body, battering all my senses but I persevered and eventually it dwindled, fading in relinquishment.

My eyes darted open, my vision burred, but strong prying fingers held my kneeling form still against the wild tremors.

"Did it work?" my voice cracked.

"Have a look," Jayson's bright tone gave me hope.

I'd spent all morning attempting to gouge my wings out of my human back and keep them there, but after thirteen unsuccessful attempts I was exhausted.

As I centred myself, I slowly became aware of the heavy weight nagging at the flesh of my shoulders and the hot blood trickling down my spine.

My neck protested as I lifted it, the joints clicking loudly, but a wave of relief echoed through me at the sight of my crimson wings-collapsed inelegantly across the wooden floor of the indoor training room at the Palace. I was kneeling down for balance, blistering burn marks on my knees from where I'd shaken so violently, but now I tried to stand. Jayson supported me by the waist and I finally managed to straighten upright. My wings weighed a bloody ton but I could just about manage.

"See if you can walk." Jayson suggested.

I staggered forwards precariously, but soon got the hang of it and even though my muscles ached tremendously I eventually managed to move my wings freely. I knew that after a bit more practice, I would be fine. Once I discovered how to make my tail feathers come out too.

Loud footsteps behind us made us turn. To my surprise it was the Water-Elder I vaguely recognised from the High-Council. With a swift step she moved over to Jayson, whispering something in his ear. He nodded respectfully, placing his crossed fingers over his forehead then heart in a conventional gesture then smiled at me, "I'll see you tomorrow."

"Um...okay." I frowned, confused, as he left the room.

The woman looked at me with a mixture of weariness and politeness. "I am sorry for the intrusion," she began, "but I have some important matters I wish to carry out."

"Okay," I said, then thought of my wings, "Should I Change back?"

She shook her head, "No, it looks like you need the practice."

She took me away from my ever-present Protector, instantly explaining, "It is not long until the Winter Festival and I need to make sure you know exactly what you will be doing on the night. From now on, you shall be practicing every afternoon with our musicians so you are prepared. They'll travel here."

I nodded courteously, but asked, "Shouldn't I be practicing at the venue?"

Her eyebrows knitted together a fraction. "No, definitely not," She said, "Nobody can see the Festival Palace until the night; it isn't fully complete yet."

How on earth would they be ready for the Winter Festival when the venue had not yet been built? I wondered. The Elder lead me to the massive golden hall of my Palace. It was filled with theatre chairs and a group of people with peculiar musical devices–along with drums and string instruments-who I presumed were the musicians.

"I will supervise your practice personally, and we will finish when I am satisfied," warned the Water Elder to the entire room-including my already-miserable Protector who had just followed us. She had a distinct powerful presence about her which I couldn't help but like in a nervous way.

So I dropped my bag onto a nearby cushioned seat and went to stand with the band. I took a deep breath and waited for my cue to begin, as I did every day until the eve of the Winter Festival. Despite him having hits to deal with again, Jayson continued to train me in the morning. I didn't see the others much at all. I didn't have time to be honest. It was very lonely. Without Jayson's morning company, I doubt I would have survived.

Thankfully the Festival came pretty quickly.

"There is no way in hell I'm wearing that."

I swear I saw little Ellie roll her big black eyes. "Lady Ruby, it is just for one night," she assured me, "it will not kill you."

Looking at the thin scraps of material and jewel-enlaced golden cords that were somehow supposed to classify as clothing, I disagreed entirely.

"Come on Ruby," Chara said. She and Briseis had come over for the unveiling of my outfit, possibly just to mock me. Lynk didn't know, they'd have to be gone before he got back. I hadn't seen much of him either recently. I'd hoped Chara would be on my side, but apparently not, "Just try it on."

I grudgingly picked it up with the very tips of my fingers, holding the glittery contraption at arm's length like it was made of a poisonous substance.

"It's not that bad," Bris agreed, her face appearing from underneath the silk sheets of my bed which she had a new found love for.

This wasn't fair; they were ganging up on me.

"Okay, okay," I surrendered, following Ellie and Trixy into my dressing room with an expression that resembled thunder.

After a lot of moaning, swearing, and breathing in to the point that my stomach was somewhere in my thigh, I had managed to get into the thing. Jesus Christ it hurt, they'd pulled the strings so tight I may never be able to get out of it again. Talk about cutting off circulation. When I came back out again, I heard Briseis giggle and Evelyn laugh helplessly, though I think it was my red face they thought was funny.

"You're walking like a moron," Chara commented.

"That's because my body has been smushed in several unnatural places," I grumbled, "and these shoes are seriously uncomfortable." They were sandals made with a golden string that wrapped in elegant twists all the way up to my bare knees. Then I saw the mirror and was shocked.

What was I wearing? Or, more specifically, what wasn't I?

There wasn't much to Brellusk; a long draping piece of silky red fabric covered from just under my belly button, swaying all the way to my shins. It was held there by a golden cord which dangled ruby-encrusted strings over my bare hips, and at the back was another strip of material. It was like a skirt with the sides torn off. There was enough space above the skirt for my ridiculously-long-draping on the floor-tail feathers to spread fantastically.

My stomach–which had miraculously toned, a little, after the hours spent rigorously training-was bare, and my chest was supported by an excessively sequined top. It was held up by a fancy jewelled halter-neck and golden string that crisscrossed down the bottom of my back, leaving room on my shoulders for my wings to come through. The whole ensemble was ludicrous; I looked like a belly dancer. God I hope I wasn't expected to dance in it. Or be able to walk in it. Or breathe.

"What's wrong?" Chara asked at my expression, "you look amazing."

"What happens if it's windy?" I explained, a little hysterically, "The whole world will see my...nakedness."

"You can wear a thong." Ellie reminded me.

I frowned, and said sarcastically, "Thanks for the reassurance."

"Just imagine Jayson's face when he sees you in this," Briseis said.

To be honest I couldn't really care less.

"Or Kieran's," Chara added quietly.

To be honest, I doubted *he* could care less. He hadn't spoken to me since our last argument. Whenever I went around he ignored me completely.

"Anyway, we've got to go," Chara said brightly, "the men will be home soon. We'll see you tomorrow and don't worry about it. You look fine."

"See you babe," Bris kissed my cheek before dancing out the door behind Chara.

"See you," I muttered to the closed door, and then I turned to a patiently-waiting Evelyn, "Do I have to wear it?"

Evelyn nodded, "Yes my Lady, you do."

I didn't know what I'd expected, maybe reindeer on the roof or something, but I was actually quite disappointed the next morning; the day of the Winter Festival. The Fire Palace wasn't decorated, it was as dreary and empty as usual, nothing at all seemed spectacular and the only gift I received was a message from the Ashaiks.

It was snowing again today, so I went out to sit on my sheltered balcony to watch the intricate flakes fall. Then I heard something.

I shuffled back instantly; away from the railing where I could be seen. Pressing my back against the wall I listened attentively, focusing my impeccable hearing on the sounds above me, closing my eyes.

The voice I could hear was deep and quiet, horribly rough; barely understandable. "It'll not take long, once Lynk's made his announcement." I think it was saying.

"We'll go home then?" asked another voice.

"If it all goes well," answered the other.

The other voice laughed quietly, "And if it doesn't?"

"Then we'll have our own little party."

"Good! I haven't eaten in far too long."

"Phoenix flesh is tainted," disagreed the other. "It isn't pure."

I shivered at those words.

"That's what makes it taste so good," sniggered one.

"Brother, you have forgotten the taste of human, haven't you?" Its voice rose in shock. "I know it's been a while since our last slave…"

"I could never forget."

There was a brief silence and then, "We'll both be reunited with it soon, anyway, Brother, thanks to Lynk."

"After tonight," purred the voice. "It all begins tonight".

I heard the glass door slide shut above me. It went quiet. I didn't like the sound of 'it all begins tonight.' Automatically I rushed back into my room–realising to my startled horror that Lynk was in there. I froze in stunned fear.

"What do you want?" I asked cautiously as he stared at the fat white snow lashing down from the grumbling sky.

"I just came to wish you a good winter," he answered, seemingly authentic–though I didn't believe him for a second. "I brought you a gift." He pulled out a wrapped box from his pocket. I glanced at it sceptically, why was he giving me a present?

"What is it?" I honestly tried not to sound so apprehensive.

"It was your mother's," he told me, smiling. I really wanted to believe his smile was genuine, but knew it was plastered on like a theatrical mask.

Lynk offered me the box and I slowly opened it. Inside was a gold necklace from which hung a feather-shaped garnet stone and several golden quills. It was a beautiful gem, deep crimson, and the chain was delicately engraved with ancient patterns.

"Do you like it?" he wondered, his voice dark and unfathomable.

"It's beautiful, but why…"

"Would you wear it?" he interrupted me, his voice strangely demanding.

I nodded frantically under pressure, "It's lovely. But why..."

"It's a gift. I realise that we didn't really start well, so this is me saying sorry," he answered, sounding earnest, his eyes uncharacteristically sincere. "You're mother would have wanted you to wear it tonight."

I was dumbfounded, completely confused, but I nodded.

Lynk looked at me, his topaz eyes unreadable, "By the way, Kian shall not be your protector tonight. He needs a day off too."

"Really," the immediate future suddenly brightened, "I don't have to be followed around?"

Lynk smiled and then said, "Yes, we're leaving at seven."

"Erm, actually," I added nervously as he turned to leave the room, "I'm going to go with Jayson Wanowa, he's meeting me here."

I'd expected him to get angry and yell at me, but he stayed in absolute control. His face didn't even twitch, "Okay, that's fine. I have a few things to sort out so I'll probably just see you there." With that, he strolled through my room and shut the door behind him.

I stood there unresponsively, staring bewilderedly at the necklace.

What the hell? What things did he have to sort out?

It all begins tonight.

I rushed into my room, unsure of what to do. I couldn't send a message. I think Lynk reads them when he's here. This was important; I needed to tell the Ashaiks what had happened, not only Lynk giving me an unexpected present, but what I'd heard when I was on the balcony. Why were those cannibal Phoenix or half-breed monsters-I wasn't quite sure which-going to have human flesh soon? No humans live on the island except the slaves. Those words echoed in my head like a fearful promise. *It all begins tonight.*

My maids came in around half-way through the afternoon; apparently it was time to get ready, starting with a bath. The rest of my time was then spent with my maids rushing about around me with cosmetics and lotions and various other beauty therapy devices. I'd been demoted to toy doll.

I closed my eyes to it all, listening to music, letting them tug at my hair and mess with my features. It was only once we'd struggled into the Brellusk–belly dancer outfit-that I properly woke up. I didn't wear my mother's chain, instead I kept it safely hidden in my pillowcase so I couldn't lose or break it.

I was instructed to Half-Change downstairs because there'd be more room.

Ellie then came forwards with the gold necklace Lynk had given me, placing it neatly over my curling crimson hair onto my neck. I didn't dare glance in the mirror.

I heard a knock on the door. "Come in," I called, and Evelyn entered.

"Jayson's here," she explained. "And you look lovely."

"Thanks," I smiled appreciatively, "but I can't move my head."

She smiled, "You ready now?"

I nodded, feeling the nerves constantly winding up my bare back.

We headed downstairs, into the Hall. I stopped. Evelyn nodded in understanding. I closed my eyes, thinking of fire. I'd been practicing Half-Changing twice everyday for the past week and had just about mastered the skill. My shoulders and the base of my back still bled from it though, and Evelyn had to carefully wipe the blood away. I took deep breaths then finally went to the main entrance to meet Jayson, my sweeping tail feathers gliding across the floor like a wedding train, my wings folded delicately.

Jayson looked amazing, he was wearing traditional golden trousers stitched with a red string...not that he didn't usually wear trousers or anything. His beautiful golden wings stretched out and his pale muscled chest was bare and painted with crimson symbols of fire; his marks. His blond hair was styled perfectly. He had an excited brightness in his eyes.

He looked like an angel. It was only then when looking at Jayson, I truly understood why people thought we were Angels; who wouldn't?

"You look beautiful," he told me as I came closer.

"Thanks, so do you." I smiled.

He laughed, "Shall we?" he gestured towards the door.

I nodded, waving goodbye to Evelyn. We made our way outside. I knew I should have been cold–though it had stopped snowing and the sky was filled with twinkling stars-but I felt as if I were on fire.

"How are you feeling?" Jayson asked.

"Terrified," I responded. I could feel myself shaking.

We were travelling quite far, so my feet were killing me by the time we reached the centre of the city–to the gardens behind the gemstone tower. I was so dizzy with nervousness that when I stopped, I tripped slightly on the grass.

"Wonderful entrance there from Ruby," a familiar voice called.

Without looking up, I answered, "I must keep up my reputation."

I stood up straight, realising that the whole family was there; Chara, Nik, Ebony and her husband, Adrian. They all looked great, Chara dressed in a short backless satin dress with only her wings out, and Ebony in an emerald Brellusk, her gorgeous black tail feathers sprouting everywhere. Nik was shirtless like Jayson, wings from his shoulders and brownish trousers covering his legs; Adrian wingless and human. Then I saw Kieran.

I think my heart stopped beating. I felt an awesome gush of...*something* flood through me, trembling my stomach. It was kind of like the feeling when you suddenly drop on a rollercoaster, only a million times better.

He strolled towards me with that cocky swagger and stood still just a metre or so away. He was wearing all black, and he'd never looked hotter.

His cinnamon skin was bare, Earth symbols freshly painted over his prominent muscles, mingling with his tattoos already there from the Half-Change. His obsidian wings danced behind him. I couldn't actually believe my eyes when I saw his familiar biker leathers, hanging low on his hips, the bottoms tucked into his black chunky boots that possibly hid something deadly. Had he really brought them all this way? On a dark belt strapped to his hips hung a long curved Gaborah blade; this was a sign of royalty. It was certainly an interesting combination with the leather. His onyx hair had been spiked up in gorgeous disarray, making him appear like a hawk. His piercing emerald eyes only added to the dangerous-and-knowing-it look.

Then Ebony moved into my line of vision. I blinked like a statue coming to life, the enchantment broken.

"Ruby, you look amazing." She enthused brilliantly.

Chara swept forwards too, hugging me fiercely. I must admit, I was still a little star-struck. Nik came forwards as well, wrapping his arms around me in a brotherly way. Jayson abruptly put his arm around my waist.

I looked at Jayson, suddenly remembering his existence and smiling reassuringly. Kieran glowered, almost baring his teeth.

Apparently people were just noticing Jayson.

"Oh Mother," Chara said, "Jayson. You look like an angel."

Jayson frowned slightly, as if unsure if she was complimenting him. "Is that good?" he wondered good-naturedly.

"No," Kieran delivered before Chara could reply, "Angels have no reproductive organs. Do you see what she's implying," he shook his head in mock seriousness. "I wouldn't stand for that."

"I didn't mean..." Chara began, flustered.

"You wouldn't stand for anything, Kierakai," Jayson intercepted angrily, tension was rising like the calm before the storm.

"No," Kieran considered calmly, "but I'd stand *against* you being within a hundred mile radius of me and civilisation."

I felt Jayson tense beside me and gripped his arm warningly.

Kieran noticed this and smirked, "Don't get your feathers in a bunch because of me. Just leave if you want to."

"Kieran, Adrian," a vaguely familiar voice spoke. Garnha suddenly stepped through the trees, her husband–Kieran's awful father-shortly behind her. "Let's go."

Kieran turned to look at his mother and father, "I didn't realise this was a family event." He smiled coldly at his father. "I should have brought my father-son friendship bracelet."

The man with salt and pepper hair grunted, "Kierakai…" threateningly.

Kieran sighed, his face going startlingly serious, "Look, oh noble sperm donor, it's not that I don't like you or want to be seen in public with you, it's that I *really* don't like you or want to be seen in public with you; so keep moving." He gestured towards the numerous Phoenix making their way down the path to the surprise venue.

Kieran's father's face was a thunderstorm of furious incredulity but before he could do anything Garnha ushered him away, giving Kieran a stern look.

Once they'd disappeared into the crown, Kieran turned happily to the rest of us, "Anymore unwanted family reunions? No? Okay then, let's get going; I know Jayson's *dying* to show us his new moves on the dance floor."

Wisely, Jayson didn't rise to the challenge.

I gasped in astonishment as the Winter Palace came into view. At the top of permanent stone steps was a great expanse of flat stone, built on it was the beautiful artistic venue structured entirely out of incandescent blue ice. Massive transparent shards scraped the heavens, and four main columns of ice supported the entire glittering mass, like a massive frozen gazebo.

Jayson nudged me along and I followed him up the steps.

Inside it was even more spectacular. The whole area was embellished with winter decorations, scintillating crystal chandeliers, snowflake ice sculptures scattered between burning sapphire-coloured bonfires and marvellously scented white winter flowers. It was like being in a fairy tale.

The room was absolutely huge and streaming with exotically dressed people; no Phoenix felt the cold. Round tables were dispersed around. Dominating the centre of the room was an upraised rounded stage; I gulped.

Suddenly a woman rushed towards us, she looked stressed but smiled, "I'm Savannah, and I can show you your seats."

Then a vaguely familiar voice sounded next to me, it was the female Water-Elder who'd supervised my singing practice. Her name was Katrina. "You take them," she told the other woman, nodding towards the rest of my party, "I need Ruby. We have to start early, people are arriving too quickly."

I nodded, feeling panicked butterflies flutter in my stomach. I unhooked my arm from Jayson's, quickly saying, "I've got to go, wish me luck."

He smiled, and to my surprise, suddenly bent forwards to lightly kiss my lips. Before I had chance to react he pulled away again, "Good luck."

Blinking like a madwoman with a nervous twitch I followed Katrina away from Jayson and the Ashaiks, feeling eyes boring into my back.

She led me around the bustling room-I'd never seen so many Phoenix in my life-to a tiny room at the side of the ice building. Inside I found at least twenty scantily clad female dancers of different Tribes, each displaying their wings. It was an art to dance like that apparently. At least I wasn't the only one hardly dressed. Then my stomach dropped, Sofia was one of the dancers. And she looked breathtaking.

I waited there, nerves bubbling in my chest until somebody called "Ruby?"

"Yes?" I said, despite knowing what was coming.

"We're ready." Katrina said, looking purposefully at the dancers.

Good, I thought, *at least somebody is.*

Chapter Twenty-Seven

Incandescent light burned brightly in spheres, the brilliant rays flickering down from the ceiling like trapped stars. They hung from the decorated ice rafters like raindrops on blades of grass, dangling precariously in their thousands. I blinked against its blinding harshness, but unfortunately I still saw my waiting audience.

My heart pounded so strongly it was like a fierce battle cry. Beads of sticky sweat formulated across my back, tumbling down my naked spine. I clasped my hands together; interlacing my fingers tightly like they were the only things keeping me clutched to earth. The drums began beating, imitating my pulse and the beautiful wind and string instruments soon followed.

Suddenly a blank wall hit me. What was I doing? I don't remember the words! Seizing hold of my panic before it would grow overwhelming, I opened my mouth and began the song. The first word choked out, the next sounded like a strangled cat, but by the third I'd controlled myself.

The rest of the lyrics flowed out like water, shimmering and mesmerising. The music slowly melted through my hesitant system, my body awakening, reincarnated by the sound. My voice wrapped around me, around the open room, around every individual; gradually strengthening. The world and its inhabitants were at my fingertips, ready to grasp.

No, these people were not mine to take.

The dancers spilled around me as the chorus kicked in. Automatically, they captured attention and all my nervous ideas vanished. Feeling relieved that the crowd was mostly distracted, their intense gazes divided, I continued my song while keeping my voice firmly under control.

The dancers moved seductively, alluringly, in a sexy way that I could never *ever* pull off. They swayed their bodies back and forth tantalisingly, leaping elegantly into the air with their impressive wings. The dance was like ballet with wings and sass. And, of course, Sofia was phenomenally talented and looked so beautiful that my self-confidence shrivelled and died.

I bet Kieran was watching her.

The song came towards the climax and I released my voice to its enchanting potential-mostly because Sofia was stealing my limelight-and then *everybody* was looking at me. The weaker Phoenix had blank faces.

Shit.

Not again.

Thankfully the music came abruptly to halt. There were a few seconds of startled silence and then the room burst into enthusiastic applause.

It was over. I'd done it.

I could feel my pulse racing. My lungs frantically gasped for oxygen. Exhaustion suddenly consumed me, smudging my vision and swaying my body precariously. I hadn't realised how much effort it took to keep my voice under control for such a big crowd. Vaguely I heard surrounding noises, like the screeching of chairs on the stone floor but my head swam irrationally. I could feel myself falling...

Strong arms caught me. Feeling that I'd played this scene before, I looked up. In a daze, I felt almost confused when I realised that the eyes I saw weren't green. They were amber.

"Are you alright?" Jayson asked, concern etched across his features.

I frowned as my vision slowly adjusted. I heard a hollow ringing in my ears. I could also hear that the music had awkwardly started up again; the dancers were now joined with male dancers and were currently gliding gracefully across the room. This music wasn't painfully intense, it was as smooth and tempting as chocolate.

"I t-think so," I spluttered shakily, then I shook my head and forced my unstable legs to hold my weight as I carefully straightened up.

Jayson looked uncertain, a worried frown creasing his forehead, and he reluctantly removed his hands from my waist. Grimacing, I followed as he led me to a nearby table.

Jayson sat me down on an unoccupied chair-not glancing at the other twelve people who were gaping at me like I'd just drank mayonnaise through a straw-instead he gazed anxiously in my eyes like he thought I might shatter. "Are you sure you're okay? You look kind of green," he queried probingly.

"I'm fine," I answered honestly, the dizziness had completely subsided.

He offered me an expensive-looking crystal glass filled with a bubbling pink liquid. I made a face, but took it off him. It tasted like fizzy grapefruit.

"You were fantastic, by the way," Jayson complimented. "Up until the point you nearly fainted."

I laughed, "Up until that point." I glanced at the dancers enviously, wishing I could look so graceful, and wondered "So what happens now?"

"Well, now, there will be games, fireworks, flight displays, food." I turned back to him; he was raising his eyebrows, "dancing; that kind of thing."

"Food sounds good," I volunteered, suddenly ravenous.

He smiled, standing up, but when I stood up too he shook his head and pushed my shoulder down again. I frowned at him, confused, and he said, "You just sit there, you still look pale. I'll get you something."

"I always look pale," I objected, but he grinned then walked off anyway.

"That's very true," said an annoying, familiar voice "Bleached almost."

"Are you being racist?" I wondered, not looking at him.

"I just came to check if my damsel in distress is okay," he answered innocently, with an irritating edge. "I know how difficult you find it to stand completely still and not find something to injure yourself with."

"Is it because it's a special occasion that you're being doubly annoying, or are you just unsuccessfully trying to be conversational?" I enquired, finally turning to look at Kieran.

"Oh Princess," Kieran retorted sarcastically, "every day's a special occasion when I'm with you."

"How sweet," I said through gritted teeth. I glared angrily at him.

"Sarcasm really isn't that attractive on you," he said lazily. "Leave it to professionals like me, who use it as an art rather than a final resort."

"Kieran, I'm hungry," I moaned, "can't I ignore you some other time?"

"You know, if I actually cared about your opinion, I might be offended," he said. "I'm a very sensitive person after all. I might be crying inside."

"Oh yeah, I can see how emotional you are," I muttered furiously.

"Yeah," he smirked, "it must be hard for you to take it in. After all, most emotion can't fight through the gooey black stuff surrounding your heart."

I glowered at him, but he looked at me with that superior arrogance flickering in his eyes. A smirk rested on his flawless lips, a cocky lean in his stance. Jayson returned, staring pointedly at Kieran. Warning bells chimed in my head, but Kieran didn't seem remotely fazed.

"Alright, that's enough," Jayson said, a firm warning tone saturating his voice, an edge I'd only heard once. "You shouldn't speak to her like that."

Kieran examined him calmly, like he was merely curious. "How did you get here? You know you shouldn't be wandering around without your owner." Kieran put his hands on his hips, shaking his head with dramatic eyes. "Did somebody let you out of your cage again?"

I saw Jayson's eyes flash, but he composed himself-barely-before he spoke, "What do you want?"

"To talk to Ruby," he answered. Everybody could hear him. "You know, what I was doing perfectly well before you came."

"Your definition of talking is very different to mine," Jayson responded.

"Simple verbs like 'talk' can confuse some people; I'm sure you're just a late developer." Kieran assured him patronisingly, "Just sit down before you wet yourself in embarrassment."

"Kieran," I said warningly but he ignored me.

"Ruby's right here," Jayson said, not moving an inch or taking his animalistic gaze from Kieran as he gestured towards me blindly.

"I know. I was speaking to her before you rudely interrupted."

"*I'm* rude?" Jayson scoffed.

Kieran nodded, his face mockingly delighted. "There you go; acceptance is the first sign on the road to recovery. Soon you'll have perfect manners."

"Did you learn that at anger management?" Jayson retorted bitterly.

Kieran just looked at him, "You know, usually I don't judge why parents keep their unwanted children, but with you, I can't help but wonder what the hell they were thinking." He said it so calmly, so factually.

That was when Jayson snapped.

"What were *your* parent's thinking when they kept that human," -he nearly spat the word- "your *brother*, alive? It's disgusting."

My jaw dropped open in astonishment; shock froze my limbs where they were beginning to hastily stand. I gaped at Jayson. It was ten times worse than anything Kieran had said. I really couldn't believe he'd just said that.

"What did you say?" the quiet nonchalance in Kieran's velvety voice didn't fool me. Jayson had insulted his brother; that was unforgivable.

"Everybody knows your brother is human," Jayson answered. I moved to jerk forwards but my bones wouldn't respond and I staggered into the back of a vacant chair. *No Kieran*, I thought pleadingly, *people are watching*.

"I thought you did," Kieran said, his voice way too rational. "I just needed confirmation before I beat an apology out of you."

I shoved the chair back, but I wasn't fast enough. Even Jayson–the assassin warrior-wasn't fast enough. Kieran brought up his arm, as fast as lightning, and a millisecond later I heard a loud crack as his fist connected with Jayson's jaw. Jayson rolled back on his heels from the impact, his expression almost surprised and then he pounced forward like a cat.

"Kieran!" I shouted as I rushed over.

Jayson went to hit Kieran but he somehow managed to dodge out of the way. The scene blurred as fists flew at speeds too quick for my mind to comprehend. Charging at

Jayson, I yanked him back as hard as I could, trying to avoid being accidentally hit myself, probably by my own arm. I was knocked to the side and Kieran furiously beat Jayson to the floor, growling. Jayson somehow managed to kick Kieran's ribcage, the impact forcing him backwards into a table; the plates and glasses going flying. They charged at each other like wild animals, their faces unrecognisable with fury.

Suddenly Adrian was there, grabbing the back of Kieran's shirt with his iron strength and hauling him off Jayson. For once, Kieran actually looked like Adrian's younger brother. Flint, Jayson's friend, moved to restrain Jayson. Kieran was struggling viciously to escape Adrian's frantic grasp. I could see the animalistic glint in his emerald eyes; they were unfocused and malicious, beyond the point of reasoning. Adrian was saying things in his ear but Kieran blatantly couldn't hear him. He looked possessed.

I went to stand between them with my back to Jayson-whose face was already swelling. I stared at Kieran carefully, waiting until he finally noticed me. His burning stare almost passed *through* me. A shudder rippled to my core. The hostile contempt wasn't aimed at me but it was still hurt to behold.

"Kieran," I spoke his name quietly, reassuringly so he knew I was there. And then I breathed that significant ancient word before I even realised I had said it. My instincts took over entirely as I gently whispered "Sungha."

His eyes flickered with a spark of comprehension, and then shifted to mine. I gazed into his eyes until eventually his dilated pupils shrunk and he looked slightly less insane. His perfect features softened, the tense muscles of his shoulders seemed to sag like rafters in an old cottage. Adrian's strained-white knuckles relaxed slightly. Adrian looked at me for the first time without any hate. He looked almost grateful.

"Sungha," Kieran repeated quietly.

When Lynk's voice suddenly was in my ear, I jumped, startled.

"Now boys," he said, "don't you think you're a little old for bickering?"

"If so, we're also too old to be called boys," Kieran snapped, bluntly, thoughtlessly. I exhaled in exasperation, mentally cursing.

To my surprise, Lynk seemed almost amused. Well that was a first, that someone was actually *impressed* by Kieran's bad attitude.

"I suppose you're right and therefore I won't need to remind you, Kierakai Ashaik, that if you are brought before the High Council one more time, you won't just be leaving with a few scars that your mummy can heal," he warned delicately. "In fact, I doubt you'd leave at all."

"You want to keep me?" Kieran inquired, his voice laced with mocking amusement, "Well I'm flattered, but unfortunately I'm also straight."

Lynk stared calmly at him, "Pass me your sword."

"Excuse me?" Kieran seemed surprised, "I thought we'd just made my sexuality quiet clear. I'll save my sword for the ladies, thank you."

Adrian reached down to Kieran's dark belt and withdrew his Gaborah blade, muttering something nasty in Kieran's ear. He passed it to Lynk without a word. Lynk held the blade tightly, "I suggest you disappear, now, Kierakai."

I shivered at the black threat in his eyes but before Kieran could say anything Adrian answered, "My Lord," nodding respectfully, he shoved Kieran away. I watched as he left, feeling strangely numb.

Lynk then turned to Jayson. "I would have thought better of you, Wanowa."

"Apologies," he grunted, "It won't happen again."

"Ruby," at the sound of my name my attention snapped to Lynk. "Why can I not help but think you were involved in this?"

"Kieran was being rude," I told him, "and Jayson was just sticking up for me." I didn't feel it was necessary to mention the finer details.

Lynk shook his head disappointedly, but then something caught his eye and he seemed distracted. I turned to see what he was looking at, but frowned when I saw nothing. Lynk said, "Be careful; all of you. I don't want anyone messing up the plan."

"What plan?" I inquired, instantly suspicious. *It all begins tonight.*

Lynk glanced back at me, as if he'd just realised I'd been standing there. "The plan for a successful night, of course," he answered guardedly. "Excuse me," he said before walking off into a sea of constantly moving people.

I turned to Jayson, suddenly realising just how angry I was. "I can't believe you," I scolded. "Why did you do that?" He looked almost shocked at my outburst but when he opened his mouth, I interrupted him, "Why would you say that? You know what Kieran's like, he's not exactly a friendly person on a good day; you knew he was going to be pissed; like really pissed."

"I don't know what I was thinking," he answered pathetically.

"Well, obviously." I retorted grumpily, feeling exhausted. I plonked myself down on a chair, digging into whatever was on the plate Jayson had brought me. I couldn't taste anything; like the food turned to ash in my mouth.

"I didn't know you were close to Adrian as well," Jayson said slowly, sitting.

"I'm not really, but as a whole I'm close to the entire family." Chewing something that tasted like chicken, I swallowed hungrily without savouring. I wondered, "Is that, like, abnormal?"

"Yeah," he sighed. "It really is."

I mulled that over as I shovelled food into my mouth. I'm even less of a lady when eating, especially when I'm angry. When the plate was empty, and the silence become too awkward for me to stand, I downed the rest of my glass; hoping it was filled with alcohol.

"Hey," Jayson said warningly, "Steady on, that's stuff's lethal."

"I'm no lightweight," I snapped, "I'll be fine."

"Look, I'm sorry about Kieran, okay?" he gushed suddenly, his words practically spilling out. "Just please stop giving me that look."

"It was more what you said about Adrian than anything else," my eyes narrowed. "Do you really think that?"

He shook his head, "I was just angry. Kieran just...*gets* to me. You don't understand. We go so far back. They hurt me I hurt them."

I nodded, wondering why he said 'they' instead of 'him'.

"He gets to me too," I sighed eventually.

When I didn't say anything else, Jayson asked, "Do you want to go for a walk? I could use some fresh air."

I stood up and followed him around the outside of the Ice Palace. There were less people outside than inside and eventually we found a more secluded section. I sat down on some stone steps, Jayson sitting beside me. Our wings spread out behind us, interlocking like a plaits.

It was darker outside. The music was muffled by the frozen walls. I glanced at Jayson. He was looking at me already, those sweet amber eyes staring directly into mine. He really was beautiful. I knew it was true. He had his flaws, I know, but he had been a really good friend to me over the last couple of weeks. It was nice to be with someone so relaxed and laid back–despite his questionable occupation and disputes with the Ashaik brothers. I felt truly calm around Jayson.

I finally plucked up enough courage to ask him, "What did happen between you and Kieran?"

He took a deep breath, glancing away, then returned his vision to me, sighing eventually, "It's complicated, and, in all honestly, not much at all to do with Kieran."

I analysed his expression. He seemed suddenly deeply sad, "Adrian?" I guessed. "You found out about him being human?"

He shook his head, eyes wide. "No!" he said honestly, almost shocked at my accusation. "What I said to Kieran just now was in anger. I never meant it. I knew about Adrian all along. It didn't bother me. It was them it bothered."

I frowned confusedly, "So what did happen?"

He withdrew a shaky breath; his usually relaxed face was utterly devoid of emotion. "I can't tell you Ruby."

I pulled a face, "Why not?"

"It's just so shameful," he answered. "It hurt me so much I did something stupid. I told Lynk that they were leaving." He put his head in his hands, his shoulders sinking. "I was just so angry. I regret it so much."

"Lynk?" I felt horrified, "Why?"

"He's our Elder," He frowned then looked down at the floor. "I thought he would just bring them back and punish them. I didn't expect him to send so many after them, with death warrants..." he trailed off; shuddering. "I went to Lynk after, trying to find out what had happened but he refused to see me. I assumed they were all dead." He looked up at me. "When I saw Kieran during your First Flight it was like seeing a ghost. I didn't know what to think, to say; I think I just got angry again."

I placed a hand on his, knowing that this was really hard for him to admit. "I believe you," I sighed eventually. Whatever had happened between them was just between them. Maybe I'd be told one day, but I knew it'd be a while.

He looked up at me from underneath his long ashen lashes, those amber eyes sparkling with an orange flame. "Really?"

I smiled, "Really."

The next thing I knew he was leaning in closer to me, his lips coming dangerously close to me. I froze where I sat, astounded and confused, unsure of what to do. I liked Jayson, but could I do this? I didn't have much choice in the end, my body reacted for me.

His lips were soft this time, tender. He was being careful to erase my memory of our last drunken kiss. It was sweet, easy. It wasn't all wild and passionate like it had been with Kieran, it was slower, more a build-up of something that could actually happen. Would the feelings and the passion come later? Was it okay to be doing this now? It was so relaxed, easy, like our friendship. I was so confused. It felt wrong. Seriously wrong. It wasn't Kieran I was kissing, but I couldn't be with Kieran, so should I settle for the next best?

He lifted his hand to my face, carefully entwining his fingers in my hair, pulling me closer and kissing me again, our mouths moving together. What was I doing? Why was I letting him kiss me? I was so confused.

I pulled back suddenly, looking at Jayson. He smiled that soft easy-going smile. I looked away, a million emotions and questions running through me.

Then my heart lurched as I noticed Kieran standing at the bottom of the steps.

His face was incredulous, dangerous. He turned and walked off. Without the slightest hesitation I left Jayson, instinctively running after Kieran and apologising as I went. I ran down the stone steps into the forest-like gardens. Kieran wasn't hard to find because wherever he went he left a path of destruction, ripping up the roots of several large trees with his mind and his Earth Affinity, sending them loudly catapulting to the snowy earth.

I followed the devastation, then his footprints when he stopped killing the greenery. His footprints disappeared. Sighing, I went and sat on the ledge of a nearby water fountain. A beautiful stone Phoenix was positioned in the centre; water trickled from her slender wingtips. I put my head in my hands, listening to the water.

Why did Jayson have to do that?

A sound of rustling splinters made me glance up. Kieran stood there, looking at me. I looked at him. The large moon shone in the sky like a magnificent opal, casting the world in a mysterious silver ambiance. Kieran was like a shadow in the ominous atmosphere. His black hair was inky and luminous; his darkly tanned skin standing out against the snow, but his emerald eyes remained as clear and fluorescent as normal.

He stood silently for a long moment, his feet planted uncooperatively to earth like they were undecided if they wanted to move.

I rose quietly. "Kieran, I..." I didn't know what I was going to say.

"Just shut up for a moment," he demanded furiously.

I shut my mouth obediently, awaiting his harsh words.

He strode over to me and swiftly bent down to kiss my unsuspecting lips.

I gasped in surprise, and he made a rumbling noise in the back of his throat, almost a growl. One of his hands fiercely cupped the back of my head, his fingers intertwined in the bright curling strands. My heart hammered erratically, my head whirling dizzyingly. I wrapped my shaking hands up around his shoulders, kissing him back with equal passion. The hand that was in my hair moved down my bare back, his rough fingers tracing over my tattooed spine. I shivered ecstatically at his touch, my defences crumbling.

Kieran pulled back less than an inch. Leaning his forehead against mine and holding my face in his hands, his large fingers spread protectively. His deep green eyes held a strange distant light, a flicker of silver sparkling within his black pupils; like he was showing me his soul.

"You are mine," he whispered, leaning forwards, his voice tickled my neck as he nuzzled his nose against my ear. I shivered and his voice came again in a deep seductive murmur. "No one can touch you but me. And if I can't touch you; no one can." He said sternly, his expression ferociously protective.

I smiled helplessly. And he launched at me again.

He pushed me back with his body, against a nearby tree, his fingers moving across my body with a fierce hunger. His hands were in my hair, pulling at the curls almost painfully, forcing my face to his. He kissed me wildly, fast and strong and unpredictable. My hands danced across his chest, feeling the hard muscles there and the contraction of his lungs as he breathed heavily. My body seemed on fire, sensations spreading though me like wildfire. My skin burning in ways I'd never experienced before.

"You're too beautiful tonight, Ruby," Kieran murmured, pulling back to stop himself from going too far. "I completely blame you for this."

"I don't mind taking responsibility," I offered contentedly.

Abruptly Kieran leaned back a fraction. "You will," he disagreed seriously, "if somebody finds out."

My eyes widened in astonishment as the image of the pregnant woman on the Wall sprung across my vision. The thought was horrifying. I'd be cursed before we'd even get to that stage too; made human again, but this time permanently. I couldn't imagine never flying again, to once again feel secluded and not belonging to anything. To me it was the worst thing imaginable, and I'd barely been a Phoenix for a month.

It would kill Kieran.

Suddenly I heard the rush of running feet over the snow. Kieran released me instantly, straightening up. Ebony burst out of the trees, panting frantically like she'd been racing for her life. I looked at her, instantly worried by the look in her eyes. My stomach trembled apprehensively.

"What are you-" I began confusedly, but she interrupted me.

"You need to come quickly," her voice was saturated with fear and panic. "It's Lynk, he's..."

That was all she needed to say, I was already running.

Chapter Twenty-Eight

My heavy wings made it difficult to balance as I thundered up the cool stone steps. There was nobody dancing inside anymore, the various instruments lining the wall were eerily abandoned. I burst through into the centre of the ice structure, to where every Phoenix gathered around the stage in a heaving crowd. A lone figure stood on the stage with a golden breastplate covering his chest, a Gaborah blade at his hips and massive white-yellow wings released from his shoulders. Lynk was speaking calmly, rationally and I strained to catch his words.

"For too long we have been forced to remain within the boundaries of Kariak, trapped like disobedient animals. Don't we deserve to be free? Don't we deserve to know what else there is out there?" he was saying. I instantly heard the persuasive note in his influential voice. "We are all caged birds; we should fight back at those who imprisoned us. We are more powerful; we are stronger, we *will* prevail. We *will* be the higher race."

He wanted to leave the island? He wanted to go...to go to my country? And countries like it? I couldn't believe my ears. People would freak out. For a moment I imagined poor sweet Tanya, alone in her little pub, surrounded by the Angels and Daemons. She'd have a heart attack.

Phoenix flesh is tainted...you have forgotten the taste of human... we'll both be reunited with it soon anyway, brother, thanks to Lynk the monsters words were like a death sentence; humankind's death sentence. If Lynk leaves, they leave. If they leave, they'll eat humans. If they eat humans, it'll be mass destruction. And God knows how many half-breeds there are. My attacker had said an army; an army of those monsters? I shuddered mentally. It'd start a war!

Oh God, people were nodding in agreement.

It's his voice, I realised in dawning horror.

I glanced at Kieran, and he looked just as shocked as me. Without hesitation, he began shoving his way through the audience.

Lynk was still speaking, "Few have left before, but what I wish is *all* of Kariak to leave. All Karisian creatures deserve freedom." His black eyes scanned the audience, "The task isn't that difficult. All we need to do is destroy the Gemstone Towers, destroy the wards, and we'll be free. We'll come and go as we please and fly the skies of freedom."

I heard a voice speak up, it sounded surprisingly like Chara's. "There was a reason the gem towers were made, you know. Humans hate us."

Lynk barely looked interested in this. "They will fear us. And fear we can control. Human's fear their Gods as they will us, or adore us as their Angels."

Kieran reached the stage while I was still struggling to tear my way through the unresponsive bodies. Only a few still looked comprehensive. Kieran stood up straight, looking out at the emotionless faces, a spark of worried understanding lighting his eyes; he knew that the majority of the crowd were already controlled by Lynk.

But still he said to Lynk, "You could never be a God."

Lynk looked at him, merely curiously, "And why is that?"

"Well, one: you're ugly. Two: you're actually quite stupid. And three,' Kieran suddenly flipped a small knife from inside the thick leather band around his wrist, and before Lynk could react, Kieran cut the tip of his finger with it; drawing a single tear of dark blood. "You bleed. Gods are immortal. We are not."

Kieran knew what he was doing. For the second it took for the tiny wound to heal, Lynk lost his concentration, and therefore severed the connection with some of the crowd under his influence. It wasn't much, but it was enough.

Kieran turned to the heaving crowd, emitting an air of reassuring confidence. "Let's cut out the bullshit. I have lived with humans, lived *as* a human." He announced bravely, "I can tell you the truth *before* you go dancing off with the Siren over here." Kieran pointed at Lynk.

I heard a faint but authoritative voice-an Elder. "Speak, Earthbird."

Kieran nodded "Humans are simpler than us. They depend on normalcy and routine. If we knock down the wards and reveal Kariak, releasing all the monsters even *we* don't want to see they'll freak out and fight back. And there are far too many of them for our single race to fight." Kieran had a glint in his eyes, a glint that made it very obvious that he knew about Lynk's alliances.

Lynk saw this, but didn't seem remotely bothered. He answered now with a lazy ignorance. "This is the reason I have made alliances with others." He explained, and at this some of the crowd woke up.

A man next to me shook his head. I recognised him instantaneously. He was on the High Council, the man with whitish blue hair and ocean eyes, and also the one who was the harshest. He boomed, "You made alliances without consulting the Council?" his voice echoed around the room. "Who have you made these alliances with?" he demanded.

Lynk merely glanced at the man, "Daemons, or rather, my new breed of Daemons."

The man next to me took in a deep, horrified breath. "Daemons?" he bellowed furiously, "They're not to be trusted. They wouldn't help us."

Lynk glared down at him now, his eyes gave the impression that he was mentally visualizing pinning the Elder to the floor like a butterfly on a pin. Outwardly though, Lynk was as cool and calculating as usual; it was an extremely intimidating quality.

"I believe in the art of breeding to gain perfection," Lynk's lips twisted, but his voice remained unbearably beautiful. "As creator I have the upper hand."

"What have you done?" the Water Elder demanded.

Lynk ignored him, instead his gaze swept across the other faces in the audience, "Don't you all want freedom? Don't you all want to live? To know what's out there and take it for your own?"

Nobody in the audience spoke. A terrifying silence filled the air.

"Well," Lynk finally spoke, "I had hoped you would all see my point of view. I had hoped I wouldn't have to *make* you all understand."

Apprehension trembled my stomach. Lynk was going to use his voice properly...oh my God. I shoved an Airbird to the side to push my way closer to the stage, but more people swallowed me up like a constant tide.

Nikolas suddenly appeared on stage. "You won't survive out there," he said quietly to Lynk, his voice so soft that even I, only a metre away, had to strain to hear. "The air isn't pure enough for Phoenix." He glanced at me sadly, and slowly I began to understand. "We were growing weaker every month we stayed away, becoming so ill that sometimes it took hours to Change. We're not meant for that world. The land is paved over by concrete; the fire is contaminated with toxic gases. We were slowly dying."

I gasped in realisation, and finally shoved my way through the rest of the crowd to look up at Kieran. "You...were...dying?" I barely whispered the words but I knew he heard. So, after all, the reason they left wasn't because of me; it was to save themselves. "That's the real reason you left, isn't it?"

Kieran never did answer that question.

Nikolas was abruptly there, his kind eyes regretful. "It wasn't the only reason, Ruby, we *did* want to save you, but we were planning to go back anyway. We just didn't know when. You were just a..."

"A reason to leave," I finished in a whisper, "an excuse."

I could feel my hands shaking. They'd let me believe that it was for *my* benefit that they left. I'd thought they'd *wanted* to help me. I'd thought they cared about me. Really they just wanted to save themselves.

They really didn't care about saving me.

I wasn't even of Earth. I didn't matter to them.

I was such an idiot.

Lynk's harsh laughter cut deeply, "My poor daughter. Did you think you were special?" His voice was like razors. "Don't take it personally; most Phoenix are liars."

My eyes narrowed, "Including you. I saw what you did to that woman a week ago. You tortured her, then had those monsters tear out her stomach so you could get a stupid worthless key."

"Worthless?" he repeated, as if mildly surprised by my choice of vocabulary. "Do you even know what that key opens?"

"It opens the Gemstone Tower in the Fire City," I snapped.

"And what's kept in the tower?" he asked, his voice like razorblades.

I glared at him, "The wards that protect the city."

His topaz and black eyes, identical to mine, transformed. The onyx in them expanded, devouring the colour that once thrived there like sunshine. When he spoke his voice was too deep; a horribly seductive edge was creeping into it, "And how, my sweet child, is that unimportant? Don't be so naive, everything has ambiguous purposes."

His voice was like a drug; as soon as people caught a whiff of its intoxicating essence it captivated them completely. Like the siren's enchanting music that caused sailors to blissfully crash their ships into rocks. Like a vampire's bewitching smile that disguised the sharp, pointed teeth.

And he hadn't even started yet.

"The Metovah key isn't important right now, however what is important is that ridiculous proposition, Lynk," spoke the blue eyed Elder with a clear firm voice. Apparently he was still completely himself. "As a member of the Council, you have a right to express your opinion and your ideas, but as an Elder I strongly decline."

Lynk rolled his eyes. "I've had enough of you. I *am* the Council."

Lynk looked towards the ceiling, upraising his hands as if praising and making a distinctive gesture. Immediately, I glanced up into the roof. At first I noticed nothing spectacular, but then slowly, I understood.

Camouflaged high in the ice rafters, concealed by the extravagant decorations, the Daemon half-breeds dwelled.

Phoenix dazedly looked up, realisation immediately snapping into them.

There were at least twelve; some crawling down the walls to block the exits, some abseiling down diaphanous rope to hang silently above the petrified crowd like spiders. One sprang off the highest rafter, landing on the stage. It straightened up, one of its devilish horns pointing directly at me. The skin under a damaged metal breastplate was streaked with distorted tribal patterns, its sharp human cheekbones splattered with obsidian paint. Its deformed legs spread wide, its bat-like wings devouring the stage.

Lynk ignored my glare, instead acknowledging the whole crowd. "This is your last chance," he said. "Do you share my vision? Or are you against it."

Kieran smiled arrogantly, "I think I speak for everyone when I say you can shove your 'vision' up your hairy..."

Before he could finish the sentence the half-breed sprang at him, hissing something in a foreign language. Instantly Kieran dived out of the way, struggling to search for a Gaborah blade that wasn't there. The creature crept closer now. Kieran had no weapon. Why? Kieran *always* had a weapon. *Lynk took it from him earlier*, I realised. Crap, crap, crap.

Recklessly I leapt up onto the stage to stand between Kieran and the beast. A noise ripped out of my throat instinctively. I bared my teeth threateningly. The Daemon hesitated for the briefest of moments; to my astonishment Lynk put his hand out, palm up. It growled, but otherwise obeyed.

Lynk looked at me curiously, "Why would you want to protect him?"

I glared, "Nobody deserves to be eaten by a genetically modified bat."

"What do you want, Ruby?" Lynk wondered. "If you surrender, you could help bring freedom to the children of Kariak."

I shook my head furiously, "I may look like you, I may sound like you, but in my heart I'm English. And the English *never* surrender."

He shrugged, "Suit yourself."

A chant boomed out from Lynk. He spoke in a complicated ancient language. I turned to stare at the crowd, dismayed, as the pairs of eyes dimmed in synchrony, their features transforming into blank unresponsive expressions. Phoenix were strong, but still overpowered.

Panicked, I glanced to Kieran. To my great relief he didn't look affected; for whatever miracle made him immune to the noise, I was grateful.

Up until the point he grabbed someone's blade and began running at Lynk. I tried to yank him back, seeing the creature behind him, but he slipped though my grasp. Now I screamed as they closed in on him. There were too many. Suddenly something pressed against my back.

Lynk's chant was intensifying now, growing louder and stronger. Four people were climbing up onto the stage, their faces as dead as zombies. I realised that they were the four male Council Elders. The male Earth Elder was Kieran's father. He stumbled along with empty eyes.

I saw the Daemons push Kieran to his knees; their many purple eyes watching him inescapably. He froze then, defeated, if he moved he would die.

I guessed if I moved I'd be stabbed too.

As I watched, Lynk moved towards the Water Elder. The man held out his hand and Lynk drew up a dagger and sliced along his palm. Beads of bluish blood instantly formed, soon spraying out and changing to red as it dripped onto a piece of parchment Lynk held. I had no idea what he was doing. I couldn't decipher the unfamiliar symbols on the stained material.

Lynk broke his chant for the briefest of moments, "I am sorry, my brothers. You may forget legalising this, but I need your agreement to get what I want."

He returned to chanting, bringing up the knife to the next Elder. My heart was pounding; sweat coated my skin like an extra layer of slippery skin. A memory suddenly flooded through my head, Kieran was with me in my room, persuading me that my voice can be used for good. I glanced up at Lynk and thought; *this is as good a time as any.*

I opened my mouth, unleashing my voice. But as soon as the sound released I felt a sharp stab of pain shoot around my neck in a circle, cutting off the flow of energy like a choke chain.

I screamed in agony. What was happening? I was gasping, my vision distorting, my eyes uncontrollably rolling towards the floor.

"Ruby," somebody called, "it's you're necklace!" It was Chara; I caught a glimpse of her blurring silhouette.

Her words made sense despite the biting confusion and I struggled determinedly against the excruciation, trying to pry the necklace Lynk had given me off my skin. I screeched as the pain intensified and the Daemon grasped my feeble hands. Lynk was still in control. I *could* stop it, I knew I could, I just needed to get the damn thing off!

I fought against my better judgements, and the anguish, bashing my fist with all my strength against the Daemon restraining me, it stumbled back, hissing for an instant and in that second I reached to the chain around my neck. It had tightened dramatically, cutting into my skin and I struggled to get a grip as the Daemon came back to me. Just in time I looped my finger underneath the marked metal, ripping it with all the force I could muster. I heard the necklace snap. The pain instantly disappeared.

Lynk was raising his knife to the last Elder, the man with fiery red hair and a heavily lined face. I glanced down at my hands, clicking my fingers the way Jayson had taught me, to spark a flame. I leapt forwards instinctively, tearing the parchment out of Lynks hands. Instantaneously I staggered back, raising my little flame to the parchment. It lit satisfyingly fast, disintegrating into a hundred fragments of burning ash. Lynk looked at me furiously but before he could do anything I raised my voice and threw everything I had at him, screaming *stop*. He stumbled back, more in surprise than anything else, and I heard as the crowd awoke from the enchantment.

The Elders looked down at their hands in shock and sudden pain. The blue eyed Elder glared at Lynk; he shouted, so that his booming voice echoed across the room, "Warriors!"

Kieran broke free of the Daemon just as a swarm of people began to attack. Lynk was staring with his jaw gaping open as his followers were battered by thousands of avenging Phoenix. The half-breeds began climbing the walls, retreating up through the ice rafters, but going upwards isn't a great idea when fighting birds. A few people Changed fully, fighting the monsters in the air, tearing at their legs with their talons.

Lynk didn't have the time to use Chyun'ju as he was plagued by the masses. He fought back, but more Phoenix flooded though; overwhelming him. All of the half-breeds had either been killed or had escaped. Eventually the stage cleared so that only the Eight Elders, both male and female, were there looking down at Lynk on his knees with two blades at his throat. Kieran, Adrian, Nik, Chara and Bris came to stand beside me at the foot of the stage.

"Your offences are unforgivable, Lynk," snarled the blue eyed Elder. "Not only did you break the law on several different accounts, you invaded every Phoenix in this room in the worst possible way. Also creating those *things*," he shuddered. "It's an outrage. For this you shall receive the Ultimate Curse."

Lynk looked barely bothered by this, or the Gaborah blades. He answered simply, "I doubt that's going to happen."

I saw it before anybody else did, I sprang forwards to try and stop it but was too slow. Kieran's father, the Earth Elder, had plunged a knife into the Water Elder. The blue eyed man sunk to the floor immediately, blood spurting from his chest. Kieran's father now had a knife to the ancient red haired woman.

"That's why." Lynk said calmly.

Why hadn't I predicted this?

I heard people gasp in horror, staring down at the body of the dead Elder in disbelief. Adrian ran towards his father but he clutched the knife closer to the Fire Elder and wailed, "If anyone comes any closer, I'll kill her."

Adrian froze. I froze. Everybody froze.

"Let him go, now," snapped Kieran's father and automatically the guards released him, backing away. Lynk slowly straightened up.

"Everybody stay back," Lynk ordered. "It seems that things haven't exactly worked out as I hoped," he said composedly, "but I will get what I want. I had tried to make you see, but you are all too foolish to understand."

"You don't understand anything!" I screamed, "Anything at all."

He didn't even look at me as he said, "Briseis, get Ruby, we're leaving."

This stopped whatever words were formulating on my tongue.

What?

A knife was pressed against my throat, strong arms wrapped around me, restraining my powerful wings with supernatural strength. A terribly familiar scent filtered through my system.

Briseis.

She was working for Lynk.

From the corner of my eye I saw Kieran move towards me but Briseis screamed at him, "Hold still Kieran or I swear on my life I'll kill her."

"That isn't much of a promise," Kieran said, "You're life means nothing to me anymore." But he held still.

I saw Adrian gaping at Briseis. "Bris?" he asked weakly, the look in his black eyes was devastating. "Briseis. What are you doing?"

"What does it look like I'd doing idiot?" she snapped, her voice had harshness in it that I'd never heard before.

"I don't understand," he said quietly.

Her face was so close to mine I could actually feel the snarl in her words, "I'm not surprised. Humans *are* less intelligent."

A sound rippled through the crowd, like gasps of surprise. That was it, Adrian's secret was out. The look on Adrian's face was heartbreaking.

"Enough, Briseis," Lynk commanded. "Stop playing with the boy, and get what I want from his brother."

"Go forwards," Briseis hissed in my ear, shoving me towards Kieran. "Drop your blade," she told Kieran, who didn't respond. His Gaborah blade stayed firmly in his hand, his knuckles clenched white over the silver pommel. "Drop it," she said more sternly, "Or you know what I will do."

Kieran glared at her, but dropped the blade.

"How long have you been working for Lynk?" Adrian suddenly demanded.

Briseis laughed harshly, "I'm not working for him. I'm working *with* him. If you remember, *I* was the one who got you access to the scrolls that got us out of Kariak. *I* led us all to the Lake District; to Ruby. *I* was the first to agree to go back to Kariak. And *I*," she paused dramatically for a movement, "poisoned you all. It was me who put the idea into your heads that the reason you were getting ill was because the air on earth isn't 'pure'." She sniggered nastily. "I just wanted to come home sooner."

For once Kieran looked speechless. I must admit, I didn't exactly know what anyone could say to that. She'd been betraying us secretly from the beginning. My body felt numb. I didn't know what to think. All those times I'd spoken with her as a friend, trusting her, laughing with her, sharing my secrets. It had all been a lie. Lynk must have known everything. Why had she done it? How could she? I didn't understand.

"Briseis," Lynk said patiently "enough boasting and get the chain."

"My Lord," I could feel her nod. "Kierakai, give me the chain from around your neck."

Kieran looked down, artificially confused, "I don't think now is really a good time to compare accessories."

"Do it, now," she ordered, the blade at my throat tightened. I winced as fresh blood trickled down my neck. Why does this always happen to me?

Kieran read the pain in my eyes, carefully unclasping the gold chain from around his neck. He clutched it tightly in his palm, not moving. "What do you want with it?"

"No questions, give it Ruby," Briseis snapped, then spat at me, "Hold out your hand."

I held out my trembling arm, palm upwards.

I didn't feel anything fall onto my hand.

"What do you want with it?" Kieran repeated firmly.

Briseis produced another knife in her other hand, slashing it across my bare arm. I screamed, and then tried to bite my lip against the noise, my jaw clenched determinedly. Tears swam in my eyes, but I looked pleadingly at Kieran. *Don't give it her,* but a weight fell onto my hand.

As soon as I saw it there on my palm I realised something.

The markings were exactly the same as those on the chain my mother gave me, only arranged in a different order.

I was roughly yanked towards Lynk and he snatched the chain from my grasp. My heart was beating so fast I thought it might explode. Kieran's father still held the Fire Elder at the tip of his blade. Lynk, Briseis and Kieran's father silently exchanged a significant look.

Briseis held me still for a moment, as if waiting for something.

A loud shrieking noise punctured the tense silence. I winced, instinctively covering my ears with my hands. It did nothing against the unanticipated explosion that suddenly erupted. A powerful wind collided with the crowd, sending people crashing and toppling into each other. The earth shuddered, savagely quaking the delicate building. I glanced towards source, my heart clenching as one of the four columns that supported the ice structure, cracked.

Time seemed to slow down. There was a terrifying, unforgettable moment where everyone took a deep breath, and then the column began collapsing.

Discordant screams escaped terrified lips as people rushed to get out of the way of the shattering building. Dangerous fragments of ice broke from the ceiling, plummeting to the ground as huge deadly icicles. A high-pitched shrill sound rose above the noise, and to my horror I recognised it.

Half-breeds flew through the air, shrieking with demented delight. Two scooped down, grabbing me as Briseis let me go. They hauled me into the air with their strong sharp claws and inhuman vigour, their leathery wings beating fast. We were free of the tumbling ice in seconds. They didn't stop flying despite my furious protests, and clutched tighter when I kicked at one of them; sinking their sharpened claws into my flesh.

The Winter Palace was disappearing rapidly behind me, along with many lives that had been trapped underneath it. I screamed over the chilling wind, struggling to get free, but then they dropped me. The drop was sudden. I screamed as I landed on the dirt, my head connecting with a rock. I felt myself being dragged away as the impact stole my consciousness.

Darkness wrapped around me like a pair of black wings.

About the Author

Stephanie Harbon was born in Hartford, Connecticut, in 1994, while her father was working there. She moved back to beautiful Derbyshire at the tender age of three and lives there with her parents, German Shepherd Max and snake Chara. When not writing she likes to practice Taekwon Do, of which she has now been a devotee for nearly ten years. (She has a 4th Degree black belt) From a young age she loved reading and writing and decided, when just thirteen, to write her first novel. She loves fantasy but wanted to write something different from the usual crop of vampire, witch and werewolf stories. **Ashes** her debut novel has taken a long time to write but she is now planning a follow-on story and once readers have become involved in the amazing world that she has created, they will be waiting impatiently for her second book.